THE CANTERBURY TRAIL

ANGIE ABDOU

the canterbury trail

BRINDLE
& GLASS

Brindle & Glass Publishing Ltd.
www.brindleandglass.com

LIBRARY AND ARCHIVES CANADA CATALOGUING IN PUBLICATION
Abdou, Angie, 1969–
The Canterbury trail / Angie Abdou.

Print format: ISBN 978-1-897142-50-9
Electronic monograph in PDF format: ISBN 978-1-897142-65-3
Electronic monograph in HTML format: ISBN 978-1-897142-66-0

I. Title.

PS8601.B36C36 2011   C813'.6   C2010-906352-X

Editor: Lynne Van Luven
Proofreader: Lenore Hietkamp
Cover image: from "Fernie Three Sisters," painting by Laura Nelson, www.lauranelson.ca
Interior design and chapter illustrations: Pete Kohut
Author photo: Judy McMahon

Canadian Patrimoine
Heritage canadien

BRITISH COLUMBIA
ARTS COUNCIL

Canada Council   Conseil des Arts
for the Arts   du Canada

Brindle & Glass is pleased to acknowledge the financial support for its publishing
program from the Government of Canada through the Canada Book Fund, Canada
Council for the Arts, and the Province of British Columbia through the British
Columbia Arts Council and the Book Publishing Tax Credit.

MIX
FSC FSC™ C016245

The interior pages of this book have been printed on 100% post-consumer
recycled paper, processed chlorine free, and printed with vegetable-based inks.

1 2 3 4 5 14 13 12 11

PRINTED IN CANADA

For Marty Hafke, Amanda Racher, and Ryan Merrill—
still ski bums at heart and inspiring in so many ways.

The Pilgrims

Heinz, the hermit

F-Bomb, the ski bum

Loco (Antonio Ragusa), the local

SOR, the trustafarian

Sancho, the trustafarian's whippet-like mutt

Shanny, the rad chick

Alison, the urbanite journalist

Kevin, the redneck

Fredrik ("Apple Cake"), the foreigner

Claudette, la Canadienne

Cosmos, the hippy

Ella, the hippy's Bear-Aware girlfriend

Findley and Rider, the hippy's huskies

Janet, the mother

Michael, the developer

Lanny, the miller

Sitka, the miller's golden retriever

PART I

If you don't have a story, you don't have anything.

—Paul Ragusa

1. The Hermit

 **Heinz pounded the** last nail into his makeshift sign and stood back to assess the results. The statement sat dead-centre of a towering larch. Maybe the sign should be a bit slanted, more irreverent. Already, though, Heinz wondered at the pretension of "yer." He was no illiterate, why should he pretend to be? But carving the apostrophe in "you're" had seemed like too much work—or, more specifically, like it would *look* to have been too much work, a disproportionate amount of care taken.

And, he'd *never* succumb to the "your" of the real illiterates, the impossibly lazy sloths of the text-messaging age. Heinz Wilhelm Wittiger knew the difference between a possessive pronoun and a contraction, thank you very much.

Who would see the sign anyway? Who was this imagined reader who might stumble across Heinz's hidden mountain hut and think, *what kind of weirdo troubles himself carving apostrophes?*

Heinz cocked his head to the left to assess whether his sign might look better if it were a bit off-kilter, if it would seem a little angrier somehow.

He'd considered putting an apostrophe on "paying." "Payin'" to match the colloquial tone, the redneck forcefulness, of the "yer." But having ruled out the contraction, he didn't see how he could justify introducing an apostrophe for the sake of slang.

He sounded pedantic even to himself, but good writing, as he'd always told his students, was in the details, in all those little decisions that no one else thought about. In fact, good—truly seamless—writing allowed a reader the privilege of not noticing.

Tell me you're not serious. Puh-leeze. Apostrophes? Give me a break. An anonymous grade ten student's voice rang in his head. He'd quit teaching more than a decade ago, but the students' voices never left him. They lived in his head, mocking his tendency to linger on the details of language.

Gawd, that's soooooo stupid. Punctuated with a pop.

Even the snapping bubblegum lived on with him. He'd withdrawn from society as far as he knew how, and still he wasn't alone.

He fired up his rusted-out, unlicensed Ford only when he absolutely needed to stock up on groceries. He'd drive the twenty minutes into Coalton on rough forestry roads, brave the looks of suspicious bank tellers, then load his beaten-up truck bed with canned beans, canned tomatoes, canned fish, canned everything. Or dried. Dried milk, dried fruit, dried beef. Those trips were the only time he saw people at close quarters—sometimes he even had to talk to them—and they always stared. He imagined them wondering where he came from, constructing a narrative around his odd, unshaven appearance, his dirty clothes, his downcast eyes and gruff manner.

But maybe they only noticed him because he smelled. He had to smell. He hadn't had a real shower in years. Years and years. Why should he care? No one asked a bear to shower. Nobody expected the wolf to bathe. He was of nature now.

Let them sniff.

When Heinz first moved out here, he'd planned to write a novel. Finally in retirement, as a widower, he would pen the great masterpiece he'd dreamed of throughout his teaching career, the book he knew himself capable of, if only he could find the time to dig it out—something about small-town mountain life, the competing claims that resource management, tourism and recreation made on this finite Canadian space, sort of Stephen Leacock meets Michel Foucault meets David Suzuki. But it'd taken him a full year to get settled, to bang together a shelter, dig an outhouse, stockpile supplies. That year of introspective digging, banging and sawing made him realize that he hated all his potential readers—those Internet surfers, Amazon.com buyers, iPod listeners, all plugged-in and wired-up—hated them. When he left Coalton, he smashed all his electronic devices—his computer, his stereo, his television. He brought his axe in from the woodpile and swung hard, slamming the wide, blunt end of the axe full force into the middle of each wired-up monstrosity. He left the whole mangled mess for his son to find. Let that be his goodbye. To his son and to that whole world.

So, he asked himself, how could he write a book to a world he'd abandoned? If a writer types in the forest, does anyone hear?

Really, after spending a full year with nothing but his own thoughts, he had to admit that he really had nothing to say, nothing worth the trees needed to make the paper. No, he decided, his withdrawal would be complete. What stories he had, he would tell to himself, the words threading themselves to each other in his mind as he hoed a new trail, or roasted elk meat on a spit above an open fire, or drifted off to sleep with wind coming through the cracks in his wall and tickling his cheeks.

Heinz sniffed the spring air.

It smelled like dog shit. Even out here. Melting dog shit. The first sign of spring in the mountains. Was it too much trouble for people to clean up after their bloody dogs?

Yes, he supposed it was. Hikers weren't going to pack in baggies in order to pack out crap. They were in nature, the logic went, and nothing was more natural than animal shit.

No one cared that this was his home, his particular little piece of nature. They trekked by on their skis or snowshoes or roared by on their snowmobiles, and they must've noticed his ramshackle hut, his rustic signs, the evidence of his existence, but they left their shit anyway.

He supposed his signs were a bit of a cop-out, a compromise on his initial plan. He hated the world, but still he posted his little messages. And they'd spread like dandelions during his five years in the bush, inching back into the woods and eventually all the way up the mountain, to the very summit, and over the crest to the well-used backcountry hut. If Heinz wasn't going to write, he needed another hobby. He picked trail building.

At first, he just wandered—finding the quickest way to mountaintop, then the most scenic, then the most likely to spot wildlife, then the path with a well-placed swimming spot or a nicely shaded nook for an afternoon nap. Eventually, he began marking his routes—more to leave evidence of his existence than to save himself from getting lost. By then he knew the way—*all* the ways—but naming a certain incline or a particular creek-crossing gave him an inexplicable satisfaction. He didn't want to name the squirrels and birds. He didn't need a "Chip" and a "Chirp," and he had no interest in being the crazy old hermit who deluded himself that the animals were his friends. Instead, he named the land.

He chose a medieval motif in homage to his repulsion for the modern world. The steep incline straight out his backdoor was Pilgrim's Progress. The small lake five kilometres to the east was Grendel's Mother's Mere. He'd called the backcountry hut just off the back of the summit Camelot, whereas his own hut carried the grimmer title of Heorot: leave the stuff of medieval romance to the hippy ski bums, he'd take Anglo-Saxon tragedy. As he etched "Camelot" into the warped sign, he couldn't resist invoking Monty Python and adding "it is a silly place" in blocky script at the bottom. He imagined grown men dressed in nothing but long-johns, gorging themselves on boxed wine, and dancing the night away as they waited for the sun to rise on a new ski day.

Heorot was a dark and deathful place, not a silly one, and this, to him, was the key distinguishing feature between himself and the town-dwellers who visited Camelot. He had left silly behind. Those skiing fanatics from Coalton lived for silly, and when they came out here to the backcountry, they brought silly with them.

As Heinz amassed summers in the bush, his signing system grew increasingly complex. He engraved posts distinguishing invasive weeds from indigenous plants; he mounted placards bearing lengthy explanations of the role of fire in the natural lifecycle of a forest; he painted angry warnings that feeding wildlife was dangerous for everybody, animals and humans alike. Eventually, he wore a well-grooved trail from his backdoor straight up and over the mountain to Camelot.

People from town found his trail to Camelot. It became increasingly well-worn and the maintenance more and more demanding. Every season he removed several defaced signs, replacing them with new ones. Skiers never seemed to tire of changing Pilgrim's Progress to Pothead's Progress or Camelot to Smoke-a-Lot or Grendel Mother's Mere to Grendel's Mother's Muff.

Heinz had never got the mother jokes. Still didn't. And now these perverse, immature attempts at humour—or aggression disguised as humour—had followed him out to the middle of nowhere.

Rather than giving in and leaving the ruined signs to fall down and decay, Heinz grew ever more rigorous about maintaining his kingdom according to his exact vision, no matter how much work it took. At the trailhead, he mounted a huge sign—the size of a van—mapping the full route up the mountain, past the lake, and over the summit to Camelot. He named the whole thing The Canterbury Trail.

That would be his novel.

He wondered if legends had grown up around him—the weird recluse living in the woods building a kingdom of forest trails. As much as he hated people traipsing through what he viewed as his backyard, he did derive some enjoyment from their use of his trails. Yes, Heinz hated the ski bums with their graffiti and their dog shit, but, in the end, he needed them. They were his readers.

His only readers.

And already they'd defaced his CANTERBURY TRAIL sign, employing the most offensive of English words in the new name. To them, The Canterbury Trail was known simply as "The Cunt."

2. The Ski Bum

WAKE & BAKE

Preparation time: 5 minutes

Take one gram of world famous BC bud.

If the weed is dry, crumble between thumb and forefinger to loosen. Otherwise, use a coffee grinder or pair of manicure scissors to cut it into small pieces.

Lay one ZigZag rolling paper across pointer finger and middle finger so fold runs between the two, lying parallel to fingers. The paper's sticky seam must be at the top, facing you.

Sprinkle marijuana liberally into trough.

Close thumb and forefinger of right hand on one end of the paper and thumb and forefinger of left hand on other end of paper, pinching both ends just above the marijuana in trough.

Roll back and forth, packing marijuana into small cylinder centered in rolling paper.

Be careful not to pack too tight—must allow space for air to move through marijuana freely.

Once marijuana is centred and packed, roll downward with thumbs, securing marijuana at bottom of paper, tucking bottom edge tightly.

Hold bottom half of paper with thumbs, keeping it tight to marijuana. With forefingers, push top of paper over the bottom. Roll into a cigarette shape.

Once all paper is rolled into cigarette except small sticky lip, moisten remaining paper with tongue and continue rolling until sticky lip adheres to bottom of joint.

Ready to serve. Filter optional.

NOTE: Goes well with coffee. Guaranteed to make the morning go oh-so smooooooooooothly.

An unexpected dump of spring snow had put smiles on everyone's faces. Loco posed knee-deep in the snow bank, one hand pointing at the *"I Love Big Dumps"* sticker on the back of his truck, the other holding his huge skis high above his head, tips pointed heavenward. His ski pants sat low on his hips revealing the waistband of his Patagonia underwear, and he wore a long-sleeved blue T-shirt with GIV'ER LIKE YER MA ON PROM NIGHT in loud red letters across his chest. SOR captured the moment on his new video camera, a bargain on e-Bay. A good shot of Loco holding his skis like they were weapons and he the blood-thirsty warrior would be the perfect opening frame for the film they planned to make this weekend. Coalton's backcountry terrain begged to be captured on a kick-ass ski video. The rugged rock faces, chest-deep powdery fluff, twenty-foot cliffs wide open for hucking yourself off: you couldn't ask for a better setting. They planned to set the whole thing to Rage Against the Machine's "Killing in the Name of." They'd include all the mandatory footage—steep descents, huge drops, wicked stunts, gnarly crashes—but they'd do it with their own special Coalton, "Rippy" style—a sort of Redneck/Hippy fusion.

While SOR and Loco worked out the details of their masterpiece, F-Bomb occupied himself loading their three pairs of skis and other skiing paraphernalia into Loco's rusted truck bed. It was too late to ride the lifts on the local hill—it had all shut down a week ago—but there's no way they'd miss out on this phat offering from the snow gods. They'd been awake since seven this morning, packing their gear. One last hike into backcountry, one last weekend shredding the pow, would cap their season perfectly. One last crusade up The Cunt into Camelot, then they'd go their own ways for the summer.

F-Bomb knew he was in for three months of hell—tree planting up in northern BC. Shitty weather, no showers, no chicks, no breaks. Muscle spasms, breakfast in the dark, sun blisters, cracked dry hands, soggy tent-living. And fucking mosquitoes. Mosquitoes in his ears, in his nose, in his eyes. He wouldn't be able to sit still for a second or he'd be black with the ravenous little parasites. One slap on his thigh and his hand would be a stewy mess of bug guts and human blood.

But F-Bomb was going back. Realistically, nothing else would give him the cash he needed in order to dedicate himself to another winter of Living the Life. Every year, he wished summer would never come. Perpetual Canadian winter would be his idea of heaven. Perpetual *Coalton* winter. Coalton—a place famous for its big mountains and non-stop precipitation, a place where how fast you could ski was the best measure of your worth as a human being.

"I'm on The National Ski Team," he'd say with a smirk when people asked him what he was doing for the winter. "National" only in the sense of funded by the nation's tax dollars. A spring and summer of tree planting and a winter of Employment Insurance would keep him in Kraft Dinner, beer and lift tickets for one more season. Then he'd figure out what to do next.

Loco and SOR's off-season looked to be shaping up better than his, or easier at least. Loco's dad managed a crew at the mine and had landed them jobs driving truck. Supposedly permanent jobs. The word—permanent—had a sickening flow to it, causing a pain that radiated out from F-Bomb's liver, spreading slowly through his internal organs and grinding its way along his limbs. Permanent, as in starting this spring and lasting, ever so torturously, through eternity.

That was Loco's dad's intention anyway, but both Loco and SOR let on that they might work (another awful word—*work*) for the spring, summer, and maybe even the fall, but they'd for sure fly as soon as the snow did. SOR'd be able to get away with that, but F-Bomb wondered if Loco would really stand up to his miner father.

At twenty-three, Loco had already stolen more than his share of time to rip around the mountain. If he was going to try for another season of pure skiing, he'd have to find another ski town, far away from Coalton and his father.

On this glorious snowy April morning, though, no sign of worry over future employment showed on Loco's face. He and SOR hovered above the three backpacks that slumped gape-mouthed on the porch of their rented miner's shack, the piece-of-shit house slanting to one side as if someone had kicked in its right kneecap. F-Bomb knew the foundation had to be sinking. It sure wouldn't be the only rental property in town with a sinking foundation, all the landlords holding fast to their slums, waiting for the new golf course, the ski hill upgrades, something to drive real estate up, up, and up. Soon the land would be worth a fortune, and the landlord would sell to some city slickers ("shitty" slickers, more like it) who'd tear the shack down and build themselves a million-dollar mountain chalet to match the million-dollar view—shimmering snowcapped peaks in every direction. Then they'd act like they'd discovered Coalton, like the whole place sat empty before they arrived. Columbus had nothing over these arrogant pricks from the big shitty.

F-Bomb joined his roommates on the porch for the last-minute avalanche gear review, fast tracking procedure with his "Beacon? Probe? Shovel? Check. Check. Check. Fresh batteries? Done." Of course, they needed other stuff too—they weren't getting anywhere without skis or poles or gloves—but the avy gear was the easiest to forget, a potentially fatal omission.

"All right, then! Check. Check. Check. Let's get at 'er!" Loco easily picked up on F-Bomb's quickened pace, missing more syllables than he hit, so that "all right, then" came out more like "ahrt, en." He sounded like his tongue couldn't reach the roof of his mouth, and F-Bomb sometimes wondered if maybe it couldn't. Maybe that piercing had fucking paralyzed it.

Nothing else about Loco was paralyzed, though. He bolted full speed for the truck, but came to a forced stand-still as SOR grabbed the back of his jacket, "Slow down, buddy. Let's think this through.

First things first—how 'bout a little wake and bake." SOR let himself fall butt first in the snow bank, pulling a baggy from the zip pocket on the bib of his snowveralls. The steep snow banks on either side of the sidewalk testified to the great ski season past. SOR moved his ass side-to-side digging himself a good cushy spot, at a safe distance from the ubiquitous dog piss—much of it the work of SOR's own dog, a scrawny whippet-like mutt named Sancho. "Ah, my good friend, Mary Jane. Come to Dada." SOR placed a fat joint between his lips as F-Bomb and Loco dropped down on either side of him, Loco passing over a lighter shaped like a naked lady with flame shooting out from her ass.

SOR lit the joint, closing his eyes and sucking deeply. SOR stood for "Stud on Rockets"—the weakest of their nicknames. He'd been in Coalton all of six weeks, fresh from the farm in Orillia, Ontario, when he started making fun of newbies on the hill, calling them GORBs (Geeks on Rental Boards) or JONGs (Jerk-Off Newbie Gapers). "SOR" was supposed to be his own flip of "GORB"—its polar opposite. Instead, it sounded like a venereal disease—a bloody, festering wound.

Laid back on the snow, sucking on his breakfast joint, SOR looked too relaxed to be the kind of guy who made up his own nickname. F-Bomb had tried "Thor" for awhile—he almost looked like a Thor with his six-foot-three, wide-shouldered build, his shoulder-length blond hair—but the others had mocked F-Bomb, talking with their tongues between their teeth as if "Thor" was just "SOR" with lisp.

F-Bomb watched SOR take another long toke off the morning spliff and wondered, not for the first time, how lucrative the Ontario farming business was. SOR's source of income was never clear, but he always had the latest in hiking boots, skis and trekking gear. Whenever they asked him where he got all his cash, he just shrugged and mumbled, "It's just paper, man." Only people who had a lot of such paper had the luxury of being so dismissive. Maybe SOR was one of the "trustafarians" who arrived in Coalton every year with knotted hair, deep pockets, and a wide open skiing schedule. Maybe SOR should stand for Skiing On parents' Riches.

The demented grin on Loco's face as he took the joint from SOR would stop anyone from asking where he'd gotten his nickname. Loco couldn't smile without looking slightly crazed; ever since a nasty fall down the headwall earlier this season, his mouth had more gaps than teeth. He'd lost seven in the fall, and had three more pulled out because of cracks.

"You don't need teeth to ski," he'd said, sticking his tongue through the unsightly space. "Plus, now I can make cool whistling sounds."

"Now you look like the crazy fuck you've always been," SOR assured him. Crazy, toothless Loco. Clearly, nobody ever felt the need to ask, "Why you called Loco?"

As with any good nickname, though, the true story had an unexpected twist. Loco grew up in Coalton and couldn't be prouder. Must've been a dozen times a day, you'd hear him say, "I'm fucking local, man. I know." What exactly it was he knew varied. What creates the worst avalanche conditions? He knew. Where do you hide from the Mounties when they spot you drinking in public during Ull Dayz? He knew. Which tree in town is the best place to hide after last call, so you can throw eggs at drunk tourists? He knew.

He was fucking local, man. He just knew.

"More like fucking loco!" F-Bomb couldn't resist, and it had stuck.

F-Bomb pulled off his glove and took the joint from Loco, careful not to burn his fingers and drop it in the snow. Raising the spliff to his lips, he watched Sancho lift a leg and piss on the corner of their piece-of-shit house.

Man, he hated that dog. They'd have to take him touring with them today. The last time they'd left him at home, he'd shit from one end of their shack to another in protest, and then ate a hole in the drywall just in case they'd missed his point. F-Bomb stifled a cough as the smoke burned his throat.

Truthfully, he was the one who really had best claim to the status of "local," more than Loco, but when you're local in the sense of Cree, you don't brag about it the way you do when you're local in the sense of third-generation Italian immigrant miner. While Loco could go on and on about his grandfather who'd practically built the city hall, F-Bomb didn't want anyone to get wind of just how local his own grandpa was, didn't feel the need to go on and on about some priest diddling his young grandfather at the residential school down the road.

He couldn't deal with all that "your people" shit. *Your people have suffered. This land belongs to your people. Your people deserve so much more.*

Fuck that.

Next thing, his so-called buddies would be wanting him to build them a fucking sweat lodge, bake them bannock or some other fucked up shit. And every time he got drunk, it'd be "lookit the drunk Indian, can't hold his liquor." The rest of them could barf all over themselves three nights a week, and they were just young, just having fun. But his drunkenness would suddenly be a genetic defect. His rye would suddenly be firewater. Fuck it. Let Loco be the local.

Easing himself out of his bum-shaped snow seat, F-Bomb passed the joint back to SOR, who'd let his head fall to rest in the snow bank so he looked like a dead snow angel, his blond hair splayed above his head creating a sort of halo.

F-Bomb headed back to the shed to find some extra touring gear for Alison. He doubted she had skins or trekkers. Probably, she had nothing but the standard on-hill skis and poles. He had no idea how she planned to make it up the mountain today.

Shaking the rusted lock loose, he squeezed into an almost negligible space between a broken snow blower and a garbage pail full of mismatched ski poles, letting his eyes adjust to the light. What a mess—a graveyard of ski seasons past. Years' worth of ski bums had passed through this rental house, each group leaving its unwanted gear for the next. As he picked through the bucket of poles, he wondered at his hands seeming so far away from him; he had the eeriest sensation of disembodiment in the dimly lit, claustrophobic space, until he remembered that he was just a little stoned.

Clumsily digging in the chaos, he managed to find Alison some touring gear—a pair of frayed skins and some rusty trekkers to throw on her skis for the uphill—and wondered how to get it to the truck without SOR or Loco seeing. How could he explain something to them when he couldn't even explain it to himself? He planned to postpone his little revelation as long as possible.

As he came back around the corner to the front yard, he watched Loco regale SOR with his boundless local knowledge—telling SOR where exactly in his pack to place his avalanche shovel for easiest access and least discomfort, what clothing layer to wear next to his skin, and what food served as optimal mid-trek refueling. F-Bomb wondered, not for the first time, if there was anything Loco didn't think he knew.

F-Bomb passed unnoticed and threw the extra gear in the truck bed, giving Sancho a nudge with his foot to stop him from pissing on the tire. He'd never seen an animal so eager to mark territory. Though Loco wasn't far off—in February they'd had a big yellow mess in the backyard for weeks after Loco demonstrated his long-touted ability to write his name with his own urine.

"Ahrt, Professor Loco," F-Bomb muffled his syllables imitating Loco's sloppy accent. "You have six hours on the hike-in to bless us with your endless supply of local lore. Less talking, more moving."

SOR still had the camera in his hand and zoomed in on F-Bomb's face.

"Less talking, more moving—cut to skiing. Perfect frame, F-Bomb! Thanks."

The flakes fell heavily, sticking to F-Bomb's eyelashes and blurring his vision. He grew eager to be out in it, not standing around here posing for SOR's camera. He grabbed his slumping pack from between his two friends, cinching the top and buckling it tight, moving toward the truck bed. "Let's go!"

God, life was perfect.

Except one thing.

F-Bomb needed to tell them that he'd invited Alison, the neighbourhood cougar. He didn't know how she'd fit into the truck cab, let alone into their skiing plans. She must've been practically forty, but was always prowling around their yard, a predator on the hunt for loving. He knew she'd even found it at least a few times. What could a forty-year-old woman want with their ski-bum miner's shack, filled with soggy beer cases and sweaty ski socks? But every now and then her sleep-creased face would show up at their breakfast table, and F-Bomb was pretty sure it wasn't because she couldn't find any Captain Crunch at her house.

He never knew whose bed she shared—Loco's or SOR's—and he never asked. Maybe both for all he knew. Maybe they took turns. He didn't need to know.

He hadn't taken a turn yet and didn't plan to—he'd invited her on their ski trip out of pity alone.

By eleven last night, it'd been clear that things were looking up for a truly epic ski day—the solitary thing that would motivate this trio to rein in party plans. Not that anything too exciting was happening socially these days anyway—the ski crowd pretty much cleared out last week when the lifts closed, like someone had hung a CLOSED FOR THE SEASON sign at the town limits. So it was just the three of them sitting around the sticky kitchen table, playing quarters and guzzling beer. They should've been doing an end-of-season clean-up and getting ready to move out, but that mission got aborted when F-Bomb opened a barf-filled cooler in the corner of the kitchen—a leftover from SOR on last month's "Pick Up or Puke" night. After each of them had had a good gagging look at that mess, they threw the cooler in the backyard and decided clean-up could wait.

Loco had noticed the snow first, "Fuck man, it's chugging like a three-dollar whore out there."

After that, they took turns running to the living-room window every ten minutes, monitoring the accumulation on their walkway.

"It's horfing like SOR on cheap draft night."

"It's dumping like F-Bomb after two-for-one burritos at El Guapo."

"It's gonna be fucking sick tomorrow."

By the time the puke-filled cooler had disappeared in the white fluff in the backyard, they'd curtailed their drinking and planned an early morning take-off for Camelot.

Just after midnight, while SOR and Loco hunted down transceiver batteries, F-Bomb wandered out to the road, holding his face up to the barely visible street lamp to let the fast-falling flakes pelt his bare cheeks. He felt the cold, fresh liquid melt on his hot skin and trickle toward his ears, breathed deep through his nose, inhaling the snow particles into his very being. Tomorrow, he'd be balls deep in it. Tits under even.

Hell, if this kept up, he'd need a fucking snorkel.

He slowly opened his eyes and turned back to the house, starting when he saw shadowy Alison sitting on her front porch watching him. She wore pajama bottoms freckled with pink hearts and an oversized puffy down jacket. She looked all of twelve, crouched there alone in the dark.

"Fuck! You scared the shit out of me! What're you lurking out here for?" He heard his own voice, a rough snagging against the soft velour of snow. He wouldn't apologize, though. She scared him first.

She aimed her gap-toothed smile up at him and holding out a hand as if to catch the falling snow, "Awesome, hey? I can't believe the hill closed already. How can we miss out on this? Just when I was getting the hang of powder."

He couldn't have pinpointed what exactly, but something lusty in her voice combined with her bare hand reaching for the elusive flakes got to him. This aged, newbie skiing spaz, of all people, had The Powder Fever. She wanted to ski.

Wanted it so bad she couldn't sleep.

Before his good sense could rescue him from his kind heart, he had heard himself saying, "Come with us."

SOR and Loco would kill him. Any idiot knew the rule—*bro's before ho's*—and she wasn't even his ho. *No friends on a powder day*, and he'd committed himself to babysitting someone he didn't even like.

STUPID.

That single mistake last night would have him hauling a newbie gaper around the mountain all weekend. His so-called friends would take off and beat him to first lines, then brag about being unable to breathe 'cause of all the powder up their noses, while he hand-held a petrified beginner.

As SOR and Loco loaded the last of their bags, F-Bomb searched his brain for a way out. Could he tell her there wasn't room in the truck? The ski-hut wasn't co-ed? He didn't have any extra touring gear for her? Sancho was allergic to chicks?

If only he could forget that image of her bare hand reaching for the snow, he'd just tell her—*you can't come, we don't want you.*

He and SOR were arguing about which of them had to straddle the gearbox, when she showed up, tripping across the snow with her skis fallen off her shoulder into an X across her chest, gripped at the cross point with both arms. She'd clumsily draped her pack over her elbow, and clasped her helmet strap between her teeth. Her poles and gloves had fallen on the sidewalk between their houses, and were quickly disappearing in the accumulating snow.

"Ready to shred the phat pow pow, boys?!" She spoke between clenched teeth, but still her helmet fell to the ground.

F-Bomb relieved her of her skis, noticing beads of sweat on her upper lip. "You're gonna fucking hurt someone with these." He threw them into the bed of the truck, where their bags were already dusted with white, and easily grabbed her pack, swinging it over after the skis so it landed with a thud (a worryingly breakable sounding thud—he wouldn't even ask what she had in there). "Grab your shit and get in the truck. Put your gloves up against the heater—they're going to be wet before we even get started." He ignored the bewildered glances of SOR and Loco. "SOR, get your fucking mutt in the back of the truck. Let's go."

F-Bomb jumped in next to the driver's seat. He'd let SOR have the window seat, sort of a peace offering. "How many times today do I have to say it? Let's fucking go."

Alison trotted down the sidewalk in her black Lycra ski pants, bending over to retrieve her poles and gloves. But SOR and Loco weren't looking at her. They stared dumbly at each other across the truck's hood. Loco mouthed *What the fuck?* but by then Alison had pounced into the cab, landing practically on F-Bomb's lap. Eventually, SOR and Loco could do nothing but follow.

They pushed Sancho in the truck box, and they all squished into the front. F-Bomb's elbow dug into Loco's ribs and Alison's ass slid half way up SOR's leg. Ignoring the frosted windows, Loco revved the engine and they rattled off to The Canterbury Trail for their last trek of the season.

As they pulled away from the house, F-Bomb waved over his shoulder at the neighbour shovelling snow off his roof. He stood up to his waist in it, absurd in his attempt to shovel it faster than it fell. In a few more weeks, he'd be out in the front yard with a garden hose, watering the snow off the lawn. When would these people learn that you can't fight nature?

Besides, if they hated snow so much, why the fuck did they live in a snow belt?

3. The Mother

Fat flakes drifted down from the sky, freshening all the world and the people in it. Janet held out her tongue, reveling in the sensation of fluff melting in her mouth. She loved the quietness snow brought, muffling even the deafening whistle from the tracks just down the hill, where trains ceaselessly hauled coal from the valley's biggest mine. When she and Michael had first shacked up in Coalton, she'd claimed to love the train, its romantic echo evoking thoughts of rhythmic travel through otherwise impassable mountain terrain. They'd joked about the way it vibrated their bed, saving them two quarters and a trip to a cheap motel. Now, every time the train roared by and shook their house's foundation, she ground her teeth, clenching her jaw until the muscles in her cheeks ached.

She wrapped her bare hands around her warm mug of tea and watched Michael and Lanny, bundled up in full ski gear, moving stiffly in circles around the backyard. Janet had buried their transceivers, and now insisted they take turns with hers, following the *beep beep beep* to locate the hidden signals. They'd practise single burials first and then multiples. Michael and Lanny could roll their eyes all they wanted, but she didn't want them out in the backcountry without some practice. Sure, Lanny talked the talk, but she'd bet he hadn't been on a real rigorous ski tour in five years. The size of his burgeoning belly suggested he hadn't done *anything* rigorous for at least five years. She wasn't going to have her husband—the father of her future child—lying for dead under two metres of snow while Lanny tried to remember what end of his transceiver faced forward.

She suspected they humoured her now only because she'd plied them with booze. Earlier in the cluttered kitchen, while Lanny picked through menu lists and packed dried foods, she saw Michael searching the liquor cabinet for some Baileys to sneak into the coffee. She'd come to the rescue and offered to whip up a concoction that would put their standard coffee and Baileys to shame.

She waddled around the obstacle course of boxes, grocery bags, skiing gear, plastic storage bins, and backpacks that Lanny and Michael had strewn throughout her kitchen. She picked three mismatched coffee mugs from the cupboard, wishing for the first time ever for a full set of dishware—something to hint at the organized domesticity that she hoped would arrive with the baby. For now, their kitchen—with its hints at their hippy past and its gestures towards their mainstream future—looked like it didn't know what kind of people it belonged to. She grimaced at their Sally Ann cups ("World's Best Lover" in bold black against a chipped red heart on one, "Coalton Centennial" in a dignified script on another) and then pulled three bottles of fancy liqueur from an oak liquor cabinet that they couldn't have imagined owning five years ago. Back then, if they had booze, they drank it.

She put the tea kettle on the stove to boil, breathing in the odor of gas as the flames shot up under the burner, and measured out a mix of liqueurs into the two cracked mugs. Like a priest obsessed with pornography, she'd acquired a strange fascination with bar-tending since falling pregnant. Her creation of tea combined with whatever bits of liqueur remained in the liquor cabinet—sort of a makeshift blueberry tea—did keep Lanny and Michael from rushing off to the backcountry. Instead, the boys happily sipped and searched in the backyard, raising their steaming cups to her in a toast whenever they caught her looking.

She watched Michael turn his back and sip on his blueberry tea while Lanny shuffled off to bury the transceivers about six feet apart in the far corner of the yard between two pines. His golden retriever, Sitka, followed close at his heels. Lanny had the oddest habit of talking for the animal. He'd bend over and scratch Sitka's neck, asking "How 'bout a ski, old girl?" Fair enough. But then he'd scrunch up his face like Scooby Doo and answer right back, "Rooray! Riing, I ruv it!"

Janet asked Lanny about this bizarre habit years ago, and he'd told her that Sitka was the only one worth talking to and it was no fun if she never talked back. Then he'd walked away muttering, "Ralk? Of course, I ralk! I'm not roopid."

Now, Lanny stopped and packed a tight snowball, throwing it far across the yard, and laughing as Sitka bounded after it. He yanked on Michael's sleeve and pointed at the dog. The snow was so deep that Sitka had to tunnel her way across the yard, only the black tip of her nose visible in the white.

Janet congratulated herself on their laughter. They looked to be having fun, despite their initial "Right, you have it—safety first, Mom!" mockery.

Janet's bum was growing cold inside her ski pants as she leaned against the ice-covered deck. Soon, she'd either have to go inside or join them in their backyard games. She slid her hands up under her ski jacket and massaged her warm belly. Kodiak (as Michael had named the fetus, in honour of his favourite ski run) seemed pretty mellow today, taking a break from the usual nonstop mogul skiing.

She and Kodiak were going on this trip too. No one would be

digging her and her baby out of anywhere, though. That was for sure. She'd take zero risks. She'd already made that much clear. She and Kodiak would stick to low-inclined slopes with heavy tree coverage, and if Lanny and Michael had to wait, they'd wait. Simple as that.

Being a mother didn't—or *shouldn't*—mean she suddenly got left out of everything; she'd insisted on establishing that right from the start—even before the start, while she was still a mother-in-waiting.

She sat her empty mug on the deck, and leaned over to retrieve a shovel and probe from the ground. Heaving her cold butt from the deck, she moved toward the men. Sitka rolled on the ground, rubbing thick winter fur off her back onto the sticky snow, and then burrowed across the yard to Lanny. The dog's lopsided waddle reminded Janet of Lanny's crisis last winter when he'd learned that the animal had the hip dysplasia so common in retrievers. Suddenly, Lanny had to decide whether to fork out eight thousand dollars' for a hip replacement. In the end, he must've decided that he didn't love the dog quite *that* much. Anyway, the dog was nearly seven years old—it didn't have eight thousand dollars' worth of life left.

Now, Lanny and Michael both held their transceivers as if about to strap them on their chests, done with the practice runs. She trained her eyes away from Lanny's right hand. Even though it was covered in a thick black mitt, her gaze was drawn to what she knew was hidden beneath. He'd lost three of his fingers in an accident at the mill nearly five years ago now, and still she couldn't stop staring at the deformed stumps that remained. His index finger had been sliced off close to the first knuckle. The remaining skin stretched taut across the malformed knuckle, sucking tight into a little dip in the middle of the amputated joint, puckered like a kiss, she always thought. Fingers three and four had fared better, chopped off just above the middle knuckle, but that didn't make them of any more use to him. He never said anything about the accident, but he sometimes made a joke of propping the finger nub on the base of his nostril so it looked like he had the whole finger stuck all the way up his nose.

Now, he used his injured right hand only to hold his transceiver firm to his chest and used his left hand for the finer work of fiddling with the buckle clasp on the transceiver strap.

Janet clapped her hands together and announced, "Okay. Before we take off, let's try actually using the avalanche shovels. Don't huff, Michael. I read an article about a man who'd carried the same shovel around in his pack for a decade—without *ever* assembling it. He'd never had to use it, so why would he? When he actually had an emergency, it turned out the handle didn't even fit, was the wrong brand, of all things. He had to dig out his friend holding the shovel blade in both hands." She held her red shovel between her palms as if to demonstrate the awkwardness, but both men had already obediently turned to find their own shovels. Clearly, they knew the pregnant woman would win this one.

"He was too slow," she continued triumphantly at their backs. "Not the right time to be too slow. Try explaining that to the family at the funeral." She dropped the shovel blade to the ground and held her cool hands to her forehead. "Without the right shovel, a transceiver offers nothing but social grace, only helps you find the dead body." She knew those words weren't her own, and tried to remember which mountain guide she'd stolen them from. "So, let's practise with our probes too."

Lanny and Michael sighed audibly, but both turned back to the porch to fetch their probes. *At this rate*, she knew they were thinking, *we'll never get to Camelot.*

Maybe that's what she wanted. Let's be honest—she was six months pregnant. It's not as if she was dying to lug this belly up a bloody mountain so she could sit in some falling down hut all weekend while her husband and his ex-roommate pretended they were twenty-one again, calling each other Cheech and Banger, stoned and skiing from sun-up to sundown.

And if they were out skiing all day, she'd be the one stuck preparing the meals, washing the dishes in melted snow, dealing with the grey water, boiling down snow for fresh water, folding stiff ski clothes after they'd dried over the fire, cutting the wood, stoking the fire, keeping the hut uncluttered—in short, she'd be acting out the very role that she'd insisted on tagging along in order to avoid. She'd be the typical, boring house wife. Only without running water or electricity.

How, again, was this a win?

Kneeling in the snow to dig out Lanny's transceiver with her quickly assembled avalanche shovel, she wondered why in god's name she put herself through this. Why did she have to pretend to love it all—the wild, the adventure, all that back to the earth bullshit? She hated almost everything about ski touring—right down to the minor inconvenience of outdoor urination. The guys had it easy, where the women had to pull off layers of clothes and squat half naked in the snow, buttocks brushing against the sharp ice crystals on the ground.

And now she'd be doing it six months pregnant. Her feet hurt, her back ached, and she was thirty-eight years old. Why couldn't she go to Chateau Lake Louise, spend a day getting her shoulders rubbed and her feet soaked? Her goddamn cuticles fixed, if that's what she felt like. Would that make her a bad person?

And it's not as if Michael was the exact same man she'd married. People were allowed to change—to *grow*, for god's sake.

She'd married a tree hugger, a *skiing-fanatic* tree hugger. The change in him had happened so gradually, so insidiously, she couldn't mark it—couldn't say when or why it occurred. When they started dating, he skied a hundred days a season, picking up night shifts at the local pub to make rent payments (more often than not, at least). By the time they married, he'd taken an online investment course and worked three days a week at the bank downtown, but still skied the other four. Now, he worked for the town's biggest real estate company. His posters declared "Coalton's Ski-Bum Realtor" and showed him tearing down the slopes, waist deep in powder. Fluff flying right over his head.

But in reality, the picture was eight years old and had very little to do with Michael LePlage, Coalton's "Pow(d)er Realtor." The whole thing was an illusion. Michael-the-Ski-Bum had long ago been absorbed into Michael-the-Realtor.

Last week, he'd reprimanded her for buying mere grocery-store carnations at the Overwaitea for a show suite. The Michael she knew didn't have the foggiest clue of the difference between carnations and orchids. And now he was a flower snob? Everything was done in the name of development—of Coalton's *progress*—and apparently even a person's flower tastes had to develop in order to attract the "right" clientele. She couldn't help herself asking him if they themselves qualified as the right clientele and if so when they'd fallen into that category. And why no one had asked her if she wanted to move. These were the kinds of questions Michael hated.

"We're just progressing the progression," he'd respond and turn back to his laptop.

Even this trip was designed in the name of development. Coalton Valley Forestry Company had just leaked that it would be dividing and selling giant parcels of land immediately west of town, a last-ditch attempt to fight the devastation of pine beetle and trade tariffs. Simply put, property was valuable; trees were not. The land included a favourite local ski spot. Janet felt sure the old Michael would come out of hiding and object to the potential loss of a Coalton gold nugget. He wouldn't lose Camelot to a condominium development. Would he?

He'd proposed to her there, after a six-hour snowshoe under a full moon, his pack jammed full of heavy luxury items. Wine, candles, a stereo. "I don't have money for a ring," he'd said softly, "but I have a strong back. This is what I can do for you."

So, when he recently mentioned the spring pilgrimage to their old spot, she truly believed the trip to be motivated by nostalgia.

He's back flew into her head with a warm sigh. This new Michael—the one who'd wake her every morning whispering his to-do list into her ear (*get a rack of lamb for dinner, I've invited the Carmichaels; check that those ski bums haven't left all their crap littering the front yard of our rental property on 3rd; do up some invites for our open house on Sunday*)—that Michael would be gone.

But no. The new Michael appeared to be here to stay. Sentimental memories played no part in his enthusiasm over this trip.

"It's an unprecedented opportunity. We're in exactly the right place at the right time. We've gotta seize it," the new Michael said.

Those were the words this new Michael used—*unprecedented* and *opportunity*. *Capitalize* was another favourite. "We'd be crazy not to capitalize on this opportunity."

Late at night, Janet often sat up in bed and turned on her reading lamp so she could watch his face as he slept. Stripped of artifice, of all those new expressions that came along with the new vocabulary, he looked younger, freer, less posed. In short, he looked almost exactly like the Michael she'd fallen in love with.

4. The Redneck

Kevin and Fredrik had sat in the living room drinking rye and watching the sky barf until sometime after four this morning, oblivious to Claudette upstairs, banging doors and stomping feet. Their attention was directed only to the sky:

"She's a-comin' down now, boys!"

"It's squallin' good out there tonight."

"Hot diggety, she's ragin."

"Someone give that sky an atta-boy."

They even ignored the sheets, blankets, and pillows she threw down the stairs at 1:00 AM, followed by a foundation-shaking slam of the bedroom door and some guttural foreign curse that even Kevin didn't recognize.

The sheets got all caught up on the antlers of Kevin's moose mounted at the foot of the stairs. If there's one thing that pissed Kevin off, it was someone disrespecting the massive rack of his massive moose.

If she wanted them to pipe down, if she wanted Fredrik to leave, why didn't she just say so? Kevin was no mind reader. How was he supposed to know what the hell her problem was? He didn't do nothing wrong. Since when was having a drink in your own house cause for war? Him and Fredrik drove truck at the mine all week long, like a coupla damn gerbils on a wheel. A dirty, stinking wheel.

She knew he hated his job. He didn't refer to his occupation as "Driving Fucking Truck" for nothin'. But he did it forty hours a week—fill truck with rock, empty truck of rock, fill truck with rock, empty truck of rock. That oughta entitle a guy to a bit of downtime. Couldn't she just give him that without pulling her psychotic, wronged housewife routine?

Really, it was about control. She wanted to control him and every second of his pathetic excuse for a life. If she felt like going to bed, why didn't she just go to bed, why did she need him lying there counting shadows on the ceiling while she farted in her sleep? What did it hurt her if he spent a few hours hanging with a buddy? He hardly saw his friends anymore. Probably that was exactly what she wanted. As if marriage should be the end of everything else. Before-Marriage-Kevin and After-Marriage-Kevin, never the two shall meet. Might as well stamp THE END across his forehead and file him under "D" for "Done like Dinner."

Well, she could stomp her-French-little-self silly all weekend long for all he cared because he and Fredrik were Goin' Sleddin'.

Goodbye, Claudette. Oh-rev-r, as the good old Quebecois like to say. See ya, wouldn't wanna be ya.

5. The Urbanite

HOW TO IMMERSE YOURSELF IN SKI CULTURE

Learn the language: gnar, graupel, shred, sick.

Dress like they dress: baggy not tight; polypro not
    cotton; toqued not combed.

Eat as they eat and play as they play: at your own peril.

With her right ass cheek slid half way up SOR's thigh, and her left breast plopped against F-Bomb's shoulder, Alison sat exactly where she wanted to be. Sandwiched between two warm young men like these, who needed coffee? They made her blood course faster, her heart dance in its cage, her skin sing with warmth. Alison was raring to go—*take me to the backcountry, if you must, just take me.*

Loco swore under his breath and pulled his truck to the side of the road. He whistled a high-pitched protest through the big space where three front teeth were meant to be.

Alison couldn't make out the street from the parking lane from the sidewalk—all pure white, flakes falling so fast now that the headlights in the oncoming lane were barely visible. Thank god she wasn't driving. The 401 in Toronto she could handle. She could predict what inane things other Torontonians might do. That danger she knew. She could never predict what the Coalton weather might do and that terrified her.

"See all the hard-packed snow on the road? The steep hill?" Loco asked, as if to the windshield wipers, "This is when you need 4 x 4." He cranked a lever down by F-Bomb's leg, forcing F-Bomb to jump over and squish Alison so far into SOR that she could smell the plastic pine scent of his pit stick. She pushed her Lycra clad butt farther into his crotch, barely listening to Loco. He delivered these soliloquies entirely for his own benefit anyway. "That's what drives me crazy about this town," Loco continued, "all the moronic tourists who don't know 4 x 4 from their ass. 'Oh, I'm in the mountains now, I better put my shiny new SUV in 4 x 4.'" He lowered his voice an octave and continued as himself, "You don't use 4 x 4 on dry paved roads. Ever. Any mountain local knows that. Fastest way to destroy your differential. Those imbeciles from the city buy off-road vehicles when the paved road to the ski hill is as close as they'll ever come to off-roadin'."

Checking that the 4 x 4 light had indeed come on, Loco eased the truck back into the traffic, inching along so slowly that a pedestrian could've made better progress. He clicked his tongue piercing against a lonely eyetooth in a way that seemed, to Alison, at odds with his seriousness.

Alison had found Loco's tirades humorous when she first met him in the fall, but he hadn't exactly grown on her throughout the winter. If anything, he was more the kind of guy that receded on you. At first, she thought he was sort of joking, acting out a caricature version of himself, but when he didn't come out of it for a week, then a month, then a whole season, she realized he was indeed serious—the Loco you saw was the Loco you got. He truly believed himself spokesperson of Coalton by virtue of his ancestry. Unless his peers could claim a grounding of at least three generations in Coalton (which none of them seemed able to do), they had no right to an opinion on skiing technique, on gardening practices, on streaking procedure, on strip-club etiquette, on resource extraction, on anything. She slid her fingers up SOR's warm neck and tangled them into his dreadlocked mess of blond hair.

SOR's breath smelled of pot, as it usually did. Alison didn't mind. She liked the smell, though she never smoked the stuff anymore. She'd come to Coalton on a research mission and didn't need to numb her senses. Pot made her truly stupid. Just after she arrived in Coalton, she'd shared a joint with SOR, and her whole face went numb. That never happened in Toronto, but this BC stuff fell in a category all its own. The Alberta–BC border crossing should bear a warning: "Welcome to British Columbia. Our marijuana is very strong here."

SOR's plan was to smoke a little, then go for a mountain-bike ride, show her the spectacular fall colours from a nicely elevated lookout. After their "little smoke," oblivious to her complete dysfunction, he'd busied himself getting the bikes ready. By the time he turned his attention back to her, he found her tangled up in her own backpack, nearly in tears. He told her not to worry, things would be better once they got moving. He straightened her backpack, strapped on her helmet, and helped her onto her bike seat, giving her a little push in the right direction.

Things did not get better. She could barely ride off the sidewalk without falling over, never mind up a single-track mountain trail. Her bike felt ten feet off the ground. She clung tightly to the handle bars and had to consciously think through the motion of every single pedal stroke. Half way up, she'd already fallen off her bike three times and lay splayed across the trail, a bleeding teary mess.

SOR was apologetic enough, "Sorry, man. My fault. That's the wheelchair pot. It should come with a Chronics Only label." He patted her on the back. "Just look where you want to go. Same as in life. If you look off the path and down the mountain, that's where you'll go. Keep your eye on the path. You think about falling, that's just what you'll do." And he was gone, his glazed eyes, no doubt, right on the path.

Alison pushed her bike the rest of the way up the mountain, stumbling over every root, scratching her face on wayward branches, while SOR rode on ahead. At the top, he smoked a bit more weed while she guzzled water, hoping it'd have a diluting effect on the toxins in her body. She felt herself shrink in humiliation when a couple of quadders zipped by on the forestry road, likely judging her and her ratty-haired companion, passing them off as pie-eyed dirt bags.

"Redneck boozers," SOR announced to the cloud of dust left in their wake, as if naming a specific species of wild bird.

Alison had sobered enough that she did manage to ride her bike back down the hill, but her brakes shrieked in protest the whole way.

Her senses far from numb this morning, she noticed that SOR wasn't the only hard thing jabbing into her. The corner of the black notebook tucked into the inside pocket of her ski jacket poked her in the ribs. Her *Book of Great Ideas*, she liked to call it, if only to herself. For now, it contained random lists of information about ski culture. "Varieties of snow" alone filled three pages. "Graupel" referred to those sharp little ice pellets of snow that hurt when they hit your face and accumulated on car windows like lost little pieces of Styrofoam. "Wind sift" denoted the fine stuff, the consistency of icing sugar, that blew across the hill softening icy patches. "Elephant snot" meant the sticky warm stuff—good for building snowmen, not so good for skiing. "Cream cheese" fell somewhere between "Elephant snot" and "Sick powder." Sick meant good, really good. She'd begun to think of her work as translation—translating first for herself and then for the masses.

She had no idea, yet, what "gnar" meant, but she knew you were supposed to shred it.

The lists went on and on. Skis could be rockets, boards, sticks, big guns. The verbs to refer to skiing included shred, ride, charge, rip—the subtle distinctions still lost on her.

Skiing was skiing, wasn't it?

Apparently not.

And there appeared to be an infinite number of ways of saying "Let's smoke a joint." "It's 4:20 somewhere," or any other sentence containing the combination of four and twenty, was an explicit reference to marijuana. "I'm gonna go wax my snowboard" translated, roughly, to "I'm going out to the garage to smoke a joint. Come if you want." Of course "Mary Jane" meant "marijuana." And if a stranger on a chairlift asked "You got change for a nickel?" it meant "do you have some marijuana you'd be willing to smoke with me before we get to the top?" That one took Alison awhile to figure out, until SOR explained to her that people carried weed in a dime bag. The precise logic of "change for a nickel" was still hazy, but why wouldn't it be? She'd been through three months of people heading to various backrooms for "safety meetings" before she figured out that "safety meeting" was yet another euphemism. Just when she'd decided that any cryptic phrase must be a call to smoke pot, she found out that "Wanna come for a ride on the bus?" was an invitation to take magic mushrooms. New page, new list.

This place definitely had its own language, and Alison most certainly did not speak it—but she'd been working hard all winter to learn.

SOR's hot breath on her neck now reminded her of the one language they did have in common—the language of love. *La langue d'amour.*

The boys weren't speaking any language this morning, just staring silently into the snow, all of them stoned, probably. Perfect. This way, she could devote her full attention to the sweaty bodies pressed against her. She loved bodies, and wiggled a bit in SOR's lap to let him know. She'd heard of women near forty experiencing throbbing wombs, the overwhelming desire for a baby drowning out all else. Alison's desire was for sex alone, babies be damned. Call it throbbing clitoris.

Loco turned left onto the highway and picked up his speed. The constant transport traffic had packed down the snow here so the driving wasn't as sketchy as it'd been in town. At least she could see the yellow lines now.

Even the highway, though, bore no connection to Alison's previous conception of the word "highway." In the fall, when she moved from Toronto in search of new writing material, "highway" meant five lanes in each direction, a nonstop blur of vehicles in every single one. Here, there was only one lane in each direction, and if you wanted to pass, you had to wait fifty kilometres for a passing lane. The road wound through the mountains, with ever-threatening rock cuts and steep drop-offs at each turn. Giant semi-trucks packed with logs accounted for most of the vehicles. Loco crawled along between two of them, scraping his piercing angrily against a tooth near the back of his mouth, as a continuous stream of dirty slush pelted his windshield.

Alison didn't know for sure what counted as an "old growth" tree, but each of those stumps sticking out the end of the semi, hanging almost over Loco's truck hood, could've been a fair-sized coffee table in its own right. Not surprisingly, she'd never seen a tree that size when she lived in downtown Toronto, spending most of her time writing lifestyle pieces. Writing and writing and writing until there was literally nothing left to say. How many articles could you write about being a big-city mom, balancing work and career? Or about loft living, downsizing for the sake of convenience and environment? Or, "Sushi, The Fad That's Killing the Seas." It'd all been done, and then done again.

She'd pounded out the pieces, barely taking time to read them over, obsessively keeping track of her story count and of readers' responses to her stories. Home from the office well after dinner, she'd crouch over her laptop, Googling herself—always wanting more. More references to her. More uses of her name.

Googling herself. The masturbatory ring to the phrase was perfect. The elusive fit between sound and sense: Achieved.

She grew vain about her name. "Alison Batz," she'd announce to outstretched hands at social gatherings, pronouncing the syllables clear and with a force, waiting for some sign of recognition. "The Writer," she would finish when she didn't get it.

Alison had come to Coalton to find a new lifestyle for her Lifestyle Writing. Call it undercover research. She snickered to herself at this thought—"under the covers research," more like it—and then leaned to the left, pushing her breast into F-Bomb's forearm. She studied the rich coffee colour on the small exposed patch of skin at his neck and wanted to brush her lips against it, to lick and see if it tasted of cocoa. God, he was beautiful. She wondered if he was Hispanic or something.

With her breast nestled nicely against him and her ass pressed hard against SOR, pretty sure neither of them was sober enough to notice, Alison spotted someone about fifty metres ahead on the highway holding a big cardboard sign with TAKE ME TO CAMELOT spray painted in fluorescent orange.

A hitchhiker? Who hitched to the backcountry?

"Whoa whoa whoa. Halt this baby! That's fucking Shanny!"

"Easy on the f-bombs, F-Bomb. We're in the presence of a lady." SOR confirmed Alison's suspicion, drawling these words as if his brain sent them to his tongue one by one down a very long and windy tunnel. Definitely high.

"The fucking raddest, hottest chick in fucking Coalton stands right in our fucking path with a fucking Pick-Me-Up sign and you're worried about my fucking language?" F-Bomb leaned across Alison and SOR to knock on the passenger window, as if he might jump out and piggyback her into Camelot himself if he had to.

But Loco had already slowed and flipped his flashers to pull over to the side of the road, muttering, "Now I've seen everything. No local would do something as fucked up, as hitchhike to Camelot. This town goes more to shit every year." He shook his head as if listening to his brain rattle from side to side.

His truck came to a bumpy stop, and Alison recognized Shanny as she jogged toward them gripping her snowboard with one hand and cheerfully waving the other. She worked at the front desk of the gym in the evenings, prancing around in her tight yoga pants with an ass so perfectly round and hard that even Alison couldn't keep her eyes off it.

"Snowboard Your Way to Buns of Steel."

Alison had been five months away from Toronto and still her brain spewed forth an endless stream of headlines.

On first meeting Shanny, Alison had inquired after yoga-class times. Shanny had looked at her bored—as if such knowledge were far outside her responsibility, as if she were hired solely to stand at the front desk and drink smoothies.

"Oh, I don't know. I hate yoga. Too bad 'cause I love the clothes."

Alison swore Shanny had punctuated the sentence with a perfect wiggle of her perfect ass.

Even in these baggy camouflage boarder pants, Shanny's ass won attention. All eyes followed it as she ran around back to chuck her board next to Sancho, who stood on his hind legs and clawed at the truck's side, as if he were about to scramble over.

"That dog bolts, I'm leaving him, SOR. He's not ruining my ski day. He's your problem."

Alison prepared herself for a lecture about how only locals knew the proper way to handle dogs—Loco had given her more material than anyone this season—but his eyes shifted to Shanny who looked about to dive into the truck's cab, happily splaying her hard little self across the laps of F-Bomb, Alison, and SOR.

"Thanks for stopping!" she grinned at Loco, "I knew *someone*'d be goin' back there today. Let's hit it!"

Hit it? Somehow the phrase sounded natural coming from Shanny. Alison knew she'd immediately render herself absurd if she dared tell anyone to "hit" anything. She cringed at her own forced use of "shred the phat pow pow" earlier this morning.

"No way. Halt," Loco held up a hand, stopping Shanny cold. "This cab's reached her max. All guys in the back. With the mutt."

F-Bomb parted his lips to protest, but Loco had moved into Big Boss mode now, holding a hand centimetres from F-Bomb's face, "Shut it. In the back. Now."

Cool air filled the new gaps at Alison's sides as F-Bomb and SOR followed Loco's orders, peeling themselves away from her. She folded the corners of her lips up in an imitation of a smile at Shanny who sprang into the passenger seat with a waft of patchouli. Hippy perfume. Alison had to admit she liked the spicy aroma, a smoky sweetness almost like marijuana.

She'd take a bullet to the lung rather than be caught wearing it, but she couldn't help enjoying it on other people.

"You guys didn't tell me you were going out there this weekend. Thanks for the invite, man." Shanny stuck out her bottom lip in a mock pout. "More like 'thanks for nothing, dudes.'"

"Weren't s'posta be no chicks." Loco didn't look at either of his passengers, his eyes fastened on the rearview mirror as his buddies hopped in the back and squatted next to the snowy gear, SOR holding an arm around Sancho, who seemed to be shivering. "Guess someone changed the rules," he added without taking his eyes off the rearview mirror.

SOR waved a hand to indicate they were all in and secure. Loco turned to Alison and sighed a hot gust of air into her face. "Ahrt, girls, to Camelot. Let's GO," he shouted the last word as he spun his tires and pulled back onto the highway.

6. The Miller

Lanny had started to worry that he and Michael would never get where they were going. First, Janet had them traipsing around the backyard like a coupla puppies in obedience training school. They were supposed to be out in the wild already, but she had them penned up, following orders and sipping on some fruity tea drink like a pair of limp-dicked homos. She issued commands, and what was he supposed to do? Michael shoulda bin *telling* her— telling her they were Gonesville. *Kiss, kiss, hug, hug, see you on Sunday, honey*—however he had to do it, Lanny didn't care, *just do it*.

No such luck. Then Lanny learned that Janet actually planned to come with them.

On a ski touring trek.

In her condition.

Michael sure as hell hadn't warned Lanny. When she pulled out her touring pack and started stuffing it full of equipment, Michael wouldn't even meet Lanny's eyes. They were going into the *backcountry*. The *Wild*. No place for a pregnant lady.

And Lanny had *heard* about pregnancy. He *knew* they'd be stopping every fifteen minutes so she could waddle into the trees and take a leak. It'd take them a year to get to bloody Camelot. Plus, she'd talk the whole way there, no doubt. Zero understanding of the whole point—Escape, Quiet, Calm. Not ceaseless nattering about nothing. Women never understood when simple *quiet* was the thing needed, as if they had to continually talk themselves into existence, like if they fell silent too long they might spontaneously evaporate.

To make matters worse, she'd start every other sentence with "When the baby comes out . . ."

He *knew* where a baby came out *of*. Since when was it socially acceptable to talk about *that* place to your husband's best friend?

Women today had no sense of decorum.

As if all this wasn't enough, Michael hadn't bothered to reserve a spot at the hut. He claimed that it was too late in the season; *nobody* would be thinking about skiing in mid-April.

But now it was puking out. Anyone could be getting the same idea as them—one last, unexpected chance at the steep and deeps.

Without sign-ups, the hut was first come, first serve, which meant they shoulda left at sun-up to secure themselves prime beds. Instead they were playing hide and friggin' seek in Michael's backyard.

Worse yet, they pretended to like it. *Yes, darling. Whatever you say, darling. Why don't I run one more circle around the yard for you, darling.*

Lanny was never getting married.

Now it was almost noon, and he and Michael were still sitting in the backyard while Janet busied herself phoning her hippy, lesbian friends.

"You know who'd love to come on a hike? Ella and Cosmos!" She practically skipped off to the kitchen phone.

A hike? They weren't going for a fucking hike. They were going *skiing*! How often did he get to go skiing these days? Never. He worked all bloody week cutting trees for the Coalton mill. By the weekend, he was so exhausted he could hardly haul himself off the couch. This weekend was his last chance of the winter, and she would ruin it.

When she skipped off to the phone, Michael wouldn't even meet his eyes, suddenly grew fascinated with the task of folding his skins. There was no need to fold them—he'd be using them soon enough. Lanny had already started pressing the sticky side of one skin onto the bottom of his ski, putting pressure along the long strip until it fully covered the ski's base, caressing out each wrinkle, firmly rubbing the coarse hair designed to keep him from sliding down the mountain when he wanted to climb up it.

Finished the first ski, he propped it up in the snow so the skin's hair wouldn't get wet and ice up later. He reached for his other ski, looping the second skin over the ski's tip and working the sticky strip down toward the base.

By the time Janet came bouncing back to the yard, Michael had somehow managed to twist his skins together into a big sticky mess, and sat slumped in the snow, slowly working them apart. She smiled down at him as if she found nothing more endearing than his complete ineptitude.

"This is perfect!" she beamed.

For a second, Lanny thought she meant Michael's messed-up skins, but she continued.

"Ella and Cosmos were so relieved to hear from me. It just so happens they *need* to get out of town. It must've been the Universe telling me to call. I knew something uncanny was up when the sensation just came over me like that."

Lanny took a deep sip of his now cold tea, focused intently on rubbing Sitka under her leather collar, and said nothing. He'd noticed this about Janet before, her tendency to take on the language of others, to talk about "being stoked" for skiing with him and Michael, and then refer to taking instruction from "The Universe" with Ella and Cosmos.

"One of their huskies killed a sheep last night," Janet continued, hugging her bare hands around a coffee mug for warmth, "and now the farmer wants *both* Findley and Rider put down. Sounds like he might even have grounds to have them killed. The first taste of blood leads to an insatiable craving for it, the farmer says. He's sure they'll be back for more and, at two hundred dollars a head, he can't afford to take his chances. But you know Cosmos, she loves those dogs. They both do. So, the girls are taking them away—on the lam, as it were—"

She smiled over at Lanny, though until this point she'd been aiming her tale solely at Michael. Lanny smiled back and stuck his chin toward her, bobbing his head as if he'd never heard anything so fascinating.

"They'll just hide in the woods, they figure, until the farmer calms down enough to respond to basic compassion. Give them thirty minutes. They'll pack up and be right over with the dogs. Everything is working out perfectly!"

Michael looked dumbly up at her as if he'd forgotten the language. He wore the exact expression of one of those stunned tourists, jet-lagged and looking for the closest shopping mall.

Try Vancouver, dimwit.

Michael opened his mouth enough that Lanny thought he might say something, felt a moment of optimism, but with it still hanging slightly ajar Michael turned studiously back to his tangled skins.

Perfect? Lanny wanted to say. *The Universe? Two stinking blood-thirsty mutts? On the lam? And three—three!!—women?*

Fuck it. Lanny sank into the snow and waited for the lesbians to show up with their slobbering dogs. With a sigh, Sitka plopped her heavy, warm head into Lanny's lap. Now, the poor dog would be stuck with two aggressive huskies dry-humping her all weekend.

Lanny gulped his fruity tea, rubbed Sitka's bad hip, and looked anywhere but at Michael.

7. The Foreigner

YAMAHA BIG BEAR: TIME FOR SOME SERIOUS MUD SLINGIN'

Features a mid-size chassis, torquey, powerful engine,
5-speed automatic clutch gearbox with reverse,
independent rear suspension, on-command
2wd/4wd with diff lock, sealed wet brake, integrated
floorboards, large comfortable seat and more . . .

Fredrik loved the smell of gasoline and oil, especially when it hovered in cold, crisp air. He breathed deeply, filling himself with the heavy smell. Two-stroke smoke! Thick as ink, it was almost enough to cure his hangover. He pushed his thumb hard on the throttle, revving his snowmobile to answer the loud burst of enthusiasm emanating from Kevin's machine. Kevin roared back so loud that Fredrik could feel the vibration in his ear drum. *Yes sir, this was the life.* He'd moved here from Sweden for the bigger mountains and the deeper snow, and lately it just seemed to get deeper every year. This year it wasn't stopping. Let it snow right through to fall as far as he was concerned. Lately, with his job driving truck at the mine, he couldn't get in as many days on the mountain, but now he could afford this machine and get out faster and farther when he did have the time. Canada had been good to him.

They were still in Kev's backyard—one last run over the machines to make sure everything was in order before they headed to The Cunt-a-bury Trail for forty-eight hours of unbridled play. From here, Fredrik could see the peak where they'd be high-marking in a few hours. They could spend hours doing this—competing to see which of them could make it the furthest up a particularly steep slope, sometimes hammering the throttle as far as it'd go and leaning forward, forcing the machine up a nearly vertical wall, toying with gravity, waiting the whole while to feel the terrifying slippage of the machine sliding backwards. The goal was to get good and high, but also to turn around and come back down before you rolled or stalled out and had to deal with all your friends hollering about what a dumb fuck you'd proven yourself to be.

When Fredrik first started sledding, he'd head out with Kev to the popular spots. A group of guys always bunched together at the bottom of a slope, pointing up the mountain, yammering "Lookit! Lookit! Lookit!" and Fredrik wondered if they were even speaking English. "Lookit" appeared in no Swedish-to-English dictionary he'd ever seen. Their assessments of the sledders roaring upslope were about as comprehensible.

"Fuck you better turn yer ass 'round! Or the mountain'll turn it 'round for ya!"

"Yee-haw! He's goin' down even faster den he went up."

"Atta, boy! Giv'er!!"

"Dat was a killer hill climb dare!"

"A'right! Nosebleed highmark!"

Fredrik always got the English phrases slightly wrong. He'd call it a "killing climb" or a "bloody highmark"—such slight differences really. Clear as fucking sausage water, this language. Who cared whether you said "killing climb" or "killer climb"? Everybody, that's who. He'd get one syllable wrong and they'd laugh about it for a whole afternoon, making him feel like he'd been caught with his beard in the mailbox, mocking every word he said, imitating his lilting accent. He felt a nauseous rush of humiliation remembering how hard he'd tried to blend in and how badly he'd failed.

Luckily, today, this late in the season, it should just be him and Kev. The snowfall had slowed now, and the sun struggled to part the clouds, lighting up the mountain side, a pillowy white piece of perfection. Nothing made you feel more alive than roaring up a snow-covered rock face with the force of three-hundred-horse power vibrating between your legs.

Fredrik's mug of Clam and Beer sat on Kevin's back step, the cold air turning it frosty. Fredrik swung his leg off his mountain sled and jogged to the mug, took a long deep swig. It froze his throat and his head pounded, but one more of these and he'd be good as new. Just what the doctor ordered.

Last night had turned into a full-on bender. It must've been nearly five in the morning before he took the pillows at the foot of the stairs and the blankets hung up on the moose's rack draping down over the animal's eyes as if even it had been trying to get some sleep in the midst of the drunken chaos, and crashed on the couch. Kevin crept upstairs, holding fast to the banister—as graceful as a drunk elephant—and made his attempt on the fortress of the master bedroom.

Claudette clearly won that fight because this morning Fredrik woke to find Kevin snoring loudly on the recliner next to him, wrapped tight in a patchwork table cloth, and pulling his limbs fetal-position into his body in an attempt to keep warm. When Fredrik started clinking together glasses in a half-hearted effort to straighten the stinking mess they'd made of the living room, Kevin shook himself awake. He looked up from the chair, scratched his head vigorously with both hands, and croaked out his first words, "Hair of the dog, buddy?"

Definitely.

Fortunately, they both had the good sense to keep quiet— focused on battling their own headaches—until the Clam Eye worked its magic. Now they were on number three and a pleasant haze had fallen over the snowy world. Hangover be damned—bring on the sleddin'!

Claudette had peered out the upstairs bedroom window all morning, as if they couldn't see her while she held them under constant surveillance. He felt like holding his mug up to her in a hardy cheer. *Hey, Claudy-Baby, you forgot your invisible juice.*

Kev had sure upped the difficulty level with this broad—went right from a blue run to a black double diamond. When he dumped wife number one on the grounds she was no fun, he already had Claudette lined up as wife number two. Claudette seemed like a full-fledged party at first. She used to love nothing better than tipping into the booze and going for a roar around the mountain on a Yamaha Big Bear.

She could high-mark a snowmobile better than most guys—roaring up a steep slope at full bore, until even Fredrik had to be impressed. She earned the NO FEAR logo she wore splayed on her T-shirts, her ball cap and sweatpants.

Plus, she didn't give you guff like other chicks. Nobody would call her high-maintenance. She was happy to throw on a pair of Carhartts and make nature her playground. The summer before she and Kev got married, the three of them were ripping around the logging roads above town on a couple of quads, Claudette holding fast to Kevin's waist. She'd had the foresight to pack some Mike's Hard Lemonades, and they stopped for a watering break every thirty minutes or so. The day couldn't have been more glorious— bluebird sky, the slightest cool breeze spreading the wood's rich fragrance. One of those days that you forgot to go home. Forgot you had a home.

Around five in the afternoon, they ripped past a dirt bag hippy ski bum with an older clean-cut woman, around Claudette's age at least, their mountain bikes lying across the road as they sat in the deep grass pulling on knee pads for their descent. The woman had a big scrape on her knee, and blood trickled down her leg, staining her sock. She had another pretty nasty wound on her arm. They both looked liked they'd smoked their heads off, stoned shit silly. A hazy cloud seemed to cling to their bodies in the crisp bright day. Kev and Fredrik slowed their machines and said their hellos— taking in the sweet aroma of marijuana—before revving up and speeding down the road in a perfect cloud of summer dust. As soon as they were out of ear shot, they stopped to regroup. Claudette had laughed, "Good day for a little biking and smoking." Fredrik and Kevin both laughed with her, but at the same time Fredrik imagined the dirt bags turning to each other and laughing, *Good day for some drinkin' and quadin'.*

Allt är inte för alla. All is not for all. Pick your way, don't judge the ways of others. The words came to him in the phlegmy voice of his ninety-three-year-old Mormor. *Genom sig själv känner man andra*, she always added, you will know others through yourself. He decided against sharing his grandmother's thoughts with Claudette and Kevin.

The three of them tore the trails up until the sun dipped behind the Coalton ridge. Then Claudette pulled a flask of fireball out of her boot, and they sat, backs leaning against the microwave tower, and watched the sunset turn the world pink.

That Claudette had been easy to be around. But the moment Kevin slipped a wedding ring on her finger, she turned hard and intolerant. She took to pinching her lips in tight to her teeth and shaking her head, a subtle movement that got its message across perfectly clear: I'd rather eat fucking puke than spend another second with the two of you.

It didn't take much. He'd show up with a six-pack after work, just like he always had, and Claudette would pinch her mouth in so tight it looked like she was trying to squash a small bug living in its corners. She would turn her squinted eyes on Kevin and give her head one firm shake, like maybe she had a bit of water in her ears.

Fredrik knew marriage didn't come with a guarantee, but he would've pegged Claudette for a safe wife, one who wouldn't steal a man from his buddies and suddenly pronounce sleddin' a waste of productive time, who wouldn't declare female war on all things male. At least, that's how she'd played it when she was busy plotting to force out wife number one.

Well, Fredrik couldn't guarantee much but he knew one thing for sure—he and Kev were going sleddin' this weekend and Claudette was absolutely not coming.

8. Valhalla

This unexpected snow made Heinz impatient. Usually, he welcomed the snow. In spring, summer, and fall anyone could 4 x 4 their way to his hut. A forestry road—Branch C—led right to his front yard, his little hut tucked just down slope within the trees so it wasn't easily spotted. But it was right there. He could jump in his truck and drive into Coalton anytime he needed something. He didn't, but he could. Only when winter came, making the forestry roads impassable, fully burying his rusted-out truck, erasing his loose connections to his previous world, only then when his withdrawal was complete did Heinz feel content. But this year, he had plans for the spring, wanted to extend his trail system to include a cave on the other side of Grendel's Mother's Mere.

Damn the ski bums—he couldn't even think of the swimming hole anymore without the word *muff* leaping unbidden into his mind. He'd have to work harder at a name for this cave, something not so easily corrupted.

He'd spent a lot of time there late last spring. The first time, he followed the trickle of a creek up until it took him to the gaping hole in the side of the mountain. He walked in so far the light barely reached him, everything ominously shadowed, and he yelled his own name to hear it ricochet off the tight walls.

HEINZ . . . Heinz . . . heinz . . . hein . . .

He ate a piece of moose jerky at the cave's base, resting his bare feet in the snow-cold stream, letting his gaze wander up to the cave's ceiling in search of bats. After lunch, he wandered farther up the mountain, battling the hawthorn until he emerged above the cave, so that he could sit with his feet dangling into its yawning mouth. He sipped on his purified creek water and gazed across the valley, so untouched that he could convince himself he was the only man on earth. Adam minus Eve.

He knew, though, that he had not been the first. The hawthorn bushes lay trampled in spots, and the occasional boot imprint in mud, or in the few remaining patches of snow, stood as evidence that others had bush-whacked their way up here. It wasn't easy to get to, though, and only the most devout cave-spelunkers would bother.

As he sat dangling his feet and eyeing the land between Grendel's Mother's Mere and the creek bed that trickled out of the cave's mouth, he pondered the best route to lay his trail. A patch of brown entered the bottom of his vision.

A grizzly cub.

Heinz pulled himself back from the ledge, hiding from view. Where there was grizzly cub, there was grizzly mama, and nobody messed with a mama grizzly. The little fluff of cinnamon brown bounded to the water's edge, bending down as if to stare at its own reflection, leaning and leaning until its little black nose dipped into the cool liquid. It jumped back, giving its head a shake, then ever so cautiously moved toward the pool of water again. This time, it lifted a paw and splashed down hard.

Heinz almost expected the animal to roll on its back laughing, a cartoon version of itself. He could see why this species had inspired generations' worth of stuffed animals. Even knowing better, he'd grown so absorbed in the cute antics that he'd forgotten to stay on high alert for the mama, and the familiar, sweaty sensation of pure fear gripped his body when the giant beast poked its nose into the little bear, moving it away from water's edge.

Nothing turned the contents of his intestines to liquid faster than a grizzly bear. The large hump on her back made her look angry, like an arched cat.

Seven hundred pounds of angry.

She clawed the ground and snorted through her long nose, in, Heinz felt certain, a deliberate spectacle of aggression. He imagined he could feel the warm liquid spraying from her snout. Her eyes darted from clump of trees to clump of trees, agitated. She must've sensed his presence.

He hardly breathed until she and her cub lumbered downstream in the direction they'd come. He waited for a full hour before he dared move anywhere. When he summoned the courage to ease himself out of hiding, he jogged down to the creek side, looking for remnants of the bears' presence. He found a pile of scat and poked at it with a long stick, dissecting the digested roots and leaves. He rubbed and smeared the scat, driving it into the mud. He bent low to it and dipped his stick-end into the flattened mess, raising a chunk of it to his face. It didn't smell as awful as he expected. Human waste—filled with meat and processed food—stank worse.

He lifted the end of his stick to a big rock in the creek, trying to draw a line. He could only make the spindliest marking with the stick's tip, so he found a big leaf and bent back down to the scat. He scooped up as much of the bear waste as he could and used the leaf to smear a thick line down the rock face. He did the same for three dense, goopy lines, and then stood back to examine the effect.

A giant H.

H for Heinz.

On the way back to his hut, he made nonstop noise to ensure he wouldn't come upon the bears by surprise. "Here I come, bears. Here I am. No harm from me, no harm to you. I'm a nice nice man and here I come! I live here too. Just like you. Heinz Wilhelm Wittiger belongs to nature. Bear bear bear, here I come." His throat grew hoarse before he finished the ten-kilometre hike back to his home, but still he croaked, "Here. Heinz. Comes."

He used the scat-caked stick as a walking cane and imagined himself impotently holding it up in a weak attempt to fend off the bears if it came to that.

Though the encounter terrified Heinz, it also kept him coming back to the spot. Fear reminded a man that he was alive, Heinz believed.

Last week, while scouting around on snowshoes, he had noticed a hole in the cave's roof. It went clear through so the sun shone into the small, tight space, creating shadows across the rock formations under water on the cave's floor. He didn't know how he could've missed the hole before. Was it new, he wondered, the effect of recent erosion? While he stood studying the hole's dimensions, a bird flew in the mouth of the cave, fluttered around above his head, and then flew straight out the hole into the sunshine. Although the bird flew from the near darkness of the cave into the light of day, it reminded him of a line from Norse poetry, something about life being as brief as the time it took a bird to fly out of the darkness of the natural world into a warm, bright hall and back into the cold, dark night.

Who had it right, he wondered—those ancients who believed that life was a brief spell of light in an eternity of unknowable darkness, or the modern Christians who believed life to be a black torture one must endure until rewarded at death with the everlasting heavenly light?

That was the big question, wasn't it?

Heinz stared up at the hole of light until his neck began to cramp. In his mind, he christened the cave. "Valhalla."

9. La Canadienne

SHOTGUN

Preparation time: 10 seconds

Hold one can of cheap beer in the palm of your hand, so that the top is angled towards your hip (to help avoid messy spray).

Angle top of can down. Use car key (or any sharp object) to puncture a small hole in the side of the can towards bottom of can.

Turn the can sideways, with the hole facing up towards the ceiling. Place the tip of either index finger underneath the tab of the can to establish a good grip.

Place your mouth over the hole in the can.

Lift can upright, stand up straight and pop the top of the can open.

Chug. Beer will flow quickly, so open throat as much as possible.

NOTE: Best performed outdoors to avoid mess. For added style points, once beer has been drained, crush can on forehead.

Claudette was going sledding. She was still lost in her own anger, her muscles clenched, her traps so tight that moving her neck sent a cold blade of pain straight through the base of her skull. The intensity of her anger had sent her digestive acids into a furious boil, giving her a wicked case of heartburn. But she'd decided that hating Fredrik—actually, this morning make that hating Fredrik *and Kevin*—was no reason she should be stuck in the house by herself all weekend while they were out having fun. Forget it. She might not talk to either of them the whole forty-eight hours, but she was going.

Last night, she'd nearly called the Mounties on her own husband. *Get these drunken imbeciles out of here, please. Niaiseux! Esti d'ivrogne!*

She'd started the evening having a few drinks with them, pouring liberal rye and Cokes, then curling up deep in her old basket chair with a down comforter draped over her legs, ready to relax and listen to their snowmobiling stories.

But she soon realized she'd heard every word before. Heard them all and then heard them again. How much could one say about the snow pack?

Too much. She'd bet Kevin couldn't tell her if Fredrik had a love interest, when he'd last been laid, or whether or not he liked his foreman. But guaranteed he could tell you the exact day in January that the freezing rain had fallen on the mountains. And Fredrik was the same. They were supposedly best friends, but their idea of a personal conversation started and ended with "How 'bout that snow pack?"

Frozen rain layer in early December.

Bonded nicely with heavy snow fall and warm temps in February.

Another nasty ice layer in early March.

Things setting up nicely now with usual spring conditions.

Potential danger with unexpected, late snow.

Be careful of afternoon sun beating down on south facing slopes.

That's it, everything to be said. But those two found a way to turn it into a season-long "conversation."

And for all their talk, they did nothing to actively avoid the avalanche danger. They understood snow conditions, but when she suggested that they take a course and start wearing transceivers, they both laughed at her.

"That stuff's for skiers. If we get caught in a slide with these monster machines, we're goin' under. No sense kiddin' ourselves we ain't."

"But we'll die happy."

Nobody better *ever* say that Claudette died happy, croaked doing what she loved. She'd come back from the dead and tear out the larynx of the eulogist who dared make that idiotic comment.

Living made her happy—that's what she loved—but the way Kevin and Fredrik treated their lives like a video game? Three free chances. Press "Play Again" to start all over. It drove her mad.

The way they used snow as an excuse for drinking might be hilarious if Kevin were married to someone else. But since he happened to be married to her, it made her want to scream the roof off the house, slam doors until the foundation shook.

It's snowing—celebrate with a drink.

It's not snowing—drown sorrows in drink.

It might snow—sit by window in anticipation. And drink.

It might not snow—nothing else to do but drink.

When their celebration last night shifted from an It-Might-Snow Stakeout to an It-Is-Snowing Extravaganza, she'd been willing to retire with her book and leave them to it. She said her goodnights, quite civilly she thought, and headed upstairs, wrapped in the comforter, to read in bed.

But around twelve, they got ridiculous. Again. First she heard something heavy sliding across a table and glass smashing to the ground. That's what woke her. Then she heard, even felt, a body slam into a wall. *Fucking niaiseux!* She hoped they both broke their heads open on the plaster, choked on their own stupid blood. She'd just had a drywaller over last week to fix the hole Kev's head made the last time Fredrik came over.

She'd never actually seen them wrestling, only dealt with the results, but the imagined picture of them grappling was more comical than the reality of the damage. Fredrik stood at nearly six and a half feet, as skinny as a rope, whereas Kevin barely reached five feet, seven inches and seemed nearly as wide. Everything about him was wide—wide forehead, wide nose, and wide lips. His build made him seem angry all the time, as if too much man had been packed into too small a box and was due to explode any moment. Claudette always thought of his bristly red hair as the lighted fuse atop a box of dynamite. In contrast, Fredrik's lackadaisical, awkward limbs reminded her of a stuffed toy monkey. His heavy Swedish accent, his stupid sayings about shit in blue cupboards and beards in metal mailboxes, and his tendency to get vocabulary slightly wrong—"ice bear" for "polar bear" or "apple cake" for "apple pie"—made him even more absurd.

That Kevin dared to come upstairs after all that commotion still shocked her.

"Baby, push o'er. Make a little room for yer lover boy."

"You are the last person I wish for to come into my bed," she stumbled over the words, her English, as always, evading her in anger. "You stink." She kicked her foot out from under the covers, aiming for his groin, amazed at how fast she could bolt awake, anger jarring her dry eyes wide open. He smelled like he'd taken a swim in cheap beer then rolled around in cigarette butts, and maybe fallen over in barf to boot. "Get away. Out. *Maintenant!*"

This morning, Mr. Lover Boy and his Swedish monkey, Apple Cake, were back into the booze before nine. Not even giving themselves time to sober up from the night before.

She hated them and she hated this town. She used to love Coalton, couldn't believe she'd managed to create a life for herself in a place where playing in the snow took precedence over jobs, financial planning, marriages. Here, when people asked, "So what do you do?" they didn't mean for a living. They meant, do you ski or snowboard, sled or hike? Here, when girlfriends wanted to get together, it was for a bike ride or a cross-country ski instead of a coffee or a lunch. No more sitting in artificially lit bistros ordering overpriced salmon salad, chatting aimlessly about each other's bosses and boyfriends. City life in Quebec had been all about sitting—sitting at work, sitting in restaurants, sitting on busses and in taxicabs, forever sitting. Here, Claudette lived in perpetual motion, and in every direction she looked she saw another peak to summit, another forest to explore, another river to ride. She believed in the corny pamphlets espousing *Coalton: British Columbia's Hidden Piece of Heaven.*

But eventually the societal bullshit outweighed the natural splendor. Coalton was too small of a place to be forever The Other Woman. The Adulteress. People were quick to label others here, and the labels stuck.

In Coalton, adjectives did the work of last names.

"Alison—you know, *Big City* Alison."

"Oh you know Lanny—Redneck Forester Lanny, Seven-Finger Lanny."

There was "Good Posture Brian," "Creepy Kent," "Miner Mike," "Hippy Pete," "Hot Shanny," "Swedish Fredrik," "Bear-Aware Ella," "Draft-Dodger David," "Loosie Lucy," and "Quiet Kelly." You didn't have to guess what people thought of you here—they put it all in your name.

And now she was "Claudette . . . you know, *Home-Wrecker* Claudette." No one called her Home Wrecker to her face, of course, but Fredrik—big, sloppy-limbed Scandinavian buffoon that he was—had to make sure she knew.

Sometimes people were identified by their partners rather than by their characters—"Janet-and-Michael Janet," "Cosmos-and-Ella Cosmos." But never Claudette. She and Kevin could be together twenty years and she'd still be Home-Wrecker Claudette. Coalton had a good memory that prevented easy forgiveness. Seven years ago the ski hill got a new chairlift, and people still referred to that terrain as "The New Side," probably always would. She could live here with her husband until she needed a walker and kept her teeth on the nightstand, and still she would never be "Claudette-and-Kevin Claudette."

Months ago, Kev promised her they could move. She'd given up everything for him—every bit of respect she'd had in this community—but now he refused to give up Coalton for her. Last week, she'd run into his first wife at the coffee shop. The woman had bumped into Claudette, deliberately hitting her steaming tea, knocking it to the floor. It spilled down Claudette's leg, soaking her skirt. As she stood in the puddle, the ex-wife smiled at the server, "Nice seeing you," and breezed out the door. The server threw a dirty rag at Claudette, "Well, better clean it up." Claudette kneeled down and cleaned, ignoring the snickers from the table behind her.

The week before, someone had spray painted a giant, red HW on Claudette's rear window while she was in Overwaitea getting groceries.

HW for Home Wrecker.

She'd come home crying, knowing she'd made her face an ugly blotchy mess and that she spewed incomprehensible, slobbery noise as she tried to explain through her sobs. Kevin had pushed her hair back from her sweaty forehead, "Don't worry, baby. It'll all blow over."

When? When would it blow over?

"Quand?" she'd sobbed, not caring that Kevin didn't understand a single word of French, "Quand?"

Today, though, the entire world would consist of her and her sled. She'd race that machine as fast as it would go, talking to no one. She'd pin the throttle into the handle, roaring the engine until she couldn't hear her own thoughts, couldn't remember Fredrik's stupid name, couldn't even imagine what a bloody red HW might stand for. She'd climb for the sky, leaving Coalton and its small-minded, judgmental terrorists far behind.

At the trailhead, Claudette grabbed a Pilsner from Kevin's cooler. She jabbed her key savagely into the tin, and shot-gunned the whole thing in four seconds. For added effect, she crushed the empty can on her forehead and chucked it over her shoulder into the snow. *No fun anymore?*

She'd show them fun.

She hopped on her Yamaha Big Bear and tore down the trail, leaving a stunned Fredrik-and-Kevin to follow.

10. The Hippy

MUSHROOM TEA

Preparation time: 25 minutes

In one medium-sized pot of water, cook about 2 grams
  of dried magic mushrooms (collected in autumn,
  found growing on lawns, fields, and bark mulch
  throughout British Columbia, recognized by wavy
  brown cap fading to yellowish gills and bruising-
  blue stalk).

Simmer water. Do not boil. Keep the fire low and leave
  the magic mushrooms in for about 20 minutes.

Pour the water and mix with a caffeine-free tea.

Drink the mushroom tea.

After 30 minutes the magic mushrooms start working. You will grow relaxed. Everything will seem
  funny. You may experience hallucinations as the
  mushrooms transport you to a visionary state of
  consciousness. Effects last for about 5 hours.

NOTE: To intensify effects, simply eat the dried
  mushrooms. Chew well and chase with orange
  juice, since vitamin C further increases the effects.

Cosmos stood studying the giant sign at
the head of the trail, snow piled on its top edge
like a cotton-baton hat. She hoped the way she
held her hands to her hips and chewed on the
inside of her lip communicated her utter disgust. "There's nothing I like more than getting
out in the woods for a walk," she said as she
turned away from the sign, "knowing that I've studied enough that I
can take care of myself with just a pack on my back. I can live on

nettles and ginger root if I have to. You have to know what you're doing, sure, but once you do—Nature provides for Her children." She faced Lanny and Michael, "But *this* man," she threw her left hand above her head, gesturing toward the sign behind her, pronouncing *this* with as much venom as she could muster. "*This* man, I detest. He will ruin nature, our magical wilderness, one sign at a time. Inch of trail by inch of trail, he will destroy what makes this place special."

At least the crazy recluse hadn't mapped his way to her cave yet. She'd been up there early this spring for her annual Bringing-the-Sun-into-the-Cave ceremony and had seen none of his invasive signs yet. She wanted to march right up to his little hermit hut and give him a piece of her mind.

Be careful with those, Ella always said, *there're only so many pieces to go around.*

Findley and Rider had gathered at Cosmos' feet while she spoke, and Findley, the bigger of the two huskies, rubbed up against her legs, nearly buckling her right knee. She pulled two homemade organic dog treats out of the deep pockets of her wool sweater, gently handing one to each. Findley, as always, took the food from her hand first and Rider followed his lead. Feeling their warm, wet breath on her cool hand, she blinked quickly to ward off the too familiar burn of tears. She still couldn't believe she'd nearly lost them, with their thick coats that smelled of snow and grass and dank wool and everything wild and natural. She remembered holding their little paws up to her nose when they were just puppies, breathing in the popcorn smell of their warm soft baby paw pads.

The last twenty-four hours—first her boys missing all afternoon and late into the night, then all those murderous threats from the insane farmer—had discombobulated her. "My chakras have been thrown completely out of line," she'd said this morning as she flossed her teeth, looking into the bathroom mirror over her left shoulder at Ella. "My root chakra feels closed entirely."

She and Ella had combed the back roads calling the dogs' names until after three this morning, insomniac with worry. When there was nothing left to do, they went home and sat at their big picture window, watching the snow fall and drinking cinnamon tea. "For its calming effects," she'd sighed, handing Ella a deep steaming mug.

As they sipped, Ella kept running her hand over Cosmos' hair and down the back of her neck and shoulders, "It'll be okay. They'll be back."

Cosmos tried to take comfort from these words, tried to open herself to the warm strength in Ella's hand as it rested at the base of her skull, but a wet sandbag of worry sat heavily in the bottom of her stomach.

Even now, with the dogs safely at her side, Cosmos felt tired and irritable. She pressed her hands into her lower stomach. It protruded and felt hard to the touch. She pushed with her fingers and listened to it groan in response. Constipation was always her body's first manifestation of anxiety.

She stepped close to Ella, speaking softly in her ear so no one else would hear. "We should meditate when we get to the hut." She cupped Ella's loose, brown hair at the base of her neck, twirling a loose strand around her index finger. "As soon as we arrive," she added with urgency.

Meditation always helped. Afterwards, she decided, she'd perform a cleansing ritual, lighting her dried white sage and wafting the purifying smoke through the three-room shelter. She craved a ceremony to purge herself of all this anger and fear—two of the most debilitating emotions. She knew better than to let them get a hold of her like this. She had been frantic when they finally found the dogs, grabbing the loose flap of skin at the tip of Findley's ears and pinching down hard with her sharp fingernails, squeezing until he yelped. "Don't ever leave me like that again," she'd hissed, connecting her hiking boot with his wide ribcage. But she blocked that memory—she'd been upset. It was understandable. *We must forgive ourselves before we can forgive others*, she reminded herself. And she had no shortage of people to forgive. But she blocked those memories too.

Ella sat down in the snow rifling through the big knapsack between her legs, and Cosmos shifted her gaze, watching Lanny and Michael swing heavy packs onto their backs and step into their touring bindings. The sun shone brightly now, and the snow under their feet seemed almost slushy, though black clouds loomed in the distance. "Looks like Nature plans to give us a bit of everything She has to offer today." Cosmos smiled down at the top of Ella's head, noticing the slightest hint of grey—silver really—at the roots.

Lanny pointed at the clouds and grumbled. He banged his feet in the slush, complaining about "elephant snot." He was still grouchy about their late start. It hadn't taken Cosmos long to realize that he was one of those who believed that good planning and execution could save people from the dangers of Nature. Cosmos knew the opposite to be true—to thrive in nature one had to give up the illusion of being in control of one's own safety.

She smiled towards the dark clouds, refusing to let Lanny's negative energy affect her mood. He might be cranky, and certainly naive, thought Cosmos, but she could see he was not a bad man. His goodness came through in the obvious love between him and his golden retriever. The gentle animal had not left his side since they all unloaded from the trucks at the trailhead, had not bounded after Findley and Rider as they explored the surrounding woods, had not come after Cosmos, sniffing out her treat-filled deep pockets. And though Lanny glared at everyone—at Michael, at Cosmos, at the clouds—every time he turned to the yellow dog, his face relaxed and he lost the two sets of quotation marks that were normally etched deeply in the space between his eyebrows, carving distinct lines around a small hairy mole right in the middle of his brow.

"What a fitting colour for this breed," said Cosmos, speaking loud enough to get his attention, which he seemed determined not to give, "mellow yellow. As aggressive as a banana." She smiled.

He glowered.

"Mother Nature certainly does things right, down to the very detail of colour." She leaned over to pet the retriever's soft head, but Lanny called the dog away.

"Here, Sitka, here girl!"

As possessive as a jealous lover, thought Cosmos. Unruffled, she leaned against the giant sign and surveyed their group of sundry folk. Janet struggled with her skis, having trouble bending down. In the last month, she'd blossomed into a goddess of fertility. Her ski jacket barely fit over her belly, hugging Baby Kodiak snug. Janet's cheeks glowed with the effort of snapping her boots into their bindings. Michael tried to help her, but she swatted him away with her ski pole. He shrugged and moved towards the trailhead, leaving her bent over her lump of a belly, fighting with her skis.

The branches over the trail drooped, heavy with snow, and Michael occupied himself by knocking them with his ski pole, watching the snow fall to the ground. "This forest will be gone in a year," he said to no one in particular, "all condos." Cosmos imagined him hissing the final word—condos-sssssss—but Michael's tone suggested this change would be a good thing. *Development. Progress.* She knew the words these types used. *Growth. Improvement.*

Revitalization, that was her favourite, as if the condos would be more alive, more vital, than these very trees. She swallowed her words and turned away from Michael, rubbing her wool mitts across the burning itch behind her eyes.

Ella looked nearly ready. She'd found a plastic bowl in her knapsack and dropped it on the ground, filling it with bottled water for the dogs. The dogs' sloppy slurping echoed in the quiet air. Still, Lanny's dog stayed by his side, untempted by the fresh water.

Cosmos studied Ella's tired face as she bent over the drinking dogs, a hand on the back of each furry neck. Cosmos had taken a face-reading course at the community college last year and knew that Ella's full lips and small nose spoke of her honesty, her gentleness. But nothing in her face gave away the unexpected strength that rose in her during moments of crisis. That Amazonian power appeared rarely and had surprised Cosmos once more this morning.

On the phone, Ella agreed to meet the farmer about his slaughtered sheep. "Give us a couple of hours to pack up the dogs and prepare ourselves, then we'll be right over. Go ahead and make arrangements with your vet, but give us time to say our goodbyes." Her voice was deep and solemn—convincing even Cosmos—and she hung up the phone softly, even mournfully. Cosmos swallowed her shock, stopped herself from shouting *let's disembowel the bastard*!! She held her breath and watched. That's when the energy ripped through Ella, and she moved faster than Cosmos had ever seen her small body go. "Get Findley and Rider. Get your stuff. Now. We're leaving town. Fast."

The bold-faced, even easeful, deceptiveness startled Cosmos for a second, but then she realized that unconditional honesty served no one well.

People often dismissed Ella's power because of her size—*a mere wisp of a thing*, they'd say, as if she were a curl of hair to blow away in the wind. Ella was more like a loaded cement truck, thought Cosmos. Once she picked up speed, even she couldn't slam on the brakes hard enough to bring herself to a quick stop.

She'd even landed herself in the town's lone jail cell once. Two hunters showed up at her Bear Aware meeting, holding placards that read "The Only Good Bear is a Dead Bear" and "Show Me a Wild Bear and I'll Show You a Fine Rug." She approached them all smiles and sweetness. Before it even occurred to them to be wary, she'd broken the Dead-Bear placard over the tall one's head. He went to hospital for seventeen stitches. In fact, she'd hinted that her passion for Bear Aware had broken up her first marriage. A marriage to a man, of all things.

"Tea anyone?" Ella asked pulling a thermos from her backpack. "A little something to help us see Nature's true beauty," she said with a mysterious smile. "None for you, Janet—but I brought some raspberry leaf tea especially for mama. It'll strengthen your uterus for labour. Guarantee our little Kodiak a smooth entrance into this world."

Cosmos noticed Lanny cringe at the word uterus, throw his head back as if to avoid a fast left jab. It made her want to say it again: *uterus, uterus, uterus.*

Vagina, labia, clitoris.

Birth canal, menstruation, menopause.

Take that.

Janet had finally got her skis on and leaned against a tree, gratefully raising the small cup to her lips. Ella packed that thermos away and began pouring cups of earthy-smelling tea for everyone else from the other thermos.

"I love mushroom tea," beamed Cosmos, immediately embarrassed by her own enthusiasm. Why did she always have to be so emphatic? Why could she never achieve the aloof serenity she so desired? Some days, she not only loved Ella, she wished she could be Ella.

She lowered her voice and tried again. "It tastes of dirt, true, but it aids perception, making Nature's beauty fully visible to the normally clouded and cynical human mind." She heard herself saying these words slowly, airily—and inwardly praised herself for achieving the exact combination of aloofness and profundity she'd hoped for. Detached yet wise.

Michael took a cup, looked at Janet and shrugged before raising it to his lips. Lanny, however, waved Ella away, grumbling, "I'll pass on the witch's brew, thanks. I've had more than my quota of tea for today."

He turned as if talking to his dog and muttered, "Roopid Ritches."

Cosmos had noticed Lanny muttering to his dog all morning, and she'd thought he spoke *to* the animal. Now she realized that he also spoke *for* the animal. Were the "ritches" she and Ella, Cosmos wondered. And did he mean bitches or witches? And which was worse? She suppressed an urge to spit on him. She was better than that. *You're better than that*, she told herself using the strong, convinced tone she saved for her pep talks to Ella. *No man will ever make you feel insignificant and timid again.*

"I think of myself as more of a nun than a witch." Cosmos spoke calmly in Lanny's direction, though he showed no sign of hearing. "Or maybe a priestess." She arched her eyebrows. "A spokesperson and teacher for our true Goddess, Nature herself."

Lanny ignored her words. Turning away from Ella and bending down, he dug in the snow and retrieved a half-buried, crushed Pilsner can. "Pigs!" he snarled at the can before tucking it into the top of his pack, then banging his ski pole hard against a fresh snowmobile track running up the trail.

Cosmos hated snowmobilers too—their stinking, noisy machines disrupting the serenity of wilderness. But she'd resigned herself. "Anger only eats away at the soul," she said in Lanny's direction, though he appeared determined to pretend she didn't exist, at least not on his ski trip. She suspected he felt invaded. His aura glowed an angry, sulking purple. She smiled at him.

He snarled at her and returned his attention to the snowmobile track.

Now, she saw it—his grey-blue eyes, the slight graying at his temples, the powerful nose that overshadowed his mouth, the thick chest. Some of the wolf definitely dwelled in Lanny. That explained his impatience, his eagerness to be in the woods, the way he fidgeted and avoided meeting eyes with any of the humans. Lanny the Wolf. Of course.

Ella packed up the empty teacups and swung her pack on her back. Seeing that people were ready, Lanny started up the trail, sliding forward on his long skis. Michael followed, then Janet. Findley and Rider ran up ahead after Lanny and his dog. They pounced playfully on the smaller animal. The yellow dog rolled subserviently on her back.

Let water find its own level, Cosmos always said. Don't interfere with Nature. The dogs would work out their own way of dealing with each other. She'd let Findley and Rider stick with Lanny. They liked being at the front of the pack. And they probably identified with the wolf in him. They'd all be great friends by the end of the weekend.

Her own pack felt heavy on her shoulders as she followed Ella up the trail. She'd stuffed it full of spiritual equipment: tarot cards, animal cards, dried herbs, calming teas, incense sticks, meditation stones, and healing crystals. Even though she had packed in a rush, she brought her entire bag of tricks. She'd never been "on the lam" before and couldn't anticipate what she'd need.

Plus, she'd promised to do Janet's tarot. Janet wanted to know about Baby Kodiak, of course, and about some investment opportunity Michael was looking into. As if money mattered in the big scheme of things. She sensed Michael had lost his way on that count.

That's what else they could do—a sharing circle. Some heartfelt sharing would help them all re-center themselves and remember what truly mattered. Clearly, Michael needed a nudge in that direction, but she'd find a way to present the idea so he'd think it was for all of them.

She fell into a steady walking rhythm, enjoying the scraping of her snowshoes on the spring snow. She had no problem with following behind the others and set herself an easy, leisurely pace. No need to hurry; they had a long walk ahead of them. In twenty minutes or so, Ella's magic tea would kick in, opening a new window into the magical wonders of Nature.

As she waited, Cosmos went through her plans for the weekend. A plethora of invigorating activities in the hut. There'd be so much positive energy that Michael and Lanny would forget all about their macho big mountain skiing. What a great weekend it would be! She felt the knot at the base of her skull ease. All really was working out for the best. Each step took them farther away from the farmer's murderous threats and from her own violent outburst. Findley and Rider safely bounded up the trail, stopping occasionally to sniff at their new golden-retriever friend. Cosmos breathed deeply, consciously releasing tension with every exhalation. One simply had to put faith in the Universe. Mother Nature always took care of Her children.

11. The Rad Chick

MARY JANE'S COOKIES

Use any cookie recipe and substitute pot butter for
regular butter at same quantity.

Preparation time: 5 to 7 hours

Collect marijuana-shake from local pot grower. Since
it is not good enough quality to sell, it should be
available for free.

Melt 4 pounds of butter in a pot slowly, careful to
avoid burning.

Take a large pyrex lasagna dish and fill it to the half
mark point with shake.

Pour the melted butter over the shake. A perfect mix
should be butter almost to the top of the dish, and
the shake should be mushy and fairly dense.

Cover the dish with aluminum foil (very important),
then put in the oven at the lowest possible setting,
preferably 175 farenheit.

Cook for 4 to 6 hrs (until the smell of marijuana
permeates house).

Take dish out of the oven and immediately strain
butter. Don't let it cool. [Note: First, strain melted
butter through a fine collander then strain it
through a pair of fine-mesh pantyhose to remove
final, small bits of shake.]

Pour melted, strained butter into white styrofoam
cups since they are exactly 250 mL or 1 cup. At
this point, the butter should be fairly clear green
liquid.

NOTE: Special butter can be used on everything from
Christmas turkey to morning toast.

Shanny was stoked that they got off to a relatively early start this morning. When Loco pulled his beater over to the side of the road in view of The Cunt-a-bury Trail sign, the snow was still chugging down at warp speed. They parked and unloaded their gear in the snow bank, Shanny's mouth salivating at the virgin blanket of sparkling white fluff covering the ground, piling up high on the road signs, coating the branches of all the cedar trees, transforming them to shimmering ghosts. The gradual slope before her beckoned, completely untracked, a perfect marshmallow landscape with not a single footmark in sight. If she squinted up at the peaks in the distance, the snow looked like stiffly beaten meringue.

She hurried, strapping her snowboard to her pack and then throwing the pack on her back, jamming her feet into snowshoes. She wanted her footprints to be the first, each step up the mountain clearly marking her ascent, nothing but untracked beauty before her and only her own imprints in the fresh snow behind her.

She looked over her shoulder at the guys, who goofed around, not keeping her pace. SOR held a ski up, caressing it like a lover. "These babies are perfect for today. Picked them exactly for the conditions." He liked to say that any real skier needed a quiver of skis. These ones were long and stiff for the high speed ripping that was synonymous with spring skiing—good for going fast, not so easy to turn. "You gotta show these skis who's boss. You don't make love to these skis. You fuck them." He threw them both down to the ground, egged on by laughter. Shanny knew F-Bomb had heard this routine before, but he still laughed hard enough to turn his face red with the effort. Fueled by his audience, SOR leapt on top of his skis, gyrating his hips wildly. "Today, me and these skis are gonna tear this mountain a new asshole. They wouldn't be called mountains, if you weren't supposta mount them."

Though SOR was only just warming to his performance,

Shanny took the opportunity to hustle ahead and break trail. She knew she wouldn't stay out front for long—the guys would be faster on their skis.

That old chick—Alison?—was a wild card, though. She looked to be a bit of a GORB with her Lycra pants and baby blue headband, perky ponytail bouncing at the top of her head, flying this way and that, as if it were battery operated. And what was up with the way she kept pulling out a notebook, scribbling frantically each time one of the guys said anything remotely funny? Shanny still hadn't figured out who was responsible for her. She'd seen the type before, though—moved to a ski town with no real interest in skiing. Here just for the guys. Coalton bore the nickname Sausage Town for a reason. There were enough guys here in Coalton that *every* girl got treated like the Prom Queen.

Shanny hoped this new Prom Queen would slow down all three of the guys, so she could get a healthy lead and be alone in the candied landscape, globs of vanilla ice cream plopped on top of fallen logs, perfect strips of whipping cream sitting along every tree branch. She imagined herself the Queen of the Jujubes, rolling through her Candied Kingdom.

Snowy mountains and wintry woods were simply good sweetness for the soul. Backcountry touring could easily be the missed solution to the world's problems. All those politician dudes and terrorist nut-jobs just needed to chill out, and nothing said "chill" like a couple hours sliding around on a snowy mountain.

She took a deep inhalation of the fresh, crisp air, holding in the subtle perfume of pine trees before exhaling and watching her frosty breath hang in the air. She enjoyed a good forty minutes out front alone before Loco came gliding up past her, his skis leaving two thin tracks through the icing sugar at her feet. He said nothing on his way by, and she followed behind him another hour without speaking. As they headed into steeper terrain, she grew too winded to talk anyway. She heard her heart, a hollow ache deep in her eardrums, and she unzipped her waterproof jacket to let the cool breeze greet her skin. She wiped her running nose on the collar of her fleece shirt.

Loco cut a zigzag up the mountain, easily sliding on top of the snow in his skis, and leaving a smooth trail like two parallel fingers running through frosting. The terrain quickly grew too steep for him to slide straight up the slope, so he worked his way upwards in gradual switchbacks, angling up in one direction for a hundred or so metres and then doing a steep kick turn so he could face his skis in the opposite direction and angle back up the other way. Soon he was far enough ahead that Shanny could imagine he was just a plastic figure decorating her perfectly iced angelfood cake.

She knew nothing made skiers angrier than a snowboarder stomping holes in their skin trail. Even in snowshoes, she'd ruin the two perfectly smooth and parallel tracks, so she stayed to the side of Loco's trail, leaving it fast for the others, but followed his zig-zagging pattern of ascent. She couldn't go straight up anymore. When she tried, she slid back two steps for every three she took forward, huffing and grunting with the effort of stopping herself from falling farther down the hill. She didn't want to sweat too hard or she'd be wet and cold as soon as they stopped moving, so she followed Loco's more gradual path.

She noticed Loco holding up to wait whenever she fell far enough behind to be out of his sight. They'd entered into steep enough ground now that travelling alone could be dangerous, even though they stayed in a treed area where slides were unlikely.

Every time she got back within Loco's sight, he'd start trudging uphill again, not waiting for her to reach his side. He seemed no more interested in sharing the day than she was.

The clouds broke quickly in mid-morning, and as the sun gradually climbed straight above Shanny's head, marking the noon hour, the hum of snowmobiles shattered her illusion that this mountain was hers to consume in its frosting-covered entirety.

Snowmobiles weren't all bad, though. Maybe she could catch a lift. She didn't try to kid anyone—sure, she enjoyed the uphill trip, but she lived for the pure exhilaration of the downhill ride, and the faster she could get up, the more times she could rip down. If a snowmobiler offered her a ride, she'd have her inner thighs hugging his ass before he'd even come to a full stop.

As her ears strained to locate the approximate distance of the snowmobiles, she heard the faint barking of dogs in the valley below, farther down than the hum of engines. She guessed that the low deep woofs belonged to some big, aggressive dogs (shepherd or husky, maybe) and the occasional high pitched yelp to a more submissive animal not faring so well with its travelling partners. The new snow and spring sunshine were luring everyone out to the mountain today. Soon, her little ski group would have company. She hoped not everyone planned to go as far back as Camelot, or there'd be more bodies than beds.

The sun began to feel surprisingly warm against the skin of her face, and she pulled off her toque, ruffling her short hair with her fingertips, her scalp itchy with sweat. She bet that the snow lower down had started to turn to slush, but up here the crystals still fell loose like white sugar around her snowshoes with every step.

Ahead, Loco hadn't continued uphill when he saw her coming as usual. He'd propped his skis into the snow and sat on his pack, using the skis as a back rest. The beige of his toque matched his skin so that the BULA logo stitched in black looked, from a distance, to be tattooed right into his forehead. She laughed at his choice of spot—just under the POTHEAD'S PROGRESS sign. Legend had it that a backwoods creature—half man, half giant—maintained these signs. Everyone referred to him as The Ull, in reference to Ullr, the Norse god of snow. Each November, the local ski crowd partied around a giant bonfire, burning old skis in sacrifice to The Ull in hopes He'd bless them with a winter of non-stop white stuff.

Loco lifted his head and smiled, holding a water bottle out to her. She coughed a little at noticing her throat's dryness, but she shook away Loco's bottle. Instead, she reached down to the ground and grabbed a handful of snow, scooping the loose particles in both hands. Her tongue lapped up the cool flakes and she closed her mouth, feeling the liquid melt on her tongue. "This'll do me." She smiled at Loco before lapping up another mouthful of snow. Though the icy crystals felt good against her tongue, cooling her from the inside out, she felt no less parched. The snow coated her mouth but did nothing to relieve her body's hunger for liquid. The sensation reminded her of dreams. She could never quench her thirst in her dreams.

Loco shook his head, shoving the water bottle into her chest. "Sucking snow doesn't help anything. Your body uses energy to melt the snow. It'll take more from you than it'll give."

She knew he was right. She took his bottle and drank deeply, savouring the delicious sensation of the cool liquid on her lips, around her tongue, pouring down her throat. Water always tasted best half way up a snowy mountain, under the warm spring sun.

"Good pace," Loco nodded his approval as she came up from the water for air. "And with snowshoes no less. We're making awesome time." Loco took the bottle from her and tightened the lid with an extra twist before he sat it in the top pocket of his pack. "We better wait for the others, though. Alison was having a tough time even way back when I left them. Can't imagine she's doing any better now." He pulled an energy bar out of the zipped pocket on the front of his snowpants, ripped the tinfoil wrapper, and bit hard. Twisting and pulling at the goopy bar with his back teeth, he looked more animal than human. "Shit. Frozen." He'd managed to break a piece off into his mouth but chewed with exaggerated emphasis. "I thought it'd stay soft if I kept it close to my skin. Not close enough, I guess."

Shanny eased her pack off her back, careful not to smoke herself in the head with her own snowboard. She unstrapped the board, burying it a third way down in the snow, so she could sit on her pack and use the board as a backrest. Leaning back in the sun next to Loco, she listened for the others.

Sancho wasn't much of a barker so she couldn't hear any sign from him. She'd expected him to bolt to the front of the line and keep pace with Loco. With his short coat, Sancho was a complete write-off as a snow dog, but he was definitely fast. He could probably run to the cabin and back six times to their once. But he must've been loyally sticking next to his master because she hadn't seen him since she'd left the truck. She remembered a hike she'd done with SOR earlier in the winter. At the summit, they'd lost track of Sancho for a few minutes; when they found him, he was sitting far out on the windblown snow that arched over the edge of the mountain. Nothing but seven metres of suspended-snow between the dog and a six-hundred metre drop to the slope below. Follow that with one nasty avalanche ride. Both she and SOR had been scared to breathe. She imagined the cornice cracking under the dog's weight, Sancho tumbling to his death as they watched, completely helpless.

Dog there, dog gone.

Goodbye, puppy.

What would you even do in a situation like that? Shrug and walk back down the mountain, she guessed. Nothing else to do.

Without speaking, SOR had reached into his bib pocket and pulled out a Beggin' Strip, holding it out to the dog. Sancho happily bounded over, oblivious to his narrowly avoided death. After that, she and SOR always referred to Sancho as "The Avalanche Dog."

Inspired by their joke, SOR actually disguised Sancho as an avalanche dog when he travelled home to Ontario to visit his family that summer. Air Canada wasn't throwing any pet of his under the plane with the luggage. Cold, dark, noisy—that was no way to treat an animal, SOR argued, forgetting the times he'd left Sancho alone locked in the house for three day stretches while he'd gone ski touring (times Sancho had repaid him by shitting on his bed and eating his Italian leather hiking boots).

So, SOR borrowed a Canadian Avalanche Dog card from a buddy who worked at the ski hill, mocked one up on the computer, cut and pasted a photo of Sancho—using his full name, Sancho Panza, for a more distinguished effect—and threw the card through a laminating machine. As the *coup de grace*, he bought a little felt doggy vest at the local pet shop and sewed a big red cross onto each side.

"It's a working dog," he'd said at the check-in. And he and Sancho were through, easy as that.

Sancho got his own seat in the back row right next to SOR, and he sat bolt straight, serious face staring directly ahead, as if living up to his new role. The flight attendants called SOR "Sir" all the way to Ontario, extra attentive and bringing Sancho cookies. The vest-clad whippet-mutt refused every one, turning his head away in disgust—*can't you see I'm a working dog?*

Shanny'd love to see the bimbo stewardesses who could possibly mistake this short-haired skinny mutt for a mountain rescue dog. Who'd fall for that? SOR said he couldn't even enjoy the joke because he prayed ceaselessly the whole way to Ontario—a two-word mantra, *Don't shit. Don't shit. Don't shit.*

Even though Loco'd probably heard this story a dozen times, Shanny thought of sharing it with him again now just to hear him rant about proper skiing dogs versus dogs that had no place on a trip like this one, but he didn't seem inclined to talk today, and avoided looking at her, occupying himself working out the snow that had accumulated between his skins and skis.

Too bad. She got a kick out of the way Loco went on about Coalton forty years ago as if he'd actually been alive to see it. As he told it, everything was better then—more snow, fewer tourists, cheaper houses, longer winters. He acted like he could remember snow piles so high that people had dug tunnels to get in their front doors. Shanny wondered if there was such a thing as inherited memory. Maybe he was on a second or third life in Coalton.

He still dressed young—pierced tongue, raggedy hair, loose pants—but on him, it all seemed a disguise, like he could step into a phone booth, twirl around, and walk out looking more like her dad than like SOR. He'd exit the booth wearing a golf shirt and a leather jacket, combing his hair back smooth behind his ears and complaining that the problem with today's youth was a limited capacity for responsibility.

Take the other night. SOR and F-Bomb had picked a perfect line, running off the highest peak of their roof and into a billowy soft cushion of snow on the front lawn. Loco hung back. The guys taunted him with the usual cracks (mostly to do with the size of his sexual organs), but he turned his back to them, grabbing a shovel and focusing on cleaning the driveway. After a few trips up the roof with their skis, SOR and F-Bomb decided jumping off would be less work and nearly as fun. Each time, they'd leap from the roof, splaying their limbs and landing face first in the snow like suicidal snow angels. Shanny joined them and did a few dives. Loco stopped shovelling, but still he just leaned against his truck and watched, clicking his tongue piercing on his eyetooth. He didn't move even when F-Bomb took the taunts to a new level ("what's the matter, your pussy too sore?").

Shanny, though, sensed that Loco's reticence had nothing to do with cowardice. He lived with SOR and F-Bomb, dressed as they dressed, mostly acted as they acted, but she couldn't help but feel he was simply killing time until the moment when he pushed his way out of the baggy pants and logo-covered T-shirts, got new teeth, and emerged a completed adult. Like a regenerating worm, he'd chop off his piercings, his chain-link jewellery, his brightly coloured handkerchiefs, and grow into a new Loco. Shanny had noticed that, unlike F-Bomb and SOR, Loco didn't have any tattoos—none of Loco's gestures towards The Good Life, the ski-bum life, were permanent.

Shanny shook her head and pulled her eyes off of Loco. She was creeping herself out staring at him like that, his eyes closed, his face turned up to the sun. She turned instead to the massive mountain wall in front of her, its rock face rising steep and ominous. Her eyes searched the rock wall, looking for routes that she might be able to descend. One route—a mere streak of snow from this distance—bore the name "JI-JO" for "jump in, jump out." The line was ski-able, but with a mandatory cliff-drop to get in and another to exit. She'd done it last year, and it both scared the shit out of her and made her long to do it again. Once you jumped the first eight-foot cliff, you were committed. Second thoughts could mean death. She got that familiar tingling feeling across her chest and along her scalp, a buzzing pins-and-needles sensation deep inside her, as if her thighs had fallen asleep. Fear or excitement? She never knew the difference. Maybe she'd do it this weekend for SOR and his camera. She let her eyes skip away from the run before she had time to pussy out.

At the mountain's summit, the sun lit up the billowing cornices, turning them into glazed icing atop a giant cake, making them seem a photographer's dream rather than a backcountry enthusiast's nightmare. Even she, who knew better, felt drawn to the gravity-defying pile of snow. She understood Sancho's urge to run out on the lip of white fluff, suspended on nothing but snow and air, miles above the earth. Out there, she'd be an angel, part of the miracle and closer to the divine.

Shanny made a mental note to steer clear of the slope just under an especially threatening hang-over. If that thing slid, it could rip right down to the valley bottom and cause an avalanche with enough force to bury a house. With the non-stop snowfall, it'd been a great ski year—best in almost half a century according to Loco— but an awful year for avalanches.

Her gaze fell from the cornice at the crest of the mountain to a lower pass where she and her crew would cut over the summit and descend to Camelot. Impatience to get there made her jump up from her resting spot and try to catch sight of SOR, F-Bomb, and Alison. She could hear their voices now. They must be close. She couldn't hear the snowmobiles at all anymore and wondered if they'd gone off in a different direction or stopped for a lunch break.

She strapped her feet back into the snowshoes and jogged over to the nearest clump of trees for a pee. She unzipped her pants, and pulled a long, clear tube out of her fly. Immediately she relieved the tension on her bladder, watching the stream of urine spill down the trunk of an old cedar.

The voices came closer, chatter breaking through the natural quiet that Shanny and Loco had silently agreed upon. Shanny couldn't quite make out all their words, but SOR's laugh boomed loud and clear, "then she fell. Hard . . . skis buried . . . steep slope . . ."

To hear him tell it, nothing had ever been so funny. From what Shanny could piece together, F-Bomb had tried to help Alison, who'd somehow got herself buried up to mid-thigh with her head facing down the slope and one ski popped off, but when she grabbed his pole to right herself, she'd applied too much force and pulled him right on top of her. Only SOR found this tangled mess of limbs funny. He actually snorted when he told Loco how Alison's pack—stupidly heavy, jammed full with bottles of wine, *actual bottles of wine*, he stressed—dragged her and F-Bomb farther down the slope. When F-Bomb disengaged himself from her, she'd lain with her feet up and waving in the air, like a potato bug flipped on its back.

"Fucking funny, SOR. I didn't see you offerin' to trade her packs. Now I'm stuck carrying her hundred-fucking-pound load. I have half a mind to leave the wine right here—a treat for that old hermit guy, the so-called Ull."

Shanny flicked her wrist, shaking the last bit of urine from the tube, then tucked it back in her pants. She bit her lip, remembering how frustrating—and *exhausting*—it was to be knee-deep in snow, struggling up a slope, while trying to keep loose gear from careening down the mountain into permanent oblivion. She jogged out to hear the rest of the story face-to-face.

When she emerged from the trees, she saw that SOR lay on the ground waving his arms and legs in the air, imitating his imagined potato bug. But F-Bomb, Alison, and Sancho ignored him now, gathered around Loco who handed out strips of beef jerky. But SOR didn't care—his jokes were mostly for himself. He continued to flail his limbs and giggle. "Potato bug!" Flail. "Potato bug!" Flail.

Alison's clothes were soaked. She must've been wet through to the skin and would freeze if the group stopped too long. She chewed ravenously on one strip of jerky and clasped another tightly in her hand as if someone might try to steal it from her. She rattled off what sounded like newspaper headlines between bites, small bits of shredded jerky shooting out from her mouth.

"Toronto Urbanite Saved by Dried Cow Flesh."

"Middle-Aged Woman JONGs Herself to Death in Canadian Rockies."

"Kick Turns: A Sure Way to Instant Death."

"Medieval Motif, Medieval Torture: Coincidence?"

Ignoring her, SOR emerged from his potato bug routine and smiled widely, lifting both arms up to the sun, "Ah, spring skiing—my bread and butter!"

Shanny had spent enough time on the hill with SOR to know that everything was his bread and butter. He was the only guy she knew who could be sitting on the chairlift in the pouring rain, rust dripping off the cable above and staining his three-hundred-dollar jacket, and he'd still find a way to smile. "Skiing in the rain—my bread and butter."

She'd heard it all from him: "Elephant snot—my bread and butter," "Freezing ice crystals whipping me in the face—my bread and butter," "Gale force winds threatening to blow pine trees over into chairlift and send helpless skiers plummeting to their deaths—" SOR's bread and butter. It could be forty degrees below Celsius and, while everyone else squinted their eyes shut, tucked their chins to their chests, muttering "fucking cold, fucking cold, fucking cold" into their balaclavas, SOR'd be admiring the way ice crystals hung in the air shaping perfect rings of light around the sun.

Shanny plopped down next to F-Bomb in the soft snow, which had started to turn slushy under the powerful midday sun. He handed her his piece of beef jerky without speaking. He'd already taken a couple of bites from it, but she happily took it anyway, "Thanks, dude." She never felt hungry while she kept moving, but as soon as she slowed down, the hunger pounced upon her. Once after getting home from a ski tour, she'd eaten three fully dressed burgers, a plate of poutine dripping in thick gravy and cheese curds, and a giant slice of lemon meringue pie. She'd demolish F-Bomb's jerky. It had some spice to it, burning her tongue, and the large pepper flakes made her nose run. She ripped another piece off in her teeth, thinking of how savage Loco had looked tearing at his frozen Power Bar.

"Not exactly the model of ladylike manners, am I?" she asked F-Bomb, holding her hand slightly in front of her mouth so at least he didn't have to look at the mess of chewed-up dried meat.

"You're perfect," F-Bomb said loudly enough that everyone turned. Shanny watched a flush crawl up his divinely tanned neck to his hairline. "I mean, you're fine."

"Uh-Huh, BABY! Oh so FIIII-INE, hey F-Bomb?" SOR guffawed, dancing with his own ski, then dipping it low and diving in for a kiss.

"I mean, I like your manners." F-Bomb raised his hand towards SOR to silence him. "Oh god, never mind what I mean." He held his hands over his eyes, like a kid believing what he couldn't see just went away. He lifted himself from the snow, walking awkwardly over to his pack, sinking deep with each step. "Worry about your own girlfriend, why donchya," he muttered without looking up at SOR, making "girlfriend" sound like an insult. For the first time, Alison's presence on the trip made sense to Shanny. SOR always said a chick's horniness added to her hotness. "Take a six who's super horny, she's an instant eight. Easy." This Alison broad must be especially horny.

"Once everyone's done their lunch," Shanny belted out, keen to take the attention away from poor F-Bomb, "I've got a little something special for dessert." She pointed at the POTHEAD'S PROGRESS sign above Loco's head. "Perfect place for it." She pulled a zip-lock baggie filled with sugar-coated ginger cookies from her pack, and swatted away Sancho, who'd taken his nose out of the snow and aimed it at her baking. "Mary Jane specials—we've got enough to last all weekend and then some."

The guys all knew what made these cookies special because she'd baked them at their house and the smell of well-cooked marijuana had lingered for a full week afterwards. A marked improvement over the usual smell of cat piss, she thought. She didn't know how a house without cats could smell so much like a litter box.

She held a cookie to her nose and sniffed the skunky weed aroma before taking her first bite. "I never smoke—" she said, reiterating a familiar speech, one she'd probably already given them when she made the cookies at their house. "That shit'll kill your lungs, especially all this hydroponics, indoor grown crap, filled with toxic chemicals. Just look at the black tar in any roach—that's what you're breathing into your bodies." She sank her teeth deep into her ginger cookie. "But I love eating it. Easier on the lungs and a way better buzz." She noticed SOR had pulled out his camera and zoomed in close on her face. "Great footage, buddy," she said into the camera with her mouth still full.

When Shanny smoked, her mind got foggy, but when she ate weed, it sent her whole body into lullaby land.

Everyone took a cookie but Alison, who held her hand up in front of her nose like she'd just opened a barf-filled cooler at the guys' place. "I'm fine thanks."

"We's all *fine*. These'll just help make us a little finer." SOR popped the whole thing in his mouth.

"Great." Alison sighed the word, lifting her head to the sky, as if speaking to God Himself. "Toronto Woman Dies in Care of BC Stoners."

Shanny wasn't surprised that Alison had taken a pass. That made sense. Old people weren't supposed to do drugs. Drugs were for kids.

"Those Lycra pants hot? Don't let in much air, do they?" Shanny addressed Alison directly for the first time, running her eyes up and down the woman's legs rather than meeting her eyes. "And they're soaked. You're gonna frickin freeze when it cools down."

"How much farther?" Alison asked, ignoring Shanny. Even her ponytail seemed less bouncy. Maybe she'd run out of batteries.

Loco pointed up to the top of the mountain, where Shanny'd been scouting out runs earlier. "That much farther."

Motivated by Loco's gesture that drew attention to their ultimate uphill destination, everyone moved towards their gear, readying themselves for the final ascent, everyone but Alison, who lay curled on top of her pack, tucking her knees into her chest, banging her forehead on them, and hiding her face from the others. Shanny wondered if she was crying.

"Hey, it's not as bad as it looks. We've already come two-thirds of the way. We're on the final push."

Alison lifted her head, and her wet eyes worried over the mountain-face towering above them. She looked like she'd just realized where they were. She pointed her nose towards the steep slopes loaded with snow, "How do we know that's not all going to avalanche on us?"

"We don't," Loco said simply, sliding his ski forward and breaking new trail. "That's why you follow us. Stay on safe ground."

"And he's off . . ." Alison whispered at his back, as she dug her fingers in the snow, showing no sign of moving to stand up. She sniffled a bit and then, pulling herself together, said with renewed enthusiasm, "Well, at least I can feel safe that we have an avalanche dog with us." She smiled unconvincingly, showing a big pepper flake lodged in the gap between her two front teeth.

Sancho shivered, dropping his head to the ground and chewing on the little balls of snow stuck in his paw pads.

"Avalanche dog!" SOR snorted the words as F-Bomb and Shanny shook with laughter, neither of them making a sound but bent right over, convulsed and grabbing their guts. Just the idea of being high had already made everything funnier. The laugh overtook Shanny's whole body, like an orgasm.

"Safe ground," Alison shouted after Loco. "How do I know what's safe ground?"

SOR grinned. "Just stay high, always stay high."

It was true—up on a ridge, snow had no way to fall but away from you—but the simple word "high" started F-Bomb and Shanny into a new fit of laughter.

"Don't worry," SOR addressed Alison with mock seriousness. "Everybody's nice and high now. We'll be getting *real* high soon." With each repetition of high, F-Bomb and Shanny laughed harder. F-Bomb gasped for breath, and Shanny even surprised herself with two spit-soaked snorts.

After the second, she put her hands on her hips and took a deep breath, huffing her exhalations and leaning backwards, arching, as if she could stretch the silliness out.

If you don't take the drugs, the drugs take you, SOR liked to say. Taking drugs—his bread and butter.

Shanny reined in the corners of her mouth. "Okay. Okay. Let's get where we're going." She huffed once more and leaned down to buckle her snowshoes, her balance almost perfectly steady. She passed by Alison with a pat on the head.

Loco hadn't made too much progress. Shanny could still hold him in her sight as she plodded up the mountain. She focused on directing the drug. Pot didn't have to hamper her backcountry performance. If she focused, she could let it make her more aware of her body, her energy more intensely directed towards her ascent. Only if she let it run wild—like she had back there—did it turn her silly.

She still hadn't exactly figured out Alison's deal. It seemed like F-Bomb had invited her—and that's why he got stuck with her heavy pack—but she was sort of SOR's girlfriend and that's why he hung back with her now.

Whatever the reason, F-Bomb left them behind and fell comfortably into stride with Shanny. He could've easily slid ahead, gliding smoothly in Loco's ski tracks, while Shanny trudged behind in fresh snow.

"Don't worry about me," she said in the slow even voice she used to convince herself and others that she wasn't high. "Go on ahead with Loco. I'll stick as close as I can."

"No prob," F-Bomb said without looking at her. "I got this heavy pack anyway." He kept his sentences short as if he was afraid of a repeat performance of his *You're PERFECT* debacle. Shanny felt sorry enough for him, but she really didn't want him stuck to her now. She could hear the snowmobiles coming up behind them again. How was she going to catch a ride with him glued to her? *Thanks for the company, but . . . see ya!* That'd be rude, but if a free ride presented itself, she was jumping on. Guilt or no guilt.

She tried slowing her pace to fall naturally behind him, but he slowed his to match. "Fucking redneck pigs'll probably drive right over our fucking skin track," he muttered. "If you can't get there of your own power, you don't deserve to be there."

When Shanny's cheeks began to vibrate from the hum of the snowmobiles, she knew they were nearly close enough to see her. She let her posture sag, as if weighed down by the burden of her board and pack, slowed her walk, lifting each foot clumsily, pretending her feet were encased in cement slabs rather than cutting-edge carbon fibre trekking gear. She made herself look like her very survival depended on this ride. She stuck her arm out at a ninety degree angle, balled her hand in a tight fist, and pointed her thumb at the sky. The universal sign for "Please give me a free ride, please." But rather than coming to a standstill and turning to face the snowmobilers, she kept trudging up the mountain.

Shanny McCrea would never beg.

As the snowmobile pulled closer, she felt the familiar tingling in her skin, her muscles throbbing with desire—*please, please, please,* she thought, waving her thumb ever so slightly—but just when she expected the engine to quiet, the machine to pull in smoothly at her side, it revved louder than ever and flew by her in a gust of air that nearly toppled her over.

She stared in disbelief at the skinny legs clinging tight to the sides of the seat, the narrow hips and tiny bum, the ponytail flying out the bottom of the helmet.

It was a chick.

Shanny let her hand fall to her side. She knew more sleds were coming but even if they were guys, there's no way they'd be stopping when they were following a chick. It looked like Shanny'd be walking the whole way to Camelot today.

She shrugged at F-Bomb. "Ah well, another two hours and we'll be at the hut. We hustle, we can even get a run in before the sun goes down."

She straightened her back and quickened her steps, leaving F-Bomb to hurry after her.

12. The Developer

Usually Michael's mind as he made his way up a mountain was consumed with the simple right, left, right, left, right movement of his feet.

It'd become a standing joke between him and Janet. After a lengthy silence on every trek, she'd ask, "What're you thinking about?"

His answer was always the same: "Right, left, right . . ." He knew she'd posed the question in hopes of more intimacy: *I've been thinking about our relationship . . .* Or, *I've been giving some thought to our future . . .* Or, *You, of course, I'm thinking about you . . .*

But really he thought about nothing. He suspected that over the years, she'd come to believe him. She still asked, but now she laughed, answering with him, "Right, left, right . . ."

If the climbing became exceptionally strenuous, he'd switch from the plodding *right, left, right* to counting his steps, as if concentration on simple numbers could force out thoughts of fatigue. He'd let the numbers push the temptation to stop and rest from his mind, while he focused on manageable goals—fifty steps, then one hundred steps, then one hundred and fifty steps—never allowing himself to grapple with the reality of his far-off ultimate destination. He couldn't let himself contemplate the mountain ridge where he planned to end up. If he lifted his head to look at the summit, the impossibility of it made him dizzy. How could he ever *walk* that far? Surely, no one could.

Instead, he'd let his neck slump and his head fall so that his only view was of his skis, the right sliding forward against the snow (one!), then the left (two!).

He'd become so absorbed in his immediate task that when he

did occasionally lift his head—to relieve an uncomfortable kink in his neck, say—the view surprised him, as if he'd forgotten there was a world beyond him, a wild and magnificent world that had allegedly drawn him out here in the first place. The enormity of the mountains, the blinding sheen of perfect new snowflakes, crystals like countless crushed diamonds on untouched snow, the impossible height and circumference of the four-hundred-year-old cedars, the emerald green lichen—the colour as vibrant and unreal as lime sherbet—hanging from every branch and turning the world into something straight out of Tolkien—a setting so surreal and colossal that it overwhelmed Michael, threatened to catapult him whole into an alternate universe where humans played no part, where they carried less significance than an ant stuck to the bottom of a sneaker. To keep hold of his own sanity, he looked down and counted. First foot forward. *One.* And then the other. *Two.*

But today their pace was slow and Michael let both his eyes and his mind run free. He ignored a slight ache in his cheeks, where he held his muscles taut to avoid unseemly—even slightly hysterical—laughter. Low down on the trail, he'd let out a giggle when Findley and Rider ganged up on Sitka—Findley dry-humping the golden retriever's ass and Rider its head—and Lanny had snapped. "I've put up with enough of your shit. I'm not dealing with you acting like a tripped-out hippy all the way to Camelot. So shut the fuck up." Lanny continued walking as he talked, not reinforcing his threat by stopping to meet Michael's eyes, but he smacked Rider hard with his pole for emphasis, as if he'd rather smack Michael himself.

Barely registering the abuse, Findley jumped back on the slobber-caked yellow dog and Rider followed suit.

"Roopid rapists," Michael said through pinched cheeks in his best Scooby Doo imitation. He needed to laugh so bad that saliva filled his mouth. He swallowed hard. Normally, he found it infantile—embarrassing even—when Lanny talked for his dog, but today it was hilariously funny. Belly-shaking, eye-watering, uproariously funny.

"Real hysterical, Mike. These dogs are your fault." Lanny had stopped on the trail and looked back at Michael, now meeting his eyes in an implied threat. "Didn't I say to shut the fuck up?"

"Reah, real runny, Rike!" Michael heard himself answer in Scooby-Doo's voice again. He raised his hands to his aching cheeks, holding his laughter in. Lanny was joking, right? He couldn't be that angry. He looked like a twenty-two-year-old version of himself, filled with testosterone and ready to start a barroom brawl, his fists clenched tight around his ski poles.

The image of the two of them fist-fighting out here in the snow, sliding around on their skis, weighed down under their packs— Cheech versus Banger—released a new rush of giggles. Laughter welled up in Michael, filling him like water and pushing against his sides to escape. He managed to hold it in his gut, but imagined it spilling over his mouth and down his shirt, staining the snow at his feet.

Simple, he told himself, it was like being the only drunk person at a dinner party. Just pretend to be normal. Avoid talking. He pinched his lips tight together to stop himself from speaking for Sitka again (*Reeze! Righten up, Ranny!*), and he watched Lanny pick up momentum, gliding along the skin track, increasing his speed as if eager to put as much distance as possible between himself and Michael.

Findley and Rider finally ran on ahead, disappearing into the thick woods, while Sitka stuck close to Lanny's side. Despite the new snow, Lanny didn't have to break trail. Some keeners had set out earlier than them today and a firm skin track was already set, a ready-made escalator up to the summit. At this thought, Michael stood up straight, putting his poles under his armpit as if they were an umbrella.

"To the top please," he announced to an imaginary doorman. His giggles seemed to echo in the valley, bouncing off the ridge to the east and then the one to the west. It seemed the very sky laughed with him.

Or was it laughing at him?

He sat down in the snow. Reaching up, he pulled lichen from a cedar branch just above his head. He dropped his gloves to the ground and rolled the dried tendrils in his hands. The green was called Old Man's Beard and the black was Witch's Hair. He raked his fingers through the black lichen, as coarse and dry as an old man's facial hair, and held it up to his face, felt its itchy scratch against his chin.

What would be really funny—he laughed aloud just thinking of it—would be to fill his toque with green lichen. Stuffing piles of the ratty moss deep into his hat, so it trailed down to his shoulders, making him look like an aged Aerosmith groupie.

Just wait 'til Janet caught up and saw him. He flopped on his back in the snow giggling as he imagined her expression. Why hadn't he noticed before—just how funny everything was. This tea really was the ticket. Too bad Janet couldn't have had some—she'd lost her sense of humour recently. Worse, she'd replaced it with a state of continual panic. She thought too much—analyzing every little detail—*should we do this? what's the best way to do that?*—instead of just moving along the intended line. He rolled a strand of Witch's Hair into a tight ball and stuffed it up his right nostril. A single tendril hung down toward his mouth like a dangling piece of snot. He curled his tongue up toward his nose, trying to catch the flaccid piece of lichen and pull it into his mouth.

All that thinking would send anyone into a panic. He had a saying that held his own panic at bay—"Keep progressing the progression."

High school
↓
University
↓
Job
↓
Marriage

↓

House

↓

Promotion

↓

Bigger house

↓

Pregnancy

↓

Nursery

↓

First baby (boy)

↓

Bigger house (promotion here would come in handy)

↓

Second baby (girl)

And so on down the line to retirement. It wasn't that hard if you knew what you were supposed to do. He'd like to put his slogan on bumper stickers and T-shirts, wave it from flags. "Progress the Progression." He twirled the strand of Witch's Hair hanging out of his nose.

As he sprawled at the foot of the tree, gazing up its trunk, lichen stuffed up his nose, the pattern of bark caught his attention. So perfectly symmetrical. The way one engraved line against the rough surface led to another and another and another, never giving the eye a resting place but dragging it up and up the tree, swirling one way and then the next—as if this towering giant were alive with movement.

And—of course!—it *was* alive, the whole world was alive; if he closed his eyes to the swirling cedar tree, focused his senses and opened his ears, he could hear the mountain singing, a low deep hum—*hohm, hohm, hohm*—in time with the beating of a human heart, of *his* human heart . . .

"Hohm, hohm, hohm" he chanted along with the singing mountain, "hohmmmmm."

And this was how Janet found him. She came up the skin track—out alone ahead of Ella and Cosmos—to the sight of her husband sprawled on his back in starfish position, his fists clenching lichen, and a mock booger trailing from his nose. His eyes were still squeezed tight but the sound of Janet's breathing above him was enough—enough to remind him of who he was and what he did and did not do. He stopped his chanting and opened one eye.

Janet's face loomed above him.

He looked to make sure it had a neck.

It did. He followed it back up to her face, noticing that her eyes and nose made a perfect triangle, exactly in the top third of her face.

"You're quite symmetrical," he announced, lowering his voice to a somber and serious pitch.

Janet did not respond.

Taking in the cross squiggle of her eyebrows, he remembered that only people who were not sober worked so hard at sounding sober. He tried to relax. "Don't be mad. Symmetry is beautiful." He still made no move to lift his body from its splayed pose in the snow. "Lines are beautiful. Lines make things easy. Always remember: progress the progression. Follow the line . . . line . . . line . . . line . . ." He forgot about Janet, tracing his finger along the grooves in the cedar trunk.

"Cosmos . . ." Janet exhaled the word so it sounded like something between a sigh and a reprimand. The word struck Michael as hilariously funny because, after all, Cosmos wasn't here. It was as if Janet addressed her reprimand to the singing mountain, to the swirling tree, to the multitude of mirrors beneath her feet. At this angle, every snowflake was a house of a thousand mirrors. He rolled on his belly to stop the laughter, opening his mouth to the cold snow beneath him. He lifted his chin to stop himself from choking.

"Cosmos," he repeated into the snow through his laughter. "Cosmos!" The word fell apart—torn to pieces with laughter. "Hey,

Cosmos, I'm talking to you, Cosmos!" The snow got in his mouth, mixing with the words, wetting his laughter. He felt ready to choke and coughed into the ground.

He wondered if he could work this adventure into his marketing: "Coalton's Ski-Bum Realtor, tasting every inch of our backcountry." To sell land, a man had to know the land, and Michael LePlage had experienced this particular piece of property through all of his senses. He held his ear to the ground, listening for the snow's song, wondering if it matched that of the mountain.

"Okay, Mr. Mushroom Head. Pull it together." He felt Janet's hand on his shoulder, rolling him over to face the sky. "I can't carry you up this mountain. I can barely carry myself today." She plopped her pack on the ground, and pulled out some water. "Sit up and drink this."

He did as told, saying nothing.

She rubbed her belly, staring at the sky. He held his hand out to meet hers, letting it rest where he could sometimes feel a kick. She turned her eyes on him then, and he felt them petting him softly, pulling him into an embrace as full and real as the hug of a grandmother. He could smell fresh baked cinnamon buns. "My Banger," she smiled, tracing a finger along the edge of his ear, "long time no see." But then she stiffened, the smell of cinnamon buns disappeared, and she looked down at her belly. "Kodiak, meet your wasted daddy."

Reprimanded, he pulled his hand away.

"Real nice, Michael. Some real-estate scouting trip this is turning out to be." He saw her jaw working and heard the grinding of her teeth—always a good gauge of Janet's stress levels. She put her bare hands to her cheeks, massaging as if to force her jaw apart, and began nibbling lightly on her bottom lip. He imagined her biting a chunk off, gnawing at it, chewing until little strands of sinew stuck in her teeth, blood pooling at the corners of her mouth. He saw her biting again, slowly chewing off as much of her face as her teeth could reach.

He closed his eyes to ward off the rush of nausea engulfing him. *Don't do that*, he tried to say, but he gagged on the words.

13. The Local

HOW TO MAKE A SKI VIDEO

Ingredients: Rad lines, bottomless snow, sick cliff
hucks, wicked stunts, gnarly crashes, gruesome
injuries, trippy camera angles.

Mix randomly and back with trendy tunes.

"Fucking rednecks. You can fucking bet they'll all expect a fucking bed, but won't do a fucking speck of the fucking work." F-Bomb stood waist deep in a hole of snow, digging out the front door of Camelot. He stopped to point his shovel toward the snowmobile tracks running away from the hut, then shook his head at an abandoned machine, parked diagonally at the front door. He raised his fleece-clad arm and rubbed the sweat from his forehead. "They'll be back. At the most convenient time for them. Yeah, they'll be back with their obnoxious machines and their beer guts and their big fucking mouths. We can fucking count on that." His sunglasses slid forward on his nose as he bent back down to dig. "After *we* have dug out the eight-foot hole. After *we* have chipped out steps. After *we* have wasted our whole fucking day. *Then* they'll fucking come back."

Loco felt his neck muscles pull tense with each profanity. F-Bomb's swearing had never grated on his nerves like this before, but lately he felt about to explode with annoyance. And it wasn't just F-Bomb's swearing; it was SOR's joking, Shanny's flirting, everybody's simplest act of *being*. And as soon as he interacted with them, even *he* annoyed himself. The best thing to do, he'd decided, was stand back, be a passive observer. Recently, he approached his own life like someone watching a movie. A mockumentary.

"The Coalton Story: tripping into the pie-eyed zone."

"Okay, jump out, cry baby. I'll dig." Shanny leapt into the hole with her avalanche shovel and pushed F-Bomb up and out by the seat of his pants, each hand cupping a buttock. They were deep enough now that only one person could dig at a time, and as Shanny squished into the tight space, her whole body pressed against F-Bomb's back.

Loco stood at the rim of the hole, flattening the snow that piled up around its edges, making himself look busy. He noticed the way Shanny pushed her tits into the middle of F-Bomb's back, the way her hands lingered on his ass, and knew already that everyone in the hut would be up all night listening to a bed frame of two-by-fours banging against sheet-thin walls. With Loco's luck, he'd get it in stereo: Shanny and F-Bomb on one side and SOR and Alison on the other. He felt the familiar heat of anger at the base of his neck, and braced himself against the rush of red at the edges of his vision. They all acted like a pack of animals, ready to rub themselves up (and off) against anything handy.

Though, at the moment, getting off seemed to be the last thing on Alison's mind. She slept curled in a small ball, her knees pulled tight into her chest, right next to the hut—six feet from where Shanny dug. She hadn't said a word to Loco, SOR, or F-Bomb when she arrived. She'd thrown her pack off her shoulders to the ground, where it quickly became her pillow. She fell to it as if drop-kicked, briefly looking up at Shanny, and whispered through clenched teeth, "What kind of girl pees standing up?"

She went to sleep without waiting for an answer and hadn't opened her eyes since. Loco had imagined them arriving at Camelot under warm spring sun, sitting in the slushy snow, sipping on a cool can of beer, while the smell of sunscreen hung heavy in the air, his own skin sticky with it. Maybe they'd build a little kicker and take turns hucking off it—180s, 360s, spread eagles, front flips, back flips. In his imagination, the scene played out with them wearing T-shirts—no need for fleece or down—their flesh glistening a golden brown in the glaring sun. When they got home and watched the video of themselves, the sun would shoot bolts of light from their ski tips, from their sunglasses, from their watch faces. On television, they'd be luminescent, superhuman, godlike, unbound by the laws of gravity. Rarely would the solid ground feature in the shots; instead, flying young bodies would shine out against pure blue sky.

Loco knew that one day he'd be an old man like his dad and he'd pull out these tapes for his kids—proof that there was a time that the divinity of youth had shone through him too.

But while his imagination ran ahead of him, he—who should've known better—had forgotten that April was still winter up in the mountains. In the brief time Alison had lain at the hut's edge in the snow, the temperature had dropped sharply. Though it was only late afternoon, the sun had already fallen behind the ridge to the northwest, bringing a biting sting to the air. Afternoon ended abruptly in this valley.

Loco dug into his pack, reaching for the puffy jacket stuffed in the bottom. He pulled it out and laid it over Alison. In the occasional quiet lulls between the noise of the scraping shovels and SOR's chatter, Loco could hear the faintest whistle of a snore emanating from Alison's nose, a high-pitched imitation of the never-ending train whistles at the valley's bottom.

Sancho, who'd logged more feet of elevation than anyone, had finally run out of steam too. All the way up from their rest stop at POTHEAD'S PROGRESS, Sancho'd bolted out ahead, racing through the snow until it practically buried him, charging far out of sight but then circling back to see what was keeping the humans. When he and Loco finally arrived at Camelot, Sancho ran frantically around the hut three times before slowing down and pissing systematically on each of the hut's four corners. For a while, he made ineffectual attempts at digging with F-Bomb and Shanny but eventually he couldn't resist Alison's curled warm body and finally collapsed at her side.

Now, he snuggled up against her chest, his scrawny ribcage rising and falling in time with her snores. She slept so deeply that Loco wondered if she'd have to be carried in for the night once true darkness fell.

Shanny, on the other hand, showed no signs of fatigue. She dug with a deep, even rhythm. She seemed focused on her task, eyes steady on her shovel blade, never lifting her head, as if she were completely unaware of the three men standing above her at the hole's edge, staring down at her.

No rest for Hot Shanny. If she wanted to play with the boys, she better play at the boys' pace. Loco agreed with Big City Alison for once. What was with the pissing standing up? On their lunch break, Shanny had walked into the trees to relieve herself, but not far into the trees. It was as if she'd wanted him to see. He remembered the ad he'd seen for "female backcountry convenience"—*You Go, Girl* written in deep yellow against the sparkling snow. But geez—just because you *could* do something didn't mean you *did* do it.

As she peed, he'd faced directly away from her and focused on chewing his beef jerky, filling his ears with the gnawing of his jaw against the rough, dry meat. He held the stick of meat so close to his face that salty fat rubbed off on his nose.

Coalton had changed—five years ago, they wouldn't be hauling two chicks on a trip like this. Coalton had been MansLand at its best, but girls had got word and they'd started to flock.

Shanny and Alison might think they were different. Shanny saw herself as oh-so young and athletic, hotter than all the chicks and radder than all the guys. "She's got bigger balls than I do!" F-Bomb would say, after she'd hucked off a cliff. And Shanny would smile and gyrate like she'd just received the best compliment. Whereas Alison passed herself off as Ms. Maturity—a little too good for this life, a little too grown-up, a little too well dressed, a little too well off. And yet, she'd deign to immerse herself in it for awhile, to jot her little notes, capture a slice of their life to package up and take home with her to sell.

Alison maintained that pretense of objective distance, as if life in Coalton was nothing but field work to her, where Shanny, just as new to town and likely just as transient, threw herself into the ski-bum life with a ferocity, as if she alone *was* life in Coalton. But, and here's what neither one wanted to hear, really the two of them were just the same. Here for the dick. Both of them.

He felt the cruel tug of anger and focused his attention on the cool white snow capping the mountain peaks, felt the purity wash away the bleeding red.

These bursts of anger embarrassed him—even when nobody but him saw any sign of the ugly emotion. He knew there was an irrationality to his raging possessiveness. That was his problem. He saw himself too clearly.

When he'd turned eighteen, he couldn't wait to get out of Coalton. Since grade ten, he'd been counting the days until he could graduate and put provinces of distance between himself and the suffocating insularity of Coalton. "Everyone knows you here," people said in celebration of Coalton's unbeatable "community."

Well, he was tired of everyone knowing him. Tired of the grocery clerk who knew his family had roast pork every Wednesday—a four-pound boneless roast so there'd be plenty of leftovers for Thursday. Tired of the choir leader at the Catholic church who insisted he had a beautiful voice just like his mother (and her mother before her) and that he had equally beautiful Italian eyes just like his father (and his father before him). Tired of the grade one teacher who bragged she'd always known he'd be an engineer and make his parents proud—coming back to work at the mine where his forefathers had been mere truck drivers. All of it tired him to the point of sickness.

There was more to the world, he'd insisted, than Coalton. But most of the kids in his graduating class had never been out of the province, let alone the country. Hell, the farthest some of them had ventured out of town limits was the bumpy drive down Coal Creek Road—as black as its name—to the bush party field just past the rifle range. They believed a man's worth was measured by how fast he could shotgun a beer. And that alone showed just how much a guy needed to be on the ball to succeed around here.

But Loco vowed he'd never be like that. He'd show everyone he was better than life in Coalton. He'd leave and he'd go far. He'd send back those Christmas cards, formatted like newsletters, telling of his promotions and showing pictures of him with a wife and two kids, all of them wearing well-pressed, matching clothes bought at a big-city mall. Coalton didn't even have a mall.

That's how he pictured life playing out. But during his first week away at university in the big city, he'd experienced unprecedented terror.

His classmates mocked the way he spoke, saying "gunna" for "going to" or "supper" for "dinner" or "show" for "movie." As if using one word instead of another made him stupid. The endless list of things he said wrong filled his mind, pushing out mathematics, taking precedence over physics.

And he didn't know anyone. Unfamiliar faces everywhere—grocery stores, restaurants, gas stations, classrooms. Room after room, filled with people he didn't know. He hadn't imagined there could be so many different faces. Where were all the people he knew? *His* people.

So here he was, back at home. A small-town chicken-shit hick. A big-mouth, know-it-all blowhard with a dad who cleaned his black fingernails at the kitchen table with a butter knife.

He hated the big city but suddenly couldn't help himself from measuring every thing and every one and every word by its standards. Even here, as far as he could get from the stupid city, he still knew what those people would say of his toothless grin, his ski-goggle tan. He pretended not to care, had even refused to get his teeth fixed, but still he heard the voices.

He pulled his attention away from them, his constant judges, and back to his current travelling companions. But he couldn't help turning the same evaluative gaze on them. Small, insignificant dropouts. That's what they all were. Crapping on the big shitty, but only because they couldn't cut it there.

Just like him.

Shanny was now just shoulders and head, the rest of her sunk deep in the hole of her own making. SOR and F-Bomb had given up all pretence of looking busy and were sitting in the snow, letting their legs dangle into the deepening hole. Both had pulled down-jackets out of their packs and put them on over their damp climbing layer. Shanny's face glistened with a layer of sweat, even though she was still in short-sleeves and bare headed.

Loco—suddenly embarrassed by the docile, limp way he hung about the others, with them but not of them—stepped back from the group to organize the clutter of skis and poles strewn on the ground. He stuck each pair into the snow, shaping a neat line with all tips pointing toward the sky—a multi-coloured picket fence in the middle of nowhere. Somehow it made him feel calmer to fence himself off from Shanny, F-Bomb, and SOR, like they'd be less likely to notice his brooding if he kept himself quarantined.

Loco ran his hand over the smooth surface of his newly erected picket fence. The cool skin of the skis enthralled him, captured his full attention—*Wow, soooo smooth. Cool!*—and he realized how stoned he was. Damn Shanny's cookies. He should tear himself away from himself and just go be with the others. He ran his fingers back over the fence of skis, trailing an intricate swirl of loops and bows across the shiny top sheet of each. A bumper sticker peeled at the edges on one of SOR's skis: "Why's it called tourist season, if we can't shoot them?"

Loco snorted a puff of air into the space between the back of his throat and his nose. He meant the sound to come out as a laugh, but even in his own ears the snort sounded anything but merry. He defended his own bitterness by rehashing a well-used rant against SOR's sense of entitlement—here for only one season and already considering himself a rung above the common tour-ist, granting himself a quick ascent, despite the long-established Coalton hierarchy.

Only when Loco saw his own breath hanging in the air, evidence of his heated words, did he realize he'd been talking aloud, muttering to himself like some wronged and senile great-grandfather. He pulled off a glove and held his hand up to his cold cheek for the pinch-test—his face felt numb and far away. He pushed harder, moving his hand around as if his face were made of play dough.

He'd promised himself he'd stay away from the weed. His father would kill him if he failed the mine's drug test, would literally kick his scrawny ass all the way uptown, drag him by his hair the full length of Victoria Avenue, and then drown him in the wishing well in the middle of Coalton town square.

SOR could resort to the cheap tricks: magic urine-cleansing drinks, hidden bladders to carry untainted pee, herbal detoxification remedies. Metamucil, B-complex vitamins, cranberry juice, and TUMS. But Loco swore he wouldn't. The websites said the urine of even the most frequent user would come out clean after seven weeks, and he knew he could manage that. Only a loser couldn't manage that. SOR could cheat on his drug test if he had to, but Loco was different. He'd spent two decades in Coalton having his father point out the hippy losers who had nothing better to do than slouch on benches in front of coffee shops, their eyes glassy and nearly swollen shut, barely seeming to take in the world around them.

People want to live in Coalton, they ought to contribute to Coalton.

Coalton's a special place—people should have to earn a home here.

No free rides. In Coalton. Or anywhere.

These were the slogans of Loco's youth, and he could mock them when he joked around with his roommates, could put on his miner's swagger, pulling his pants up high and sticking his tongue deep under his lower lip, digging at some imaginary chewing tobacco. *No free meals around here, kiddos.* But deep down in that space at the pit of his stomach that told him what he had to do, he felt his dad was right. He could goof off for a few years—

give himself a break, "the transition years," he called them—but it was never meant to be forever. Growing up was built into his genetic code.

As if pushed to the earth by the weight of this conditioning, he let himself slump cross-legged in the snow, his face inches from his new fence, pressed his nose right up against the cool top sheet of his own ski. He could see the others through the spaces between the skis. His left eye took in the pure red of his ski while he lined up his right eye with a space.

Shanny had stopped digging, and F-Bomb, from his seated position, pulled her out of the hole, grabbing her arms, tugging and leaning backward, until he was flat on his back in the snow with her on top of him. Loco shifted his eyes so he could only see the tangle of their legs, Shanny's feet kicking playfully for escape.

"Geez, get a room, you two! What'd you put in those cookies, Shanny? Testosterone? F-Bomb's finally brave enough to talk to you without choking on his own Adam's apple." SOR stretched out each of his words, but Loco couldn't tell if he was really all that stoned or if he'd just gotten so used to sounding stoned that he didn't know any other way to talk. He'd reclined in the snow with his head rested against the hip of Alison (his not-girlfriend) who still slept. He rattled off jokes. Silence, for SOR, was an impossibility.

"What's the difference between a beginner snowboarder and an expert snowboarder?"

"Three days." F-Bomb deflated SOR's predictable punch lines, exhaling them in a bored sigh. Shanny took the opportunity to wiggle away from him, hop back into the hole, and resume her digging.

"How many snowboarders does it take to change a light bulb?"

"Three. One to hold it, one to videotape it and the other to say 'AWESOME, DUDE!'"

Nobody made a move for the cabin. SOR's voice was the only animated thing about him. His limbs hung loosely at his sides, legs and arms splayed away from his body, his toes falling heavily into a duck-footed flop. Even his head lolled to the side so his right ear nearly rested on his shoulder, his neck as lifeless as if he were a puppet made of stuffed socks.

"You know what I'm going be, man? Fuck this miner shit. I ain't no redneck miner. I'm gonna be an inventor. I got some great ideas. And you know what, just today, I'm gonna share them with you. You ready for it?"

"I doubt it, but hit me anyway." F-Bomb didn't even shift his eyes to SOR, so fixed were they on Shanny's ass.

"Okay—get this . . . spray-on socks." SOR paused, waited for a reaction. "Huh? Spray-on socks. It's brilliant. A million-dollar idea. Better than what's-it, those little bread-tie do-hickies . . . or milk bags. Someone made billions on those. Who likes putting socks on in the morning? After a shower? No way. Spray-on socks. Trillion-dollar idea, I tell you. Mark my words."

"Consider them marked, SOR." Shanny laughed the words out in short huffs of breath, the digging giving her a workout.

Loco lifted his one eye up the column of space between two skis, all the way up past the hut to the steep mountain ridge that loomed above. Locals called this ridge The Sleeping Giant. A steep peak at one end was said to be the giant's toes, pointing to the sky. A bump at the other end resembled a nose. A little dip above the nose could pass for an eye socket, and a ridge somewhere between the two peaks looked just like a pair of hands folded across a sleeping man's chest.

They'd all climbed miles up and away from Coalton, but with The Sleeping Giant before him and another steep mountain wall on either side of him, Loco suddenly felt caged in. He'd climbed all this way to end up in a hole.

He shifted his gaze to see if Shanny had hit the bottom of the doorframe yet, but before his eye got to where he imagined them to still be, F-Bomb's words caught him off-guard.

"What the fuck are you doing now, you weird peeping Tom?" F-Bomb pushed over three skis with one swipe, dismantling the fence and exposing Loco sitting cross-legged and staring at them. "Get your ass out here with the rest of us."

Loco did feel weird. Physically with these people but not like them. Not on the inside. He ran his index finger back and forth across his numb lips as if he were thrumming a guitar. Even in the cool air, heat rose to his face, burning his numb cheeks. Afraid of looking ridiculous, he climbed to his feet, stumbling in his stiff ski boots, knocking over another of the skis in his dismantled fence.

He and F-Bomb were almost the same height, and they suddenly stood awkwardly face-to-face. Loco looked at F-Bomb. A question mark hovered in F-Bomb's features as if he were waiting for something—a joke, an insult, an explanation. *Remember, this is what you say, this is your line.* F-Bomb seemed so uncomfortable with the silence that Loco had a feeling that if he could hand him a cue card, he would.

And that was just it. Too often these days, Loco *couldn't* remember what he was supposed to say. The things that came to his mind now—"Your swearing embarrasses me" or "Life's no joke" or "There's more to living than fucking and skiing"—were all wrong. He knew that.

Instead, he bit the inside of his mouth with his surviving back teeth. His piercing clicked against his eyetooth and suddenly he couldn't stand it. Couldn't stand being here but not being here. Couldn't stand being dressed one way but having forgotten the whole entire fucking script. He opened his jaw right there, stuck out his tongue and pulled the whole piercing out, threw it in the snow. There had to be a time and this was as good as any. He squished the hard heel of his ski boot on top of the silver post and ball, both of which looked so small now, and pushed the piercing deep into the snow pack. He looked up at F-Bomb, expecting some understanding reflected in his face—something that would explain what he'd just done.

F-Bomb stood with his hands on his hips, a cloud of bewilderment shadowing his features for only an instant. "Jeezuz, Loco."

"My name is Antonio. That's what my mother calls me. Her mother too." He tried in that instant to think of himself as Antonio, but the only Antonio he could call to mind was the one in frames around his mother's house, with a tidy haircut and shirts buttoned right up tight to the neck. That "Antonio" had nothing to do with the toothless version of himself that hung around smoking pot and skiing with this crowd.

F-Bomb rubbed his eyes and let his gaze fall from Loco's face. He scratched his head through his toque, simultaneously pushing it down lower on his forehead, almost right to his eyes. At least, Loco thought, he'd quit staring.

Still, Loco wanted more, craved an incident that was truly reality shifting. Maybe Loco *wanted* to be excommunicated from the group once and for all, something that would free him from this nightmarish limbo state. Maybe they would send him packing, bag slung over his shoulder, making his way down the mountain by himself, skiing alone as his ex-friends shouted taunts at his back.

But those sorts of things never happened. Not in real life. Instead, F-Bomb just shook his head and walked back to the hut. "Loco's cut off. He's having some kind of bad fucking trip."

With nowhere else to go, Loco shuffled over to the hole at the door and sat with his feet dangling over the edge with the others. He kicked one heel into the snow, then the other. F-Bomb put a hand on his shoulder and lowered himself to sit next to him, almost apologetically. Nobody said anything.

Where SOR was concerned there was only one reason to be sitting in a circle. He reached into his bib pocket and pulled out a joint.

"No way, man!" Shanny yelled so loud that Loco couldn't believe Alison didn't budge. Everything Shanny did was loud. He bet she was one of those girls who shrieked the whole time you were fucking her—*do this, touch that, poke here, lick there.* "I'm done with the pot—" she continued just as loud, "I'm so high. I can't even feel these." She held a hand over each breast, squeezing like they were tricycle horns. "Those cookies always give me the full-on body buzz. There's more here if anybody wants 'em." She stretched out to grab her backpack and pulled out her zip-lock baggie, while SOR took the inaugural Camelot toke from his new joint.

Loco sucked on the warm blood trickling from his tongue where he'd yanked out his piercing.

Holding the smoke deep in his lungs, SOR pointed across the valley to the south of the hut, making wide sweeping gestures with his hands so their eyes would take in the large slope. "Clear cuts are kinda pretty in the winter, once the snow fills them in," he said as he exhaled. The land was a patchwork quilt—exact squares of white where snow had covered the clear cut stitched neatly to the exact squares of green of the forest.

"Pretty?" Shanny said angrily, passing the joint to F-Bomb without sucking. Here we go, thought Loco. These people moved to Coalton as if they'd fallen into a paradise born from nothing—if it weren't for mining and forestry, the town would not even be here. Newbie Gapers took the end, forgot about the means.

F-Bomb held the joint smoldering between his fingertips. "We get too excited about clear-cutting. A mountain without trees is natural. I remember when my grandmother came back here. She stared at the mountains, baffled. Finally, I asked, 'what's wrong, grandma?'—'the mountains have grown hair,' she said. In her time, all these mountains were bald—forest fires, beetles . . . man's not the only thing that destroys forests. Forests were never meant to be forever."

Loco felt himself recoil, a shudder so severe he wondered if the others had seen it. He hated the mysterious way F-Bomb talked about his grandmother, about his family's past in the valley. *My people were here before coal mines, my people were here before tourism*, but never once saying that he was an Indian—everyone tiptoeing around the word like it was a curse. Anyways, being Indian didn't give him any better understanding of Coalton. His connections were to the Coalton of *yesterday*, not of *today*. *Coalton is a coal-mining town. Coalton is a skiing town*, he'd like to say, *Coalton is not an untamed wilderness, home of the buffalo hunt.* F-Bomb could take his stupid stories about the mountains growing hair and tell them at the local elementary school during First Nations Week.

Yeah! "Why don't you take your sorry-ass tale to Mrs. MacDonald's Ethnic Pride Day." Loco heard his own words as if they'd come out of somebody else's mouth. And then as if he'd been the one insulted, he jumped on F-Bomb, pushing his hands hard against F-Bomb's chest, forcing his friend's torso against the icy snow, jumping on top, straddling his waist and forcing both hands against F-Bomb's face as if he'd like to rub off F-Bomb's nose, his mouth, his eyes.

"What do you know?" Loco heard himself ask in a high pitched squeal, like a crying girl. "What do you know about this place?"

"Whoa, buddy. Easy, man." Loco felt SOR's hands on his shoulders, pulling back. SOR yanked him off of F-Bomb and to his feet. Together, they fell back until they were sitting on the abandoned snowmobile.

SOR started to laugh, to dismiss the whole episode, but then F-Bomb exploded, running at Loco, driving his head into Loco's middle, pushing him off the snowmobile and pinning him to the ground, knees digging into his chest, strong hands forcing down his arms. SOR scattered out of Loco's vision. Ice crystals dug against the back of Loco's hands.

F-Bomb lowered his face to meet Loco's. "I know as much as you. Exactly as much as you. This is *our* place. It belongs to *all* of us."

Loco squirmed to get loose, but F-Bomb was stronger. Loco felt as effectual as a frog pinned to a dissection plate. F-Bomb's face came closer and closer, suffocating Loco. He braced himself for a bite, already experiencing the sensation of sharp teeth sinking into flesh, but instead F-Bomb brought his lips to rest on Loco's sweaty skin, planting a sharp wet kiss in the middle of his forehead. "It's not just yours," he said. "Relax and share."

At that, SOR let out a barking noise—part cry, part laughter—

that must've resounded all the way to Coalton at the mountain's base.

"Fuck, you guys, grow up." Loco had forgotten about Shanny. "I thought we were here to ski. Ten more shovels and we're in. What is this shit, anyway? Foxy Boxing comes to Camelot?" She swung her shovel hard into the snow near the door's base.

The three men froze, Loco stretched out on his back in the snow, F-Bomb sitting upright across his chest, and SOR fallen awkwardly against the abandoned snowmobile. An embarrassment so rancid he could taste it had descended upon Loco. SOR and F-Bomb studied the ground, avoiding each other's eyes but eventually, as if there was nothing else to do, they both started to giggle.

"Hey, look. I'm F-Bomb—the kissing native healer." SOR pursed his lips, directing loud smooches toward the nose of the snow-mobile. "Relax, man, it's all of ours." He planted his lips right onto the snowmobile, shook with laughter. "My lips alone will free you from the white man's rage." He clumsily climbed to his feet, pushing up off the machine to steady himself. "That's just awesome, dude. Awesome."

F-Bomb joined SOR's laughter, rolling off of Loco and right-ing himself to his knees. "Ah, can it, SOR." He brushed his hands together, as if he'd just finished cleaning stables. "Geez, maybe we're all having a bad trip." SOR and F-Bomb both turned to Loco, and he knew that they waited for him to dismiss the episode with laughter just as they had.

And suddenly, Loco needed to dig. Saying nothing, he pushed himself to his feet, squished into the hole next to Shanny and swung his shovel into the hard snow. Their shovel blades clanged against each other with every swing, but Shanny worked alone, not even looking to him. Loco's shovel was the first to scrape against the door's base. He moved his body closer to the door, expecting her to move away, leaving him to finish, but she kept time with him for the final strokes. Then, just as he reached for the knob, Shanny's shoulder bumped him out of the way. She pushed her whole body into the door, jarring it loose.

"Voila!" She swung the door wide open and a waft of stale, moldy air greeted them. She turned her face away from the dark insides of the hut, toward the bright blue sky, and deeply breathed the fresh spring air as F-Bomb and SOR clomped their way past her and Loco into the small sitting room, their hard ski boots rattling the plywood floor. She entered right on their heels, leaving Alison sleeping with Sancho on the snow above the door. Loco looked at Alison for a moment, watched her twitch and frown in her sleep, then followed the other three into Camelot.

14. The Urbanite

When Alison heard Loco's boots clomp onto the hut's floor, she rolled onto her back and opened her eyes. She wrapped an arm around Sancho, hugging his small warm body into her side. She hadn't been sleeping at all. Just hiding. Hiding in the face of humiliation and disappointment. She'd embarrassed herself today—completely incompetent on her skis. If she wasn't doing the wrong thing, she was saying the wrong thing. And now that she'd actually gotten up the blasted mountain, she had no idea how she'd get back down. She contemplated waiting for the spring thaw.

And—all that effort to arrive here? At some glorified shack? She'd seen bigger, more well-maintained tool sheds.

What had she expected? A five-star lodge? A dishwasher? A man in a tuxedo serving her red wine while she lay in front of a roaring fire on a bearskin rug?

She wasn't sure, but she knew she'd expected a washroom at the very least. Where was she supposed to pee? She was afraid to ask. Even the promise of SOR's young hard body wasn't enough of a distraction from the despair she felt when she opened her eyes to this half-buried shack.

Not sure what to do next, she stayed on her back, looking up at the blue sky, and clicked the hard heels of her ski boots together three times.

There's no place like home.
There's no place like home.
There's no place like home.

15. The Redneck

Kevin pulled up to Camelot in the late afternoon to find the whole place under snow. Snow packed right up and over the whole doorframe. Claudette had already arrived and pulled off her helmet, sitting astride her machine with her head thrown back, taking a long drink of water from a bright pink Nalgene bottle. He inched his machine over to hers, pulling it in so the two snow machines sat nose-to-nose. He watched Claudette's long neck muscles work with each swallow and resisted the desire to reach out and pet it. That's what he loved most of all about Claudette—her length. Long neck, long legs, long hair, long nose. In bed, he often told her so. *I love your long legs wrapped around me* or *I love your long fingers stroking my thick cock.*

The very sun seemed to be loving her at this moment, playing in the auburn highlights of her hair, bringing out the perfect glow of her cheeks, her forehead. This late afternoon light turned everything golden. She could be a poster girl, hanging in the garage above his workbench.

"It's hard to stay mad at you when you's lookin' like that," he met her eye and held it, eventually cracking a smile as if their whole spat had been a shared joke. The moment she let him meet her eyes, he knew the worst was over. She'd never resisted his smiles. That's one thing Claudette wasn't: long-suffering. His last wife had been the opposite, always furious about one thing or another. Some women seemed to enjoy being mad, as if they'd like to curl up in a tight hole of their own anger and live there.

Give credit where credit was due. Claudette was never like that. Claudette, at the very least, *wanted* to be happy.

She dropped her bottle into the snow and leaned over her handlebars, smiling up at him from under her long bangs. She shook her head at him a little bit, but the smile had already given her away. He knew any gestures towards anger now would only be playful. Still, though, she didn't speak. She always considered her words first, translating maybe. He jumped into the silence.

"Donchya think you could drive that thing a bit faster?" he teased. "Geez, why the lollygagging?" He lifted his leg from his machine and nudged the nose of her machine with his foot.

"Kicked yer ass." She dropped her Quebecois accent, drawing out the words in an exaggerated imitation of his local redneck drawl.

He knew the drill from here. They'd be back where he wanted in no time. "You kicked everyone's ass," he smiled again. Smiles couldn't hurt. "Sure not arguing that." He stood up from his black leather seat, warm with the heat of the sun, and took the short stride to her side, grabbing her gloved hand and holding it up in victory, running his other hand slowly along the inside of her long arm. "You win, baby." He leaned his head down to the space between her neck and shoulder, and took a deep breath of her hair. "Nearly ran over those skiers too. Beating your husband, crushing his fragile male ego, weren't enough? You had to take out some ski bums for good measure?" He swung a leg over her machine and sat behind her, straddling her narrow hips between his legs. She didn't move away but didn't come any closer either. He ran his fingers down her long hair scooping it together in a ponytail with both of his hands. He lifted it up and touched his lips ever so gently to the exposed base of her neck.

Not a kiss.

Not yet.

Just a promise of one.

He rested his chin on her shoulder and spoke softly into her ear. "Get the hell out of this woman's way when she makes up her mind ta git somewheres."

She pulled away from him a bit, drawing out their make-up ritual. "I'm surprised you don't stop to give a ride for the hot little hussy snowboarder." The words came out as *'ot leetle 'ussy*.

"Wouldn't dare." He lifted his chin and opened his mouth to her earlobe, letting his front tooth rub across its soft skin. "Wouldn't even have crossed my mind with your *'ot little ha-ass* in full view," he copied her accent, letting his hand fall down along her spine and rest on the seat, gently brushing against her buttocks. "I was chasing *this* down the whole way up." On the word *this*, he kneaded her buttocks, working his fingers out towards her hips. At her hips, he squeezed tight, then slowly—so slowly—slid his hands across her belly. Then down. Lower—gently—and lower— softly—and lower. He felt her body relax against his and her knees fall apart. Without a word, she twisted her neck and lifted her warm mouth to meet his.

That's how Fredrik found them. Kevin heard the mechanical roar while his tongue was still deep within Claudette's mouth. He gave her one last nibble on the bottom lip, then looked over her shoulder to see gangly Fredrik ambling towards them, bulbous black helmet tucked under his arm, taking his usual long strides as if he were desperate to arrive at his destination in as few steps as possible.

"Good. You two made up then. One problem solved. Now what are we going to do about this." Fredrik gestured towards the buried hut. Kevin always wondered at Fredrik's lack of a strong accent, still expected him to talk with the typical Swedish lilt, the *bjorg-dee-bjorg-dee-bjorg* of the chef from *The Muppets*, like he had when they first met. Instead, Fredrik's pronunciation was overly proper, careful to a fault. He rarely collapsed his words into contractions, but left every single syllable its own breathing space.

"I don't know what Apple Cake here is *go-ing* to do," he whispered in Claudette's ear, "but I sure know what I'm gunna do." He snuck a hand under her bulky jacket, snaking his way through her many layers of clothes and bringing his palm flat on her warm belly.

Watching Fredrik kick at the snow surrounding the entrance to Camelot, Kevin felt Claudette's body soften against his.

"Look at all this snow! My contributions to The Ull must have paid off this year." Fredrik pointed at the snow piled high on Camelot's roof. "We're going to have fooling winter sledding conditions. In April. Somebody has made The Ull happy this year. A happy Ull is a generous Ull."

"*Sacrifice*, Fredik, not *contributions*," Claudette corrected. "And *full-on*, not *fooling*."

Kevin flinched at each of Fredrik's mentions of The Ull, but said nothing. He pulled his hand away from Claudette and silently watched Fredrik set his helmet on the ground and crouch to perch upon it before he continued.

"When I came up here in February, we dug for two hours to get in. I knew it'd be even higher in April—not even starting to melt down until May or June. But I hoped by now someone else would've been up to dig it out and we'd be climbing up to the front step."

Dragged away from Claudette by Fredrik's words, Kevin jumped off her machine, searching through his avy-pack for a shovel, then stood up, hands on his hips, thinking better of it. "Why don't we go for a ride and let the young punks dig it out? Chances are good that this is where they're headed. If we already have to share the place—strike one—why should we do all the work and make it two strikes? Be a good workout for the lazy pothead ski bums anyways."

A smile spread across Fredrik's giraffe-like face. "I like the way you think." He sat with his knees bent to chest and nodded vigorously like a bobble-head doll. "And there are more of them than—"

"Lazy jerks!" Claudette was at Kevin's side and said the two words into his face, her breath warm on his cheek. He could hear her smile. It was no reprimand. Claudette could pull a fit with the best of them, but when she came around, she really came around. He already looked forward to being snuggly zipped into a sleeping bag with her later tonight. He hoped Fredrik had brought ear plugs.

"Let's go play then!" Kevin grabbed Claudette's helmet from where it hung on her handlebars, shoved it at her, and started to move toward his own snowmobile.

But Claudette clasped her helmet, placed a hand in the centre of his chest. Before she spoke, he knew what she'd say.

She twisted her mouth in the way she did when about to say something he didn't want to hear. "We could go see your—"

"Uh-uh." He cut her off quickly, turning around and slapping his hand up against her mouth, harder than he intended. Worried that he'd hurt her, he lightened the pressure of his hand, but not enough that she could speak. Fredrik didn't need to know this little family secret. Their friendship worked just fine at the snow-pack-discussion level.

She pulled his fingers off her mouth. "Kevin, he's all alone. You can't just leave him out here and forget about him."

He lifted his hands to the back of his neck, massaged the muscle knot of tension that felt like it had settled in there for good, radiating sharp twinges of pain up the back of his scalp and down his right shoulder. "C'mon baby," he heard the desperation in his own voice. "We just made up. You know I don't want to talk about this." Kevin didn't look at Claudette, but pushed the heel of his hand into his own forehead, pressed down hard as if the pressure might rub out the fat folds in his brow and, along with them, the tension that had caused a slow ache to creep across his scalp. He knew Fredrik would be watching them, perplexed, wanting answers, but he refused to look in his friend's direction. He hurled his anger at Claudette instead. "That was *our* secret. Fredrik didn't need to know." He bit off his words before he added *I trusted you*. Women's words. A woman's trick. He was starting to sound like his bloody manipulative bitch of an ex-wife.

Fredrik had developed an intense interest in his handlebars. He'd pulled a pair of underwear—it looked like—out of his pack and rubbed the silver frantically, as if his very existence depended on the sheen of those handlebars. Claudette grabbed Fredrik's arm, pulled him into Kevin's vision, lifted Kevin's chin, forcing him to look at his good friend.

"You two are best of friends, oui? Yes? You can tell him." Kevin felt like he was in a soap opera. This was not a scene he'd choose to live.

Damn his father.

Fredrik pulled his elbow away from Claudette, almost violently. "Tell me what? He's not obligated to tell me anything." *Ob–li–gate–ed.* Even in the middle of this drama, Kevin noted Fredrik's stiff pronunciation, his formal choice of words, imagined how he'd imitate his friend when they rehashed the scene later, turned it into a funny story about how they missed optimal sledding time due to typical womanly craziness.

Fredrik pulled his arm away from Claudette, pointed up. "Snowpack there looks pretty stable, Kev. We could go for a quick rip."

The good old snowpack. Kevin felt Claudette's sigh. He thought about turning away from her. But it was too late for Kevin to accept Fredrik's offering—he could already taste the familiar sourness of guilt.

He looked at Claudette instead of Fredrik. "I guess I don't need to tell him if he's going to see for himself." Before Claudette even realized his acquiescence, Kevin was on his machine, roaring the engine. "You ride with me." He felt himself relax slightly as she, without a word, wrapped herself around his back.

"Let's go!" He yelled over the engine's noise to a stupefied Fredrik. "You follow."

He didn't look back but could picture Fredrik—all knees and elbows—scrambling for his helmet and then his machine.

16. The Miller

NUSTY RAILS

1½ oz Scotch whisky

½ oz Drambuie

Peel of lemon for garnish (first one only, then fuckit)

NOTE: The first five are called "Rusty Nails." The sixth, seventh and eighth are "Nusty Rails." After that, call 'em whatever you want. No one understands you anymore anyway.

Lanny hated these two butt-fucking, head-fucking huskies, would like to see them both disemboweled by a giant cougar. He'd never thought of himself as the kind of guy who'd hurt an animal. He'd grown up on elk steaks, deer roasts, and pheasant breasts, but when he was ten, his dad had taken him hunting. "A rite of passage into the double digits," he'd said, handing him a rifle almost too heavy to carry. His two older brothers had followed the same progression: potato guns in the backyard, to pellet guns at the rifle range, to a .22 in the woods, to this.

Most of Lanny's friends started with deer—a whitetail or muley, midsize, not too intimidating. Not Lanny. On his day, Lanny and his dad tracked a towering five-point elk. His dad was fierce on that point, refusing to even follow the animal until Lanny counted each of the points on its antlers. When they found the right size, they used a bugle to call it away from its herd. Then they stalked it for at least thirty minutes, weaving around towering pine trees, tripping through tangled hawthorn brush, making sure always to stay downwind of the animal so it wouldn't catch a whiff of their scent. They waited to raise their guns until the elk stopped, lowering its head to drink from an ice cold mountain stream. That's when Lanny's dad nodded his chin towards Lanny's rifle. *It's yours.* A gift. The golden key to adulthood. To manhood.

Rules skittered around Lanny's skull: *Always take two shots, never trust that one will do the job. Use the back of the free hand as a rest. Once you get a scope on the elk, DO IT and DO IT NOW. Aim for the heart/lung area, right behind the shoulder.*

He held the elk in his scope, watched its chest rise and fall with each breath. Saw its coarse tongue lick its lips as it finished drinking and lifted its head, ears perked.

Lanny couldn't do it. What he wanted more than anything was to pet the animal's long neck, kiss its wet nose. He slowly lowered the barrel of his rifle to his shin. Without making the slightest noise, not even a sigh that might have scared off the big game, he turned to his dad, shook his head, knowing his eyes shone. He hated himself for this weakness.

His dad snorted his disdain, but quickly turned away from his son toward the animal, lifting his own rifle and tightening his finger on the trigger. Before he pulled the finger with the necessary force, Lanny clapped. Just a single smack of defiance. But it was enough. The elk shot through the woods, crashing over dead branches.

His dad said nothing. Nothing there, nothing on the long walk through the woods and back to the truck, and nothing on the whole drive back home. But he never let Lanny eat wild meat again.

"Not for the lily-livered," he'd say pushing a bowl of salad toward Lanny as he pushed a crock pot full of steaming elk stew towards his brothers.

It didn't matter. Lanny could forego wild meat before he could bring himself to shoot a defenseless animal in the woods. If those were his options, he'd take the salad over the stew.

But, lily-livered or not, he'd love to smash in the skulls of both of these huskies, jumping all over poor Sitka, pounding her into the ground, chewing on her ears, sticking their noses up her ass. Lanny had had enough. He hauled off and hit one of them—Rider?

Findley? Who could tell the difference?—right across the hindquarters, hard with his ski pole. But the violence didn't even seem to register with the stupid beast of a dog. If Lanny had a gun, he'd have shot the monster right in the ass.

Yeah! Root him right in the rass, Ranny!

Sitka was the only sensible creature on this trip. Without her, Lanny would've turned around and gone home—alone!—before he'd even gotten out of Michael's backyard.

When he and the dogs arrived at Camelot, the hut had been dug out and ski tracks and dog tracks scattered in every direction, but there were no people. An abandoned snowmobile sat diagonally across the entrance to the hut. Lanny huffed. It looked like a hundred people had been here already.

Some remote hut this was turning out to be. Some escape. Not only did he suddenly have half the town with him, but the other half had already arrived. He snapped out of his skis and inched his way down the steep hole to the door. He bumped it open with his forearm, shooing the dogs away. Huskies were outdoor animals. If he could control one thing tonight, it would be that: the damn dogs were staying outside.

He let Sitka follow him into the sitting room.

"Shit!!!!"

The smell of dog crap hit Lanny so full force in the face that he could taste it. Sitka dove for the steaming pile of excrement in the middle of room, clearly intending to put her nose right in it. "No! Sitka. No, no, no . . ." He pushed the dog away from the centre of the room. "No." He lifted his hands to his head, pulled off his wool toque and threw it hard to the ground. At the quick, violent movement he heard animal claws scratch across the floor, and followed the sound to see the skinniest excuse for a dog crouched in front of the fire, chewing the leg off of a wood stool. "Git," Lanny yelled. "Git!" He shooed the sickly thing toward the door, but couldn't bring himself to open it and throw the scrawny mutt outside. The poor thing'd freeze to death. It wasn't evening yet, but the day had turned cool and grey, as it did late afternoon in the mountains after the sun dipped behind the range. Anyways, it wasn't the stupid dog's fault. If you had to go, you had to go.

Lanny held his breath and scraped the pile of shit onto an old newspaper from the fire supplies. Opening the kitchen window, he reached out with one hand, dug a quick hole in the snow right at the window's level, and buried the shit in that.

He looked around the familiar room. People had been here. Obviously. They'd left their mess, left their shitty dog, and were gone.

They'd lit a fire already in the woodstove next to the door, over-stuffed it if anything. The hut must've been thirty degrees Celsius. Lanny opened the door a crack to let in some fresh air. Whoever arrived here before him had left a mess of dishes, open packs, and food. Someone had hung a pair of boxers to dry on the fire grate. Lanny turned his eyes away from the yellowing waistband. He sighed deeply, picking his wool toque off the floor and hanging it by the fire, being sure not to let it touch the underwear.

Now that he'd cleared out the shit, the room smelled like skunky weed. Just watch. They'd be camping out with a bunch of dropout, ski-bum punks. Perfect. The hippies were arriving any second, and the ski bums had already got here. Remembering the snow machine outside, he added redneck to the list. Why not throw everybody into mix? Some lazy, stoned ski bums, some flakey, tarot-card waving hippies, and some rye-guzzling, oil-burning rednecks. Add Michael—ski bum turned hardcore greedy developer guy—and you had a complete cross-section of Coalton society.

A zip-lock baggie with ginger cookies sat open on the middle of the table, and he helped himself to a couple as he plopped himself into the bench seat.

Even with the sun still up, the hut's insides were dark, and his eyes were just beginning to adjust. Tin dishes and packages of dry food already littered the table.

So, their companions were not tidy. Or respectful. At least they were industrious—not only did a fire roar in the wood stove, but a healthy pile of wood also sat stacked around its base. A big bucket of snow was melting in front of the stove.

The place looked almost exactly the same as last time Lanny was here, probably five years ago now. The unpainted wood of the walls and floor had turned black over the years, but that wasn't new. There was only one change. Above the wood stove in the corner next to the front door, somebody had carved CAMELOT ROCKS in block capital letters. Other than that people had kept the hut in surprisingly good shape.

Lanny did a quick count of beds—two rooms downstairs, with two beds in each, and then room for three, maybe four, sleeping bags in the loft. That was eight sleeping spots, twelve in a pinch, if you accounted for squishing some couples into the single beds.

He climbed up the ladder to peek into the loft. This was his least favourite place to sleep. With the fire roaring in the evening, this top space got stifling hot. On previous trips, he'd woken up in the middle of the night, forcing his body out the small window, dangling from his waist, desperate for cool fresh air.

The four beds on the main floor had been claimed, packs and wet clothing strewn possessively across each. Both rooms smelled of sweaty socks.

He'd just have to move the clothes, he decided. Janet couldn't be expected to sleep on a floor in her condition.

She should be sleeping at home if anybody bloody well asked him. Which nobody ever did.

While Sitka crouched in the middle of the floor chewing snow-balls out of her footpads, Lanny made his way into the bedroom farthest from the kitchen sink. It'd be loud, right next to the table and bench seats where people were bound to be drinking and playing cards late into the night, but at least it wouldn't stink of sloppy food scraps.

Six bottles of wine lay in a row across the one bed. He held the heels of his hands up to his ears, blocking the nauseating sound of the stupid shitty mutt chewing up the hut furniture.

Jeezus. Who in their right mind hauled bottled wine up to Camelot?

He grabbed the bottles' necks, three in each hand, and carried them into the main room, set them on the kitchen table, where he noticed another open, almost half drunk. He went back into the room, scooping scattered packs and clothes into his arms. Sitka banged her tail hard against the floor as Lanny tromped over to the room by the kitchen sink, his ski boots rattling the whole shack, and dropped the mess on the narrow bed closest to the door.

That was fair. The ski bums could have one room and he, Janet, and Michael could share the other. The lesbians could fend for themselves. Maybe they could sleep outside with their ruffian, blood-thirsty mutts.

He'd give Janet the bed closest to the door. She'd be up all night peeing from what he'd heard. There wasn't much room for maneuvering in these rooms, and he didn't want her waddling over him in the pitch dark.

He and Michael could rock-paper-scissors for the other bed. He hoped Michael'd be stuck sleeping on the floor.

Michael was the only reason Lanny had agreed to this stupid trip in the first place. But the Michael he'd agreed to wasn't the Michael who was here. There's a new line of work for him—contortionist. "Michael LePlage—the Man of a Thousand Faces." Lanny had never even seen this particular face before. Tripped-out hippy was a new one. Or at least, a drastic flashback to Michael (aka Banger) of the early '90s.

Lanny hefted his backpack onto the bed farthest from the door and left Michael's on the floor at the foot of Janet's bed.

"Let's go outside, buddy. It stinks in here." He patted Sitka on the head, but then turned back before heading for the fresh air. The skinny dog hardly acknowledged their presence, just continued his work of sharpening his teeth, steadily gnawing his way through the wooden leg of a stool.

Digging in the front pocket of his pack and wondering if stopping the dog from eating the furniture was his job too, Lanny waited for his fingertips to graze the cool, smooth surface of his travelling flask. He'd measured out nine Rusty Nails—three per night, carefully rationed. Normally, he'd save them for evening. One before dinner, one after, and one before bed. But this trip had turned out to be anything but normal. He'd build himself a comfy little seat in the snow and have a wee nip now. Enjoy a snippet of peace before the hordes arrived. He stepped outside the door and slammed it hard, leaving the furniture-devouring animal inside. He imagined it crouching in the middle of the room to shit again as soon as the door closed. Fine. Lanny wouldn't go back in until someone else arrived. Let them clean up the shit this time.

Sitka took an impressive jump at the steep exit, getting her front paws over the lip of the snow hole. Scrambling with her hind legs, she managed a more agile exit than Lanny hoped for and now sat looking down at the doorway. She crouched her shoulders nervously waiting for the pounce of the bigger dogs, but Findley and Rider appeared to have wandered off somewhere.

Finally some good news. With any luck they'd run into a cougar. Lanny imagined Cosmos and Ella finding the dogs' carcasses tomorrow morning, intestines splayed across the snow.

Lanny looked at his ascent and sighed. If he had half a brain, he would've dug himself a way out before hurling himself in. His pack with his avy shovel sat up above in the snow, leaning against the abandoned snowmobile. He clasped the neck of his flask between his teeth and brushed his bare hands together, warming them before reaching up to the firm snow where Sitka sat. He dug the tips of his fingers—the ones that had tips—deep enough that he'd have a chance of pulling himself up and over. He kicked the pointy toe of his ski boot into the near vertical wall of snow before him. *Stupid ski-bum punks had never heard of digging out steps?*

His belly pushed against the cold wall, and he could feel its chill through his polypro shirt and fleece sweater.

All right, he counted, *one, two . . .*

What was he weighing these days? Two-ten? Two-twenty? Two-thirty? He'd make a sorry sight hauling himself out of this death trap.

So, again—*one, two, and THREE.* With a grunt and a squeal and a groan and good deal of panting and cursing, Lanny got one knee up and over the edge to freedom. Sitka scattered from him, making room so Lanny could fling the rest of his bulk up to flat ground. With one last mighty *HEAVE-HO*, he found himself lying sprawled out on the ground, looking straight up at the blue sky. Sitka leapt over and licked the side of Lanny's face. Lanny rubbed his shoulder on his ear, wiping off the dog saliva, and then opened his arm so Sitka could curl up next to his body.

Lanny's knee throbbed but as if from a long way away. Come to think, everything felt to be happening from afar. His fingers were cold but not like someone who'd just been digging in frozen ground for five minutes. More like someone reading a book about another guy's fingers being cold. He burped up the odd skunky taste of that ginger cookie, covered his mouth with his hand. "Scuze me," he smiled to Sitka. He shook his hands in front of his face. They buzzed, a distant pins and needles sensation. He hoped it wasn't MS.

Lanny's flask had fallen from his mouth with the final heave ho. He retrieved it with a simple stretch of his numb arm. Without bothering to sit up, he twisted its lid with his teeth until it came off in his mouth. He spit the lid to the ground and took a healthy swig as he lay flat on his back. The cool Scotch and Drambuie coated his throat in a most satisfying way, heating a space deep in his ears. He took another swig, staring straight at the sky. A trickle of Rusty Nail ran out the side of his mouth toward his ear, but he didn't care. For the first time that day, Lanny felt unclenched. He stretched out and enjoyed the loosening sensation blanketing his body.

▨ "Don't be a hypocrite," Janet had snarled at Lanny when she, Michael, Cosmos, and Ella finally arrived at Camelot. He'd ousted the ski bums, saved her a bed, cleaned up steaming shit, and helped carry her barf-coated husband to safety. For what? For a snarly reception. All's he'd said was, "Looks like the King of Real Estate don't handle his drugs too good anymore. There's a reason that shit's for kids." But again he had that weird feeling. His words echoed in his own ears. This day was getting to him.

When he saw them coming, he'd been laid out on the snow. Relaxing. He'd managed to roll onto his side into a sort of half fetal position. Sitka backed into him, snuggling her rear end into the warm spot between his chest and his lap. Lanny propped his head up on one hand and sipped happily on his Rusty Nails. Rationing, he'd decided, was for pussies.

He expected to hear the others coming before he saw them, but he saw Ella's red toque first. Gradually, the others joined her at the summit, an easy ski down to Camelot. Still no huskies, though. No doubt Cosmos would find a way to hold him responsible for her stupid, slobbering, foul-breathed beasts.

Lanny forced himself up to a seated position, stretched his legs out straight in front of him, and pulled Sitka's warm body across his thighs. What was taking them so long up there? Michael could've straight-lined it in one minute flat. Come to that, Michael and Janet should've reached the summit an easy hour before Ella and Cosmos, who were on snowshoes. Lanny stretched his eyes and squinted his ears.

Ah, shit. He pulled himself to his feet, tightened the lid on his flask, and shoved it into the waist of his pants. He flinched as the cold metal pressed against the flesh above his groin. He held one hand to his hip and the other above his eyes, level with his eyebrows. There was no sun to block anymore—it had fallen behind the ridge hours ago—but standing here with one hand on his hip and the other shadowing his eyes, he felt like captain of a giant sea vessel. Captain Lanny—able to search out all obstacles, big and small, and crush each with unwavering fortitude. He wobbled on his feet, but caught himself.

Damn knee. It really was sore.

"Hi ho! Landlubbers!" He yelled up to Michael and Janet. His words bounced back at him, sounding just a little silly, but what the hey. They were on holidays after all. Nothing wrong with a little fun. Fuck them if they couldn't take a joke.

He took another step in their direction, but the land weaved and bobbed, as if he really were Captain Lanny at sea.

He lifted his gaze back to the summit, took some time focusing on his stranded friends. Michael didn't look to be moving of his own accord at all. His skis were pointed in one serious snowplow. All pizza, no french fries. Plus, he had one arm flung around Janet's shoulders, and she was snowplowing just as severely, with her knees bent in awkwardly as if the weight of her husband and her belly were too much for her little frame. But she wasn't actually skiing down. Lanny had to squint hard to determine that she'd moved down slope at all. For god's sake, the lezzies on snowshoes were holding pace with Janet and Michael. Cosmos stood at Michael's other side clutching the crook of his elbow. Red-toqued Ella stood behind him and looked to be holding him up at the middle, one hand on each hip.

Lanny tried to get annoyed. Tried to work up some of the fury he had at the bottom by The Cunt's trailhead, the fury that propelled him the whole way up the mountain. But he could feel his mood shifting. He didn't have the energy for anger. Felt too lethargically powerful here at the helm of his imaginary ship.

He surprised himself with a cold puff of laughter. *Jeezus, they're really carrying him down the mountain.*

If down was what'd you'd call it—easing him on a gentle slant across the mountain to the right and then (with all the grace of a four-headed, eight-legged, beached sea creature) making the slightest turn downhill and coming back across the mountain to the left. They must've been heading downhill, however gradually, but the grade was imperceptible. These misfits would turn a three-minute ski into a full-hour torment.

Captain Lanny to the rescue. He lumbered over to meet them at the foot of the slope. Even Captain Lanny's altruism had its limits. He wasn't snapping back into his skis and skinning up to help them. For what—to make it a five-headed unwieldy beast?

But when the crew made it down the hill, Lanny stood with open hands to relieve them of their burden, the semi-conscious Michael LaPlage, Coalton's only Ski-Bum Realtor.

And that's when he said it. "Looks like the King of Real Estate don't handle his drugs too good anymore. There's a reason that shit's for kids, eh Banger?" Harmless really. Understated if anything. Michael didn't seem to mind. He glanced up under heavy eyelids and slurred, "Right on ya, Cheech." But Janet clearly didn't think Lanny's statement harmless.

Hypocrite? What'd she mean by that? He hadn't done drugs in nearly a decade. Not in public at any rate.

He'd of asked her too. *What d'ya mean by hypocrite, lady?* But by the time his brain warmed up to the question, she'd stomped off with Ella and Cosmos following at her wings, leaving a pukey Michael draped across Lanny's shoulders.

"Don't worry about me, ladies, I'll just take care of everything," he yelled at their backs. He doubted his words, all fuzzy as if he'd spoken them through a bag of cotton batton, even got to them.

Something was wrong with him. Not enough air to the brain or something. Geez, he'd only had two or three Rusty Nails. Nothing to make his whole tongue go numb (let alone his whole brain).

Fuck it. He wished he'd just drunk their whacked-out tea. He couldn't feel any worse.

"Hold on, little buddy," he said to Michael, who seemed barely aware of Lanny's presence. "Here's how it goes. No way I'm carryin' you. Bum knee or something. I'll just lay you down here on your back." He dropped Michael to the snow, stifling laughter at the sound Michael's air made coming out of his body. He snapped Michael's boots out of the bindings, leaving the skis where they'd fallen. "Now, we just grab your feet like this, and I'll drag you back to the hut. Pretend you're on a toboggan."

And that's what he did. Labouring the whole way, sinking deep into the snow with each step. The ride seemed to jolt Michael awake and he sang a deep "hohm, hohm, hohm" in time with each of Lanny's steps.

When Lanny got Michael to the front door of the hut, the ladies all hovered around Michael, the two crazy hippies so happy to have a project that they ignored Findley and Rider, who came bounding from the forest. *So much for Sitka's saviour, the intestine-eating cougar.* Lanny swore that both huskies had traces of blood on their slobbery jaws, and he wondered if they'd run into his hoped-for cougar after all. If so, they'd obviously fared better than the wild cat. He said something about the blood to Cosmos, "Looks like your savage beasts have been on the kill again," but she simply stared down at Michael, scratching her index finger against her chin.

"We shouldn't be letting them run wild," Ella said in a near whisper. "It *is* a major grizzly corridor." But she did nothing to restrain them.

"Oh Ella," Cosmos sighed, her voice full of air. "The bears are under three metres of snow, no more aware of the dogs than the dogs are of them. Relax."

Lanny pulled at Michael's foot until his head lay right on the precipice of the steep icy hole that led to the hut.

"Well, we'll have to get him down and in," pronounced Cosmos from the doorway, holding her hands on her hips and twisting her lips toward her left ear.

"Don't worry if it involves bruises," Janet muttered. "He deserves them. What a stunt." She and Ella stood squished shoulder-to-shoulder into the small space below Michael. "Michael!" she reached up and flicked a finger at his head, hard. "Michael! Can you walk yourself down here? Somehow?"

"Hohm . . ."

"Look, I got him this far, I can . . ."

But the women paid no attention to Lanny. Cosmos reached up and maneuvered Michael's head and shoulders to the side, so his ear was parallel to the hole. She pulled on a leg until his foot and knee dangled over the icy edge.

"I'm going to get his skis." Lanny turned away. "If anyone cares . . ."

But nobody answered. As he stomped away through the deep snow once more, he felt himself flinch hard at the sound Michael's body made as the women dragged it across the plywood floor.

By the time he returned, they'd laid Michael down on the bed he'd cleared for himself. Nobody said a single thank-you to Lanny either, mind you. The skinny dog had curled into a tight ball on the other bed and slept, moaning and twitching. Lanny noticed its coarse grey hair had shed all over, sticking to the sheet thrown over the dirty mattress. That's where he'd end up sleeping. On a dirty mattress coated in the mangy hair of some stray shitty orphan dog. That's what good ol' Captain Lanny'd get for his troubles.

"He'll be fine in an hour or two. The tea was a bit much for him maybe," Cosmos pronounced with the authority and gravity of a doctor. She corralled Lanny and Ella into her arms, swooshing them out of the room to leave Michael and Janet alone.

"Bit much for him? Ya think?! Geez."

Lanny wasted his sarcasm on Cosmos. He saw a flurry of aggravation scurry across her face, but then she simply took a deep breath, looking at him with her lids heavy, and scratched him behind his ears, patted him on the head.

"Sweets for my sweets," she said, digging deep in her pockets and then handing out dog cookies: one for Rider, one for Findley, one for Sitka, and one for him.

Weirdo.

He threw his dog treat high in the air watching Sitka leap to catch it, only to be tackled mid-jump by one of the bullies.

"Ruck off, roopid rutt!"

"Lanny, it's about time we spoke about the way you project your anger. The sooner you claim it, the sooner you can cure it." Cosmos held her hands in front of her, palms up as if she were cupping water.

He swore he saw Ella wink at him as she silently brushed past his shoulder and bent down to retrieve a giant, blackened kettle. She filled it with melted water, poured noisily, using an old yogurt container.

Cosmos had picked up the baggie of cookies, holding it at a distance between two fingers as if it were a shit-caked rag. "Probably filled with white sugar," she said in disgust. "Sugar: the gateway drug."

Right—mushroom tea good, white sugar, bad.

Freak.

He turned away from her towards Ella who splashed water into the large kettle. "You don't think everyone's had enough tea?"

Ella smiled. "Just making peppermint tea this time."

"You're pretty." That's what he said next—in that odd distant voice, ringing hollow in his own ears. "Specially the lips." He reached out the stub that used to be his right index finger, ran it across her lower lip. His hand still tingled. She grabbed his whole hand in her fist, then waggled a finger at him. *Naughty naughty.* As if she were forever dealing with strangers caressing her lips.

"Okay! Out with you!" Here came Cosmos again, with that same sweeping trick she'd performed in the bedroom, catching everything up in her arms and moving it with her, but this time she'd only corralled him.

"What? How's that fair? All huskies inside, all conscious men out?"

But she said nothing. Just left him out in the hole of snow and closed the door behind him.

This was not working out.

He turned around and banged on the door. "Let me in! I'll huff and I'll puff and I'll . . ."

He stumbled and grabbed the door frame. Ella had opened the door just a peep, and stuck her head and shoulders out to the fresh air. She stretched an arm straight out, dangling the bag of ginger cookies. "Look familiar?"

He nodded.

"How many?"

"Two."

She opened the zip-lock, held the bag open in front of his face. "Smell." He breathed deeply through his nose. Felt his stomach heave. *God, no more cookies.* He remembered the skunky burps. "Smell like anything you know?"

He stretched his hands out in front of him. Clenched and unclenched his fingers. The pins and needles weren't getting better. "Least I don't have MS."

Ella turned her perfect lips up in a smile. Lanny noticed she had beautiful big white teeth. Like a beaver, he thought. She could chew right through that front door. "Cosmos wants it good and quiet in here for Michael," those lips were saying. "How about if you hang outside for a bit? You might feel better in the fresh air anyway." Her head and its red toque disappeared from the door crack. Just when Lanny thought he'd been dismissed, she reappeared, holding out a steaming travel mug of peppermint tea. "Take this with you."

He reached for the mug, scalding his wrist with the splashing liquid. "How'm I going to get up that with this?" He nodded toward the steep, icy exit.

"We need to dig that out." She made a clicking noise with her tongue as if calculating her options on a hidden calculator. "Later. I'll give you a push this time." She opened the door all the way, so Lanny could see Cosmos behind her, waving a bundle of smoking dried herbs above her head. Ella was right—he needed some fresh air.

She stepped into the tight snow hole with Lanny. Her head reached exactly to the middle of his chest.

"*You* are going to push *me* out of here?"

She nodded, no hint of a smile playing at her luscious mouth. "Give me that." She pointed at his tin travelling mug, and took the steaming cup of tea, reached it above to flat ground, pushing it far into the snow so it wouldn't fall over. "Now you."

Some of Cosmos' smoke drifted out the door, swirling above Ella's head. It smelled like burnt oregano. "Me what?"

She made that clicking noise in her mouth again. "You what . . . ?" She spoke as if to herself. She bent down, clasped her fingers together to make a foothold. Bent like that, she barely came to his groin. And she wanted him to plunk his big, ski-booted foot onto her tiny hands. He lifted a leg and swayed like a pine tree in a windstorm. He stumbled and bumped his shoulder into the wall of snow.

Ella's tongue was clicking again, her red toque back level with his chest. "Okay, let's do this." She grabbed his shoulders. "Turn around." She faced him into the snow wall. "Just grab the top, dig your toes in, and I'll help push you over. It won't be pretty but we'll get you up there."

He felt her two tiny hands pushing into his ass.

Mother of God. His hind legs scrambled. He flew up and over and away from her. An alarming twinge called out from his right knee but he ignored it, mumbling his thanks and rolling away from the hole until Ella couldn't see him. He didn't return for his tea until he heard the door close behind her.

Crawling, his knees crunching across the frozen snow and the right one throbbing with each stretch forward, he made his way back to the steaming mug, cupped it in both hands, and lifted it to his lips. The strong smell of peppermint assaulted his senses. He dropped the cup to the ground as he felt his mouth fill with saliva. He swallowed hard, fighting the overwhelming sensation of nausea, but it was too late. His stomach heaved with each gag reflex, a groaning sound emanating from his very innards, as he clenched his face and throat, trying desperately to hold the contents of his stomach down. He half stood, and stumbled to the snowmobile parked at the hut's entrance, hugged his arms around its seat, pressing his face against the cool leather.

Another massive gagging heave wracked his body, and he lurched forward, pushing his face hard into the snowmobile's seat, spilling a barfed-up mess of half-digested ginger cookies onto the black leather. Another giant heave waved through him and his lunch—tuna salad sandwiches washed down by a thermos full of hot chocolate—followed.

He rolled on his back away from machine, pulled his knees into his chest, rubbed his fleece arm across his face, wiping cold sweat from his face. He breathed deeply. "Sitka! Sitka!" The dog had limped around the corner of the hut, scared off by the sound of his retching, but approached him cautiously, and sat at his shoulder. "Oh, Sitka . . . your poor old master is dying." He rolled onto his side, squeezing himself into the fetal position in the snow. "Come here, baby. You're limping. We'll get you some anti-inflammatory treats or you'll never make it through tomorrow. They're just in my pack in the hut." He closed his eyes and breathed. The cool ground against his cheek refreshed him, and he felt the waves of nausea subside. "Really, barfing my guts out was the best I could do," he told the dog. "Rid me of this poison. Michael and me—we're too old for this hippy shit."

He pushed himself to sitting. "Sitka, no!" He lunged at the snow machine, pushing Sitka away from the steaming barf. She returned, exploring the mess with her tongue, and he pulled on her paw. "Yuck! No!"

He grabbed her by the collar and dragged her to the side of the hut. The wind had picked up an angry momentum, and he hugged himself tight, grateful for the bit of shelter provided by the hut's walls. "Well, Sitka. It's out here with the wind or in there with the stupid mutts and the crazy bohemian broad." He scratched Sitka's neck and the dog leaned heavily into him. "At least out here we won't choke on smoke." He climbed to his feet, a droning headache reminding him of the tortures of this day, and moved close to the cabin, where he'd at least be a little sheltered from the wind. Sitka sprawled across his lap and he pulled the heavy dog into him for warmth, wishing he hadn't spilled all his hot tea. He could feel the cold, wet tea slowly seeping through his old ski pants.

His eyes scanned the ridge above him and then the gentle slope down to Camelot where he'd first spotted the four-headed beast of Cosmos-Ella-Janet-and-Michael. He foggily remembered standing like a captain at his helm and cringed in embarrassment. What else had he done? He'd lost at least an hour. Nothing compared to the years he'd lost in his twenties, he supposed. He hadn't meant this trip to be like that, though.

He squinted at the wood sign pointed at the hut, CAMELOT engraved in big square letters, "it's a silly place" in parentheses below—the work of old Heinz Wittiger, according to the Coalton rumour mill. The widowed school teacher turned crazy hermit. Sad story that—losing his wife and all, nobody watching out for him. Lanny scratched his fingernails in the fur at Sitka's chest. "Maybe not so sad, hey Sitka? Maybe you and me should escape just like that. Get way out in the wilderness, where . . ." He slid his hand under her collar, let the heat of her body warm his amputated fingers. *Where what?* ". . . where nobody would bother us."

Music had started to play inside the hut, that Middle Eastern, whacky shit. Music that belonged in a place where the air was so dense and steamy that you swam through it instead of walked, not on a snowy mountain just above Coalton.

A sound in the other direction caught his attention. Up at the summit, someone had hollered. His eyes searched the ridge, and fell upon a crowd. One, two, three, four, five.

God, add that to his five and they were now ten in the cabin. And four dogs. "The huskies are sleeping outside," he mumbled under his breath, knowing he was in no position to make such pronouncements. He'd given up on his own powers along with his role as Captain Lanny.

It looked like three guys, one female (judging from the baby blue headband and the long hair) . . . and a snowboarder of indeterminate gender.

Before he could guess at any more, the three guys had pointed their skis straight down the slope and arrived metres from the cabin. Nice form. He recognized them immediately. They flew down slope so fast that their jackets pressed firm into their chests, the extra material flapping loudly out behind them. He swore the speed even distorted the flesh on their faces, like cartoon time travellers.

The Back-Seat Boys, he and Michael called them on the hill. Point skis straight down mountain, sit back, and hold on tight. These ski-bum kids were always shouting from the lifts. *Speed's your friend! No falls, no balls! Point it, you pussy!*

The snowboarder—a girl—pulled up just at their heels. The blue-headband chick snowplowed in cautiously behind the others. Nobody said a word. The Back-Seat Boys weren't rowdy like Lanny'd seen them on the hill—trash-talking their friends from the chairlift, guzzling beer for money in the day lodge, naked table sliding after they'd gotten into the tequila shots—and Lanny sat a little straighter, preparing himself for alarming news. What would it take to quiet these hooligans?

"Conditions are bad, dude, bad," the one in the fattest and longest skis announced. His voice sounded stuffy, like he spoke through his nose, and his eyes had a red puffiness to them. It could've been from flying down the hill with no goggles, but Lanny would've sworn the young "dude" had been crying. Sitka ran over to his side to greet him.

"Who brought the golden retard?"

Lanny's sympathy and concern evaporated.

"Best entrance is a fast entrance." The red-eyed boy took a running jump at the front door, slid down the hole and banged through Cosmos' barred door. As he crashed through, he released a strong smell from the cabin's innards. "Phew," he yelled up over his shoulder, "Someone's been smoking oregano in here!"

The dark-skinned, handsome one shrugged and slid down the hole after his friend.

Lanny knew the other guy, the one who hadn't gone in yet, a

little bit. Antonio Ragusa. Little Tony. His dad was a foreman at the mine. This Tony kid had been caught in a nasty fall earlier this season, lost a lot of teeth. Maybe that's why he didn't smile now.

"Tough day?" Lanny asked him. Might as well be sociable. Like it or not they were stuck up here with these young bucks.

Tony shrugged at him. "Tough as any other, I guess. We're all here." He balanced himself at the top of the hole and gingerly slid one leg over and then the other, and clomped into the cabin.

"Sociable bunch," Lanny smiled up at the snowboarder.

She allowed a small laugh, a gift. "And you're seeing them at their best." She leaned down and rubbed the top of Sitka's head. She glanced over Sitka to the abandoned snowmobile, and wrinkled her nose at the frozen mess of half-digested ginger cookies and tuna sandwiches. "Nasty, dude! Hope that's not your machine." She covered her nose with a mitten-clad hand. "Hope that's not your barf." She looked at him for a second, as if waiting for answer, then seemed to change her mind. "I gotta get these wet clothes off. Crowded in there?"

Lanny nodded.

"Ah well, what can you do?" She said it like one long word, what-canyoudo, and then popped her bubblegum, jumped down into the hole and through the door, making it look easy.

He looked up at the blue headband.

"I hate this fucking place. I hate this fucking sport," she said. With that she threw herself into the hole, as if she had no other option, and fell through the door with a howl of pain.

Lanny leaned against the cabin, called Sitka back to him, and gathered the dog's head into his lap. Together the two of them would wait it out. Tomorrow, they were going home. "Pass the Nusty Rails, Sitka."

17. To Heorot

FIREBALL IN A FLASK
Type of alcohol: whisky
Distillery: Canadian Distillers Ltd
Price: $21.25
Home: Gimli, Manitoba
Bottle size: 750 mL, 200 mL if you're a pussy
Alcohol content: 33%
Taste: Hot cinnamon (got a problem with that, homo?)

Kevin and Claudette arrived at the decrepit hermit-hut before Kevin had time to change his mind. This place didn't even deserve the title "hut"—a grandiose word for a cluster of banged together stick and boards. "Shelter" might be more appropriate, but even that didn't account for the gaps between the boards. The wind must cut right through. He pictured his father lying there on a frozen January night, his hands across his chest and his body nearly buried in snowdrifts.

But, Kevin reminded himself, this man—or whatever he'd become—was not his father. Not anymore. He pulled a flask of Fireball out of his boot, twisted off the lip and raised it to his lips, let the fiery cinnamon coat his tongue before he swallowed.

"Dad!" he called out, the burst of sound startling Claudette so that he felt her flinch against his back. He pushed the flask back in his boot and pulled himself away, stepping down and sinking into the new layer of snow. He turned to Fredrik—"Prepare to meet The Ull"—before taking his last step to the hut. "Heinz! Are you there?"

"His dad . . . ?" Fredrik's words arched upward into a question, one he clearly didn't know how to finish.

And how could he? As if Fredrik could believe that the so-called snow god of Coalton was Kevin's father. Plain old Kevin's plain old dad. Not a legend but an uncared for old guy, coping badly with undiagnosed mental health issues. It was embarrassing. People would say Kevin didn't take care of him. And this was it. The very reason that Kevin kept his secret.

It wasn't that he didn't want to dismantle the myth, was loathe to replace the magical snow god with a crazy old fuck. He didn't give a shit about the myth, and those legends would never die anyway. People needed something to believe, no matter how unlikely that something was.

What Kevin couldn't bear was the judgment. He felt it already, sitting heavy in Fredrik's two words: His. Dad.

Kevin had failed to take care of his own aging father. That's what people would say.

Other men's wives die. Other men cope. He repeated the words to himself often to ward off suffocation-by-guilt. But the words were dull weapons—ineffectual against the raging army of guilt, self-loathing, and despair.

He pictured his mother—as fragile as a dead leaf pressed against their living room sofa. She looked as if someone had sucked out all the substance between her skin and her bones. She'd turned a jaundiced yellow, as if her whole body had been stained by nicotine. He could hardly bring himself to hold her hand, so bony and cold that it was already dead. Her only movement was to roll her head to the side, toward the bucket placed beneath her on the floor, to empty the acid contents of her stomach, retching and spitting.

And for all that sickness, the thing Kevin found most disturbing was the white hair, so thin in places that her yellowed scalp shone right through.

She could have worn a wig.

She could have tried.

Neuro-endocrine cancer, the doctors called it. So insidious, so relentless, so difficult to pin down that defeat clouded their voices before they'd even begun her treatment. "It's hormonal," one doctor after another would explain, "it floats through the body, shows up everywhere." Kevin pictured them waving the white flag of surrender. "It's in her liver," each doctor told them, placing a hand on his father's shoulder as if consoling a widower, "the chances—" They'd interrupt themselves, shaking their heads.

Shut up, Kevin wanted to scream, *Shut up!*

But his mother never said "Shut up." She never said "I'm not dead yet." She never said "We can beat this."

His mother said nothing. Her red hair all gone, she looked eighty-five, not fifty-two. Eighty-five and ready to die. Kevin wouldn't be able to make the brave son's funeral speech about his mother putting up a valiant fight. He'd feel an almost overwhelming urge to stand up and scream his objections when an anonymous priest would inevitably insist that Sonia Wittiger had shown her zest for life right until the very end.

Heinz was fifty-eight when she died, so no one thought it odd that he retired. *A man can only bear so much.* Similarly, no one thought it odd when he moved to the country. Coalton was too small for someone who didn't like people, and after his wife's death, Heinz liked no one. He worked his way through friends, through colleagues, even through amiable acquaintances—always accumulating lists of underhanded slights, unforgivable annoyances, intolerable irritations.

A small town, he claimed, didn't allow the space necessary for grieving. This was the story he told, and they all bought it.

The poor man needs his space.

And so Heinz slipped away in bits. By the time anyone, even his only son, bothered to think his behaviour odd, he was no longer Heinz. No one could bring him back.

There were sightings. "I saw your dad at the Overwaitea . . ." Kevin heard the judgment heavy in their voices. They never finished their sentences: *Saw him and he's off his rocker.* It was in their hunched posture, the way they bent in towards him, clenching his shoulder and waiting for his confession, willing him to finish their sentences for them.

Some of them even reached out and held his grocery cart when he tried to maneuver around them, attempting to squish into the space between their cart and the wall of lit-up milk and eggs.

Why even mention seeing Heinz? What the fuck was Kevin supposed to say? That's how he wanted to respond, blowing a giant hole right through their watery, sympathetic eyes, "What the fuck am I supposed to say?"

As the years passed, Kevin found a way to minimize his connection to the crazy old hermit. Coalton was a town divided—locals versus transients—and Kevin used this division, hoped that the town's memory was only as long as you wanted it to be. He attached himself more and more to the newcomers, the foreigners, the people who knew nothing of the poor school teacher. Eventually, this new circle of friends included a new wife. A French wife and a Swedish best friend.

Coalton, though, was a town that talked. The grocery store, the post office, the pub: all full of people who wondered about his father, wondered what had happened between Kevin and his first wife. His ex-wife.

Perfect Ella of the deliciously full lips, the eyes that shone like a muddy river on a steaming hot summer afternoon. Crazy Ella with the neurotic energy that she focused so intently on the bears—on *her* bears—how quickly it could turn from passionate love to outraged anger. She ranted to delirium at town council meetings. Any number of things could set her off: residents' failure to clean up fallen fruit; off-leash dogs in animal corridors; mismanagement of local trash; anything. She'd actually been threatened with charges for slapping a kindergarten teacher who threw some leftover muffins into the garbage bins behind the elementary school. The worst had been the time Kevin had to pick her up at the RCMP Headquarters.

"You'd better come talk her out," the constable had said, pulling absently on the long hairs at the corner of his moustache. "She's been pretty non-responsive with us." Kevin followed the man through heavy doors and into a dim room that smelled of cold concrete.

There Ella had sat behind bars, crouching in the corner, as small as a wet cat. He'd learned more about what happened from that week's *Coalton Herald* than he ever learned from her.

Ella acted like Heinz's "relocation"—as Kevin liked to call it— was a personal slight against her and her cause, an environmental trespass instead of a personal tragedy. *I realize it's sad, Kevin, but . . .*

. . . he's just one man.

. . . he's taken it upon himself to shack up right in the middle of a major Grizzly Bear corridor.

. . . there are homes for people like him.

. . . that's bear territory. We've pushed the bear out far enough.

There were umpteen ways of finishing that sentence and Kevin had heard them all. Like the other townspeople, Ella expected Kevin to do something about his father. Unlike the casserole-carting Rotarian Wives, she couldn't care less about Heinz. Her concern began and ended with her precious bears. Soon, Heinz—with his bear-unaware ways—was with them at breakfast, was part of every conversation they had about their future, was even between them in bed.

Forcing Ella from his mind, Kevin took a deep breath and pushed aside the piece of plywood covering the hole that served as Heinz's door. He instinctively held the back of his hand up against his nose as he stepped into the living space, thankful for the fresh wind blowing through the cracks, appreciative of the cool gusts of air that didn't hold the smell as tightly as true indoor air would have.

And there sat Heinz. He had the same oversized strong hands, the same heavy shoulders, rolled forward as if in a modest attempt to diminish his towering build. But his face had changed. Patches of skin on his cheeks above his beard had turned black from frostbite.

Overexposure to sun and wind had mottled the skin around his eyes, turning him an indistinguishable age. Too fit to be old. Too worn to be young. He faced a tree stump that served as his kitchen table. A hand sat passively on each knee, and he stared straight ahead into nothing.

"Dad. How come you're not answering? It's Kevin—your son."

Heinz wore a down vest and heavy flannel shirt with missing buttons and stained underarms. The shirt hung open and underneath he had on an old long sleeve T-shirt that Kevin had given him years ago as a gift. It had once said "Jesus would've been a telemarker," and the picture had shown a thin, bearded man, skis protruding from beneath his long gown. The skiing Jesus bent a knee to the ground in the typical telemarking technique, but on him it was the pose of genuflection. Back when Kevin had the T-shirt made, Heinz had been Coalton's only telemarker. Since then, the hill had been invaded by telemarking Norwegians and their "free the heel, free the mind" ethos.

"Christ, Dad. It smells like shit in here."

Still, Heinz didn't turn to him. Kevin held out a hand, left it to hover above his father's shoulder, half expecting him to be frozen to the touch. When he clasped the meaty joint, though, it felt warm through the flannel shirt, and finally the old bear of a man turned, ever so slowly, to look at him. He looked, and said nothing.

"Kevin." Kevin said his own name for a third time, prompted by the question in his father's watery eyes. "I'm Kevin."

Heinz's beard hung, thick and knotted, to his chest, littered with leftover crumbs of food and dried traces of slime and snot.

Kevin remembered Fredrik behind him, imagined him stunned in the doorway, and felt the familiar pull of embarrassment—the snot-filled beard, the shit-reeking home, the comatose father—it was all hard enough for him to take in, but that his friend should see it and judge him, judge Heinz—it was too much. Tears rose in his sinuses.

But anger always came more easily to Kevin than tears.

"GIT!!" He quickly turned on Claudette, morphing his sadness to outrage with the practised ease of a magician, shouting at her as if she were a feral dog. "GIT!! I told you we should not come here! I told you!" He shoved her roughly against Fredrik. "Go away, both of you, go away!"

Claudette paused for only a second—just long enough to raise her chin and stand tall, as if to say *I go of my own accord. Je m'en vais parce que je veux.* But she went. She whispered to Fredrik, and they left.

As soon as they were out the door, Kevin wished them back. The space seemed closer now, he and his father too tightly squished within it. Kevin held his fists up to his mouth, bit his knuckles, breathed in the two-stroke oil scent of his own flesh. His eyes involuntarily wandered around the small space that his father called a home. Just behind the stump of a kitchen table was a wooden bench. A sleeping bag was flung open there, its insides brown with use. A makeshift woodstove sat within arms' reach of the hard bed. Though wood had been piled high on either side, the fire was unlit. Heinz's home was no warmer inside than out.

Finally, Kevin forced his eyes to the one thing he'd been avoiding. On the floor in the middle of the shack, a deer carcass lay. Its brown marble eyes stared blankly toward the hut's roof and its guts spilled onto the floor. The hind quarters had been hewn apart. Frozen blood stained the hide and the floor. Sections of fur had been torn off exposing the sinew below. Kevin swallowed hard to ward off his growing nausea. An image came to his mind of his father hunched next to the carcass, gnawing on a hair-covered hunk of flesh.

He knew this image would reappear in his dreams.

As if Kevin's inaction finally brought about the reverse impulse in his father, Heinz suddenly moved. Not quickly but suddenly. He pushed his heavy hands into his thick knees and heaved himself to a standing position. Once upright, he looked to be bent at a funny angle, like a lumbering bear more accustomed to walking on all fours. His eyes flickered back and forth from Kevin to the door, as if he couldn't remember how this strange man—a door-to-door evangelist perhaps—had arrived in his home.

Finally, he opened his mouth and Kevin leaned forward, both eager and scared to hear what sounds might croak from it.

"No. People. Here." Heinz pronounced one word at a time, like he'd lost the knack for sentences. He shook his head slightly and then tried again. "People. Here. No. Good." His chin quivered with effort after each word.

"Those machines," he pointed out the door where he'd obviously heard them roar up on their snowmobiles. "Too loud. Bad for animals."

He was an English teacher who'd forgotten his verbs. That's what had come of Heinz's retirement hobby of erecting signs. He now saw the world in shorthand, utilitarian phrases.

As if sensing that Kevin would be at a loss by now, Claudette reappeared. Quietly, she tapped his arm. "Fredrik will wait outside," she said, as if admitting her mistake. She pushed against Kevin's arm, gently maneuvering him, creating a space between him and his father. He let her fill the space, grateful that she would take over. She smiled at the old man like a nun approaching a catatonic child, as if they had no shared language. She placed a small hand on each of his hulking shoulders and coaxed him back into his sitting position. She handed him her pink Nalgene bottle, encouraging him to drink the water, while she magically produced a wet cloth and began wiping his beard.

Sickened by the sound of his father gulping the water, Kevin turned away and paced the small hut—three steps in one direction, three steps in the other, always with his eyes averted from Heinz, always with his oil-scented hands raised to his own nose.

Desperate to look anywhere but at his father, anywhere but the mutilated deer carcass, Kevin found his eyes hung-up on some sort of weapon mounted above the wood stove. He looked closer and recognized it as a plain stick.

A long stick with some dried mud on end. Curious, he moved closer and raised his finger to the stick's end. Running his hand over the dried, earth-coloured clump, picking at the caked roots with a fingernail, he felt the jolt of recognition shoot through him.

"Bear shit!" He yelled the two words, a curse and an accusation.

Heinz showed no sign of reaction. He stuck a finger deep in his nose and dug, stretching the nostril this way, then that, and finally holding a beefy finger in front of his face, examining his findings.

Unperturbed, Claudette reached out with her wet cloth and wiped the finger clean.

"You can't live like this anymore," Kevin shouted at Heinz. "You're worse every time I come. When are you coming home?"

"This," Heinz gestured around the small place, revealing a hole in the armpit of his shirt, "my home."

"Speak intelligibly!" Kevin's mind filled with an image of his real dad's face, the one who used to reprimand him for mumbling at the dinner table. "Isn't that what you used to say to me? *Speak intelligibly, for Christ's sake!*"

Kevin stopped, holding a hand over his mouth, fearing that he too would grow unintelligible.

Heinz let his big paw of a hand fall in his lap, where he vigorously scratched his groin.

"Jeezus, Dad! You're turning into an animal."

"Proud to call myself one." Having spoken his first verb, Heinz pulled at the wet hairs on his chin, and stared down at his own boots.

Kevin opened his mouth to say something, but he had nothing. He flung his arm angrily in the air, swinging his body around and heading for the door. One step outside, he turned back to look at Claudette standing over his hunched father. The HEOROT sign above the entrance caught his attention and, with an anger that surprised even him, he hit hard, smashing it to the ground. His hand throbbed in pain. He cradled it to his body, shouting, "It's not the Middle Ages, Dad. You're a retired English teacher—not a fucking snow god, not an Anglo-Saxon king, not some sort of fucking troll. A retired English teacher!"

He closed his eyes and screamed the last three words, wishing some sort of transformative effect. Hoping he could conjure what he pronounced. But when he opened his eyes, Heinz had his eyes closed, face tilted upward. Claudette stood above him focused on the task presented by his beard.

Afterwards, Kevin couldn't remember what precipitated their departure. Claudette must've given in, must've admitted their visit could have no effect. He only knew that no one said anything on the trip back. By the time they approached Camelot, a heavy darkness had descended upon the hut, a nightfall so black and deep that when he turned off his sled's lights he couldn't make out Claudette's features, even though his own face was mere inches from hers.

Kevin stopped his machine on the ridge overlooking the small ski hut and quieted his engine. Claudette still held fast to his waist but the quality of her embrace had changed. He no longer felt the heat of lust or the promise of passion. Now her hold on him felt softer. He knew its sentiment well. Sympathy. He hated to be the object of anyone's pity.

He brushed her hands away as he sat looking down the hill to Camelot. Music pounded out of the small hut. The bass-heavy boom that Coalton's young punks seemed to play at top volume every chance they got was out of place here under the dark shadow of the alpine peaks, the eerie presence of The Sleeping Giant. Candle light and head lamps flickered through the few small windows.

From Kevin's outlook, the place looked crowded. If it weren't already so dark, he could have counted the skis and boards littered around the hut's front. They were just a blurred, shadowy mess from here, but it was a mess that took up an alarming amount of space, like a bus had dropped off a whole whack of partying ski bums.

He scooped up a handful of snow and packed it tight, walloping it hard at Heinz's CAMELOT sign. If Heinz wanted to leave, he should've just left. But no, there he always was. Nowhere and everywhere.

The tune inside changed, and a familiar screaming voice rasped out *Here we are now. Entertain us.* Voices in the cabin whooped in agreement.

Just great. They'd come all this way to end up at a fucking night club. But there was nowhere else to go now. He pumped his throttle in a signal to Claudette to retighten her hold on his waist. As soon as he felt her hands at his sides, he flew down the hill to the little cabin that seemed to rock in time with the music emanating from inside.

When he pulled off his helmet, Claudette tightened her embrace rather than letting go. She leaned into him and whispered, "We can try again tomorrow. We'll go see him—take some cleaning supplies, some good food—"

"I'm done. I'll see him when he comes back to the world. *My* world."

"He's your father, Kevin. He *is* in your world. Has to be—"

Kevin talked louder over Claudette's voice, interrupting as if she'd misunderstood. "The real world. Where the rest of us live."

He bent down to his boot, dug for his flask. She said nothing as he held the Fireball up to his mouth and bent his head far back, taking in long, hard swallows—one two and three—wiping his forearm across his mouth when he finally came up for air. "That man—or whatever he is—is not my father."

He stepped off the snowmobile and towards the hut door, but Claudette held his jacket by the elbow, pulled him in. He wouldn't let her embrace him, though. He shook his arm free and slid down the hole of snow into the full-fledged party going on in the belly of Camelot. Feeling himself fall, he decided there was nothing to do but get in the spirit of things. Fine. He could play this game. He was ready to drink until he didn't remember his own name. *Kevin who? Heinz who?* As he crashed through the door, he opened his mouth wide and shouted, "Let's drink!"

18. The Urbanite

PENFOLDS RAWSON'S RETREAT, SHIRAZ CABERNET

Colour: Medium crimson red.

Nose: Aromas of red currant and summer pudding fruits
with a lift of cabernet, and appealing spicy shiraz.

Palate: Youthful and lively fruit flavours of strawberry,
raspberry, and loganberry follow from the nose. A
medium-bodied wine with a sweet-fruited mid-
palate and great balance. Fine tannins ensure a soft
and rounded mouthfeel.

After Alison clicked her heels together wishing for home, she simply stayed on her back and
stared at the sky. For a good fifteen minutes, she
didn't move, only stared at the late afternoon
sun dipping below the ridge. She had no plan.

No escape. No options.

By the time she mustered the courage to
pull herself out of the snow and into the cabin—breathing decisively
into one nostril and out the other as instructed by her Toronto Life
Coach—all the beds had been claimed. F-Bomb and Shanny had
strewn their sweaty clothes across the two beds in the room closest
to the fire, and Loco and SOR had plunked their packs in the middle
of the beds closest to the kitchen table.

"I guess I'm up there?" Alison nodded weakly at the ladder
stretching up into the loft at the cabin's ceiling.

"First come, first served, lady," SOR answered without looking
up. He squatted over the woodstove, blowing hard into its open
mouth. Smoke had started to fill the small cabin, but only the weakest flames sparked and sputtered. No one seemed inclined to help
him. "Making fire—my bread and butter!"

Loco, F-Bomb, and Shanny were squashed into the corner around the table—if you could call it that, a dirty and warped piece of plywood thrown across two stacks of cement blocks and two bench seats hammered onto the walls. Beer cans stood open before them, and they played some sort of card game that seemed to involve yelling out "Asshole!" at regular intervals and then guzzling from the frosted silver cans. Good times.

Feeling embarrassment colour her face, Alison zipped open her pack and unloaded five bottles of red wine—she'd brought her favourites—and a bottle of Baileys. She set them on the plywood table, noting Shanny finger her own, more practical can of beer and roll her eyes at F-Bomb.

"Put them in there," Shanny pointed at the bed through the door without looking up at Alison, "so at least they're not taking up the whole table."

Alison took the bottles two at a time into the bedroom, focusing her eyes on the pictures, reading the labels, to avoid meeting the game-players' eyes. She needn't have bothered. Not one of them looked up from their cards anyway.

Shanny held her newly dealt hand in just four fingers, her other hand slid under the table at her side. Alison would bet all five of her bottles of wine that the hidden hand sat teasingly close to F-Bomb's groin, the tips of the fingers accidentally brushing here, touching there. Alison had Shanny's game figured out already.

Alison eyed the wooden ladder to her boudoir for the evening—likely a thin and torn piece of foam thrown on a wooden floor. Again, what had she expected?

No feather beds here, lady.

SOR cheered to himself in the corner—"That's what I'm talking about, baby!"—as his fire finally grabbed hold of his kindling with a loud crackle.

"Asshole!" Shanny yelled from the corner.

Did that mean she drank or the boys drank? It looked like they all drank.

Alison held a rung of the ladder tightly and bent over to free her poor feet from her ski boots. These things were made for skiing down a mountain, not climbing up one.

"Uh-uh-uh . . . don't take those off. We're getting out of here," Shanny yelled, catching Alison as her fingers toyed at the first buckle. "We've gotta go *downhill* skiing, honey. That's why we're here."

SOR picked up Alison's open pack from the ground. She noticed the picture on the front of his shirt—a skier with his head buried deep in the snow and his ass pointed toward heaven, with the cheerful slogan "It's Not Fun Until Somebody Gets Hurt" scrawled underneath. With an easy overhand movement, he threw her pack up and over the edge of the loft, spraying clothes everywhere. "There. Saved you a trip."

"Hmm, thanks. That was easier. Too bad you couldn't have done that with me today." She winked at SOR, trying to work up some of her initial enthusiasm for this weekend adventure.

She wouldn't be the incompetent urbanite who couldn't do anything right. She wouldn't be the old lady who got left behind because she couldn't handle the physical exertion. "Anybody got a corkscrew?" She absolutely would not. "If we're going anywhere, I need a drink."

Wearing his usual expression of consternation—*I alone will save you idiots from yourselves*—Loco dug his snow pit. He scowled at his results, pulled out an object that, to Alison, looked like a pocket mirror, scraped a pinch of snow across its surface. Scowling some more, he studied the particles through a portable magnifying glass, mumbling words that only held vague meaning for Alison (*facet, shear, hoar*). He whistled through the space where his teeth should be.

"We had over thirty centimetres of fresh snow last night and this morning." He spoke down into his magnifying glass, but F-Bomb and SOR bent close, intent on each word. "Winds from the south swept even more snow over the ridges onto north-facing slopes."

"Sweet, sweet powder," Shanny purred, gazing up to the south-facing slopes.

"Take into account that cold spell last week, drawing all the air moisture to the surface of the snow, and now we have a nasty combo of loaded slopes with a deadly surface hoar layer buried good and deep."

Loco bent back to the ground digging at the snow and compiling another sample. F-Bomb and SOR frowned at each other over him.

Alison shifted from one foot to another, wondering if she'd ever get rid of the piercing pain in her heels. And she couldn't even feel her toes. It wasn't dark yet—she guessed it was only 4:00 PM—but it was shadowy and windy. How come nobody else looked cold? Small particles of snow pelted Alison in the cheeks, and she pulled her shoulders up towards her ears, hiding her face in the folds of her jacket.

Finally, Loco stood up straight and made the pronouncement that the others waited for. "We'll stay in the trees." His voice held such gravity that he reminded Alison of her senior editors announcing that subscriptions were down and the Internet meant the end of print media.

At this announcement, Shanny snapped her head away from Loco to glance longingly at the wide open bowl to their left. "But . . ." Alison pictured shelves full of glasses cracking at the pitch of Shanny's plea. "Please . . . if we just stick tight to the side, we'll be fine. All that powder . . . We can't waste it!"

Loco didn't even turn to look at her. "Suicide. Not on my watch," he said with a tone of grave import.

Even after a full season, Alison still struggled to figure out the dynamics of this group. How did they all come to be under his watch? Was he a self-proclaimed leader whom the others humored? Or did he stand at the top of a knowledge-based hierarchy that kicked into effect out here where such knowledge really could mean the difference between life and death?

She wished she'd clued into that whole "life and death" aspect of this trip before getting half way up the mountain. *This wasn't Disneyland*, as the winter extremists liked to say, *no guarantees on this ride, honey.* Personally, Alison was quite fond of guarantees.

For whatever hidden set of rules put Loco in charge, Alison whispered a small prayer of thanks. He appeared the most cautious of the group and she was fully in favour of caution. She tried not to think of all the terrifying reports she'd read about avalanches as part of her research—the giant cracks splitting open across the entire face of a slope, the rapid earthquake of snow and debris, a thousand tons of snow thundering down a mountain and destroying everything in its path, uprooting stumps and pushing over boulders. Mere people didn't stand a chance.

"We can do a quick lap here in the tight trees," Loco said as he repositioned his skis, aiming to snake the group up through a thick stand of firs.

"And how do we know for sure this won't avalanche on us?" Alison heard the squeak in her own voice, as well as her misuse of a noun as a verb, and pretended not to notice the hostile, dismissive humph from Shanny.

"Too mellow a grade. Too many trees. You can see how old the trees are. We're clear of any avalanche paths here." Loco started to climb as he spoke these final words, and the others followed.

"Flat gay powder, it is! Yee haw! Flat gay powder—my bread and butter." Nothing—not even missing out on thirty centimetres of fresh fluff, not even potentially fatal avalanche hazard—could dampen SOR's mood. "Nasty hoar layer? Perfect, I'm up for a good nasty whore any day!" He held his ski pole between his legs, riding it like a bucking bronco.

Alison knew she could learn something from his mood, so could Shanny. "Pull up that bottom lip or you'll snowshoe right over it," she said to Shanny. Alison kicked herself internally for saying this aloud. She sounded exactly like her mother.

"Thanks, Mom," answered Shanny, right on cue. Alison knew

she deserved that and vowed to shut the fuck up. She slid one ski forward and then the other, and happily greeted the warmth that spread across her body. She felt fine when they were moving. It was April, after all, and couldn't be much colder than minus seven.

Alison found the climbing less physically strenuous than their initial ascent, but now fear—rather than fatigue—had her heart beating so fast and heavy that she felt her pulse would break right through the thin skin in the hollow at the base of her throat. She tried to focus on the others to take herself out of her own mind. They chatted with greater energy and animation than they had all day. F-Bomb egged SOR on about ripping the mountain a new asshole and rad-lining himself right off the Rad-ometer, both of which, Alison gathered, would be hard to do on a slope that had an incline about as steep as the average bunny hill.

Even Loco, who'd finally slowed his pace to stick close to his friends, joked comfortably, seemingly relaxed by the confidence the others had placed in him. "Pick your line," he yelled back over his shoulder. "I'm gonna straight-line right between those two cedars—" he pointed at two giant trees that barely seemed to have any space between them at all "—and huck off this stump." He stopped to pile some snow that would help smooth his transition on and off his jump.

So, they would be coming back down exactly the way they were going up. Alison could use that information to prepare herself. It looked doable, mellow for sure but not too much space. She'd let the others go first so they wouldn't see her gorbing it up behind them, attempting to snowplow her way down through the forest.

"Easy to say on this fucking slope," F-Bomb yelled back up to Loco. "My grandma could ski this fucking shit. You'll *have to* straight-line or you won't fucking move through all this snow." He swiped his pole through the deep fluff at the side of their skin trail to make his point.

Alison wondered about his grandma. Did she really ski? She

could never tell when these guys meant what they said, and she didn't want to appear an imbecile for asking. Today was the first she'd heard about F-Bomb's native heritage. She tried to think about this revelation and what it might mean for her article, rather than focusing on the gaping avalanche trap to her left. They were, true to Loco's word, sticking in the tight trees where it was supposedly safe, but they seemed terrifyingly close to the massive bowl that he had proclaimed dangerous. Safe, here. Dangerous, there. It seemed too absolute to jive with what Alison had, in her nearly forty years, learned of the world. And she didn't even want to think about the weight and speed and sheer quantity of snow that could come ripping down that wide open slope just to their left. She felt tiny in size and tiny in significance, dwarfed by the towering rock face looming above the bowl.

Look where you wanna go. SOR's mountain-biking advice from the summer came in handy here too, she discovered. No point of thinking about the hole of death just beyond her shoulder. Look to the trees. Stick to the skin trail. Snow never slides here, Loco says so. Safe. Think safety. And breathe. In the right nostril, out the left.

"What does an avalanche sound like?" she'd once asked Loco. She expected the thunderous roar of crashing train cars, imagined tons of sliding snow, ice chunks, even tree trunks uprooted and hurling down the mountain.

"A whisper," he'd joked, quietly.

"Yeah—you're toassssssst," SOR slid his hand downward on the whisper of *toasssss* and brought it to a dead stand-still on the thud of *t*. "Unless F-Bomb is in the slide, then it sounds like *Fuck, fuck, fuck, holy fuck!*"

Now, Alison blocked out their chattering laughter and listened for the telltale whumphing that warned of dangerous air pockets in the snow pack below, but she could hear nothing.

"Just up to that ridge," Loco yelled loudly over his shoulder, pointing to a plateau in the trees slightly above them, a fully manageable distance, Alison realized with relief.

But her relief jolted away as she heard snowmobiles roaring above them. She felt the sense of panic she'd felt in elementary school when her grade four teacher showed a film on the Second World War. Planes attacking. Open fire. Dropping bombs. She'd run home from school that day, holding her book bag above her head for protection, eyes to ground the whole way.

The world could end just like that. She hadn't known.

Now, she felt that knowledge anew with every blast from the snowmobiles. Hadn't Loco said piles of snow on an unstable layer? And now people were tearing through that snow on fast machines. Right above her.

She would die. They'd all die. Alison Batz had enjoyed her last pedicure.

"Fucking rednecks," F-Bomb muttered above her.

"Oh right, F-Bomb," Shanny teased, poking her fingers into his ribs, "it's not that you can't afford a snowmobile, it's just that you disapprove. Keep telling yourself that, buddy. You love walking up the mountain."

Alison's mouth watered hot and fast. She tried to swallow her hysteria, breathed again through one nostril and then the other, paid no attention to the other skiers, just kept her place in the tight line as they came slightly out of the small trees on the edge of the bowl and followed Loco in a tight switchback turn to head back into the trees and away from the avalanche danger. In through her right nostril, out through the left. She was getting the hang of this. All would be well. In through the right, out through the left.

She almost felt calm enough to reprimand herself for her being a chicken shit when she felt her feet slide out from beneath her. *Potato bug, flail* were the first words that passed through her mind with an image of SOR lying on his back, frenetically waving his limbs in the air, while the others sat in the sunshine laughing. Clearly, she was gonging it up again, opening herself to the ridicule of these acclaimed under-achievers.

But then—slowly, it seemed—she realized that she wasn't falling.

Not exactly. The very ground itself was sliding, and she was sliding with it.

Toassssssssssssssssssssssssssssssss . . .

Before she had a name for what was happening, Loco belted it out in a deep boom from the slope above her.

"AVALANCHE!"

The word froze her blood. Few words could have the same effect—*avalanche, cancer, death.*

But, to her surprise, Alison found herself surprisingly calm, more calm in an avalanche than she had been while thinking about an avalanche. She knew she'd either die or she wouldn't, and the amount of pain involved suddenly bore little importance. The snow carried her down the mountain, but quite slowly. She saw a torrent of snow rushing down the bowl, while she was carried much more gradually along the edge of the avalanche path. She thought of kicking off her skis, but instead she used them to press against the moving snow to try moving herself sideways, across the mountain, to the edge and out of the avalanche, back into the safety of the unmoving snow in the trees. She could see loose snow thundering down the open, treeless bowl next to her.

Loco yelled above her and the words registered sharp and clear. "Fight it! Swim! Swim for the trees!"

"All eyes on SOR," he yelled. "He's farther into it. He's going under. Alison—SWIM! Fight it! Fight it!"

She swam. Fighting with her arms and legs, fighting with her skis, nearly oblivious to the snow flying in her face, up her nose. Was she supposed to kick her skis off? She couldn't remember. Could she if she wanted to? The snow pulled her down-slope, and she no longer thought about moving her body sideways, knew she couldn't. But she could—*would!*—swim hard to stay on top of the snow and the sliding debris. She did not climb all this way to be buried deep in a coffin of snow. Instinctively, she used her skis to push against the moving snow, try to force herself out of it.

SOR flew past her in the faster snow just inside the big bowl. He had no skis and swam frantically on the surface.

Alison's eyes caught hold of a towering tree rooted straight ahead of her, right in her path. She knew if she wrapped herself around its substantial trunk, she'd be done. If it didn't kill her—which it likely would—it'd break her back or smash in her head. At the threat presented by the tree, she felt her first panic but even still, it was clear-headed panic. She pushed hard against the snow, fighting it and willing her body away from the giant tree and out of the moving snow.

What does an avalanche say?

She waited for the final thud of the *t*.

And then suddenly, unexpectedly, she stopped.

No reality-changing thud. Just stopped.

Her body lay splayed on the ground, just outside the path of the moving debris. Inches to her right, the snow still slid, roaring down the steep bowl. Safe—here. Danger—there. An *avalanche*. The word had been the stuff of nightmares for so long that it felt weird to use it for real. But she had stopped. The avalanche was running there, and she was here. She felt her arms, her legs, her face. *Fine.* She was fine. She had been in an avalanche, and now she was fine.

Who would believe it? She began framing the tale for her Toronto friends. She admitted she'd only been taken for a short tumble, that it was a mere sluff, a minor avalanche. On the edge of a real avalanche, but not in it.

But minor avalanche was like minor leg amputation, minor cancer. Who cared? She'd been in an avalanche, and she'd survived. Here, she still was. Here she was as fine as ever.

She took a deep breath through her mouth, tasting the cool liquid of snow particles hanging in the air. She smelled the sweet green scent of the towering cedar trees, lifted her hands to her head and tugged at her ponytail. Absolutely fine. All parts working. She laid her head back in the soft snow, her ears taking in the absolute silence of the still snow. She'd experienced the *toassssssssssssss* but not the *t*.

But then suddenly things sped up again.

"SOR's down!" Loco's voice boomed. He was no longer above her. He'd raced down the slope, holding his transceiver in both hands. "Everybody switch to receive. Find SOR's signal. We don't have much time." His voice wasn't loud or shrill, as Alison knew hers would be if she tried talking. He didn't push his words together or hurry them. He delivered his instructions as calmly as a doorman after last call. "Closing time. Drink up. You gotta go." There was no implication of potential death in his words, but Alison knew death was here, right with them. She followed instructions and flipped a button on her transceiver switching it from send to search.

SOR was under. Under a lot of snow with no air. Death was everywhere. Alison became acutely aware that she didn't want to be a part of anyone's death, not today, not out here.

She got up on her feet and saw F-Bomb, Shanny, and Loco, gathered in a group just below her and to her right. The snow in the bowl had stopped moving, the scene as still as a Rocky-Mountain postcard. They'd obviously skied down past her already. In this group, she was always catching up.

"Here. He's right here. He's deep. Probe." Loco held his transceiver low down over the snow, drew an X with his finger, and struck the spot with his own probe.

Before Alison could even find her avalanche probe in her pack, let alone assemble it, F-Bomb and Loco had the long sharp aluminum sticks in their hands, using them to poke deep holes in the snow, searching for their buried friend. To Alison, the probes looked like oversized fishing rods; she couldn't imagine how those meager holes, the width of a pencil, would help them find anyone. But Loco and F-Bomb worked together silently, in a way that would've seemed impossible a couple of hours ago, systematically placing a pattern of small deep holes across the surface that Loco had outlined and cordoned off with heavy boot prints.

"Can you hear us, SOR? Hang in there. We're coming." Loco addressed his words to the still ground. Alison tried to imagine their tragedy on the cover of *The Globe and Mail.* She saw only an empty page. Her headline-fountain had shut off.

Alison finally found her probe and pulled it out of her backpack, fitting the short pieces together into a long rod and then jogging clumsily through the deep snow towards the others but knowing even as she made the gesture that she was too slow. And she had a feeling that panic at near death was no excuse for incompetence. Not in this group, not on this mountain.

"Got him." Loco left his probe standing in the snow where he'd made contact with an object beneath. "Dig."

"Dig at the head!" Loco barked in the same authoritative voice. He and F-Bomb both sprang for the direction of the voice, grabbing their shovels from the packs and attaching the handles to the blades with a firm click in one quick motion. They dug hard.

Not fast enough, thought Alison, *nothing was happening fast enough.* Shanny hovered at the edges of Loco and F-Bomb's hole, trying to get in the occasional dig between their fast, deep strokes, but they pushed her to the side like an annoying puppy. Alison held the cold blade of an old shovel that F-Bomb had packed for her that morning and searched in her pack for its handle.

Then a hulking man glided out of the forest, skimming across the surface of the snow on skinny wooden telemark skis. Alison smelled him before she saw him. Later she would try to capture this smell in her journal. More than anything, he smelled like road kill. Before Loco and F-Bomb noticed him, he'd pulled Loco's probe from the snow and reinserted it at what must've been the mid-point of SOR's body. He pushed Shanny, who stood there stupidly holding her shovel, downhill at an angle to the right and Alison, who knew she looked just as stupidly useless, downhill at an angle to the left. He rolled probes down the hill towards them. "Mark the spot with your probe," he instructed them quietly. "See the triangle the three probes make?" Alison looked at the three skinny aluminum sticks, wavering like branchless trees, and nodded. "Now dig. Clear a path from your probe up toward the centre probe."

Alison, relieved for the activity and grateful for the specific instructions, dug hard. She saw in her periphery vision that Shanny did the same from her corner. They raced to clear a path up to the probe marking the centre of SOR's body. The snow felt heavier and denser and deeper than Alison had imagined. The real work of a rescue, she realized, wasn't in finding the body but in digging it out quickly enough. The large, bearded man began to dig beside Alison, making up for her slowness. She could hear his breath gargling wetly through his knotted beard, damp from a substance thicker, more glutinous than snow or sweat. She prayed for SOR to yell, to let out the faintest whisper of "here."

She wouldn't let herself think of what the silence might mean.

The more they dug, the more the old man's strategy made sense. They stood downslope from SOR. That meant as they removed the snow, other snow fell downhill away from SOR's buried body. In minutes, enough had fallen that they could see SOR's red ski jacket. He lay on his side, and the snow had fallen away to expose his face. He looked peaceful.

He's sleeping was Alison's first thought. Then the more likely reality of *unconsciousness* hit her hard, with the even starker reality of *death* delivering a fast follow-up blow.

Shanny leaned on her shovel, panting hard from the digging. Loco and F-Bomb, who had continued digging down from directly above the body, stopped still. They hadn't even hit flesh yet. While SOR's four friends stood in stunned, scared silence, the old man bent forwards so low that his long beard brushed against the snow. He reached out his monstrous hand and, lighter than Alison could've imagined possible, brushed the snow off of SOR's face.

At the feathery, warm touch, SOR's eyes sprang open, focusing instantly on the stranger's face. He choked, sputtered once, and then spoke. "I love you," he said, smiling at the old man. "*Love you.*"

The words brought the group to life. Shanny jumped at SOR's body, pulling his feet loose from the snow, shaking his knees free, pulling on his thighs. Alison knelt at his face, holding her warm hands to his cheeks.

"Whoa, dude! First things first," Loco snapped at Shanny, pushing her out of the way and starting a body check, running his hands up SOR's legs, slowly and carefully, feeling for broken bones. F-Bomb searched the packs for a thermos of tea or hot chocolate.

Within five minutes, SOR was sitting upright and sipping hot chocolate from a silver thermos lid. He didn't say anything, just rolled his shoulders forward and slurped from the small vessel cupped in both hands. He shivered spasmodically, and F-Bomb draped a bright blue down jacket around his shoulders, then let his hand linger on SOR's arm, squeezing so hard Alison could see the hand muscles straining. "Thank god," he whispered, "thank god."

Alison sat down next to SOR, put her hand on his thigh. She didn't know how much affection she could show, here in front of his friends. She dug her fingers deep into his flesh, rubbing them against his very bones, feeling her fingers ache, already stiff and sore from the digging. He turned to her and for a moment seemed present in his eyes—less lost, less freaked. He leaned over and put his lips on hers, for just long enough that she could taste their salt.

But then he jumped up. "Sancho! Where's Sancho? He's down! Find Sancho!"

And there was Loco at his side, lowering him back into his snow seat. "Sancho's fine, buddy. We left him at the hut. He was too tired. He's fine." Alison lifted her hand back to SOR's thigh. Loco coaxed him to drink some more hot chocolate.

"Sancho's fine? He's at the hut?" SOR repeated Loco's words, but in his mouth they were empty. He'd ask again and again, not hearing the answers.

"Okay, I gotta go get his skis. I think I saw them up there, still in one piece." Loco turned to Alison, scratching the back of his ear as if baffled to find himself depending on her in any way. "You keep your eyes on him, keep him talking. I'll be back fast."

She squished in closer to SOR, watching Loco race up the slope that she had just slid down. She looked around for the old man, to say thank you, to offer him some hot chocolate, but he'd disappeared. Nobody else seemed to notice. She tried to think of something to say to SOR, but she had started to shiver wildly, all her energy sucked into the vortex of cold at her core. Still, F-Bomb and Shanny didn't even look cold. Alison tried to quiet her chattering teeth. "Anyone have an extra jacket?" She hated herself for asking this, for exposing her incompetence in this group, for asking for attention when someone else had just lain with death.

Shanny sneered at her. "Geez. What *are* you wearing? Is that a cotton turtleneck? F-Bomb, friends don't let friends wear cotton. No wonder she's freezing. She must be soaked."

F-Bomb swung his pack on his back. "We've gotta get moving anyway. If we don't go now, we're gonna get stuck in the dark. You'll be fine once you're moving. Loco'll be right back. Let's get ready." He nodded at Alison. "I know nobody's into this trek anymore, but we gotta get somewhere. We can't stay here. We'll go slow. We'll stick deep in the trees."

As if summoned by F-Bomb's words, Loco appeared at his side, SOR's skis resting over his right shoulder. "Good to go. Nary a scratch." He winked at SOR. "Okay, I'm leading. Stick with me, but pay attention to the person behind you. Let's stay tight. No more than a six-foot gap. We'll wait. We'll regroup. We'll get back to the hut together."

As he spoke, Loco watched SOR and gestured wildly, secretively, at the rest of his group, waving his hand at his side, encouraging them to come to him. Alison realized that SOR wasn't paying any attention to Loco's instructions or his crazed hand signals. SOR stared at his skis like he'd never seen them before and had no idea what to do with them now. Loco wanted to talk to everyone else without him. Alison stood up and slogged through the deep snow to Loco's side without SOR even glancing up in her direction. The four of them huddled in a tight group.

"We've gotta get him back to the cabin, and he's obviously going to have to skin up under his own power. But he's shaken. Let's keep a close eye on him. Put him right behind me, then F-Bomb, then Alison. Shanny, you bring up the back. I won't pull out ahead. Yell if there's trouble. With anyone." Shanny nodded. She'd already put her pack on her back and buckled herself into her snowshoes. Her snowboard, strapped loosely to the pack, bobbled with her nod and appeared to tap her lightly on the back of her head with each movement.

Alison noticed that she was the one a step behind, again. Everyone was in their skis and carrying their packs. All her equipment still lay scattered around her pack which was lying in the snow next to SOR. She turned back to him and started at what she saw. He sat in the same spot, but he'd pulled his video camera out of his bag, held it in both of his bare hands, pointing it shakily at his own face. His face looked wrinkled and distorted like one of those over-bred dogs whose skin didn't fit its face. His cheeks were wet with tears and he sobbed openly, choking and spitting in uncontrolled response to his throat's spasms. He spoke into the camera but the voice was not his own. It burbled up from his deepest innards and sounded too wet, too high.

"But I lived." he was saying, over and over. "It could've killed me. But I lived. It let me live."

Alison looked over her shoulder towards F-Bomb and Loco, but Loco pushed her towards SOR. *You. You do something*, his gesture said.

"Suddenly I'm of use? First sign of tears and it's the woman's job?" But she made her way over to him, clumsy as always in the deep snow, and put her own hands on the camera. His hold was surprisingly strong. She pulled, her hands tight on the cold metal of the camera, but there was no give at all. He'd stopped talking, but still sobs shook and rattled his body. He choked and sputtered, still looking into the lens, not acknowledging Alison.

"Hey," she said softly. "Let go. Let's just put this away. Let's just go back inside. There's a nice warm fire. We'll find Sancho. Come on now, let go." She pronounced each word soft and gentle as she continued to tug on the camera.

"I am here," he cried into the camera. "Here I am. Because it let me live."

She worked her way around to his side. Put an arm around his shoulder. "Let's just go, okay?" She had no idea what his friends expected her to do to fix this.

Then, she noticed—the blinking red light. "SOR, it's not taping." She tapped her finger at the blinking light next to the screen. "It's not even taping. Look. The battery's dying." His grip fell loose and suddenly, unexpectedly his full weight was leaning into her, his head fallen into her chest, shaking violently. She couldn't tell if he was laughing or crying. She wrapped both arms around him tight to keep them both from falling down into the cold, wet snow.

"We're going now, buddy."

Alison tightened her grip on SOR, grateful for the sound of Loco's voice.

"Pack away the camera. Get your shit together. We're going back." Loco turned, facing away from the spectacle of SOR, and waited for the others to line up behind him.

SOR swallowed his last few sobs, and looked up, pulling his head away from Alison. "The man . . ." His voice, papery thin, had no life left in it.

Reminded of the mysterious bearded figure, everyone looked towards the trees in the direction he must've gone.

"It was The Ull who saved me. I swear. It was The Ull."

They looked in vain for the big bearded man. Just two thin tracks disappeared into the forest, and already they were nearly filled with snow.

PART II

But the moon carved unknown totems
out of the lakeshore
owls in the beardusky woods derided him
moosehorned cedars circled his swamps and tossed
their antlers up to the stars
then he knew though the mountain slept the winds
were shaping its peak to an arrowhead
poised

And now he could only
bar himself in and wait
for the great flint to come singing into his heart

—Earle Birney, "Bushed"

19. Heinz the Hermit

Finally, Heinz stretched his legs and arched his back. He'd have to get out of this chair and get on with his day. He'd sat as frozen as an iceman since his son and friends pulled away on their obnoxious vehicles. They'd thrown off his routine, disoriented him, forced him to see himself from the outside. Until now, he'd been doing just fine.

He leaned over the deer carcass in the centre of his room and sawed off a piece of meat from its haunches. The smell of frozen blood brought a quick hot saliva into his mouth, and he swallowed hard. His knife got caught in the heavy frozen flesh, and he heard himself grunting as he forced the blade through the animal's meat.

Thanks to the assistance of Kevin's girlfriend, the embers in his wood stove were glowing a perfect hot orange, and he set the slab of flesh close to the heat to thaw. He could roast this dinner in a matter of minutes.

He forced a pointed stick through the still partially frozen hunk of meat, already looking forward to his meal. It sizzled and popped above the heat of the fire, the comforting sound of hot flesh all the conversation he needed.

He supposed he could've said something to his visitors. Kevin had come all that way. And that girl with him now—what was her name?—she seemed so sweet, her soft hands stroking his face, not flinching like Kevin did every time Heinz moved, not trying to force something from him.

He didn't even know what Kevin wanted to hear. What was there to say? Heinz Wilhelm Wittiger was what he was. Beyond words.

Except for the signs. Always he had to remember the concession of his signs.

He pushed at the animal carcass with his foot, moving it away from warm glow of the fire, shuffling it against the cold wall under his bed. A carcass in the house was maybe a bit much. He'd gotten sloppy living alone. He'd move the dead animal outside once it warmed up. He'd need to build a cold shelter. Summer was trickier in some ways—more available food but no shelf life. He was just one person, he could only eat so much so fast. And if he didn't eat it, bears would smell it soon enough and come hunting.

At least Kevin hadn't brought that Bear Woman with him. She'd have gone ape-shit hysterical at the sight of his deer. But a man had to eat, for god's sake. Nothing was more natural than eating.

He pulled his stick from the fire, admiring the perfect brown of each side. He pulled the meat from the stick and pinched it between his fingernails, keeping the heat from his bare flesh, waving it in the air to help it cool. In two long steps, he was out the front door—more of a hole, he guessed, now that he saw it through the eyes of his son and his son's friends. He lowered himself to sit on a stump, leaning his back into the trunk of a cedar. He savoured the gamey meat as he surveyed the wide face of the mountain through the forest before him. He imagined that's where his son would be snowmobiling. He hoped they'd be careful. The Ull, he Heinz, had been generous this year, and there'd therefore been a frightening amount of snow. Those imbeciles from Coalton sometimes didn't know enough to be scared. No respect for nature.

He pinned the chunk of deer with his teeth and sucked the remaining morsels of meat from the gristly flesh. A healthy-sized piece of sinews and fat remained, and he tongued it around in his mouth, enjoying its complex texture. As he chewed on the gristle, he thought about his HEOROT sign. Kevin had punched the hut so hard the sign had fallen to the ground. He hadn't even apologized or bent down to pick it up. Heinz's hard work disrespected again. He couldn't even keep the vandals from his own home. He sighed.

Kevin was right, though—Heinz wasn't an Anglo-Saxon king. He poked at the HEOROT sign with his toe, digging it deeper into the snow. He wasn't a king of anything, and this wasn't a hall. He leaned his head back against the tree and tore at the fat and sinew in his mouth with his old teeth, eventually swallowing it all. Even when the meat was done, he didn't let himself look down to his disrespected handiwork. He'd fix it tomorrow. Right now, he could tell from the hollering beyond the ridge, someone desperately needed his help. He'd go see what he could do, and then he was going to sleep. It wasn't even dark yet, and this day had already been exhausting.

20. In the Belly of Camelot

"Let's drink!"

Ella stood facing the wood stove, her head bent over the kettle, heavy warm moisture bathing her face, when he came crashing through the door. She didn't have to turn to look. She knew the voice instantly, and felt herself shrivel and disappear. She fought an urge to put the palm of her hand against the hot plate, hold it there as the skin and the sinews fried away, as if that pain would distract her from this shrivelling, this irrevocable lessening of herself.

She did not want him in her life or in her space. But Camelot was not her space. She had no control over who stayed here, and she had no place else to go. Janet and Michael had retreated to one room, and the ski bums had laid claim to the other, spreading their stinky socks across the beds like cats spray their scent to mark territory. She could stay in this room, with him, or she could go out alone into the cold night.

She turned directly away from the door to face the empty wall next to the stove, naively hoping that if he didn't see her face, he wouldn't recognize her, as if she could somehow get through to morning without her ex-husband noticing her. She heard her own breath—short and fast—and clasped her hands tightly around her warm cup of tea. Where was Cosmos? She needed Cosmos, wanted to hide herself in the bright folds of Cosmos' flowing skirt.

Now the young men were closing in on him, throwing angry words, puffing out their chests, growing bigger and louder like cawing roosters. Panic closed in so tight around Ella that she couldn't make out any of the details in the room—only sounds and flashes of colour. She caught the bright orange of Cosmos' inappropriate gown moving toward the hostile voices. Always the mediator. *Don't worry about them, Cosmos, take care of me.* Ella closed her lids and forced herself to take deep, even breaths. *Move away from the anger,* she heard Cosmos' soothing voice advising her.

Ella zoomed in on the red flash of her sleeping bag, huddled on the floor against the wall where she'd been reading earlier. She pushed her stiff legs toward it, got her back against the wall, slid down into the bright red cushion of down. Her hand groped for the book on the ground next to her, opened its cover, turned her eyes to the black and white of the page before her, stared at the blur of words and listened to her own short, quick breaths, and pulled her arms and legs into her body to make herself smaller, trying to become a hollow cave of nothingness.

🪨 "Let's drink!"

Alison had just got comfortable, snuggling into a corner of the kitchen bench under SOR's arm, soaking in his warmth and enjoying her fourth glass of wine—a full-bodied red with hints of clover—when a stocky redhead burst through the door.

Cosmos—as the aging hippy had declared that she should be called—sat cross-legged in front of the fire, eyelids closed and arms lifted out to her sides with index fingers clasped tight to her thumbs as if gripping imaginary mosquitoes that were intent on escape. The redneck nearly mowed her over, sent her tumbling onto an elbow.

F-Bomb, SOR, and Loco started to guffaw—there was no other word for it, their bench shook with the laughter—and their noise dismantled the imaginary wall that had been erected between Alison's crew (at the table) and group number two (as she thought of them) huddling around the fire. The others had been here when she and a shaken SOR returned from their afternoon Taste-of-Death ski tour, and Alison still couldn't quite figure out how the five of them fit together—hippies, business men, rednecks. Some of them hadn't even glanced in each other's direction all evening, never mind spoken. The big one with three stub fingers didn't even come into the hut until it'd grown dark out. He lumbered in, hulking over a pot on the wood stove, boiling himself noodles, shoving them into his face, talking to no one but his dog.

"Hey," Loco's voice boomed over the laughter, suddenly serious, even threatening. "You folks on snowmobiles today?" The question was sharp and pointed forcefully at the two men standing in the entrance. Alison felt SOR stiffen and move away from her on that last word. Until then, he'd leaned comfortably against her, sipping on a can of beer, occasionally rubbing the cool tin against the curve of her neck as if that were foreplay.

The first redneck, the short redhead, had pulled himself to his feet after his clumsy entrance, barely casting a look at the woman he'd toppled over. A long, skinny counterpart had entered more gracefully to stand behind him. Alison couldn't help feeling a little sorry for them, coming in from the cold, wet, and frightening hell she knew existed outside those doors, only to be greeted by this hostility. You could smell the testosterone in here. She smiled towards the skinny one.

"What if we was? You got something to say about it?" The short one pulled off his right glove one finger at a time, deliberately displaying each overgrown knuckle. The skinny one looked to the door as if expecting reinforcements.

"Good lord!" That came from Ella, Cosmos' quiet companion. She looked shrivelled, hunched into a tiny ball in a sleeping bag scrunched against the wall, like a makeshift beanbag chair. Her two words were quiet, almost a whisper. "Good lord," she repeated, even quieter, and then dropped her gaze back to a book in her lap. Alison had been trying, without success, all evening to read the dust-jacket of that book, to find some clue to the most elusive of the hut's personalities.

Cosmos stepped into the space Ella's words had made. "Ella's right. No fighting." She rose to her feet, only a little shaky, and held one hand extended towards SOR and the other towards the newcomer, as if she were the referee and they Olympic boxers. She wore a bizarre gown, so flowing and full that Alison could barely make out her substantial frame beneath. Its bright oranges and reds and pinks were bordering on fluorescent. She couldn't have hiked here in that get-up, obviously, but she'd been wearing it when Alison arrived. "We're sharing this space," Cosmos stated, shaking her arms so the material hanging at her underarms glimmered slightly. "Communication is key. Aggression shall not enter our living quarters."

Before Alison had a chance to voice her question—*shall not???*— Loco pounced in the direction of their big-knuckled opponent. "I'd like to communicate my fist right into his face if he's the buffoon who nearly killed my buddy today."

The nameless accused man cast a confused look at his lanky companion before responding to his assailant. "Killed? Whoa, buddy. We've had a rough day. Sounds like yours has been maybe even rougher. But nobody's killing nobody. We're just here for a coupla drinks and some sleep." He rubbed the heel of his hand in the space between his eyebrows, and Alison detected an overwhelming weariness.

A woman had entered quietly and stood between the two men. She seemed to be doing a quick head count, oblivious to the tension, unaware that she and her two men might be unwelcome here, beds or no beds. She unzipped her skidoo pants and stepped out of them. Her jeans were too tight and her pink T-shirt a little too short, leaving a roll of flesh exposed above her snug waistband. Did she think she was still twenty-two, Alison wondered, giving her own shirt a tug towards her hips.

"Bad?" SOR pushed out past Alison and moved to Loco's side "You think maybe my day's been *bad*? Try the worst. If you count getting buried and nearly fucking suffocating to death as bad." He still held a beer can in his hand, but now he looked as though he thought it could be used as a weapon. She wanted to lean over and remind him it wasn't glass. "You think you own the mountain on those death machines?" His voice had lost the shake that owned it earlier this evening. The words came out loud and deep, each one an assault on the recipients.

"Whoa, whoa, whoa." The tall one finally spoke, stepping slowly toward SOR, waving his hands as if he were washing windows. "I do not know exactly what happened to you today, but I am pretty sure that we were not . . . liable?" He looked toward his friend, shook his head. "Not, how do you say, at fault? Maybe somebody else caused this—" Each of his words was stiff, standing cold on its own, as if he composed his sentence one syllable at a time. "We are not the only snowmobilers on the mountain, you know, and—"

"—and if you were caught in a slide, maybe YOU were at the wrong place in the wrong time," the woman in the pink T-shirt and too tight jeans spoke up, far more aggressively than Alison would've imagined.

SOR tightened his grip on his beer until Alison expected to hear the can crinkle in his fist.

A loud clap from the direction of the woodstove interrupted the confrontation. Alison's head snapped toward the sound: Cosmos stood on a chair, towering above the angry young men. She clapped her hands again and held them out before her like a minister.

Ella barely raised her eyes from her book.

"Clearly, there have been wounds." Cosmos boomed out each word, loud and distinct. "People have been wounded." She lowered her hands slowly, wiggling her fingers as if sprinkling rain water on the people beneath her. "The time for healing is at hand. To heal, we must be a people united, not a people divided. Come. Come, my people." She swept her arms as if to gather everyone into a circle at her feet.

Alison felt her body lift from its seat and gravitate towards the pull of those arms. It would be rude to ignore this odd woman, wouldn't it? The crazy hippy would look even sillier if no one moved. Moving was the only polite thing to do. She took her wine with her, though.

"Oh no, not this shit again!" Alison turned to the unfamiliar voice of the dog-lover with seven fingers (and some bits). These words were the most life he'd shown all night. "She swooshed me right outside last time she started with this arm craziness. I had to sit out there by myself until I was nearly frostbit." But even as he spoke, he joined the others, limping his way into the circle.

Even the pregnant woman and her husband, who'd retreated to the semi-privacy of a bedroom, were pulled out by Cosmos and joined the circle.

"Sit, everyone, sit." Cosmos spoke quietly in a forced deep voice, raising and lowering her arms as if fanning a fire. Loco rolled his eyes. F-Bomb muttered, "This is fucking shit." But whether out of curiosity or boredom or courtesy, everyone began to sit. The redneck snowmobilers stood by the door muttering. The threat of violence, at least, seemed to have vanished. Loco aimed his hostile glance toward the door but stayed rooted next to F-Bomb.

"First, we will do a sharing circle," Cosmos said from up on the chair, looking down at her audience. "Turn inward for a few moments. Think of the thing that brings you the greatest happiness, the fullest peace. Each of you will have a turn to speak." Alison noticed that the chick in the tight jeans had fixed her gaze on Ella and stared with such hostility that Alison expected Ella to spontaneously combust or something, but Ella closed her lids, turning inward as directed by Cosmos.

"I've looked inward and realized that I'm fucking starved"—this from a loud voice at the door. The shorter of the snowmobilers moved toward the stove. "Grab that chili, Apple Cake." He looked down over at SOR who sat with his legs curled under him in Cosmos' circle. "If the feisty kid here doesn't have a problem with that, let's eat." When SOR didn't object, the redhead, barely audible, mumbled "—and tell your other creepy friends to quit staring at us."

Cosmos ignored this intrusion—seemed oblivious to it, in fact—and pointed towards Michael, indicating that he should be the first to "share." Alison slid a hand into SOR's back pocket and pulled him tight to her side to keep him from lunging at the ornery redneck and pushing the loudmouth right into the woodstove. *Eat that, redneck pig.*

Michael smirked and waved his head at Cosmos. "Nope. Sorry, Coz. Not happening." He put a hand to his wife's knee to quiet her shushing. He would take over from this point. Alison knew the type. "There'll be no sharing circles on my watch," he concluded with confident authority. When Alison first arrived, he'd been pale and weak, hunched over a bowl of soup, while the three women flitted about him bearing Tylenol and herbal tea. Hungover on too much Scotch, if Alison knew the type as well as she thought, but he'd come back to life now. If it were left to him, he'd control the rest of the evening.

"Your watch?" Cosmos lifted her eyebrows in a challenge, but her arms had already fallen to her sides.

"You folks never heard of washing a pot when you're done with it?" The short angry guy was standing over the sink, banging around dishes. "Like I need to do someone else's fucking dirty dishes? You think yer the only ones had a bad day." He didn't turn to look at anyone, but muttered his words to the dirty dishes themselves. His tall friend pushed him aside and poured some warm water from the kettle into the sink. Their female companion hadn't yet moved from the door, looked like she hadn't decided whether or not she'd stay.

Michael rubbed his hands across the thighs of his well-ironed slacks—even way out here in the wilds, not a wrinkle to be seen. Alison noticed that he was the only man not wearing a toque. His hair was short and tidy, fitting his head like a perfect helmet. "How about if we compromise?" He smiled up at Cosmos, who had suddenly begun blinking as if she'd abruptly woken from the deepest of sleeps, uncertain of where (or when) she was. "I agree," Michael said, rising and moving to her side, "that a game is a good idea."

"A game?" Cosmos blinked on each word. Her tone still carried disdain, but she had started to lower herself from her chair, nearly tripping over the hem of her skirt.

"A fucking game?" F-Bomb echoed in a stage whisper to Loco.

Michael offered Cosmos a hand down. "Good idea. A game. A sort of a contest," Michael said magnanimously, as if the idea had been hers.

The woman in tight jeans had made her way to the sink and whispered angrily at the shorter man, tugging hard on the sleeve of his snowmobiling jacket, pulling his attention back to her. "Did you know *she'd* be 'ere? How could you do this to me? *Kaw-liss*, Kevin. *Tabarnack*. This is no coincidence!" Alison was surprised, for some reason, to hear a strong French accent. Kevin shook loose of his jacket and her grip, then turned his full attention to the pot of chili on the stove. She bent to the floor and grabbed a silver flask from the jacket's pocket. She screwed off the lid, slid it into her own pocket, and held the flask up to her mouth, the bulge in the centre of her throat bobbing once, twice, three times. She took a deep breath, wiped her mouth on the back of her arm, and then drank again.

"How about a story contest? And—" Michael offered Cosmos a final gift, "that'll still involve sharing of a sort."

Alison muttered under her breath, so only Loco and SOR could hear her, "French Woman Drowns Husband in his Own Chili . . . Sharing Circle Derailed by Real-Estate Geek . . . Hippy Loses It: Killing Spree at Remote Hut . . . Interesting material." F-Bomb slid a Swiss Army knife across the floor to Loco, who jabbed a hole in his can of beer, then shot-gunned the whole thing in seven seconds before sliding the knife back to F-Bomb, who then did the same.

Interesting had been Alison's word of choice since they all arrived back at the hut in the late afternoon. A tiny, decrepit hut filled with wet, stinking dogs: interesting. A seven-fingered man who moped around glaring at everyone but talking to no one: interesting. A crazy hippy in a fluorescent gown conducting some sort of séance over in the corner: interesting. In the light of their close call this afternoon, she felt that nothing could frighten her anymore, nothing as simple as unfortunate bunk mates could lay claim to words like "disaster" or "tragic." She now knew that sharing too small a space with too many people wasn't the stuff of true crisis. She could cope with this. It was simply *interesting*.

Michael had walked Cosmos into the circle, opening a space for her between his pregnant wife and Ella, helping her into her preferred cross-legged position. She gathered her full skirt around her knees, shut her lids briefly as if reconciling herself to her demotion, and then raised her face to him, and surprised Alison by smiling.

"We'll need rules, of course. Cosmos?" He delegated the task—seeming to empower his inferiors while actually controlling their every move—and Alison could easily imagine him in a high rise on Bay Street. He set a hand on his wife's shoulder and lowered himself to the floor.

Alison couldn't tell if this woman admired her take-charge husband or if she were imagining him being eaten alive by rabid cougars.

"Rules," Cosmos said, lifting her fingers to the corners of her eyes as if to wipe away tears, and, Alison noticed, there was the slightest tremor to her voice. "A good story should have a valuable message, something to make us better people." Her posture improved as she spoke these words, re-gathering herself.

"And it better make us laugh our asses off," interjected F-Bomb just before letting out a loud belch.

"And sex. A good story should be sexy." The French woman added this criterion quietly, into her man's shoulder. He switched his spoon to his left hand, continued stirring his chili, while dropping his right arm around her shoulders without looking at her. She stayed tight to his side, but turned her head away so she could sip from his flask.

"For fucking sure," F-Bomb agreed, slapping Loco with a high-five.

Cosmos nodded vigorously to each contribution, asking names, repeating them loudly for the whole group. The woman in pink was Claudette, and the short redhead guy with the temper was Kevin. The tall one with them was Fredrik with some sort of Scandy accent. Alison wondered why anyone's name mattered. Surely, they'd never talk to these people again.

"Conflict," Ella added firmly, but at the same time managing to appear entirely disinterested in the exchange. "Conflict is crucial." As she shifted on her sitting bones, she lifted her book slightly off her lap, and Alison hoped to get a glimpse of the cover. All she could see, though, were big block letters—a C and an N—no picture.

"But it's gotta have people we like. If I don't like the people, I'm not reading past the first page," added Janet, the pregnant wife, rubbing small circles around her protruding belly.

"All right," Cosmos moderated. "message, humour, love, conflict, and . . . people. Sure. Yes. But . . ." Alison hated the lilt of Cosmos' voice, the way it suggested *I'm so much better than you people* or so much more *enlightened* or whatever she'd call it. "All of that is important, but I'm certain we can agree that . . . well, spiritual significance is *more* important."

"I didn't say love. I said sex." Claudette pulled her face away from Kevin's arm, and spoke loudly, making sure she'd be heard.

"If it's a contest, we need a judge," SOR chipped in reasonably. "The judge can decide what's important."

"This is fucking gay. I'm not fucking playing any fucking story game." F-Bomb stood from the floor, reached down to grab Shanny's hand and pull her with him. "Let's play cards. Asshole or something." His hand was on Shanny, but he directed his words over his shoulder to Loco. Shanny shook him off and stayed seated. He stood dumbly looking down at her, then lowered himself again to her side.

"Ella. Ella will be the judge," Cosmos spoke firmly, and Alison expected her to start doing that arm-waving thing again any second.

"A story judge. Of course. Maybe we should talk about qualifications, criteria, necessary skill sets." Michael clearly felt his leadership was needed again.

Alison had heard this "we" business all too often—editors coming into her office at closing time, "*We* have decided that this piece needs to be reworked by tomorrow," or "*We* need to reconsider the angle of this article—*we* don't want to offend advertisers." Right. We. She waited for Michael to announce *his* criteria and then fob the work off on someone else. She held some wine in her mouth, enjoying the way it numbed her tongue. Forks scraped against tin plates in the far corner of the room. The rednecks had squished around the table and had their faces inches above their plates, shovelling steaming ground beef and kidney beans into their mouths.

"How about you?" Michael turned toward Alison, and she felt herself jump, a little hiccup of startled movement. She started to sweat behind her ears.

"How about me what?"

"You're a journalist, aren't you? I saw a piece on you in the *Herald*. You work for *Globe and Mail*, right? That's good enough credentials for us, I should think. What's your name?" A whiff of sweet smoke reached Alison's nose. Good lord, not another joint. She took a healthy-sized gulp of her red wine, as Loco lit fire to the weed packed into the bowl of a miniature bong. It'd take a hell of a lot of wine to keep up with these guys.

"Alison Batz," she heard herself squeak.

"There we go. Alison Batz will be judge."

Cosmos' posture deteriorated, her spine collapsing in on itself.

Michael's wife, Janet, looked over at Alison. "My husband has a crush on all things Toronto. Big-city lust. Don't let it creep you out."

Michael ruffled Janet's hair as if she'd said something cute, but Alison glimpsed a faint blush crawl beyond the collar of his golf shirt.

"Shanny goes first," he announced, no longer inclined to maintain the illusion of sharing his power with Cosmos.

"Shanny? How does that work? Hottest ass first?" SOR jumped to his feet as he talked. "Yeehaw! That means I'm next." He bent forward at his waist and slapped his own ass. His sweatpants were cut off just below the knee, and his flawless calves looked liked they'd been shaved. He had a joint pressed between his lips and the smoke streamed up his face, forcing him to squint his watery eyes.

Alison turned to the man in the perfectly pressed pants and the helmet hair, taking in his full horror. *Control that, you self-assured ass*, she thought with surprising glee.

21. The Contest

SWAMP WATER

Ingredients: Fruit punch, 7-up, orange pop, grape pop,
     Pepsi, root beer, or whatever.
Mix randomly until none of the flavours stand out and
     the liquid turns a muddy brown.

"So how come I have to go first?" Shanny's tongue felt big and lazy in her warm mouth. She lifted it in slow circles, pushing it against the inside of her cheeks, stifling a giggle at the way her own face resisted and then stretched, like rubber.

"Well, I'm guessing at ages a bit," Michael answered, "but it's always ladies first and then I figure we'll start with the youngest. Sound fair?" He nodded at Shanny to begin.

She thought about asking him who cut his hair—nobody else in Coalton had hair like that. It looked like he actually put some kind of goop in it, the kind high school girls use. She lazily reached her hand out to touch the hardened spikes at the top of his scalp, a whole mess of dangerous barbs pointing skyward like a bed of nails, but his head was too far away, much farther than she'd thought. Her arm sat suspended, extended pointlessly in space. She let it drop to her side, registering the loud clump it made hitting the floor.

She looked down at her own hand, dizzy and surprised at the distance. She forced her eyes to focus on her far-away fingertips, reining them in closer.

Suddenly, she noticed Michael was still looking at her, waiting. She pushed some words out of her mouth.

"Actually, I have a cool story. Everyone loves this one."

"Ah shit, not the elk saga again." Loco must've drank eight cans of beer by now, but he hadn't gotten any less grumpy.

"It's a moose." Shanny dragged out the "oooooo" of moose and then took a deep drink from her own can of beer. She could hear the defensive sulk in her own voice. It made her want to giggle. She pushed her numb hand against her numb mouth.

"Can it, Loco. Let the lady tell her fucking story."

"So chivalrous, F-Bomb. Merci beaucoup, mon amour." Shanny leaned in and kissed his cheek. Maybe her French was better than her English tonight. That came out all right. She tried again. "D'accord. Je vais. Mon histoire ici." Speaking French—even broken high school French—made her feel sexy. Actually, she'd been horny ever since she'd stomped in the front door. Partly it was the pot, she knew that. She rubbed the inside of her arm across her own breast, enjoying the sensation. But maybe it was death too. She should write that down and see if it seemed as profound once she sobered up—death made people horny. Nothing more life-affirming than sex.

Shanny found herself pressed between F-Bomb on one side and Cosmos on the other. She shifted her weight so her leg pushed against F-Bomb. She pulled her spine straight and began.

"Okay, so my story . . . this one time . . ."

She knew this story so well that she could tell it without paying attention to herself. Instead, her attention fell pretty heavily on F-Bomb's hand, which had slid up under her shirt and sat on her lower back, warm fingers tickling perfect circles on her bare flesh. A nice complement to the body buzz she'd got from round two of the Mary Jane specials. But even while she practically lived in those fingertips, she felt her attention tugged every so gently to the other side, just past Cosmos, where she fantasized about leaning her cheek against Ella's ankles.

Shanny had found herself staring at Ella ever since they arrived back at Camelot after their disaster of an afternoon tour. She felt herself to be awkward, loud, and uncouth by comparison to this quietly detached creature. Shanny'd barged into the hut on Loco's heels, shaking the floor in her bulky snowboarding boots, feeling her legs rub together noisily in her oversized snowpants. She and the guys headed right for the bag of cookies. After their winter fiasco they needed something to hit the dim light on reality.

SOR ripped the bag open and shoved an entire cookie in his mouth. "That fucking harshed my mellow," he'd announced with his cheeks bulging and bits of brown dough coating his tongue. Even Alison scrunched her eyes shut, held out her hand "Give me one of those." *Middle-Aged Gorb Turns Pothead.* As Shanny stood with the guys, her own mouth packed full of cookie, she'd spotted Ella.

Ella sat against the wall, curled compactly into a red cushy sleeping bag, a book perched in her lap, the word "cunt" in block capitals across the cover. She made no effort to hide the book jacket, to cover the word, but she didn't seem to have self-consciously put it on display either.

It was as if she was unaware she had an audience at all. She simply sat and read. Sat and read her book called *Cunt*.

Unless Shanny was between the sheets, she didn't even want to admit she *had* one of those—in fact, she'd gone to great effort and expense to compensate for the backcountry inconvenience of it—and here was a book shouting the word out. She struggled to see the full cover. She felt a slow burn snaking up her neck and finding a home in her cheeks.

"*Cunt.*" She tried the sound under her breath, and wondered if there was a word in the English language likely to be more universally offensive. But on Ella it didn't look obscene. The tiny woman cocked her head to one side, her features scrunched cutely as if she had a little itch in her nose. Every once in awhile she'd pinch her bottom lip, lift her eyes from the book, and then tap her index finger absently on the page.

On Ella, the word "cunt" looked like an intellectual endeavour. She sipped on her tea, pinched her lip between her thumb and index finger, and read. Above all else, Shanny thought, noting the way Ella pushed her hair tidily behind her ears and then lifted her cup to her lips, taking the daintiest and quietest of sips, Ella looked like a lady.

No one had ever called Shanny a lady.

Suddenly being one of the guys didn't seem like such a compliment. She watched Ella lift herself gracefully from the floor and pour herself another cup of tea. She resettled into her sleeping bag, book back on her lap, not once lifting her eyes to check who might be watching her.

Ella, Shanny thought, was the exact opposite of Alison. Ella was contained—holding herself tightly within herself, leaving it to others to seek her out but not caring if they did—whereas Alison sprawled herself everywhere, holding herself up on display—*see me, applaud me, love me.*

What if she, Shanny, was actually like Alison? She didn't want to be anything like Alison. She wanted to be like Ella. Composed. Mysterious. Feminine. Not falling all over herself to impress people.

Shanny knew that Loco and F-Bomb watched Ella too, staring lasciviously at her generous bosom—nobody in Shanny's snowboarding crowd could even be said to have a bosom—but Ella didn't even look toward the guys. Or towards anyone, really. She'd pat a hand on the pregnant woman's belly every now and then, or offer to top up Cosmos' tea, but otherwise, she paid attention to no one.

Ella lost that serene detachment with the arrival of the rednecks. Shanny saw that, saw the way the yelling men made her unsteady on her feet like a sapling pine weighed down by a heavy spring snow. Ella was at the stove pouring tea when the first man came flying through the doors, insisting "Let's drink." She'd frozen, holding the kettle in midair. Eventually, she made her way back to her sleeping bag, and Shanny wondered if she'd pull it right over her head to hide inside. Unexpectedly, Shanny wanted to be at her side, arm around her in protection. There was something about her that deserved to be defended.

And now Shanny sat within reaching distance of Ella. She could've stretched her arm across Cosmos' brightly coloured lap and held Ella's hairless ankle. As Shanny contemplated doing so, she burped up some skunky ginger cookie and swallowed hard.

She'd never barfed on a Camelot trip yet. It was a point of pride. She didn't want this to be a first. She focused on the hole of Ella's ear and then moved gradually down Ella's body, focusing on the ankles, letting their snowiness wash over her.

Whatever the reason, those were the sexiest ankles Shanny had ever seen. Shanny's eyes moved up to Ella's purple Capri pants, imagining the bare calf as a dreamy ski run, perfect fall line. Her outstretched legs seemed to invite Shanny's eyes to climb up them, curling into the lap of her warm wide thighs. A long loose black tank top draped down past Ella's waist, clinging provocatively to her hips. It dipped at the neckline, showing the slightest hint of faded tan line at her breast. And then there was Ella's face—surely everyone noticed Ella's face, with the lips begging to be touched. Now Shanny noticed that these lips were slightly parted, but not in that dumb way. They made Shanny want to lean over and press her own lips hard against those of the other woman, slide her tongue into the small open cave of space. Even while she fantasized about making herself at home in this woman's warm mouth, Shanny continued to talk, though she wasn't sure if she was managing to link the words of her story—*moose, windshield, bones, blood*—together into any sort of coherent narrative.

F-Bomb's fingers had found the waist of Shanny's pants, squeezed past the elastic waist band, and tickled ever so lightly along the top of her buttocks. She let her eyes massage Ella's smooth calf, while F-Bomb's fingers worked intricate patterns along the skin at the base of her spine. She vaguely heard herself carrying on with her story—*ditch, redneck, axe, moose skull, hospital.*

"Maybe someone else should go first," Michael was saying overtop of Shanny's voice. "Claudette. How about you? Would you like to tell a story?"

Claudette humphed as she rose from the table, made her way across the room, stepping right over Shanny's lap, and throwing her dishes in the sink. "I tell no story. You surprised your first choice does not work out? Ahhh, the pothead ski bum is too stoned to talk—*Quelle surprise!*" Claudette dropped her flask into the sink next to her dirty dishes and then pulled a bottle of rye out of a bag by the front door. "Look for someone else to play your silly game." She carried the bottle of rye back to the table and squished in next to Kevin.

Pothead ski bum?

Shanny thought of objecting but couldn't quite come up with the words. Skirts shuffled to her right as Cosmos rose, moving towards the oversized kettle on the woodstove to refill her tea. Shanny quickly closed the space between herself and Ella. She slid over and felt herself bump awkwardly into Ella's outstretched legs. Ella turned and smiled. This close, she smelled of strawberry lip gloss. As Shanny smiled back, she felt F-Bomb scurry to her side. His hand did its best to reclaim its position on her upper ass.

Face, glass, fingers, broken, Shanny's story went on.

Cosmos bent down to the woodstove shovelling wood on top of the glowing embers.

"Hey, dudette! Back off! That's my job." SOR jogged the short distance to Cosmos' side, his steps shaking the plywood floor, and pushed her out of the way.

Shanny could feel Ella breathing on her right as she watched SOR stoke his raging fire, holding a hand up to block the heat rushing his face. The cabin was already so hot that Ella and Shanny had both stripped off their layers to their sleeveless undershirts, a pile of polypro and fleece scattered around them. Every inhale rubbed Ella's soft skin up to Shanny's shoulder and every exhale rubbed it back down to her elbow. Shanny had grown oblivious to F-Bomb's fingers. Up went Ella's soft skin, then down it slid. Up so soft. And down again.

Gawd, she wondered, how'd she get so stoned? She could barely feel her legs. She knocked her knuckles across her own knees, felt a hollow echo.

"SOR," she heard herself say, projecting her voice across the room, "You almost ate it today, bud."

That wasn't what she meant to say. She tried again.

"You scared the shit outta me. I thought you were dead as a fucking doornail, dude."

SOR laughed, closing the heavy door of the woodstove and crossing the room in a few steps. He sat down behind her and F-Bomb, leaning his weight into them so they formed a tight triangle. "Scary shit, hey?" He cracked a beer, took a sip and then handed it to Shanny and cracked another. "Not as fucking scary as I thought, though. It's as if when you're in that in-between space— alive but nearly dead . . ."

Shanny wondered how he managed to put so many words together. He had to be even higher than she was.

She forced her attention to him. Tried to take in his meaning. His edges—the edges of his hair, his face, his arms—were soft and began to wave as she stared at him, his blond dreadlocks turning into a hazy halo. She tried forcing her eyes toward the back of her head to pull him back into focus, harden his edges.

". . . you're in that in-between space . . ." He held his hands parallel, palms facing each other, as if holding a heavy brick, and stared straight into her eyes, like he could bring her to that in-between place in his mind. ". . . and . . . you realize . . . death is right there—scary, sure—but now you suddenly know, you *know*, that death has always been right there, death always *will* be right there."

"Real profound, kid." A heavy voice came from the table. "That whacky tabacky is makin' you smarter by the second. Smoke any more and we's all gonna hafta start takin' notes."

Alison hated Shanny. Still. And more. "Story. Story! You're supposed to be telling a story!" But Shanny just sat there, flopping heavily to one side, leaning into the hippy lesbian as if she might fall over right on top of her. Not that Alison cared about the infantile story contest to start with. She just didn't see what else was going to keep this mammoth group civilly occupied for the space of an evening. She'd been in bigger closets, and now half of Coalton was packed in here. Half of Coalton and its dogs. But there Shanny sat, her mouth slightly ajar and nothing intelligible coming out of it.

Really, Alison just wanted to polish off this bottle of wine and then drag SOR up the ladder to her loft. They'd find a way to pass the evening up there. But now he was leaned into Shanny, whispering philosophical musings on the nature of life, and she, Alison, was sitting here on the floor. By herself.

Their circle was disintegrating. She looked meaningfully at Cosmos, then at Michael. The story thing was their stupid idea. Why didn't they do something?

Alison crossed her legs and did a couple involuntary Kegels. She'd had to pee since they got back to the hut late this afternoon, but still couldn't bring herself to brave the outhouse. She looked at the big redneck splayed out on the floor next to her. He'd made a pillow of his golden retriever and stared at the ceiling, twirling his stump finger at his nostril. It looked like he was digging the finger all the way up his nose to the back of his throat.

"What happened to the other dogs?" she asked him. "I thought this place would be overrun with stinking animals."

He pointed his head toward one of the bedrooms. "The skinny one's in there, shedding all over my bed." He pointed his elbow in the other direction to the woodstove. The two huskies had slid into the corner behind it and slept sprawled against the wall. "Saving up energy for their next assault on poor Sitka." He took his stumpy finger from his nostril and put it in his ear.

Alison imagined the fingernail digging into his very brain, and took a big gulp of wine, wondering if her teeth were stained purple. "Fuck, I've gotta piss."

The man looked at her, but didn't move his finger from his ear.

She'd never used the word *piss* before. Pissing was something horses did. To piss: it made her think of drunk, old, vulgar men. But what was she supposed to say? *Excuse me, good sir, I'm off to the Ladies.'* Nobody would be waiting inside the door to hand her a fresh towel and a breath mint here. The thought of what she would face out there—piles of other people's excrement, a garbage bin of shit-stained toilet paper, a smell so foul it would make her lose her dinner—had kept her crossing her legs all evening. But if she didn't go soon, she'd be sitting in a puddle. She emptied her glass and forced herself to her feet.

"Real profound, kid."

Alison had a hand on the door when she heard these three words. She turned back to the room and saw they came from the corner table. The snowmobilers.

The shorter of the two men, Kevin, spoke loudly, but he looked at his tall Scandy friend rather than at SOR. The three snowmobilers faced each other in a tight group, laughing as if nobody else was there.

"Will there be an exam, do you think?" Claudette swung an arm around Kevin and leaned her head into his shoulder. "Death is: a) frightening; b)—"

"Was I talking to you?" SOR pushed himself up to standing, pressed his hands into his hips, looking surprisingly fierce in his Capri pants. Suddenly, F-Bomb and Loco were behind him, copying his hands-on-the-hips pose, chests puffed out.

"Oh for god's sakes," Alison sighed the words as she turned to look at the person closest to her. Cosmos stood at the sink in her flowing robes, quietly cleaning up the dishes from the snowmobilers' chili dinner. She hadn't even turned to look at the loud voices. She continued her rhythmic work, plunging her hand into the sink full of water, pulling out a dish, circling a sponge over it three times before dunking it back into the water and then dropping it with a clank to the pile of clean dishes accumulating on the countertop at her right.

"Nature will find its own level," she said as she passed a wet plate to the pile on the counter and reached under water for the next. "It's their energies. Once they recognize the other's true essence, feel it in their—"

"—Excuse me. I gotta piss." Alison stepped out into the snow and heard another plate rattle onto the pile as the door clicked closed behind her.

▓ It sounded like there might be a fight, but Shanny couldn't summon the energy to care. She felt like she'd been wrapped in piles of steaming hot towels. Pleasantly close to unconsciousness. She pulled the sole of her foot into her inner thigh, bending her knee and jutting it out to the left so it was just touching Ella's. She wanted to lay herself down in the woman's lap, roll her head to the side to bring her ear to rest on the fleshy thighs, let her fingertips trail down the woman's shin and trace circles around the bare of her ankle.

She felt Ella square her back to the loud voices in the corner as if she too had chosen to block out the rest of the world, to exist only in this sensation of skin-on-skin.

Shanny squinted her ears against the harsh words behind her, dulling them, transforming them into melodic white noise, and breathed out, long and even, feeling goose bumps turn her skin taut as her bare arm slid down against Ella's.

▓ "Look, I don't want to fight with you." Kevin addressed the tri-angle of young men approaching him, all three chests inflated with air, all six fists clenched. But his attention wasn't on them at all. His attention rested fully with Ella. He saw the way she turned her back to him, knew what she was thinking.

More proof.

She was collecting more proof that he was a barbaric oaf.

A mean-spirited, violent, dumb-ass barbaric oaf.

And she didn't have to say a word. It was all in the way she held her shoulders, turned her head.

What were the chances? How could he even have imagined that she'd be at a backcountry snowmobiling hut? This was turning into one seriously fucking shitty day. He should've called it quits when he woke up hungover and wrapped in a tablecloth.

"I said I don't *want* to fight with you, but I will if you don't get your paw off my shirt." The native guy had moved in close and grabbed his collar. Kevin swatted his hand away.

Did he really have to deal with this? Now? He reached his hand out and clenched it around the young man's throat, dug a thumb hard into one side of the windpipe. He pulled his other elbow back fast, ready to punch, to flatten the guy's nose, if he had to, splatter it right across his drunk Indian face. He didn't care one way or the other. It was all like a movie he'd watched too many times.

He watched Ella dip her head toward the snowboarder girl. Her hair swung with the movement. She'd cut it short since he last saw her so the ends just tickled the nape of her neck. Her friend Janet caught his eye. She'd been trying to look at him ever since he got here, whether to warn him away or welcome him, he didn't know. He looked away.

"I'll fucking send your nose right through to the back of your skull if I have to. You wanna fight, we can fight." As he spat the final "fight," Kevin dug his thumb deeper into the kid's throat. He heard Fredrik sliding out from behind the table and striding up next to him. Apple Cake would be doing his patented head-butt move in no time, smashing his forehead hard into the Dreadlock-Hippy's nose, spurting blood all over his pretty Capri pants.

Ella let her hand drop to the floor at her side, and Kevin swore it brushed the snowboard chick's knee. He tightened his grip on the Indian's throat.

But now Claudette was forcing herself between him and the ski bums, throwing her arms wide, making herself big. She faced him and he could smell the rye on her breath.

"Grow up! All of you. It is enough!" She put her hands into Kevin's chest, pushed him back into the bench seat. He happily let himself fall. "One weekend," she said turning towards the ski bums. "Just one weekend we have to be here together. Ignore him if you have to." She swung her fingers at them, scooting them away as if they were a cloud of mosquitoes. She pushed Fredrik's shoulder hard, turning him back to the table. "And if we have to, we will ignore you."

Kevin looked at no one, focused his attention instead on pouring some Coke into a red plastic cup. As Claudette sat down next to him, he pulled the rye bottle over to his cup. Then he thought better of it.

He pushed the small cup of Coke towards Claudette, and lifted the bottle of rye to his lips.

The whippet mutt had woken up. It had made itself comfortable on Lanny's bed, shed all over his mattress, and then slunk out here looking for something else to ruin. Lanny watched the disgusting slime of a dog. Knew it'd shit again. He was tempted to let it. Someone else could clean it up this time. Let Janet clean it up. She wanted to come, just had to be a part of their trip, leave her to it.

The dog sat in front of the fire, scratching so hard Lanny was sure it had fleas. He lifted his head off Sitka and pulled her closer into his side away from the disease-ridden mutt. *That's all we need to bring home. Fucking fleas.*

He shook his flask and heard the last remnants of his Nusty Rails slosh about the bottom. He sipped slowly, savouring the final bit, tried to ignore the broad with purple teeth who kept staring at him. First, she felt the need to inform him of her bodily functions, then she came back waving her hands around babbling about disinfectant.

"It's not a five-star resort, for sure." She'd held her hands up to her nose, sniffing loudly. "But at least they have *something* to clean your hands. Smell, though—" She pushed her palms in his face, squishing her own top lip up toward her nostrils. "Smells like rubbing alcohol." She breathed in the scent of her own hands again.

He'd ignored her, slapped her hand away from his face when she tried that again, and she stumbled back to the ski-bum kids, dropped her hand right into the crotch of one of them. But still, she trained her eyes on him like he was a T-bone steak and she a reformed vegetarian.

"Your dog got fleas or something?" He spoke in the direction of the punk kids, but nobody even looked at him.

He rubbed Sitka's sore hip, digging his fingers deep into the bone, and then scratched her ass, trying to ignore the hollow scream coming from his own knee. "Nobody listens to me, Sitka, old girl. Just you." He grabbed a dog treat from one pocket and a bottle of ibuprofen from the other; he pushed a little pill deep into the treat, then held it out to Sitka.

Fredrik had pulled out his pocket knife and sat carving deep, thick lines into the kitchen table. "I WAS HERE." He had started the "A" before the "W" leaving just a single space after his "I," but Kevin elbowed Claudette, yelling his words at her even though there wasn't room to fit a hair between them. She had her face pressed right up against his, looked to be chewing on his ear. "Get a load of Apple Cake," Kevin shouted. "'I are here?' Get something right for once, you Swedish meatball."

Kevin could be a mean drunk. Fredrik had no intention of writing "I are here." He wasn't illiterate. Just Swedish. "I am here" had been his intention.

But Claudette had laughed at that too. She was nasty, period, drunk or sober.

I was here? Why past tense? That made no sense.

You've really shit in the blue cupboard now, his father would say whenever someone in the family did something foolish. But there was no shitty blue cupboard here—this wasn't his fault.

English simply made no sense. *I AM here right now,* he thought. But still Fredrik formed his "W," angry and small, squishing it in front of his "A."

He'd do it their way. He always tried to do it their way.

Michael sat propped up against the wall with his legs splayed open in a V. He'd removed his watch and held it in both hands as he bent over the paper booklet pressed open on the floor between his legs. Janet had never seen the watch before. "New toy?" she asked.

Michael's eyebrows squished into a single line as his eyes hopped from the booklet to the watch and back again. He pushed one button, then another, shaking his head. "Equipment, Janet. Not a toy. Equipment." He reached for the booklet with one hand and flipped rapidly through the pages, as if looking for the English section.

"It looks like a watch. You already have a watch." She felt the muscles in her jaw clench into a hard line.

"Oh, this is no mere watch. This, my dear, is a T-Touch. Every mountaineer should have one—"

"Mountaineer?! You're a real estate agent. You used to be a ski bum and now you're a—"

"Titanium." He smiled the word, dangling the watch from two fingers and swinging it back and forth. "Swiss movement since 1853. Classic, durable, high-tech." He laid it out in his open palm and stroked its leather wristband. "Watch? Ha! It's got an alarm, altimeter, chronograph, compass, barometric pressure gauge, global positioning system, and temperature function."

"And you don't know how to work any of it." Janet pressed her fingers into the muscles just in front of her ears. "You could've spent the money on a new nursery. An education fund, a—"

She turned away from him and his stupid toy. This was the thing with the new Michael. The more money he made, the more he spent. The richer he got, the more things he needed.

Honestly, couldn't he tell whether or not it was cold outside without a Swiss T-Touch Altimeter GPS Watch?

Some mountaineer.

Turned away from Michael, she saw Kevin at the table pulling on Fredrik's knife to get his attention. "Hey, check out the developer dork with his new toy. Bet that set him back an easy grand. Or two."

Loco heard Kevin too. He stared across the room at Michael's new watch. "Is it a GPS?" He raised his voice, "Hey, you need directions? You need help that much, you shouldn't be here. To get home, you head *down*."

Kevin laughed, surprising Janet by turning his attention away from his own group at the table—the first time he'd done so with anything resembling good humour. "Good directions, kid. This tourist needs all the help he can get."

It seemed that disapproving of Michael was the one thing they could all agree on.

"You from around here?" Loco asked Kevin, looking up at him with a suspicious squint. "Local?"

"Coalton. A born-and-raised local." Kevin put his hand to his forehead and saluted.

Loco took in the gesture, then paused, consulting some private register. Finally, he nodded. "Me too. Local." He put his fingertips to his brow, and mirrored Kevin's gesture.

"Oh for . . ." Janet reached for Michael's pamphlet. "Here. I'll help you decode these instructions. Give me that thing." She held the pamphlet with one hand and stroked his knee with the other.

Lanny joined the snowmobilers at the table. They got there last, but were the only ones with chairs, everyone else sprawled on the floor while these three acted like they'd just arrived at the Whistler Fairmont. Well, Lanny was sick of laying his aching body on a hard wood floor. He pushed in next to the guy with the knife. He tipped his flask at Kevin and Claudette. They tipped back. Nobody said anything. Sitka crawled under the table and flopped her body across his feet.

Lanny reached for the guestbook on the nail above his head and flipped through the pages. Mostly drunken scribbles. He looked for some names he recognized. Maybe even his own. But the book only started at the beginning of this season. He hadn't been to Camelot in years. He couldn't even find any friends. He thumbed the pages, the words swerving sloppily across the lined paper. More nicknames than names proper, it looked like. There was a Cowboy, a Nuke, a Hambone. No Michael. No Lanny.

He opened to an empty page and pulled down the pen tied to

the nail just above him. He drew three big lumps, one on top of the other, and then some squiggly lines, steam rising off the top. Underneath he wrote, "SANCHO SHAT HERE" in block capital letters.

The man with a knife looked over his shoulder. "Nice," he said with a faint Scandinavian accent. "Very nice."

▨ Claudette was pleasantly hammered. It didn't even bother her when that high-maintenance Alison broad with her grape-stained teeth asked, "Where you dudes sleeping tonight?" Waving her arms around the hut. "Looks like she's booked full-out for the night."

"*Dudes?*" asked Claudette. "Bit old for that, aren't you? You've been taking speech lessons from snowboard girl there?" *And "she"? Only guys like Kevin and Lanny could get away with calling the hut a she.*

The native guy glommed onto the snowboarder laughed. "You tell 'er, Lady. Alison might talk the lingo but never lays down the lines. You should see her gorb it up on skis."

Alison slumped against the wall next to SOR. She rubbed her glass of wine back and forth between two hands. "I'm not *that* bad," she mumbled. "I just got here. I'm from Toronto, for god's sake, cut me some slack."

"Yeah." Michael had pried off the back of his new watch, and pinched a little battery between his finger and thumb, while Janet read to him from the instruction booklet. "And she has a real job. She doesn't just play all day like you . . . guys."

"If you do it right," Fredrik didn't stop carving as he spoke, just stared at the table, pushing his knife hard into the H, "playing *is* a full-time job." He lifted the knife, examined his vertical line, then turned his attention to the horizontal one. "Isn't that the Canadian ski-town way? That's why I moved here. To dedicate my life to worshiping The Ull."

Claudette felt her whole body clench on the last word. Before anyone moved, she'd already imagined the whole scene. Kevin dove across the table, sending Fredrik sprawling on the bench, his knife clattering to the floor. Kevin fell over the table on top of him, and the two rolled together, arms gripped around each other's torsos, as the ski bums chanted, "Fight! Fight! Fight!"

"I. Told. You." Kevin panted each word out between breaths as he and Fredrik crashed to the floor, Kevin's hands tightened around Fredrik's windpipe. "Never. To. Talk. About."

"Fight! Fight! Fight!"

"Him."

Fredrik managed to push Kevin off and scuttle to his feet. He ran for the door. Where did he think he would go?

Kevin ran after him, pushing his broad head hard into the small of Fredrik's back.

"Fight! Fight! Fight!" Michael and Lanny had joined in, chanting along, whether in seriousness or jest Claudette couldn't tell. Lanny iced his knee with a snowball and a big puddle of water had formed beneath him. He'd been surly all night, but he almost smiled now as he chanted, water dripping off his leg.

So this is what happened late at night, what caused the holes in their drywall. Claudette had pictured the scene many times, but had never seen it.

"Fight! Fight! Fight!"

Kevin charged Fredrik hard into the door, their bodies crashing so loud it silenced the room.

"Are you okay?" Cosmos stepped in Fredrik's direction, but Janet grabbed the bottom of her robe, pulling her back.

"Leave them." Janet clasped her hand around Cosmos' ankle. "Not our problem."

Fredrik sat rubbing his head. "Do I need a hard helmet every time I drink with you?"

"Hard *hat*!" Claudette stood pulling Kevin's elbow, though she couldn't remember having stood or crossed the room. She yanked with all her force, urging Kevin away from Fredrik, but she yelled at the skinny man on the floor, as if the whole thing had been his fault. "A helmet is already hard. You say 'hard hat.' Or you say 'helmet.' You don't say 'hard helmet.' Get it right!"

"Jyes," Alison laughed, pushing herself hard into SOR, breathing the words right into his ear. Nibbling on his lobe with her ugly purple teeth. "Eeets 'elmet not 'ard 'at," she imitated. "Jyou H-imbecile." With the huff of the H, she fell over head first into SOR's lap and breathed the last word right into his crotch.

Janet sighed and pushed herself up onto her knees, leaning into Michael until her big belly rested in his lap. *Nothing good happens after midnight,* she thought, feeling exactly like a mom. "Me and Kodiak are going to bed." She tilted her head upwards, kissing his gel-hardened head. "We're done."

"Fuck. I've drunk myself sober." Loco slumped against SOR. They both held a fan of cards, and another mess of them were strewn face-first on the floor in front of them, but Loco couldn't remember what game they were meant to be playing.

"You sure?" SOR's jaw moved against Loco's shoulder as he enunciated each word.

Loco pointed at Shanny. She lay with her head cradled in F-Bomb's lap and her legs stretched out against Ella. It looked like Ella was reading her a story. The corners of Shanny's lips curved upward, but Loco couldn't tell if she was smiling or trying to hold some barf from spilling out her mouth. "Well, I'm nowhere near as shit-faced as that."

SOR looked at his watch then held his arm in front of Loco's face. "It's not even eleven o'clock. You work at it, you could get drunk again before the night's over."

Loco squinted at SOR's watch, then at Shanny, and nodded. "D'you bring the beer funnel?"

22. Lanny's Tale

STORY

Ingredients: Childlike wonder, the Divine, death, sex.
Instructions: Mix.

"We could try the story circle again." Cosmos turned her head slightly as she spoke, directing her suggestion away from the group at the table. "Everyone doesn't have to join in. Just those who feel compelled."

Loco and SOR sat cross-legged in front of the fire. They'd rigged up some plastic contraption. Loco held one end to his mouth while SOR poured cans of beer down the other end.

She wouldn't even ask them to participate in her circle.

"Would you still be the judge?" Michael asked, pulling in close to Alison, who must've been well into her third bottle of wine. Cosmos swore his smile was almost flirtatious and she thought of jabbing him with a good strong elbow to the ribs, for Janet.

"Yeah, right, I'll be the judge. And you lose, doofus. The woman said *circle* not *contest*." Alison set her wine glass on the floor, and closed her eyes. She held three fingertips over each eye, massaging forcefully. Shanny leaned the bulk of her weight on F-Bomb, as if hoping he'd hold her up, and stretched her foot out so her bare toe rested against the jutting bone at Ella's ankle. Cosmos thought she saw Ella pushing back into her, welcoming the young flesh-on-flesh contact. She tightened her grip on her teacup to keep herself from flinging its contents into the young snowboarder's face.

"Ella," she said, hoping to ease her girlfriend away from the teasing tart. "You could tell the first story."

"I can't fucking believe this." Lanny pushed himself awkwardly to one knee and then up—unsteadily—to his feet. His dog fell lazily from his lap, lifted her head for one look towards her master, and then resumed sleeping on the wooden floor. As Lanny swayed above her, Cosmos realized that he might be the drunkest of all.

"Spirishual fucking troof," he slurred, saying each word more loudly than the last as if to compensate for his lack of clarity with extra volume. "We've heard the start of *one* story. About a fucking moosh. What troof?" He held his flask up to his mouth and shook vigorously, as if hoping to scare up some extra liquids from its hidden depths. The effort sent him toppling, and he grabbed a coat hook on the wall to hold himself up. "Troof my ass," he muttered just before the hook broke loose and he fell face first on the floor, a rusty coat hook in one hand.

"All right, dude! Now we're partying!" SOR raised his hands above his head in a hearty cheer. Alison rolled her eyes at him.

Cosmos felt as if she were floating above the others, just watching. She shook herself alert and scurried to Lannny's side, bent down and patted his head. "There, there," she crooned, and scratched him behind the ears. "Why don't you tell a story, Lanny? Get us started." She pulled him by the elbow in an attempt to right him into a more dignified position.

"I'm not telling no fucking shtory," he slurred into the floor-boards. "Shtories are for pushies." As if for emphasis, he held his absent finger up to his nose and pushed the stump hard into his nostril.

With Michael's help, Cosmos got Lanny sitting back in the semi-circle and sipping a tin cup of steaming black coffee. In the time that process took, the crowd in the hut dwindled. At the first whiff of coffee beans, SOR held a hand over his mouth and dashed for the door, F-Bomb and Loco laughing at his back.

"Chuck-fest!"

"Barf-orama, dude!"

The dogs hurled themselves at the open door. Alison wondered whether they were desperate for fresh air or just hoped to feast on barfed-up brew.

F-Bomb and Loco giggled and leaned over the guestbook, recording the details of the first puke of the trip—time, contents, puker. Information the next group at Camelot would be grateful for, no doubt.

Claudette stomped over to the door. She had changed into sweatpants at some point—sweats with NO FEAR slammed across the rear in block capitals. If there was one thing this chick wanted to advertise about herself, thought Alison, it was that her ass was not afraid of anything.

Alison had given up the pretence of a glass and guzzled her wine straight from the bottle. She'd ended up in a hut full of men and couldn't get laid. She spun an empty wine bottle at her side and waggled her finger at Lanny, who sat propped between Cosmos and Michael, coffee in hand.

"Safety meeting," she tried. "Four-twenty? Mary Jane?" She threw her hands in the air. "Nickel bag? God, I don't know. Someone just give me another fucking cookie!"

Shanny leaned hard into F-Bomb. By now, her leg was stretched out all the way, her heel resting in Ella's lap. Ella hadn't done anything to move it, so Shanny left it there.

"Why don't you tell *your* moose story, Lanny," Michael prodded. "We'll stick to a topic. What's that called?" He glanced deferentially at Alison. "A theme?"

"Yes. A theme," Alison snarled. "Give the guy a Pulitzer for Literary Criticism."

Shanny laid her head back in F-Bomb's lap, watching the ceiling move in waves. It was as if she could see the hot, thick air swirling above her. She watched the soupy air's undulations and felt her head vibrate in response to movement on the floor. Holding her hands to her forehead, she rolled her head heavily in F-Bomb's lap, rubbing her ear across the soft fleece of his pants and looking towards the door. Loco stood there pounding his feet into big rubber snow boots. Without a word to anyone, he pushed the door, stiff and noisy on its rusted hinges, and went out into the night. Shanny looked at F-Bomb, twisted her face into a question. *Should we go after him? Is he so drunk he'll freeze to death in the dark?*

F-Bomb shrugged. "He'll be back. There's nowhere to go." He let his hand, warm and heavy, fall across her left breast in a most reassuring way.

Lanny gulped his coffee, ignoring its burn on the back of his throat, revelling in the bitterness that coated his mouth. So, now he was supposed to be telling a story? He had no idea how he let Michael talk him into this nonsense. Again and again.

"You want another moosh?" he began, testing his liquor sodden vocal chords. He could tell from the sound of his voice, all loose and soggy, that he'd managed to get good and wasted on his little flask of Nusty Rails. He wondered fleetingly how much longer he'd have to put up with this "game" before he could reasonably go to bed. What was it? 8:00 PM? 10:00 PM? Midnight? He held his forearms up into his range of vision, looking in vain for a wristwatch.

"Fine. You want a moosh shtory, you got a moosh shtory. Stick with a "theme" and all of that. So, I was out on the dirt-biking trails behind coal creek—"

"—dirt-biking trails? Nice!" Shanny felt the pressure of F-Bomb's hand against her chest, pulling her back, but she wouldn't be restrained. She might be pinned to F-Bomb's lap, but still her voice rang out. "It's pigs like you who ruin it for everyone else. Ever heard of hiking or biking? I get some moron like you nearly run me over every time I go out there." Her voice rattled her own ears, louder than she'd intended it. She wondered what she'd do to fill the echo that was bound to follow her little outburst. If she were Loco or Kevin, she'd jump over and pound the guy in the head.

Ella saved Shanny the embarrassment of silence, diving in where she'd left off, loud but somehow making loud look dignified, graceful. "Motorized traffic shouldn't even be allowed back there! 'Dirt-biking trails'?! You've got nerve. Egotistical, anthropocentric nerve. Do you have any idea what noise pollution has done to our grizzly bear population? Our elk? And then it's some self-absorbed ass like you who won't hesitate to pull out a rifle and shoot the poor animal that comes limping into your yard, disoriented and scared, pushed out of its own territory by your big loud—"

"Imbecile like me? Rifle? I don't even own a rifle. Couldn't even—"

"And you know what else?" Shanny would've been on her feet by now, if F-Bomb's hand wasn't firmly planted on her knee, rooting her into the Earth. "You're supposed to fucking slow down when you see people on the trail. You can't just expect everyone to jump out of your way. Your stupid machine spewing dirt and dust and rocks and—"

"Oh, for fuck's sakes—" Kevin rose to his feet, jumping in where a stunned Lanny had failed. "What is this? Hippy and Ski-Bum Chick unite? Give the guy a break. The trails are *multi*-use. See the signs?" His hands gestured up towards the ceiling as if the whole group of them stood on the trail, under a sign, right now. "*Multi-use*, they say. Know what that means? It means he has just as much right to them as you . . . you . . . you berry-pickers do." He stared at Ella, the only one not looking at him. "Yes, I mean you."

She picked up her book, put her face down, and read. Just like that. As if it was her room and there was nobody else in the world there.

"What? You're going to hide in a book?" Kevin's voice charged after her—to whatever faraway place she'd gone. "Don't be such a cunt, Ella. Just because you don't look at me, doesn't mean I'm not here."

Her hands gripped the book so hard that her top knuckles blushed at the effort, but she didn't make the slightest motion to indicate she'd heard Kevin. He'd already turned away and stumbled toward the door. "Listening to all your crap makes me gotta take one—" He pushed open the squeaky door. "Let the poor guy tell his stupid story." The door slammed.

Lanny took a deep breath, almost hoping for someone else to start ranting. But, no, it looked like everyone was really going to let him, "the poor guy," tell his "stupid story."

Wonderful.

"So, I was out on the *multi-use* trails behind Coal Creek, riding my—perfectly acceptable—dirt bike. Okay?"

He raised his eyebrows and looked around the circle, accepting all challenges. He didn't want to play this ridiculous game anyway. He could feel the dull post-alcohol ache throbbing in his temples already and licked his parched lips, wishing for a glass of water. Ella glided by him, having filled her cup from the steaming kettle, and lowered herself back into the circle. Lanny repeated his question, aiming it at her.

"Okay?"

Unfortunately, no one said a word. He continued.

"I ran into a little trouble with my chain. It snapped once and I managed to fix it with my chainbreaker and spare master link. I get it fixed and we ride for another fifteen or so and the damn thing breaks again. Buddy says something about my sprockets are probably out of alignment—thanks for that, genius—and gives me a master link to hopefully get me back home. Then he ditches me. To tell you the truth—"

On the word "truth," SOR's body came rolling through the door. After a struggle, he managed to get to his feet. The front of his "It's Not Fun Until Somebody Gets Hurt" shirt was caked in puke, the words "Not Fun" unreadable through the mess. He made a quick swipe of his shirt, then lifted his hand to his face and, as if surprised by what he found there, started to gag again. Wiping the offending hand on his Capri pants, he slurred a goodnight and was gone into the room next to the woodstove. Lanny held a hand to his nose to stop himself from gagging at the smell of puke SOR left behind.

"Now I'm out there by myself, bent over, fiddling with my bike, oil up to my elbows, and I hear this snorting behind me." Lanny wiped the back of his hand across his nose and took a deep swig of coffee. "Scared shitless, I was."

Cosmos was about to interrupt and tell Lanny that he ought not fear Nature, when she was distracted by Shanny rolling out of F-Bomb's lap, holding one hand to her head and another in front of her, trying to regain her balance. "Whoa!" She crossed her legs and put both hands to the floor, steadying herself. "Just whoa there. *I* was supposed to tell a story. I never got to tell *my* moose story." She spoke as if she had a mouth full of molasses. She grabbed F-Bomb's beer and took a long drink before continuing. "You think *your* moose was big. *My* moose, my moose had to be eight hundred pounds of big. Too big to fit through my front windshield. Otherwise, I wouldn't be here. Rolled right across my nose and up onto the hood." She pushed two fingers into her nose, squishing it around her face. She looked ridiculous, but at least she'd finally unplastered herself from Ella.

"Just about crushed my car. Made a dent in my roof the size of a . . . The size of a . . ."

". . . The size of a really big moose," Fredrik finished for her, without looking up. He brushed his hand quickly across the table, dusting away flakes of wood and admiring his carving. "Great story." He looked at Cosmos. "We done yet?"

Claudette laughed as she lifted her red plastic cup of rye and Coke to her mouth.

"Ask Michael. He's the control freak." Cosmos reached for Alison's bottle of wine and took a sip. She was sick of babysitting this pack of ingrates. Let Michael have them.

"Carry on, Lanny," Michael said, ignoring the sulking Cosmos and the sarcastic Fredrik.

"Right," Lanny sighed, but continued. "So, I hear this snorting sound. It's wet. I can feel the saliva spraying me on the back of my neck. What do I do? What can I do? I can't just stay bent over my bike, getting snorted at, stomped to death. I take stock. I don't have a gun. I've never had a gun—not since my dad tried forcing me to hunt when I turned ten. I couldn't shoot an animal if my life depended on it."

He shot a meaningful look at Ella, aimed for menacing.

"So, I do a quick look over my tools: I've got a spark plug wrench, a screwdriver, a chainbreaker, a spare tube, one set of basic metric wrenches, a bag of beef jerky, and a two-hundred-and-forty-pound bike. And by the sounds of the hooves pawing the dirt behind me, I have a six-hundred-pound moose about to stomp me into the dirt."

"I couldn't be more fucked. I raise my head slowly. Careful not to do anything that might startle the gargantuan creature. That's when I see—a calf. The baby moose is on the other side of the trail."

Lanny paused for effect, waiting to see if anyone registered the problem here. Alison stared at him in a way that heated up a space in his lower abdomen, just below his bellybutton. He folded his arms in his lap and continued.

"That's right. The calf's on one side of my trail and—now I know—mama is on the other. So, I was wrong. I am more fucked. I start planning my memorial service, wonder what a pissed off mama moose might do to my femur, my scalp, my pelvic bone, how many pieces she might stomp me into. I say a quick prayer that she goes for my head first."

"Che-che-che-ha-ha-ha," Shanny breathed out the sound effects for *Friday the Thirteenth*, pushing the air through her teeth on each *che* and huffing it out from the very back of her throat with each *ha*. "Che-che-che-ha-ha-ha."

Lanny glared at her.

"What?! Just helping build the suspense, buddy!"

Cosmos waved Shanny down with her hand. "Let's let him

finish." Ella rubbed the arch of Shanny's foot to ease the reproof from Cosmos.

Lanny contorted his mouth in a grimace, shook his empty flask one more time.

"Keeping my shoulders hunched low, my head down, sure not to make any threatening gestures toward either moose, I slink my way along the trail sideways, getting some distance between me and both of them. I somehow pull my bike with me—it's the only thing now that might make me feel big and protected, more than a tiny human about to be stomped to death."

"I swear I don't even take a single breath as I shimmy along that trail. I don't think I took a breath since feeling that first snort on the back of my neck. With my teeny side steps, I manage to create a little distance between me and the animals and, most important, I get out from between them. But I swear I've pissed in my pants by this time."

Lanny felt a shuffle as Alison moved across the circle and pushed in next to him. She smelled like fruity wine and hand disinfectant, and he pulled away, making room for her to sit. She was fast, though, and sidled right up to him again. "Might as well use body heat to stay warm. Otherwise what good's winter?" She gave him a wink. Wine slopped out the top of her bottle and spilled onto his pants. Flustered, he restarted his story.

"I thought if I got away from the calf, she and the mama'd bolt. The weird thing is they didn't go anywhere. The mama just stood there staring straight at me, pawing at the ground, sending up big dust clouds with each stroke."

Claudette let out a big sigh. "This isn't working for me at all. I mean, we *know* you made it out okay. Where's the suspense? That's not a story."

"Well, we can wait and find out *how* he made it out. How about a little patience? A little interest in process?" This was the first assertion Alison had made in her role as judge, her hand crawled up Lanny's leg on the word "process."

"Looks to me like you're more interested in the teller than the tale, Your Judgeship." Claudette waved her red plastic cup around in quick circles, sloshing the liquid side to side, before taking a big swig.

"I'll make it fast then, if that's what you want. The moose started fake charging me. Scared the shit out of me. Somehow I managed to pick the bike up over my head—a two-hundred-and-forty pound bike. Don't ask me how. You hear about people doing weird things when they're face-to-face against death. I held it high over my head and shouted, 'Look at me! I'm fucking huge! Don't mess with me, moose. I'm FUCKING HUGE.' I remember waving that bloody bike over my head, like it was a feather pillow. The moose threw its head back with one last snort and then it and its babe loped up the hill and away from me. And here I am, living happily ever after. The End."

He lifted his empty flask up, tipped it to the group, "Cheers, big ears." He held the silver flask above his mouth and shook, hoping some liquid had mysteriously accumulated in it while he talked.

"Well . . ." Michael held out his hands to the group, inviting responses. "Alison? Our judge . . ."

"I liked it," she purred, snaking one along the inside of Lanny's thigh and gripping fast to her nearly empty wine bottle with the other.

"We see, by where you're aiming that hand, what you like. He's asking what you thought of the story." Claudette—not exactly friendly to start with—had let her mood take a nosedive when Kevin left for his crap. She eyed the door again, obviously wondering what could be keeping him.

"I like that you didn't hurt the moose," Ella said softly, her words smooth with apology.

Shanny leaned over conspiratorially, felt her lips brush against Ella's hair, and whispered, "I think I am a moose." She widened her nostrils and gave a small huff as if in evidence.

"That's it. I'm outta here." Lanny lumbered to the far bedroom, each of his steps shaking the small cabin. He grabbed his sleeping bag off the bed closest to the door. "I've had enough of this party and this party's had enough of me." The words gave him great satisfaction. *There*, he thought, *I've said it.* Tomorrow, over breakfast, he'd recall his phrase and wonder, *whatever did I mean?* "Let's skedaddle, Sitka," he called, his arm already pushing open the heavy door.

"Lanny, where're you going? You can't sleep outside." Michael's words grabbed onto him, pulling him back into the room.

"Someone has to." He let his arm perform a wide sweep of the dismantled circle. "More bodies than beds."

"But you were here first. Etiquette dictates—"

"'Etiquette dictates?' Who are you? You sound like a friggin' pansy." He nodded at F-Bomb, figuring this'd win him some points there. "It's not snowing. I'll be fine. Everyone piss on that side of the cabin." He pointed toward the outhouse. "I'm sleeping on this side. I don't want to wake up surrounded by yellow snow." And he was gone.

23. Back Outdoors

NORTHERN LIGHTS: Aurora borealis, named after the Roman goddess of dawn, Aurora, and the Greek name for north wind, Boreas. This lightshow illuminates the northern horizon as a greenish glow or a faint red. The northern lights have had a number of names throughout history. The Cree call this phenomenon the "Dance of the Spirits," and in the Middle Ages it was believed to be a sign from God.

Ella slipped out just after Lanny, assuring Cosmos that she was only going to visit the outhouse.

She had changed her mind. She would confront Kevin. She would make him see once and for all his failures, his ineptitude as a husband, as a human being. That alone would make her feel better.

"Hello, Ella."

She had barely rounded the corner onto the hard-packed trail to the outhouse when she met him. His voice was loose and sloppy, swimming in rye. He almost smiled. More of a smirk. A challenge, she thought. *What could you possibly do to me?* That's what the smirk said. Nothing was the answer. They both knew that. It'd been proven time and time again. And, out here, under the deep black sky, the towering purple mountains, face-to-face with Kevin—a mountain himself—she wondered what she had hoped to achieve.

"Kevin." She directed her face towards his, willed herself not to turn away, not to blink. "Hello."

"I see you're on a nice, romantic mountain getaway with your girlfriend." He stepped closer. She'd forgotten this aggression. The way her body responded to it. The fear melting something essential but unnamable. But she would not turn away. *He cannot do anything to me*, she reminded herself, *he wouldn't dare. Not here. Not now.*

"Yes," she answered softly. "I suppose I am." She tried to remember what it was she'd wanted to say to him, what she'd hoped to salvage.

He lifted his hand, and she noticed that it was bare, his swollen boxer's fingers exposed to the cool night air. She remembered those fingers on her, on the flat bony part of her chest, pinning her down into the mattress. Now he placed them on her collar bone, holding firmly. "I should've known something was wrong with you," he said.

Here she did step away, stumbling backward in the snow, but his words followed her.

"Muff diving, whore. Crazy cunt."

She saw herself lunge at him. "Do not call me crazy." Her words pierced her own ears. Her hands aimed at his face and her nails dove into the loose flesh of his cheeks. Clawing. Digging. Annihilating.

He pushed her in the chest, forcing her back as he yelped like an injured animal, stepping away from her and holding a hand to his bloody cheek.

"We have nothing left to say to each other. Just stay away from me," she said. Leaving him there to bleed, she turned to walk back towards Camelot, Kevin's skin embedded deep in her fingernails.

She knew it wasn't true, though, what she'd said. Why did people say things like that? She and Kevin would never finish what they had to say to each other. She should've said: you don't *hear* what I have to say to you. That was what she meant. She should've said: every time I speak to you, my words get away from me, they no longer mean what I intended them to mean. But she couldn't explain this to him. Those words too would be rendered meaningless. *Crazy*, he would say, *You're crazy.* His one word undid everything. She tied things together into tidy bundles of language and his lone word— *Crazy!!!*—had the power to loosen them.

The cool air hit Lanny full force in the face on his exit, and his nose and eyes immediately started to water, tears spilling down his cheeks, over his chin. He rubbed his face hard against his wool sleeve. With no town lights to diminish the view, the sky was a stunning thing to behold. Amazing how easily you could forget the sky's power once you were in town, numbed by human artifice. Here, the denseness of it, its unfathomable enormity, sat heavy above him, draping down to brush his shoulders. The stars—twinkling points of sharp light—leapt out of this true black, each one a wonder in itself.

He'd never heard a quiet so loud. The dense sky, the echoing silence, the cold that turned his eyes and nose to liquid—all of it made him feel that the night would swallow him whole. And he welcomed it, craved submersion into a complete, containing darkness. He opened his arms to the sky and prayed for it.

Happily, his exit to the ground above the cabin proved easy. Maybe Michael had dug the steps once he'd barfed up the last remnants of Cosmos' mushroom tea. "Nothing like a bit of exercise to freshen you up," Lanny imagined him saying. "Work does the body good." An absolute cheese factory, that guy.

Lanny headed away from the outhouse. This was a good idea. He felt better already. This is what he'd climbed a mountain for. He breathed deeply, the fresh, wet smell of alpine snow clearing his lungs and his mind.

He huddled up to the hut's outside wall and laid out his waterproof Therm-a-Rest and his down sleeping bag on the untouched snow. If he slept right up against the hut, his shoulder pushing hard into its rough wood, he'd fit under the roof's overhang. Then he'd stay dry even if it snowed a bit. Screw Michael—this was exactly where Lanny should be.

He laid back on his pillowy soft bed, a down sleeping bag atop six feet of snow, and pulled Sitka tight into his side. She'd generate the extra heat he needed. Sleeping outside was the perfect idea. His tension and anger evaporated.

Not quite ready to sleep, Lanny let his eyes play along the fluffy white landscape. He could hardly make out the mountains in the deep night, a vague purple shadow against the black sky.

Suddenly, movement caught his attention underneath the shadow of the mountains. In a clump of trees just twenty-five yards beyond him, Lanny noticed two figures. He squinted. Two people hunched and . . . he squinted harder . . . digging.

The closer figure looked like Kevin, and the other . . . well, it must be Tony Ragusa, the mining foreman's son. They were the only two unaccounted for.

He thought of yelling out *Digging for gold, you two?!* But he was finally enjoying some solitude and peace. He let it be. He pretended he'd never even noticed them, and he turned his attention back to the purple silhouettes of The Sleeping Giant, admiring the way the sky above it glowed an eerie green.

"This." He scanned his eyes across the rocky peaks, the star-filled sky, the cedars heavy with snow. "This is what I miss, Sitka. This is what I came here for. We should've left that train-wreck inside hours ago."

He thought he heard Sitka let out a deep and tormented growl in protest, and was about to question the dog's judgment, when he realized the inhuman noise had emanated from his own intestines. He held his hand to his lower abdomen, felt a raging gurgle, a boiling waterfall of intestinal juices.

"Hoo boy."

Another loud rumble rang out in response.

"Noodles and Rusty Nails not to your liking, old body? Not your idea of supper?"

His stomach kicked and lurched.

"Uh-oh. Outhouse pronto. You keep the bed warm, Sitka."

Alison had been stumbling around in the deep snow for nearly ten minutes, unable to find what way Lanny had headed, when she saw him come striding back from the outhouse.

As she got closer, Lanny stepped off the hard packed snow to let Alison pass, performing a sweeping gesture with his hand to indicate the vacated walking path to the outhouse. Off the path, he lost his confident stride. He stumbled as his feet sank into the deep snow, and seemed surprised to find himself sunk up to his knees.

Alison stopped on the path, parallel to the spot where Lanny stood rooted—trapped—up to his knees in dense, heavy snow. She placed a hand on each of his shoulders. "What a gentleman you are," she said, squeezing his shoulders hard, "emphasis on the *man*."

She bet he hadn't had sex in months, even years. First clue: no woman here with him. Second clue: no ring. Third clue: not a single mention of a woman.

Plus, he had that pent-up quality about him.

And Alison knew she was just the woman to unpent him. In fact, Alison thought, there's nothing she liked better than a good unpenting.

"You work at the mill," she said, moving her hands from his shoulders slowly, caressingly, down his arms. She trailed her fingers along his hands, moving to latch onto his fingers and hold tight, lead him somewhere more appropriate, more private, away from the path of the out-house goers. She sniffed. "The hand-cleaner!" She held his hand up to her nose. "Rubbing alcohol scented with vanilla. Vanilla's an aphrodisiac, you know." She felt the decapitated stumps on the right hand, and lifted the middle one to her lips, popped it into her mouth and began to suck.

"I do work at the mill. Yes." He tried to pull his hand away from her but she held it tight, brushing her teeth against the mottled skin of his amputation, like she might do damage if he forced the issue. "Always have worked there," he continued. "Fifteen years." That's right, talk about work—he struggled to orient himself on some kind of familiar territory. "That job can come with a heavy price, though." He nodded his chin toward his amputated fingers, two of which were now below her tongue.

She smiled, resting her teeth on the stumps of fingers. The rising moon gave off enough light for him to see the purple tint of her teeth. He watched her pull the fingers from her mouth and run her tongue across her teeth and noticed the way, for just a moment, it stuck between the gap in her two front teeth.

She held his hand up to her face, rubbing the smooth stumps across her cool cheek. "I've always wanted a miller."

Maybe always was an exaggeration, but now the imagined smell of sawdust excited her. Nothing said "man" like sawdust. She pictured herself rolling naked with him in the mounds of wood chips that must cover the ground at the mill. She bet he had it everywhere, particles of tree in his hair, coating his skin, filling his ears. She leaned in to smell him, expecting the scent of falling timber, and wrapped her arms around his tree trunk of a body.

"God, I just want to climb you!"

She pushed her hands into his chest, but felt no warmth of flesh, held at bay by layers and layers of down, fleece, wool. She fumbled at the zipper of his down jacket, as he tried to shake her off. "No one will even know we're gone." She pulled on his arm, nodding her head toward Camelot. "You can fuck me up against that shed." She grabbed his full-fingered hand, put it between her legs. "You can have me however you want me."

He grabbed his hand back and struggled to get a foot loose from its holding of snow. He did briefly manage to step up and out but sank just as deeply in a new spot. He looked to be rooted into the ground. Right, she could play this game—a man at her mercy. The Coalton version of handcuffs. She ran her hands down the full length of his torso, sunk her teeth into the flesh between his neck and shoulder.

"Around that corner. No one will see us." She leaned back, grabbing his hands and pulling with all her force. He pulled away from her, but she knew his gestures towards escape must be a game. Surely, every man wanted sex. The timid man clearly needed some encouragement. But his body was a cement pillar, refusing to budge from the steep holes that his feet had pressed into the snow.

"Don't worry. We'll get you out of here in a jiffy."

He opened his mouth like he might call for help, but no sound came out. He stiffened his legs, locking his knees and rooting himself to the spot. Never mind. She had enough strength for both of them. Hadn't he just said that a human could lift a three-hundred-pound motor bike over his head when a crisis called for it? This was a crisis if she'd ever been in one. She *would* free this man. And then he'd owe her. With a mighty heave-ho, she pulled, yanking like she'd pull his forearms right out of his elbows if he didn't follow.

Gravity was on her side. His heavy body began to sway forward as sure as falling timber. "That's it big boy, here we go," she encouraged him, pulling with greater force yet. She planted her hands on his hips and swung her body round behind him, pushing forward full force with both hands.

He landed in the downward dog position, his hands rooted just as deeply in the snow as his legs. She couldn't resist clasping a hand to each of his butt cheeks sticking high in the air. "Don't be scared," she said, "It'll feel nice." She maneuvered in close to him, wrapping her arms around his waist like a Greco Roman wrestler.

And he responded, suddenly every bit as agile as a wrestler, diving his torso forward and out of her grasp, landing face first in the snow across the hard-packed path. That was all the leverage he needed. He braced himself on the firm snow and wiggled his legs free of the deep holes. Shaking Alison off his back, he forced a knee forward onto the path and scrambled onto all fours. She grabbed his foot, but he had his strength back now. He gave one firm kick and, not looking back, he ran into the woods as fast as a deer startled by the oncoming headlights of a semi-truck.

Alison let herself fall to the ground, the snow cold against her ass. She sighed and glanced up at the cabin, light flickering out of the front windows.

It really did look like she'd be sleeping alone tonight.

"I remember when the river ran black. Black. You could swim in it." Loco had returned to the hut and was doing that thing where he talked like he was seventy-five instead of twenty-five. Alison tried to ease the door shut. If she could get in without anyone noticing, maybe she could zip past everyone and up the ladder. She'd given up on this group and was ready for bed. She was actually glad that puke-covered SOR had headed to the bedroom instead of her loft. She wasn't desperate enough to put up with barf-breath. Having given up on sex, she found that the alcohol had turned her angry and mean. She hated SOR, hated his friends, hated all these stinking animals, and hated this piece of shit of a place.

"We're pulling two million tons a day of rock out over there," Loco continued, gesturing towards the range where the valley's biggest mines were located, the ones where he'd find himself working soon enough. "We're tearing down the whole fucking mountain. And people are going to have a cow about this new thing down there," he gestured toward the bottom of the valley, and Alison pictured the river, running cold and pure on a scorching summer day. She could go for a drink of that right now, would like to stick her head right in it, feel the water bend her ears as it raced by. "Only because it's new. People can't handle new."

They were talking about coal bed methane, of course. She was surprised it'd taken this long to come up. Coalton's go-to news story, Coalton's go-to coffee shop debate, Coalton's go-to barroom brawl. "What?!" she always felt like saying, "Coalton's thinking of drilling for coal bed methane? I didn't know that." You'd have to be deaf, dumb, and blind not to know that.

"Tourism," Michael responded calmly, catching Alison's eye and waving her over to the corner table around which the late-nighters had gathered. "Tourism is Coalton's future. You're not going to have tourism when mining has turned the landscape into a moonscape, when all the fish in the river have died. We put up with traditional mining because it's already here. We can't do anything about that."

"Can't do anything about that? Fuck, it makes me insane." Loco turned his crazed gaze at Alison, as if in hopes someone with a single ounce of sanity might have joined the conversation. "People have no idea how much this town depends on coal. *Depends* on it." He banged his fist on the table, rattling it so hard a half a dozen empty beer cans tumbled to the floor. He left the cans, spoke as if only Alison were hearing him, as if she were on his side. "They don't remember. They don't remember when the mine closed and women were selling their wedding rings to buy clothes for the kids. Or when we kids were fishing in the river to get food for dinner. Because there was no money. That's what happened when the mines closed. Without mining, we have nothing." Alison saw the beginning gleam of tears coating Loco's eyes.

"People come to the mountains for serenity. They don't want trains rattling by every hour, blasting their horns, rattling nearby houses right off their foundations. Ever since mining hit a boom, the coal trains run nonstop. Hollering all day and all night. How's that serene?" Michael tapped his finger rhythmically on the table top as he spoke.

"Are you fucking retarded? You have any idea how much one of them trains is worth? *Five million dollars.* Five million dollars of coal in each train. That's what you should hear—not *chugga, chugga, chugga* but *CHA-CHING, CHA-CHING, CHA-CHING.* That's the sound of money, dude. Nobody in Coalton—nobody with half a brain—would complain about the trains. Filled with *pay dirt.*"

"Coal didn't put this place on the map," Michael used the same soothing voice, but addressed his comments to the rough-hewn table top. "Skiing put this place on the map. Tourism."

"What language do you fucking speak? You know, just 'cause you open your mouth and noise comes out doesn't mean you're having a conversation. Are you listening to anything I'm saying? The place is called *Coal*ton, you moron. Of course coal put it on the map."

Alison felt Michael's body grow rigid. He turned to her, as if she must be on his side. "Why am I arguing with this punk?"

"Dude, little tip—if you don't know who the Trip Asshole is, it's probably you." F-Bomb stared at Michael and popped open another can of beer, the sharp exhale of the lid punctuating his sentence. "There's always one."

"Punk? I'm the punk?" Globs of spit pooled in the corner of Loco's mouth. "You're the one forcing development down everyone's throats like it's some kind of solution instead of the problem. Tourism doesn't keep a community alive. Those jobs—$8.50 an hour. That's what they pay. You tell me how you're gonna support a family on that? Not when the houses cost a million dollars. The only ones making any money on your scheme—the only ones *living*—are the punks selling those million-dollar houses, the *punks* like you."

Cosmos came swooping across the floor as if from nowhere. She'd changed into plaid pajama pants with a matching long-sleeved shirt and no longer had her long flowing skirts swishing around her ankles, though her languid way of walking, her habit of brushing her hands in the folds of the material as they swung this way and that, suggested that she still did, that she always did.

"Look," she said. "Ella and I will have to sleep out in the common room." She waved her hand behind her, gesturing to the floor in front of the fire.

"You can sleep with me," Shanny blurted out, the pitch slightly hysterical.

"*Tokahontas Leaves Indian Prince for Gay Lover,*" Alison snorted into Michael's ear.

"We've laid out our sleeping mats." Cosmos ignored Shanny and Alison, but stumbled a bit here, as if unsure what to say next, as if someone else might, by now, have deduced her request. "I would . . ." She dug her fingers into her lower abdomen, pushing so hard it looked like she'd force her way in and rip out her own intestines. Finally, she found her words and delivered them evenly, with authority. "I would suggest that you respect our needs."

F-Bomb leaned into Loco, "Translation: Shut the fuck up, we need to get some fucking sleep."

"Ya fucking yah-hoos," Loco added, cracking a toothless grin.

"Language! Does *everything* have to be fuck, fuck, fucking?" Cosmos held a hand to her brow, squinting as if they'd thrown the words at her. "The hostility . . . Michael . . ." She turned to him then, and Alison could see that she was so tired and desperate that she was willing to bow to Michael's self-proclaimed authority. That was bad. "Please," Cosmos concluded, breathing the word in a single worn out sigh.

"Language? Give me a fucking break. This from the lady whose girlfriend's reading a fucking book called fucking *Cunt*." F-Bomb spat the word, collecting saliva from the back of his throat on the hard "c" and projecting it into the air on the final "t."

"Cunt," Cosmos sang the word, drawing out the *unnnnn*, "is not a curse. It's a word of reverence and respect, a word denoting the place of female power, the place from which all life comes." She rubbed her chin as if in deep thought. "Only the Western Patriarchy has turned it dirty."

F-Bomb elbowed Loco in the ribs then held a hand up to his face to cover his own smirk. "All right. How about this? *Shut the cunt up. We need to get some cunting sleep. Ya cunting ya-hoos!*"

Michael to the rescue, thought Alison, watching him clasp his hands together at his new challenge. "Cosmos is right," he nodded. "It's time we all headed to bed. But," he looked back up at Cosmos, "let's not end the day like this. Let's end on a good note. We never finished our story contest. And you never got a chance to tell a tale." He held his hands out to her, welcoming her into the group. *He's selling her a community, a sense of belonging*, thought Alison. *He looks just like a real-estate agent.*

"Why don't you finish us off with a winner?" Michael pushed over next to Loco, patting the now empty plywood seat on the end of the bench, encouraging Cosmos to sit. She pulled her hands into her sides, as if gathering her skirts about her, and perched on the bare spot next to him.

"A fucking, cunting bedtime story?" F-Bomb directed his comment to Loco as if they weren't all packed into a six-foot square space, as if everyone couldn't hear him.

Cosmos shot him a quick glance, and Alison prepared herself for another piercing, *Language! Please.* But Cosmos said nothing, just tilted her head back in Michael's direction. "I could tell a little one." A train whistle rose from the valley's bottom, a hollow echo from this distance, to mark the beginning of Cosmos' tale.

24. And They Sleep

 **As soon as** Cosmos started her tale, Alison climbed out of the bench seat and ascended the ladder, no longer concerned whether the others saw her go or wanted her to stay. Michael and Cosmos could judge their own stupid contest. Alison Batz was a *Globe and Mail* reporter, not a day-camp co-ordinator.

She squinted into the front pocket of her backpack, straining in the dim light radiating from the fire and candles flickering in the room below, and pulled out a pen and notepad. There was so much she wanted to capture. She hadn't yet written a word about the avalanche or the rescue involving the mysterious man of the woods, nothing about SOR sobbing his prayer of gratitude and humility into a camera with dead batteries.

Settling into the loft, she squished into the corner farthest from the noise, stretched out her legs, and set her notebook across her lap.

She pointed her pen to the page, but her thoughts kept drifting. Red wine and pot had made her so desperate for sex, she'd nearly raped a deformed, drunken, small-town hick on his way back from the outhouse.

Some people claimed that your true self was what came out when you drank. *In vino veritas*. If that were true, the real Alison was a horny Alison. For her, the only point of getting drunk was to have sex. Wild, uninhibited, athletic, noisy sex. She'd got rather pragmatic about it in her single Toronto days. When she started feeling the buzz of booze, she'd look around and see if there was anyone worth fucking—let's call it what it was—and if not, she'd quit drinking and switch to coffee, so she could at least get some work done when she got home.

She pulled a flashlight from the floor. It must've been SOR's. It was attached to an elastic headband, so she strapped it around her forehead, suddenly feeling very industrious. The headlamp splashed light onto the page, adding a luminescent quality to the blank white before her. She found that this spotlight brought to the writing process an even greater than usual performance anxiety. Her pen hovered uncertainly above the glowing white page.

She reminded herself that she was only experimenting. It wasn't as if her words would go to press tomorrow or anything. She wrote for herself.

"I write for myself," she said, willing her pen to spill its ink.

Still nothing.

She was so high that her teeth buzzed. She ran her tongue over them, enjoying the sensation, as if the tongue belonged to someone else. She slowly touched each of her teeth with the very tip of her wet tongue—the most intimate of kisses.

Interesting. Maybe when high, one could actually make love to oneself. She twirled the pen in her left hand—she should really write about this—but her hand too seemed like it belonged to someone else. She couldn't resist lifting it to her mouth, tracing her lips with her index finger, gently sliding the finger into her mouth, and sucking. The harder she sucked, the more the rest of her body buzzed, heat spreading down her to her groin, a deep throbbing as if all her energy had been drawn to that one spot. With one last hard suck, she pulled the finger out of her mouth, sliding it over her chin, down her chest, lingering at a nipple and flicking it through her sweaty cotton turtleneck. Arching her back, she slid her hand down her torso and tucked it into her pants, inching the still-wet finger toward the insistent throbbing.

But no.

She was here to write.

She let her body relax, her right hand pushing her left out of her pants.

She dug her hands under her legs, searching for the pen. It had slid between the sleeping bag and the floor. She wrote "Camelot" across the top of the page. She'd never before noticed the sound of her pen as it moved across her paper—a pleasant scratching like a man's fingernails tracing circles against the skin of her lower back. Just as when a man scratched her back, she could now hear the scratching of the pen from the inside out.

She traced ink across the page in incoherent squiggles, feeling its sound. Writing had never been so sensual. She lifted her pen to her lips, resting its end on her bottom lip.

So hard and so close . . . she couldn't resist, she plunged the hard pen deep into her mouth, sucking until all but the very tip was curled in her wet tongue, she twirled the pen, aroused by its cool plastic.

She pulled the pen from her mouth and quickly guided it into her pants where it found the small wet opening that was, at the moment, the very essence of herself. She plunged the pen inside of her, again and again, until her body convulsed in pleasure. "Stop," she whispered, "enough, stop."

Eventually, she fell asleep in the fetal position, her left hand down her pants, cupping the assaulted pen against her warm cunt.

Shanny couldn't follow Cosmos' story. She couldn't hold onto words at all, even though she willed her ears to take in Cosmos' words one by one, then link them until they added up to some sort of sense. But it was as if she saw Cosmos through a room filled with water, her face wavy and opaque, the sound gurgling slowly in incomprehensible bubbles.

Shanny turned toward Michael, looking for something to help focus her vision, to ward off the nauseous panic panting in her ear. But his face looked the same, all wavy and distorted, like the water had entered him and his skin rolled with it. She felt her head wave and bob loosely on her shoulders in response.

Shanny pushed out of the bench, scraping her hot, sweaty body over Loco's lap and falling to the floor, where there was more air. Cool air.

Cosmos' voice bubbled on above her.

She smelled strawberry lip gloss and let her ear fall to her shoulder so she could look in the direction of the sweet smell. Ella had knelt beside her and held a cool hand to her cheek.

"You don't hafta to sleep on the floor," Shanny tried to say, "You can sleep with me." But her words sounded just as disjointed, just as bubbly, as those of Cosmos.

"C'mon, sweetheart. To bed with you." Shanny felt a hand tighten under each of her armpits. The ceiling moved in gentle waves as her feet dragged heavily across the floor.

Janet was still awake when Michael crawled onto the double sleeping bag and snuggled up to her, placing a cool hand across the wide girth of her belly. She'd unzipped the bag and thrown the top cover wide open. With the fire stoked to maximum capacity in the next room, she might as well try to sleep in the belly of a stove. She was way too pregnant for this shit.

"Awake?" he whispered, his breath wet against her ear.

"How could I be anything else?" She knew her words were soft with good humour. She liked to have Michael with his cool hands here next to her, after lying an hour by herself, sweating while she listened to him manage the all-too-rowdy affairs in the next room. He'd been kind to Cosmos. She loved him for that.

She patted his hand splayed open over her protruding belly button, stroked it like she'd stroke a cat.

He flipped on his flashlight, holding it under the top cover of their sleeping bag, dimming it so it wouldn't hurt her eyes. "Sorry," he said, as she blinked uncomfortably, "but I want to see you." Dropping the flashlight on the mattress, partially covered by the sleeping bag so that it glowed red and turned their faces a subtle pink, he placed a fingertip above each of his wife's eyelids.

"Sorry," he said. "I went backwards today."

She was quiet for a moment, his fingertips resting on her eyelids. "Not everything has to be measured in lines, Michael. Not always."

He gently dragged his fingers across her face, closing both her eyes, and then traced two lines down her cheeks, down her neck, all the way to her belly, cupping a hand to each side of the giant mound where she held their future child. He lowered his face until his forehead rested just above her belly button, bowed as if he were praying.

She said nothing. Michael had barely touched her belly during her whole pregnancy, and she felt like he was now executing something that absolutely needed doing, something of ceremonial import. She petted the hard bristle of his hair, let her fingers toy with the tops of his ears.

After fifteen or twenty breaths, he rolled his head to the side, pressing his ear into her tummy, listening for Kodiak.

"Hear anything?" She'd lowered her voice to a whisper, not wanting to interrupt whatever ritual he'd begun.

"Yeah, the pounding of my own heart." He lifted his eyes to meet hers. "I'm terrified."

She sat up, surprised, cupped his face in her hands, pulling it closer to her own. "Terrified? Of what?"

"Of being a dad. If I can do it. If I'll be any good."

"Michael. What're you talking about? Look how far you've come. Look what you've made for us—our house, our security. You'll be a wonderful provider."

"There are many things a dad can provide. Many *ways* a dad can provide."

She waited, knowing he'd explain what he meant when he was ready. She just kept holding his face, not letting him turn away.

"There's all this." He pointed out the dark window, to nothing but blackness. "I just . . ." He pulled her hands from his face, held them between both of his. "I just wonder if I've left too much behind."

That was not a question that could be answered tonight. Janet had learned there were times that marriage called for silence. She pulled him over next to her, so they were both sitting against the headboard, with their legs stretched out before them, entwined.

She put his hand back on her belly. He tugged up her shirt, tracing his finger along the line that had appeared from her belly button to her vagina, cutting her torso exactly in half.

"What's this called again?"

"Linea nigra." She pictured the phrase written in her pregnancy manuals, but didn't know if she'd pronounced it right at all.

"What does it feel like? Does it hurt?"

"No."

"Does it hurt when Kodiak kicks?" He ran his finger up and down the line.

"No. Well, a little. Enough to make me jump, not enough to make me scream."

"Are you scared?"

"No." She shook her head so hard that her hair swung out to the sides, brushing him across the face.

He looked at her. Waited.

"Of course, I'm scared." She smiled. "But it's something that needs to be done. Something that will *get* done." She could see her words had no reassuring effect. "Many women have done it and lived to tell. It'll hurt, it'll be hell, and then it'll be done and we'll forget about it. Human memory never does justice to pain." She smiled at him again, concerned by the rapid way he ran his finger up down the line on her lower abdomen. He brushed the other hand over his eyes, and Janet wondered if they were wet. Could this be the same Michael who had spoken with such authority all night?

"You're just feeling the after effects of the tea—depleted serotonin. A little sad, that's all." She ran her thumbs along his bottom eyelids, drying them as if he were her child. "I'll tell you what," she continued. "I'd rather be in pain than have to helplessly watch you in pain. I have the easy job—I go there to get the baby out, and I grunt until the baby's out. That's easier than watching someone you love suffer. Don't worry about me, worry about you."

"Right. So you're the lucky one." He spread his fingers wide, until he was palming her belly, like he was trying to hold all of her and all of Kodiak in the protective space of a single hand. She thought of the way he'd just pointed at the dark window to everything that he'd imagined to be out there, the way he'd said, "All of this."

This was the Michael who would make a good father. She thought of telling him so, but decided instead to put her hand on his and enjoy the sensation of warmth spreading across her entire body.

When Kevin clomped into the hut, his snowy boots shaking the very walls, the smell of fresh snow filling the room, Claudette and Fredrik were the only ones still up. He warily scanned the small space, expecting to see Ella and her girlfriend curled together asleep in some corner. Nothing. They must've scored a spot in one of the rooms. Or gone to camp outside. Who the fuck knew? Or cared.

Fredrik curled into the corner of the kitchen bench next to his I WAS HERE engraving, a sleeping bag wrapped around him like he might actually spend the night right there. His legs didn't come close to fitting in the tight space, and his knees were pulled up awkwardly, his head tilted at an unnatural angle. His eyes were closed, but he looked far too twisted and uncomfortable to be asleep.

Claudette had spread her fleece blanket before the fire and laid stomach down, propped up on her elbows, playing solitaire. "Look who enters," she snarled without looking up. "Have a nice walk?"

"Little do you know what awaits you," crooned Kevin in the voice he often used as an antidote to her snarl. "Come. I've got us five-star sleeping quarters." He looked at Fredrik stuffed into the corner, hesitated. "You'd better come too. I can't let you sleep like that."

"What? Somebody opened a Chateau Coalton just around the corner?" Fredrik's face showed no sign he'd told a joke. He pulled the sleeping bag tight around his waist, and got unsteadily to his feet, before hopping one foot out, then the other.

Kevin silently led them into the night. A full moon had risen, turning everything blue with its light. He pointed to a bump in the distance. Neither Claudette nor Fredrik said a word, just trudged through the deep snow behind him.

At the edge of the trees, they discovered where Kevin had disappeared to all evening. The bump turned out to be a home of sorts. Kevin pointed to the doorway and all three of them crouched down and crawled in.

Kevin, with Tony Ragusa's help, had dug a room big enough for all three of them to sleep. He had carved two benches into the wall, and even shaped out small lumps for pillows on the hut's floor.

Claudette touched the cold walls, glistening in the light of Kevin's headlamp, "We're sleeping here?" She smiled up at Kevin. She ran her fingers along the snow ceiling, then held her tongue out to taste a cool wall. "I feel like a kid." There was a perfect space for the two of them on the snow floor, and she imagined candles lighted, flickering golden from the carved benches, making shadows of their bodies on the cold, white walls. She exhaled, watching her own breath.

Kevin had already spread out their Therma-a-Rests and sleeping bags on the floor, and now he grabbed the sleeping bag from Fredrik and squished it down next to the others. "Better than sleeping in a stinky kitchen, isn't it?" His smile revealed the pride he felt in his creation, and Claudette held her fingers softly up to his cheek.

He kissed her fingers lightly and then lay down on his back, looking up at the icy roof of the shelter he'd built. Claudette lowered herself to the ground and spread her body out on the sleeping bag next to him, wrapping her arm across the breadth of his strong chest. She felt wild, like an animal curled into its den, ready to hunker in for a long winter. She pulled tighter to Kevin's solid warmth.

And then Fredrik lowered himself to the bed next to her. She sighed—loud enough that everyone would have to notice.

"What's the English saying? Two's company, three's a . . . ?"

"You want that I should leave?"

"No," Kevin answered before Claudette had a chance. "There's room for all of us. Where else are you going to sleep?"

Claudette swallowed her objections. She knew this was supposed to be their trip, Kevin's and Fredrik's. She was the intruder. She tightened her grip around Kevin's chest and tried to focus on his shadowed face. She thought she saw two deep wounds running parallel down his cheek like claw marks from a wild cat. A trick of the light perhaps? She held her fingers to his cheek and the lines felt rough to the touch. She expected him to flinch, but he was already asleep.

Claudette rolled onto her back, let her lids fall closed, and tried her best to fall into unconsciousness, sandwiched tightly between the snores of two drunken men.

Shanny slept hard, squished between Cosmos and Ella, her nose nestled into the soft flesh at Cosmos' shoulder and Ella wrapped around her back, a hand tucked into her T-shirt and resting on her hard abdominals. If she were more conscious, she would've tried to keep from kicking F-Bomb who slept curled into the fetal position at the foot of the bed, whistling loud bursts of sound with each of his exhalations.

PART III

It took the sea a thousand years
a thousand years to trace
the features of this granite
cliff in scrag and scarp and base

It took the sea an hour one night
an hour of storm to place
the features of this granite cliff
upon a woman's face.
—E.J. Pratt, "Erosion"

25. The Morning After

Loco's first thought upon waking was that his tongue had permanently glued itself to the roof of his mouth. His lips, similarly parched, stuck to his teeth. He tried to move the sick and lethargic animal that was his tongue around his mouth to create some kind of moisture. "Water," he croaked, clasping a hand to each of his shrieking temples.

"No hired help around here, buddy."

Loco squinted one crud-caked eye enough to see SOR bent over the packs, digging for Tylenol no doubt. SOR may have been more alert, more upright at least, than Loco, but he definitely wasn't cheery. A canteen of water was strapped to his chest. Loco closed his eye. "Just give me a sip of water." His own voice rattled his brain, intensifying his headache. He felt the canteen hit him across the chest and had to suppress an abrupt gag. His hand flew to his mouth, holding his lips tight over his teeth.

He managed to pour some water over his lips and down his throat. He rolled to his side and eyed the bed next to him. F-Bomb curled there with a sleeping bag pulled over his head and his naked legs uncovered. Loco swore that in the night there'd been at least three people in the bed. A party of sorts.

"Feeling too rough even to swear, F?"

F-Bomb groaned in response and pulled the blanket tighter to his head.

"Eureka!" SOR stood up straight, pill bottle in hand. "Want some?" He shook the little bottle so the hundreds of tiny painkillers rattled against its sides.

Loco and F-Bomb simultaneously held out their hands.

"Oh, look what the dog barfed up," Cosmos beamed as the three young men came out of the bedroom, dressed in their ski pants, toques pulled down to their eyebrows. Loco felt his stomach make contact with his throat as the sour smell of the overcrowded room hit him.

Cosmos, Ella, and Shanny sat squished tightly together in the corner of the kitchen bench. Each had a hot bowl of lumpy oatmeal before her. He forced his tongue hard against the roof of his mouth and concentrated on not gagging.

"Man, you guys look like shit," said Shanny, spraying oatmeal flakes into the air. "You gotta watch out for that cheap canned beer, hey?"

"Not to mention the endless stream of marijuana cigarettes," agreed Cosmos.

"You two," Ella reprimanded softly. "Nice welcoming party." She lifted her arms and dropped a hand on the back of each woman's neck, squeezed gently—part restraint and part affection. "Good morning, boys." She lifted her full lips into a smile. Even Loco had to attempt a smile back, though doing so shot a bolt of pain through his temples. Just then a loud clap rang out from behind him, tightening the corset of torture clasped around his skull. *C'mon, Tylenol,* he silently prayed. He held his hands to his cranium and turned to the noise.

Michael stood hovering over the wood stove, waiting for the kettle to boil. His hands were clasped together. He wore baby blue ski pants and a white, polypro turtleneck. The suspender straps hung down around his hips. "What we need," he said, "is a game plan." The kettle let out a high whistle of steam, and Michael lifted it from the stove top and poured the bubbling fluid into the clear pitcher sitting on the window ledge. The strong smell of coffee instantly filled the hut. "Conditions are bad. Really bad. I think we should all stick together today." Obviously taking in their non-comprehending faces, Michael added, "In a group."

Loco and his toque-clad friends stole glances at each other. *Huh?* Loco willed one of the others to speak. Neither did, so he finally forced his uncooperative tongue into action. "A group? We? That means, like, you *and us*?"

"Yes," Michael said, pouring his steaming coffee into an over-sized mug that read "I love big dumps." "Us and you. Together."

Loco looked at his mute friends and then back to Michael. "Can I have some of that?" he said weakly, lifting his finger towards the muddy-looking liquid, his stomach lurching slightly at the dirty flecks of coffee grounds stuck to the side of the glass. "And can someone throw those dogs outside?" He pointed at Sancho and the two huskies sprawled in front of the fire and taking up most of the room. "They stink like manure."

Alison woke with a start and leapt for the loft's window. She pushed it open with a force she didn't know she had and thrust her body into the cool air just in time. Her guts heaved, and she spilled their contents onto the white snow below. Normally the distance to the ground would be three full body lengths, but because of the tremendous snow fall this year, the snow sat less than five feet below the window's ledge. She could've almost dangled herself to the ground and buried herself in the cold purity of snow to ride out this hangover.

With another subhuman grunt, half-digested wine the colour of blood poured onto the snow, bits of it splattering the window sill and her chin. She heaved with such force that she swore she'd pop the blood vessels in her eyes, and she upchucked a chunk so substantial and grisly that she feared it was a tonsil. She wiped her face on the back of her hand and retched again, managing to aim the putrid liquid out the window. God, what had she drunk—a full gallon of wine? It appeared so. She stayed at the window, gagging and spitting until she had nothing left.

Then she crawled into her ski clothes, feeling the pre-nausea saliva gather in her mouth as she pulled the sweaty cotton over her head. Ski clothes were the last thing she wanted to don this morning. But what choice did she have? There was only one way out of here. She eyed the ladder down from the loft with fear. How would she get down a mountain, if she couldn't even get out of her bedroom?

She shakily descended one wooden rung at a time. The heat of a blush rose to her face when she reached the main floor and became aware of the room full of breakfast eaters, all of whom had just been audience to her spontaneous purge.

"Good morning, sunshine," Michael said as he handed her a cup of cowboy coffee, grounds clearly floating on top.

"Fuck off," she answered.

But she took the coffee.

Lanny awoke to a splattering noise just around the corner. It sounded as if someone had just dumped a pail full of human waste out of the upstairs window. He breathed deeply, stretching as he pulled himself to sitting, and he was hit full force with the smell of rancid wine. His stomach convulsed in response. He held a glove to his face, breathing in its smell of old leather. Once he reined in his rebellious innards, he moved the glove slightly away from his face and scooped up a snowball, holding it near his mouth so he could suck on it.

Somebody upstairs was dying. Those sounds were barely human. He peeked around the corner but immediately regretted it. A mess the colour of grape juice had dirtied the snow and more fell from the sky. He drew back around his corner, gathered Sitka into his side and leaned back against the hut, sucking on his ball of fresh snow. He grabbed another handful and held it against his knee, which was sending sharp rods of pain down his calf. He pushed the icy ball hard against the pain, scared to look, preferring oblivion to any serious assessment of the damage.

"Hoo boy! And I thought I was feeling rough!" Lanny heard Kevin before he saw him. He walked toward the hut, Claudette and Fredrik in tow, and pointed up at the back window. "That's what you call rough. Turns out I'm doing all right." He waved at Lanny. "I feel like a small animal crawled into my mouth, took a shit, and then died. But I'm better than she is." He stopped at the foot of Lanny's bed. "Coming in for breakfast, fella? Nothing quiets down a hangover better than some greasy bacon and eggs. I got just the thing to make sure we don't end up like Exhibition A." Kevin gestured at the heaving noises around the corner of the hut.

Lanny pulled himself to his feet and limped along behind them, relieved that Kevin didn't notice the half-digested ginger cookies and tuna sandwiches caked across the seat of one of their snowmobiles.

Janet pushed her nose into the crook of her elbow and breathed deeply. She knew she'd smell like bacon for a full week. Nothing clung like the scent of fried pig fat. Michael sat at her side eating a peanut butter sandwich. She moved her nose to his hair. It smelled the same. Dead, fried animal.

Lanny, Kevin, Fredrik, and Claudette sat on the floor, backs against the wall. Plates covered in a mess of egg yolk and grease perched on their laps. Forks and knives clattered and scraped against the glassware. Ella refused to look in their direction. Janet had noticed this ever since Kevin had arrived. Ella dealt with him the same way Sitka dealt with the huskies—*maybe if I just don't look at them, they'll go away.* And so far it seemed to be working.

Janet held the back of her hand up to her nose, trying in vain to block the smell of fried pig fat. She turned her attention to Michael's words, hoping to tune out the background noise of screeching knives.

He held a pad of paper in front of him and had sketched out a rough map of the surrounding terrain. "All of this is going to be out of the question," he said to the three ski bums who sat in a mute line on the bench beside him. "Absolutely too dangerous to ski. With the recent snow and that nasty frost layer, forget it. If we want to ski," here he looked up at the boys, "which we obviously do, we're going to have to stick here. I say we all stay together. If we know where everyone is, then one group isn't off triggering an avalanche just above the other group."

"Safety first, that's our motto," F-Bomb said, but to Janet he sounded as if he were mocking Michael. She stiffened, but she felt Michael's hand patting her knee, letting her know that it wasn't worth responding. These boys spoke a different language. That was all. Michael would handle it.

"He's right," the one called Loco mumbled into his own chest. "We don't need a repeat of yesterday. We'll still get in some skiing."

"I don't want to 'get in some skiing.' I just want to go home," Alison's voice came up from the floor, where she lay on the bare wood, curled on her side like a caterpillar poked by a stick. The coffee hadn't helped her at all. If anything, she looked even greener than when she'd first descended the ladder.

"Well, you've gotta get out of this hut. That's obvious." SOR got off the bench and lowered himself to the floor, sitting next to her, holding a hand to her lower back. Janet wondered if he were her boyfriend. Must be, she guessed, though she wouldn't have thought so last night. These people confused her. She missed her gas stove, the new wooden hutch in her living room. "Come for a little tear around in the snow," he continued. "The fresh air will fix you right up. If you're not feeling better by lunch, I'll bring you back for a nap." Janet spotted his fingers dip lower on the ill woman's buttocks on the word "nap."

Were these kids for real? Did everything have to be about sex? Couldn't they ever give it a rest? Last night, Ella had patted Shanny on the back, reassuring her for some insult during her humiliating attempt at a story, and Shanny had—of all things—lifted Ella's fingers to her mouth and kissed them. Not the back of the hand, but the very tip of the middle fingers, in a way that couldn't be anything but erotic. Nothing made sense in this place, with these people. Part of Janet wanted to play big sister, to pull Shanny to her side and tell her, "You're more than a sexual being. You don't have to reduce everything to sex."

But in the end, Janet did nothing. She simply tried her best to ignore the whole drugged and horny reality that had enveloped Camelot. It all left Janet happy for her age and her traditional marriage, happy she could pat her belly and rest assured she was well beyond all of that.

"So that leaves you guys unaccounted for." Michael turned to the clattering of silverware against the wall. "Lanny, obviously you're coming with us, but what about the snowmobilers? What's your plan for the day?"

Kevin bounced an amused glance between Claudette and Fredrik before answering, "Well, Sir, our plan would be exactly none of your fucking business."

Michael put the cap on his pen and slid it back into the bib of his ski pants.

26. The Mother

Janet stuffed the already raging fire full of wood and opened all the windows. She would chase that smell of bacon out of here one way or another. She rifled through Cosmos' pack looking for incense, grabbed two sticks called "Tulasi Moon Scent" and lit one on the counter next to the sink and another on the kitchen table. Just for good luck, she pulled out another—this one called "Mattipal Song of the Soil"—and carefully climbed the stairs to the loft, clenching the stick of incense between her teeth. She sat the stick upright by jamming its base into a crack in the floor and kneeled above it as she struck a flame. That smelly pig didn't stand a chance.

She had to admit that it was a special kind of bliss to finally have the small hut to herself. She had been dressed for skiing, her ever growing belly stuffed into ski pants, a fleece shirt tight, too tight, around her middle, when she pulled Michael aside. "I just can't do this, baby, not today." She rubbed her hand across the back of his head and neck, ruffling his bristle of hair. "You're coming back for lunch anyway. I'll stay and relax. Warm soup and a warm hug will be ready when you get back."

"You sure?" he'd asked, concerned, resting his hand across her belly, just as he had in bed the night before. She felt a surge of affection for the man. These surges never failed to catch her off guard.

"I'm sure. You have fun, though. Do a lap for Kodiak." She winked at him and pushed him toward the door. "And play safe."

He looked back over his shoulder. "You're okay, right? There's nothing wrong? You just want to relax?"

"I just want to relax," she assured him, giving his butt a pat as he headed out the door.

She thought of telling him to take extra care today, that she sensed Nature was restless this morning—snow, sun, cloud . . . changing from one to the next and back again as if She couldn't make up her mind. But Michael would've laughed: *you're spending too much time with Cosmos, talking like Nature is a person.*

She is, Janet would've answered, *she's a woman, and she's pissed off*.

After Michael left, Janet noticed his coiled pad of paper on the kitchen table. She picked it up and flipped through the musty pages, a diary of ski trips long gone. His small, tight script filled each page. It was information that seemed useless now—a record of weather conditions past, predictions of weather conditions to come, tallies of rising snow packs, a running count of how many feet he'd climbed each season. The book must've contained information accumulated over the past decade. And she couldn't see how any of it mattered. But he'd saved it all. She flipped to the inside cover and found there, carved in deep letters pressed down into the cardboard, "If you're lucky enough to live in the mountains, you're lucky enough."

He'd saved that too, she thought. All was not lost. He would make a good father.

She put her feet up on a stump in front of the fire and rested a mug filled with chamomile tea on her belly. "Namaste" was written in swirling script across the white surface.

The light in me recognizes the light in you. She remembered it from an introductory hot yoga session in front of the woodstove in Cosmos and Ella's garage earlier this winter. Cosmos' attempt to lure Janet to the dark side, Michael had teased. As if it always had to be about sides. Us versus them.

There could've been a little more light recognition in the hut this weekend, that was for sure. Everyone here had their good: Michael trying so hard to do what was right by growing into a proper, responsible adult; Cosmos desperate to elevate the everyday and find a spiritual dimension in even the most mundane details; Lanny, as loyal to his old, lame golden retriever as he was to his best friend, Michael.

Even the rednecks were alright. She had hated Kevin when he was married to Ella, thought him volatile bordering on dangerous, but now—when she thought about him here in this empty room— he seemed like a vulnerable child, his loud aggressiveness nothing but a shield. Of course, such friendly assessments were easy enough to make at a distance, now that they weren't packed so tightly around her that she could barely breathe.

Really, the constant struggle stemmed from their love of this place. The rednecks, the hippies, the ski bums—each claiming the land as their own, insisting upon the right to name it, the power to decide how to use it.

The ski-bum kids were really okay too. Her own kid could be like that. Her own kid could be like any of them. Raised here, the child would be a product of Coalton as much as it would be a product of Janet and Michael. This was their world. They may as well embrace all of it.

She leaned back in the chair and closed her eyes. Absolute silence. She'd get to preparing lunch in an hour or two, just to make sure to have it ready when the skiers returned, sweaty and hungry. For now, she simply wanted to close her eyes and celebrate the silence.

27. The Ski

"That poor scrawny mutt is actually trembling. Someone get the pitiful thing a jacket or something." Lanny lumbered over to Sancho and bent down, like he might actually scoop up the animal and tuck it into his warm armpit. "I don't even like the stupid beast, but if nobody else'll take care of it, I will."

But SOR quickly swung his leg out, pushing Sancho out of Lanny's reach. "No dog of mine is wearing some pansy ass jacket." He stared at Lanny, focusing in on the painful looking mole in the middle of Lanny's forehead, the coarse hair sprouting from the centre of the grotesque pink and brown lump. He wanted to pluck it. *Ever heard of tweezers, guy?*

"Pitiful thing? He's an avalanche dog, dude." Shanny chewed the inside of her lower lip and winked at SOR. Her toque was pulled low down over her eyebrows, her eyes dried out and shriveled, her lids protectively squinted shut. At breakfast she still seemed half-drunk, squished between her two new pals. But now she looked like a corpse propped up on snowshoes.

"UGH . . . SICK!!" F-Bomb pointed his ski pole at the seat of the snowmobile parked between him and the door to the hut. SOR looked up the pole to the frozen mess at its tip. Someone had emptied his guts all over the machine, and over night the mess had frozen solid to the black leather. "Hey SOR—get this on video," F-Bomb shouted, as if they weren't all standing right there. *"The Morning After—Witness the Carnage."*

"Can't. Forgot the spare batteries," SOR spoke the words into the collar of ski jacket, said them quickly to get it over with. He didn't want to be here today. He felt like someone had taken a vacuum to his internal organs, sucked out all his life juices. All he could think of was the pressure of snow piling up on him yesterday, the weight of it heavy on his chest, and everything slowly turning dark as a coffin. He wanted to be under a warm blanket, in somebody's embrace. He wanted his mommy.

He wiped his snotty nose across the back of his glove and looked around the group for Alison, his bedmate of late. He said the words to himself in an exaggerated beat, making a rap of them. *My bedmate of late, how'd you like a date, I need me some bait, rid me of this hate . . .*

It needed some work.

That's what he wanted, though. A warm bed, not a snowy mountain. Sex, not skiing.

"You lugged a camera all the way up here with no extra batteries?" F-Bomb briefly turned his attention away from the frozen barf. "Serious?"

"Yep, serious. Wouldn't have said it if I wasn't serious, would I?"

Loco ignored the irritable banter between his friends and poked at the barf with the tip of his ski pole.

"That your puke, SOR?"

"Fucked if I know. Don't think so." SOR wouldn't let himself look at it again, held the back of his hand across his mouth and nose. Loco did the same.

"Let's go. What're we waiting for?" Loco slid out to the front of the group, past Michael who was fiddling with the shiny altimeter strapped to his wrist, and pointed his skis at a gradual grade up the slope before them.

F-Bomb scraped his pole through the frozen gunk one more time, then flicked the dirty tip through the loose snow at his feet. He spat and turned to follow Loco. "I'm not waiting for nothing. Let's get outta here before those rednecks show up and blame us for upchucking on their shiny toys." The two of them started sliding quickly up the mountain without looking back to see if anyone followed. SOR swallowed hard, thought about his next joint, and waited for Alison.

Shanny hauled her pack and her snowboard up on her back, clumsily pulling the straps over her shoulders, and trudged along behind the others on her snowshoes. This part was almost enough to convert anyone to skiing. Maybe next year. The thought of learning a new sport—of sucking for a full season—had kept her plodding along on snowshoes—*carrying* all her equipment no less—for long enough. Despite the clouds, she pulled sunglasses out of her jacket pocket and slid them gently on her aching face.

Better.

She was way too hungover for this shit. Her skin even hurt. She swore her hair hurt. Hiding behind her glasses, she watched Ella and Cosmos snowshoeing off in the other direction, into the trees on the far side of the hut. Their pace looked more leisurely. Shanny imagined them stopping for educational interludes and tree worship, for pleasant little picnics in the woods. She bet they were loaded down with peppermint tea and whole wheat scones. She rolled her eyes.

But last night they'd been her new best friends in the world. Even this morning—while her head still swam thick in the after-buzz of too much beer and bud—the three of them were pretty cozy. Now with the warm spring breeze blowing off the last remnants of her alcoholic fog, she watched them move away from her and wondered what had ever come over her. Maybe the witchy one had cast some kind of spell.

Seriously, being wasted was one thing, but suddenly she was . . . .

Was what? A lesbian? A lesbian groupie? A lesbian wannabe?

Bi-curious, was that the new word? That version appealed to her least of all, bringing to mind big-city raves, lipstick lesbians kissing for an audience of guys.

She knew she'd acted smitten, even in love, with the younger of the two. Her stomach clenched in embarrassment as fragmented images of the previous night bumped around her aching skull. Half mangled footage ran uncontrolled in her memory—her kissing Ella's fingertips, her letting F-Bomb slide his hand all the way down the back of her pants, Ella carrying her to bed, her pulling Ella down and under the covers beside her, Cosmos angry but joining them anyway.

Did she, Shanny, actually whisper "Please stay"? The memory was like a videotape left too long in the sun, whole sections running blank, hissing nothing but static. She'd never know for sure what actually happened. But she'd love to rewind that movie twelve hours and start the tape over. If she had any sense, any control, she could've just slept with F-Bomb like she meant to.

"Who could *sleep* with all that *sex* going on," she imagined SOR correcting her.

Make a plan and stick to it, that's what she should've done. That way nobody would've been talking—big surprise, Shanny finally bedded down with F-Bomb. Nothing to talk about there.

"Hey, ain't you goin' with your new girlfriends today, Shanny?" SOR yelled back over his shoulder, puckering his mouth and sending kisses down the mountain in her direction.

"Fuck off, SOR." Shanny dropped her gaze to the snow and kept on trudging, ignoring the heat rising in her ears.

"One of those fuckers shat all over your machine!" Kevin bent over the nose of Claudette's snowmobile and then bolted upright as if kicked in the chest. "Fuckers!" he yelled at the line of skiers snaking their way up the mountain single file. "Fuckers," he said again more quietly pounding his fist hard into his open palm.

Claudette waddled up behind him, awkward in her skidoo pants and big boots. "Let me see." She gently pushed him aside. "Well, it's not shit. It's puke. Could be worse." She opened the compartment at her machine's tail and dug through for something to scrape the mess off with. "Oh, quit huffing around, Kevin. I'm sure nobody did it on purpose. Targeted puking incident? I don't think so. Go sit. I'll clean it off, and we'll get out of here."

Fredrik already sat astride his machine, its nose pointed uphill, the engine revving.

Kevin moved to his machine but kept a close watch on Claudette, yelling instructions. "Watch the enamel! Careful! You're gonna scratch it to shit with that. What about hot water?"

Claudette gripped the butter knife, held her breath and started scraping. "Fuckers is right," she muttered under her breath, feeling her eyes water in disgust.

In truth, Michael was glad Janet had decided not to come. It had only snowed a light fluff last night, five centimetres at most, but that was on top of the thirty from the night before. It all amounted to conditions that made for epic skiing, definitely, but let's face it—there was a substantial avalanche risk involved. As the day heated up, there'd be sliding.

Taking a calculated risk was one thing for a bunch of snow-wise, agile young men—he laughed at still counting himself in that group, *young*—but quite another for his six-month-pregnant wife. Better that she herself had decided to stay back at the hut and warm the soup. She probably had her feet up and her knitting needles clacking already.

A nasty roar of engines interrupted his thoughts. He looked over his shoulder to see the three snowmobilers whizzing up a slope to the left. He held his hand out in a wave, a friendly salute with the ski pole dangling from his thumb, but the heaviest of the group (Kevin, was it?) flipped him the bird. The other two ignored him. Michael let his hand fall stupidly to his side. Their engines seemed to roar even louder, then they were gone. He hoped they'd be careful. They didn't seem to take the threatening conditions very seriously. Sure they were jerks, but nobody needed to get hurt today. He didn't need to be involved, however remotely, in that.

He let his neck relax, dropping his face to look at the ground, watching his skis slide through the loose sugar. The snow had started just before sunrise and had stopped falling not long after, but the sky still wasn't clear. No bluebird day for them. Instead, the cloud cover was thick and low like a tight lid. He unzipped his jacket, letting in some air. The low ceiling kept the temperature significantly higher than yesterday. It also decapitated the mountains, cutting them off just below their peaks, robbing them of their majesty and power. It wasn't a photo-perfect day in the Rockies today.

"How you doing Lan-ster?" He called out the question without looking over his shoulder. He could hear Lanny breathing hard right on his tail.

"Ugh." Lanny followed the sound with extra hard breathing, as if the one syllable had pushed him to the far outside reaches of his physical ability. "Ugh-ly." Another long and breathy pause. "Exactly like I deserve to feel."

"No kidding! Boozy night at the old cabin. Good news is nobody's going to be climbing anywhere too fast today. Anyway, there's not much to rush for. We're not going to be doing max vert or max downhill in these conditions." Michael's words came easily as he slid his skis one at a time up the smooth skin trail. He silently praised himself on his own physical conditioning. He wasn't officially old just yet. Tony "Loco" Ragusa and his native friend were pushing up the hill a bit faster than him, sure, but they were still well in view. He could catch them if he turned it up a notch.

But he'd hang back with his friend Lanny. "How far behind are the others?"

He heard Lanny use this question as an excuse to rest. The crinkling of his arm brushing against his side stopped, and his breathing grew more distant. Michael turned to make sure he was okay.

"Thank God," Lanny breathed up at him, pulling his pack off his shoulders, then leaning forward, a hand on each knee. Sitka limped up beside him and looked just as grateful for the excuse to plop down in the snow. "Just let me get some water. The uphill wasn't too bad yesterday, but today I'm dying. I'm too old to pull a bender like I did last night and follow it up with this." He lifted his hands slowly from his knees and dug into his pack for a bottle of water, quickly emptied half of it down his throat. "Plus, my knee's friggin' killin' me." He took another long drink of water. "The others are coming," he announced, as he came up for air. "I can hear that nutty journalist broad and her ski-bum boyfriend just behind me. They must be keeping a look out for the snowboarder. She stopped to retch up her breakfast," he laughed. "But she can't be too far back now."

Michael turned away from Lanny to watch Loco and F-Bomb vanishing up the mountain, and thought about leaving his friend, charging after the two young bucks in vicious pursuit, breaking a good sweat, hearing his heartbeat pound in his ear drums, but he dropped his pack to the ground. "Think I'll do the same," he said, reaching for his water. He didn't have anything to prove, he told himself, he was going to be a father soon. Who cared if these young punks could beat him uphill?

Anyway, all of them would get to the summit eventually. There was no rush. He pushed his pack upslope off to the side of the skin track and sat back onto it, smiling up at Lanny and inviting him to do the same. He lifted his water bottle in Lanny's direction. "Cheers, big ears. Take a load off. Remember, we're on holidays."

"Skiing hungover—my bread and butter."

SOR's little wake-and-bake seemed to have perked him right up, and Alison briefly considered partaking herself. She couldn't feel any worse. But then she remembered their mountain-biking fiasco in the fall. Pot's the last thing she needed. She could barely manage this Bizarro World maneuver—travelling uphill on downhill skis—when she was sober.

"You got anything milder?"

"Milder 'n me?"

"Pot. You got any pot that's not . . . That's not labelled Wheelchair Pot?" She wiped her arm across her eyes, stinging with sweat, and craved the cold cleansing air of yesterday. Today's warm air felt heavy and dirty, hugging her tight in her own hungover filth. She wanted to take off her clothes and roll in the snow. Anything to feel fresh and new and clean.

"Now why would I have anything as useless as that? You gotta lighten the load when you're ski touring, baby. Only brought the essentials. Weak, lame-ass pot—not on *my* essential list." He smiled lazily up at her, his eyes looking thirsty. Sancho shivered right on his heels, so close that he looked as if he were chewing on the plastic shell of SOR's boot. "Keep on trudging. One foot in front of the other."

SOR had stayed back with her this morning when F-Bomb and Loco raced on ahead. She didn't feel quite as clumsy on her skis today—had sort of got a handle on the smooth sliding uphill motion—but she had no idea how they did it so fast. "Go on ahead. You don't have to wait," she told SOR. And she meant it. She'd rather suffer on her own, didn't need any witnesses.

"Course I'm gonna wait." He smacked his ski pole firmly across her Lycra-clad ass. "You go first. This hangover and pot combo's got me in the mood for some lovin'. I like the view back here."

She appreciated the clarification—she was third on his list. Yesterday afternoon he was more into skiing. Yesterday night he was more into drinking until he barfed. And finally this morning he was into her.

Ah well, she could go for a little afternoon action. She deserved some sort of reward.

On she climbed, sure she could feel the caress of his eyes with every step forward.

When Michael, Lanny, and Sitka finally grunted their way to the summit, F-Bomb and Loco looked like they'd been there for hours. Their skis were off and F-Bomb leaned against a tree, eating a sandwich. Loco's red shovel was flying, and he already stood chest-deep in a snow pit.

Michael slid his sleeve up his arm and looked at his watch face. "Seven thousand and thirteen feet. That's a healthy little climb." He smiled at the boys. "Good work, Lanny," he patted his huffing friend on the shoulder.

"Seven thousand and thirteen feet, hey?" Loco asked but didn't stop digging. "Is that what your two-thousand-dollar toy tells you? Any local could've told you that. The Cunt Ridge has an elevation of seven thousand feet. No news there."

"Digging a snow pit?" Michael stated the obvious, trying to draw the surly ski bum into conversation. Michael remembered being that young—vaguely—remembered thinking that nobody over thirty knew their ass from their elbow. The kid couldn't hold a misplaced grudge forever. Michael thought about saying, *I'm just a guy. A guy like you. You don't have to make me the representative of everything you hate, everything that you think is destroying Coalton.* Instead he said, "Digging a snow pit? How's it look?"

Loco still didn't look up, but he pointed his shovel blade at the pit wall. "Definitely an ice layer down here, but it looks like the snow above has bonded well to it. At least right here."

"Need some help digging another sample?" Michael pulled his shovel out of his pack and jumped into the hole next to Loco. "Hey, Lanny—get a picture." He held his shovel blade up above his shoulder, in an energetic digging pose. "No wait." He brought his arm down and pushed up his sleeve, revealing the face of his new titanium T-touch. "There," he said, holding the shovel blade back above his shoulder, keeping his wrist turned toward the camera. "Okay, shoot! I got a new slogan idea. 'Michael LePlage: Digging Coalton!'"

Just as the light flashed and the camera clicked, Michael heard F-Bomb cough and choke. He looked over to see him spitting his sandwich in the snow.

It was nearly midday when SOR and Alison pulled up to the summit, the tail of the group, even after hungover Shanny. They'd stopped to rest about half way. Alison was actually laid out on her back with her head in SOR's lap, when Shanny stomped by them. "Thanks for keepin' an eye out, guys. Feeling really safe out here today. Really looked after. Thanks a bunch." She spat in the snow on her way by, horking up phlegm from somewhere deep in her chest. "Thanks a whole fucking bunch."

"You're welcome, dude," SOR yelled belatedly at her back.

SOR wanted to trade positions, wanted his head cradled in Alison's lap, wanted her arms around him. He rolled her off him as if he'd wrestle her right here in the snow and she moaned in protest. Nobody felt their best today. He let her get into sitting position against the tree and then laid his head in her lap, pulled her hands around his head.

Better.

He'd considered pulling her off into the trees before they even summitted. He knew exactly what he wanted to summit. He would've too if he thought she'd be game. Normally she ate up that stuff. The crazier, the better. But today she was suffering. He'd get her up the mountain, down the mountain, and then back to Camelot for some afternoon indoor exercise. He focused on that to forget about yesterday's burial and ward off his new fear.

He kept Alison pushing onwards and upwards with a running commentary of his afternoon plans—special rewards accumulated for each of her successful kick turns.

When they joined the group gathered at the summit, he felt a change in atmosphere, like he'd pulled up into a cloud of denser air.

"What's it lookin' like out there?" He directed the question to Loco, the self-proclaimed king of the mountain.

"Poor? Shitty? Dangerous? Pick your word."

"Perfect. Variable. Variable's my bread and butter."

"No time to be a smartass, SOR. It's heads-up hockey out here today. Straighten out a bit and pay attention. And . . ." He pointed his ski tip at Alison. "Buddy system. You're responsible for her."

SOR looked around the group. Everyone else had already paired up. F-Bomb and Loco were obviously together, and it looked like Shanny was sticking with them. The two old guys'd obviously ski together. Loco was right. That left him and Alison. "All right, baby, get ready to point 'em." He swung his pole out in the direction of her ass, but she intervened with her own pole and the two metal sticks clanged together loudly.

"Quit it. I'm going to be black and blue by the end of the day." But she smiled the words, and he could tell that the fresh air (and, of course, all his fancy foretalk) had improved her mood.

"So. Here's the story." Loco had backed himself towards the downhill run so that he faced the group. "This slope down is not too terribly steep. It's tucked into tight trees. It'll be fine. We'll regroup just at that bottom." He swung his torso around and pointed at a clump of trees a short way down slope. "See the big spruce with the bend three-quarters of the way up, in the group of three? Nobody goes past that." He swung back around, making meaningful eye contact with everyone. "Nobody. Got it? SOR— got it? Shanny?" He pointed his pole to the left to a bigger, more exposed slope. "I skied out there a bit. Did some stomping around just before the real steep grade. There's serious whumphing. The snow is deep and there's air pockets. No fooling around today. Ski side by side with your buddy. Stay where I tell you to stay. Stop where I tell you to stop." He swung his torso back towards his chosen slope, pointed his pole from side to side. "Don't go outside of this line I'm drawing. Stay inside the trees. Ready? I'll go first. SOR, you bring up the rear."

"Bringing it up the rear is definitely in my plans today, buddy."

Shanny rolled her bloodshot eyes at SOR. He jeered back, and pulled out cloth to wipe out the foggy insides of his ski goggles. The slope actually looked all right. Short but not too flat. It was steep enough that he could pick up some good speed if he weren't waiting for Alison. Enough to get a good rush of adrenalin anyway. He spat in his goggles and wiped the saliva into the plastic with a pretty nasty piece of cotton rag he carried in his pocket for just this purpose. He ignored Shanny's snorts of disgust. "All right, dudes and dudettes, I'm ready."

He looked at the two old guys. The one called Lanny was a fat piece of shit, jammed into ski pants two sizes too small. SOR wondered how he even managed to drag his sorry ass up here. SOR vowed he'd never let himself go like that. Pathetic. Even his dog looked half lame.

SOR thought about pulling his one-hitter out of the bib pocket of his snowveralls, could already imagine the cool blue tube in the palm of his hand, his bare fingers tapping the dried weed into its tip, the almost erotic anticipation of sliding the end between his lips. Just a little something to sweeten the ride down.

He feared his morning buzz might be starting to fade. He didn't want to be caught sober on a dreary, hungover day like this one. But just as he reached for the zipper on his chest, he noticed Loco pushing off downhill. F-Bomb and Shanny pushed off at his wings and the three formed a tidy V heading down the hill. Loco performed tight, controlled turns, sticking right in the thick of the trees, but with each bouncy turn, he nearly disappeared into the bottomless snow. Sancho, as excited as anyone, ditched SOR and flew down the hill in Shanny's wake. He seemed to float in the snow, surfing the mountain.

"Yee haw, buddy!! So deep you can taste it!" SOR turned to Alison. "Like a baby in a Jolly Jumper, that's what it's like. Best sensation in the world." Then he let his eyes run down the length of her Lycra pants. "Maybe second best." He aimed his pole at her ass for the umpteenth time that day.

Midway down the slope, Shanny started to pick up some speed and loosen up, she leaned back to let it ride, but when the nose of her board started to edge past Loco, he erupted, "Back, Shanny, back!" And Shanny immediately reined it in.

Why everyone bowed to Loco's will out here, SOR would never know. What made him king of the mountain? The guy acted like a decrepit senior citizen, like it'd kill him to take a risk, like he might shit-up his last pair of Depends.

The trio reached the bottom in a matter of minutes. Loco's voice echoed back up at them, "Group two is good to go."

"That's you, dudes," SOR said, without turning to look at Lanny and Michael. He was gazing over to the right, scouting out his own line. His eyes had landed on an untracked road of white heaven. He could sneak between some trees on the outside edge of Loco's boundary and have unlimited powder to himself. "Bring on the snorkel!" he said to nobody. Perfect. He hadn't climbed all the way up here for nothing.

The chubby old guy waved his pole at the fitter one. "You go first, Michael. I'll get Sitka to follow you, then I'll come up behind."

Michael nodded, took a quick look at his two-thousand-dollar watch, and pointed his skis down slope.

"Go, Sitka! Go, girl, go!!" Lanny pushed on the dog's rump, forcing it downhill after Michael. And the dog, eager to please, did take two steps but then stumbled in the deep fluff, yelping. It tried again but its front feet were ineffectual in all this snow. It fell forward clumsily, its chin tilted as it tried to keep its nose above the suffocating powder.

"It's okay girl, just a little ways. It's okay," coaxed Lanny. But the dog's yelps got louder and more insistent. Lanny sidestepped through the fluffy snow to her side. "C'mon, girl you're okay." The dog refused to move, its sharp complaints giving SOR a headache.

Shit—he really was starting to sober up.

Lanny looked uphill at him. "Sorry, guys, I should've left her at home. This is too much snow for her. She's getting old. Her hips—she can't take it. She can't even get down through this." He looked like he might start crying right along with his sorry ass mutt. "I don't know what to do."

SOR swore he heard a quiver in the poor fat bastard's voice. "No, no, no—the dog's not crying, dude. Nobody cries about powder. It's saying 'Woo hoo, powder, I love it! Woo hoo!!'"

Lanny smiled back up at them. *"Roo roo! I rove it! Rowder!"* He laughed and wiped the back of his glove hard against his eyes. *"Roo roo!* Hey, Sitka, old girl? *Roo! Roo!"*

SOR turned to Alison. "Give me two of whatever that guy just had."

Alison had pulled a hard-covered black notebook from her inside pocket. She held it in the crook of her elbow and scribbled frantically, not pausing to look up at SOR.

"Okay, Sitka, we have to get down this hill somehow." Lanny skied out in front of the dog, shaping his skis in a wide V, attempting to plow a smoother path for the animal. "Come on, follow me, girl, that's it. C'mon, sweetie." He came to a standstill in the deep snow and switched to side-stepping his way down the mountain, packing the snow down for his dog. "We'll make it, girl. That's it, nice and easy."

"Is this guy for real?" SOR reached for the one-hitter in his chest pocket. "Give me strength." The dog took a step in the path Lanny had packed down for it. Its head was above the snow now, but still it stumbled, its front feet sinking deep, even in the cleared path. Actually, now that SOR looked closer, the poor animal did seem to be limping. Michael had already reached the bottom and was, no doubt, receiving a lecture from Loco about leaving his buddy behind.

SOR breathed deeply from his little pipe, letting the sweet smoke burn his lungs. *Yes.* He tapped the tip of the pipe into his bag of weed, packing the dried herb into its small tip, and then held the pipe out to Alison.

Now the fat man was stopping again.

Alison stopped writing and reached her hand toward the pipe. "God, I'd love to. But I can't. You'd have to carry me back to the cabin."

"More for me then." He slid the cool blue pipe back between his lips and took one more suck, watching the man tuck his ski poles between his arms and lean over to pick up the dog. "Am I seeing what I think I'm seeing? Is the crazy dude actually gonna carry his dog?" And Lanny scooped the animal up in two arms, flung it over a shoulder, holding it tight with both arms around the middle as he snowplowed awkwardly through snow up to his knees down to the group at the bottom, the dog whimpering the whole way.

"Group three. It's you." Loco yelled up at them, and SOR knew he could hear the laughter in his friend's voice. How did they ever find themselves grouped with these incompetents?

"Alrighty. That's my line." SOR jabbed his pole in the direction of the far trees. "No friends on a powder day. See you at the bottom."

He pointed his skis downhill and let them run, feeling the pressure of the moving air distorting his cheeks. With each long, fast turn he sank deep into the bottomless fluff, his body suspended, weightless and free. The loose soft powder flew over his head, bringing icy freshness into his face, his mouth, his eyes. The cool wetness enveloping him washed last night's excess away. Washed everything away, leaving only him and the snow. Him flying unrestricted down the face of a mountain.

"Face shots, I love 'em," he shouted to no one, opening his mouth wide to the flying snow surrounding him.

Only when he slid to a fast stop at the bottom and looked back up to see Alison sliding sideways through the trees midway up the run, did he notice that it had started to rain and little drops of moisture stuck to his cheeks and blurred his vision through his splattered ski goggles. He turned to Loco, wiped his sleeve against his wet goggles, "She'll be all right. She's just behind me."

"I can't make it back up that slope. Not with Sitka. Too deep and too steep. To you guys, it might've felt like a nice enough grade coming down, but you all know it's going to seem three times as steep trudging back up through this deep snow."

Loco had never heard anyone fill the words "deep" and "steep" with such remorse. "We've got to stick together. That was the plan. Right from the start of the day."

"And what? We're all going to turn around because of a fucking dog? He should've thought this through before he headed up The Cunt in the first place. This is no place for the lame—man or fucking dog."

"Pipe down, F-Bomb. It's getting too wet to go straight back up that way anyway. The snow'll be wet and heavy. We can jump on our skin trail from yesterday. It'll be a bit farther back to the hut, but it's more gradual. We can move faster. It won't take so long." Loco pointed down at their tracks from yesterday as he talked, looking to make sure the bit of snow from last night hadn't entirely filled in their trail, but the smooth skin track was still distinct, just dusted by the slightest layer of new snow. He turned to Lanny. "The dog can come at the back and follow us on the skin track. It'll be good and hard packed by the time we all slide over it." He ran his eyes over what he could see of the trail from here, then turned back to Lanny. "The dog won't have as much trouble there."

"You're leaving the stupid dog inside for the afternoon." F-Bomb scowled, but Loco knew he was angrier about Shanny than he was about the dog or the ski conditions. Poor F-Bomb had let himself get all riled up for nothing, had let the anticipation build all afternoon and all evening. And then she'd made him look stupid by crawling into bed with the two crazy hippy chicks. Sure he was in a pissy mood, but it had nothing to do with skiing.

Truth be told, nobody really cared about the skiing today. They'd all filled themselves with poison last night and left themselves no reserves for today. They'd forgotten the very reason for their trip out here. Stupid. They could've got wasted at home. They didn't have to climb a snow-covered mountain for that.

"Don't worry," Lanny snarled back at F-Bomb, just as ill-tempered. "The dog'll stay inside. Inside with me. I'm leaving *myself* in for the afternoon. In case you hadn't noticed, I wouldn't exactly be missing anything." He swung his pole up towards the sky.

"Hey, I sense a trend." SOR's voice was the only one that carried any buoyancy. "I'm leaving myself and Alison in for the afternoon too." He ran a hand down her back, let it rest gently on her ass.

"Good idea, 'cause Alison ain't making it up that slope any easier than the dog is. *Of course* you're not complaining about waiting— you got just as heavy a load as he does." F-Bomb didn't look at SOR as he talked, but focused on his ski pole which he was smacking hard into the snow at his feet.

"Geez, somebody needs to get laid. Little crabby 'cause your lady turned out to be a dyke, F-Bomb?"

"Fuck off!" Shanny and F-Bomb spat the two syllables at SOR in unison.

Loco was relieved when the group spread out single file along the skin track and he could finally lose himself to the quiet of the mountains, where all he heard was the gentle pat of rain on the waterproof shell of his jacket.

How could he have forgotten about this? Loco stood at the edge of a gaping hole in his plan: a wide open face that he and the others would have to cut across to get back to the hut. This one bowl, the ridge on the other side, and an easy, short ski down were all that separated him from a warm hut and some dry clothes. Rain pounded down hard on his already soaked jacket. The hair on his forehead was soaked and water dripped from it, streaming down his face as if from a dozen eyes. And he really could cry. At least, in all of this water, nobody would notice.

Gradually, the others filed in one by one behind him, nobody saying anything, just staring with him across the terrain trap that stood between them and some hot soup.

Loco shook his head, brushing away the temptation to despair. He was leading this pathetic group on its misguided and ill-fortuned pilgrimage. All he had to do was get them home for lunch. They were almost there. He pulled up his drenched sleeve and looked at his watch through its misty face. Noon. His stomach gurgled in response. He'd worked his way through all his energy bars on this last elongated uphill push. He was flat out of food.

His eyes drifted once more into the open bowl between him and lunch. He scanned the peaks above and performed a quick assessment, the words clicking in place neatly, the tidy list of considerations activating his brain and transforming his fear to order. South-facing bowl. Loaded slopes. Avalanche path. A dusting of new snow last night, on top of the thirty centimetres from the night before. Winds from the north had swept more snow over the ridges onto the south-facing slopes.

The short of it was that there was a shit-load of snow piled above them and now it was raining like a mother fucker, turning the whole mess of it to cement. They had come across here fairly easy yesterday. But that seemed like a century ago. And in terms of weather conditions, it really might as well have been a hundred years. Weather-wise, today was a different mountain in a different world. The twisting in his stomach told him he didn't want to mess with this snow in this rain. His neat little list confirmed what his intuition had already made clear.

He looked behind him and saw that everyone had assembled in a tight group. They all looked like they'd been fully submerged in a lake. "I don't know if this is a good idea," he said quietly, making eye contact with nobody.

"What're our options?"

Loco moved slowly, pulling himself out of his own mind and its complex web of considerations. This question had come from the man with the dog. Before Loco had time to answer, the other old guy—the real estate agent asshole—jumped in.

"We don't have any options. We're here. We have to get there. Straight line. Pretty clear to me."

"No," Loco forced himself to speak, shaking himself free of the fog that had gathered around him as he climbed up the trail immersed in silence, and had grown denser as he stood on the lip of this bowl, assessing their sodden situation. "There are always options. We could cut back down there. Snake around that way. Come back up to the cabin from a safer angle in the next drainage over." He pointed his pole vaguely at geographical features that only he was familiar with. He didn't need anyone else figuring out how much energy was required in this new plan.

"That'll take all day." Michael leaned down to his pack, pulled out a folder full of topographical maps. He spread them on the ground before him, reminding Loco of Cosmos reading tarot cards at the hut last night. Rain speckled the shiny, laminated surfaces of the maps. Michael leaned down and retrieved one, wiped its rain splattered surface across his arm. The wet sleeve of his jacket just smeared more water across the glossy surface. He held the map in front of his face with two hands.

"You can save yourself the trouble. You'll go cross-eyed like that. I know exactly where we are. I've put in enough time in these mountains that we don't need your maps. Or your overpriced watch." He wiped a sleeve across his wet eyes, muttering "The map is not the terrain, you moron" under his breath.

Michael squinted once more and then lowered the map. "We won't be back until dark."

"Near dark. I could've told you that if you would've just asked. Would've saved you some unpacking and repacking."

"And all for no skiing . . ." F-Bomb's voice carried the slightest whine, but SOR interrupted him before he got anywhere.

"We skied! What do you call that sweet powder lap in the trees? That was tits deep, dude. As good as it gets. You might've pansied your way down, but I *skied*, I tore the mountain a new—"

A crash halted SOR just as he was about to start fucking his skis again. Shanny had thrown her pack to the ground—her board slamming loudly into a tree—and then fallen heavily on top of it. "I can't do it." She turned face down into her pack, laid out as if sleeping. She lifted her head and spat in the snow. "I've dry-heaved my whole way up here. I'm fucking hung, dudes." She spoke without lifting her head and the words were a barely comprehensible muffled mess. *I can't do it.* The admission clearly killed her.

Shanny wasn't the kind of girl who admitted to not being able to do anything. SOR, F-Bomb, and Loco all stared at her, as stricken as if SOR had just announced his intention to give up smoking pot.

"I'm on snowshoes, guys." She rolled onto her side, pulling her knees into her chest, looking up at them. "Remember, I'm the only one walking. Your climb is cruisy next to mine." She reached into her pack, pulled out a small piece of soft cloth, wiped it across her wet face. "And I drank my body weight in cheap beer last night. Can't do it, dudes. Can't walk all the way back up again. I'm almost done as it is." She looked done, too, crouching there on the snow, limbs pulled in tight to her body, huddling like a sick animal. Loco had never seen her look this beaten.

"How's Sitka going to make it across that?" Lanny bent over and hugged his wet dog, pulled tight in against his legs.

In the long quiet uphill push, Loco had almost forgotten that these guys too were his problem. Them and their pathetic excuse for a dog.

Before Loco had time to organize a response in his mind, Michael spoke loudly as if making a public announcement to a theatre full of people rather than six huddled wet skiers. "She's right. Shanny, is it? Shanny's right. Might as well progress the progression." He pointed out across the bowl, waving his sopping glove to indicate the cabin just beyond their vision. "If that's the direction we're going, that's the direction we're going. Progress the progression. No sense moving backwards."

"Right, words of wisdom from the guy who once said 'Coal didn't put Coalton on the map.' Let's leave your words of wisdom out of it, buddyroo." Loco turned to Lannny. "Progress the progression? Is that what his collection of laminated topographical maps told him? His fancy T-Touch watch?" Loco dropped his gaze to the tips of his skis, shook his head. "Fuck." He looked out across the bowl and then down at Shanny huddled against the trunk of a massive cedar. He didn't dare look at Alison. If rain and hangover had reduced Shanny to this, there must be nothing left of Alison. "Fuck and fuck again."

He sighed deeply, crossed his arms in front of his chest, squeezing himself warm as he concentrated on isolating their options. He tongued his gums where his front teeth should be. The gap was sensitive to the cool air, sending shivers down the back of his neck if he left his mouth hanging exposed too long. "Okay. Here's how it is. Avoiding this slope means backtracking—going back the way we came and then climbing up on a more gradual treed slope in the other drainage, the same drainage as Camelot. That'll take a couple hours. More than a couple maybe. The other option . . ." He swung his pole out to indicate the bowl in front of them.

Nobody said anything this time. Loco stomped his skis around, listening for telltale signs of what was going on below. He heard nothing. "Anybody bring lunch?"

Heads shook. Still nobody said anything.

"If we backtrack, we won't get back to the hut until four." He looked at Michael, whose mouth twitched as if it might open and release more senseless noise. Loco held up a hand to silence him. "Maybe later than four. There'll be no lunch. We'll be cold and wet. And hungry." He looked back across the bowl, his hand still held out to quiet Michael. "And, yes, it could even be getting dark." He paused, pushed his chin hard towards his left shoulder, releasing a loud crack in his neck. "Those conditions could introduce a whole new set of problems."

Nobody spoke, everybody waiting for someone else to make the decision. Loco's eyes flitted around the group but nobody would meet them, everyone pressing their lips together, studying their own feet.

"It's probably okay," Loco finally said. "It just started raining hard. Better now than in two or three hours when that snow's as heavy as cement." He stomped his skis on the snow again, listening for the threatening whumphs.

The snow said nothing.

Loco jabbed his foot once more with all his might. Nothing. He shrugged. "I guess we're going for it. We'll go across the slope one at a time. The group waits here in the trees and reconvenes in the trees on the other side. That way, if one person goes down, it's just one person. With the group of us, we'll be able to do a rescue, if we have to. Worse-case scenario. Everyone pay attention. All eyes on the skier in the bowl. Always."

He scanned the group for dissenters. Alison had turned almost the colour of the snow itself, only slightly greyer, like snow in the shadows. SOR stood right next to her, holding tight to her elbow, as if propping her up. Loco looked for a sign of panic in SOR's face. After yesterday, it'd be expected. But SOR seemed intent on looking out for Alison, if for no other reason than to get her back to the cabin for his afternoon festivities. Good. That would keep him distracted from his own fretting. Everyone else looked okay. Serious—which was good—but okay.

"All right then," Loco said, slurring the syllables together, in his most practised imitation of casual, "who wants t'go first?" He turned his head to Lanny. "How 'bout you and the dog? We're kinda goin' this way for you . . ."

Lanny bent over and rubbed his knee, wincing noticeably. But he nodded.

"You have to let it go. It's making you sick. A man's value is not determined by the worst thing he's ever done. Hating him is not going to do anything positive for you. You weren't good together. Why not leave it at that?" Cosmos leaned against a tree nearly as wide as a car, holding a thermos lid cupped between both palms. Steam floated up towards her nose, and she sniffed. "Mmmm. Peppermint." She smiled at Ella. Her hood was pulled tight around her face. Even though she sat in the shelter of the tree, water dripped off the brim of her hood, streaming down her cheeks. "Cheer up, sweetie. It's a coincidence that they're here. Coincidence always means something. Take it as a chance to resolve your issues with him, put them to rest once and for all."

Ella wanted to kick hard, hitting the bottom of that thermos lid with the tip of her foot and splashing the steaming hot tea right into Cosmos' stupid face. *A man's value is not determined by the worst thing he's ever done.* Drivel. Kevin was Ella's ex-husband. She'd measure him however she wanted to measure him. It was none of Cosmos' flakey business.

Not for the first time, Ella wondered about the worst thing a man had ever done to Cosmos. Nobody would ever know—Cosmos had exorcised that part of her life when she reinvented herself as Cosmos. But something had to have happened to make her believe in her own self-protective idiocy. Ella sent her most hateful look in Cosmos' direction.

"Don't pout, Ella. Look—they're gone now. Let's forget about them. Why let them ruin your day when they're not even here? Drink some tea." She scooped up a handful of slushy, wet snow and lopped it playfully towards Ella. It broke apart across the tip of Ella's snowshoe.

"Yeah, they're gone now. But they'll be back. We'll all be back this evening. Rooming with my ex-husband and his new wife. Honestly, does it get any worse?" She shifted in the snow, could feel the cold making its way through her thick pants and numbing her ass. The weather had turned. Ella had complained as soon as Cosmos suggested stopping to sit in the rain: why not go back to the hut and have some warm soup with Janet? But Cosmos believed you took whatever Nature handed you and took it gratefully. Rain was no reason to change plans. They'd have tea here, lunch in a few hours, and carry on their circuitous hike through the dense forest to arrive back at Camelot around four. Rain or no rain.

They'd taken their morning tea inside the mouth of a cave—the one where Cosmos had performed her annual sun ceremony in the fall. That would've been a perfect shelter from the rain now, but Ella wouldn't suggest it. Cosmos had freaked out there this morning, and right now Ella wanted to focus on her own issues. Cosmos had looked at a boot print in the mud and had grown hysterical, forcing out the words "That. Man. That. Man. That. Man" between breaths. What man? Cosmos had never been married, never had a brother. Never even spoke of a father.

Ella took a bite of her wet sandwich and tried to wipe her wet brow with the wet arm of her jacket. She knew that the plan to stay out for lunch—rather than going back for hot curry soup—was made because of her, in deference to her desire to avoid the cabin and thereby avoid a potential run-in with Kevin.

"Ella, they probably won't even be in the hut at lunch. On those sleds, they could be *anywhere* by tonight. Why would they come back here? They don't want to hang out with us anymore than we do with them."

Cosmos had been all reason, Ella all emotion. But right now in the cold and the rain and in the miserable hangover of a violent confrontation with her ex, Ella felt like blaming someone, and Cosmos was the only one here.

Ella pointed her face towards the sky and felt the drops pelting her. "Life could not be worse."

"Yes, Ella, it could be worse. We could be home with a crazed sheep farmer determined to see to it that both of our dogs get butchered." Cosmos reached her arms out wide, embracing the big dogs lying spread out in the snow at her sides. Findley rolled belly-up, and Cosmos, obligingly, scratched. "You always get like this when things don't go your way. Instead of just admitting the one thing that's bugging you, isolating it and then resolving it, you decide you hate everything and everybody. It's simple. Problem: you were forced to spend the evening in the company of a man with whom you have a bad history. Resolution: put that history in the past where it belongs. Instead, you let that one thing colour your view of everything. You don't hate me and I'm not your problem. Quit acting like it." She poured more tea from the thermos into the lid and stretched her arm out toward Ella, ignoring the rain slapping against her jacket sleeve. "Are you sure you don't want some? No sense turning this outing into a suffer-fest."

"*I* am turning it into a suffer-fest?" Ella didn't reach for the lid. She felt the threat of tears, and refused to turn into a giant bawling mess. Then she'd never be able to sustain this anger, and she knew anger was the only thing holding her together today.

Cosmos opened her mouth to speak but then closed it again, looking abruptly over Ella's left shoulder. She crinkled her brow. "Hear that?

Ella listened. A burst of rowdy noise echoed across the bowl behind her. One person, at least, had not let the rain dampen his enthusiasm. Ella leaned into the tree and pushed herself to her feet, stepped gingerly through the deep snow and out to the ridge to look across.

"It's the skiers," she said. She met Cosmos' eyes. "What's the chance of running into them today? In all this space. Another of your coincidences?" She smiled a little bit. *Just be nice, Ella.* How many times had people (her mother, her husband, local policemen, even her Cosmos) spoken those words to her. *Just be nice.* She leaned her shoulder heavily into the gargantuan cedar at her side, letting it hold her up. Sometimes being nice was harder than it sounded.

Cosmos stood at her other shoulder, and seemed to accept the smile as a fresh start. They both knew Cosmos wouldn't be getting an apology or an explanation. She'd have to take the smile. She put her hand on Ella's shoulder, leaning with her toward the cedar as they looked across the bowl at the skiers on the other side. "You *are* wet, aren't you? We'll get moving and warm up right away. With any luck, by the time we stop for lunch, it'll have stopped raining. Just think of how great the warm fire and some dry clothes will feel this evening."

With Cosmos' wet mitt on Ella's wet shoulder, they watched the skiers. Cosmos lifted her arm in an enthusiastic wave across the bowl that separated them. The group had lined up single file, with the front skier just at the edge of the ridge. Lanny, at the front, seemed to be the only one who saw them. He barely raised his hand, a minimal acknowledgement, and then pointed his skis down in the snow before him.

"He's not skiing in there, is he?" Ella looked at the wide open space. No trees, only piles and piles of snow. She felt dizzy watching him move down into the open space. She could see that he slid forward slowly and with great control, but she felt dizzy nonetheless. She tightened her grip on the cedar.

"It looks like they're all coming." Cosmos pointed to the next skier in line. He'd pulled the tips of his skis up to the edge, taking Lanny's spot. Everyone else huddled close behind him.

Ella held a hand over her brow to block the rain blowing in her eyes and looked up at the snowy peaks looming above the bowl. "Is that wise? Isn't it dangerous in the rain?" Ella didn't have any formal avalanche training. She only snowshoed and always stayed on easy graded slopes in the trees. She'd been told many times that her worry about skiers was misplaced. *Measured risk*, they said. *Informed decisions*, they said. They also liked to talk about *minimizing danger through education and preparedness*. It all looked dangerous to her.

She tilted her ear toward Cosmos, waiting for a response. But Cosmos stared soberly at Lanny edging his way deeper into the bowl with a dog yelping at his heels. She said nothing.

"We can't do anything to help. Let's just go," Ella whispered in Cosmos' ear. "I can't handle standing here watching them. They'll be fine. Let's go." Cosmos didn't budge. Ella sighed dramatically, and let her forehead fall against the rough bark of the cedar tree. "What else can we do but go?"

"We can add our positive thoughts," Cosmos insisted. "We can keep an eye on them until we know they're okay."

Ella pushed her head harder into the tree, feeling the deep impression the wet bark made on her clammy skin.

28. The Crossing

Lanny is the first to feel the snow move. He knows they shouldn't be here, but he ventures out into the slope, with Sitka close at his side, holding his breath. He thinks of making himself bigger—"Look at me! I'm FUCKING HUGE!!"—but he can't intimidate the mountain like he did a moose. *Don't mess with me, mountain.* He knows himself foolish as soon as he thinks it.

He grips his ski poles tight and slides forward. It's a calculated risk, he tells himself. People take bigger risks every day. Getting in a car is a bigger risk. That's what he tells himself as he cuts onto the snow-loaded slope, his instincts buzzing on high alert. They just have to get across this mountain face—that's all—and then they can ski on the other side, in the safety of the big trees. They'll be back at the hut sipping on hot soup within thirty minutes.

He offered to go first. If it weren't for Sitka, the rest of the group might have decided to turn back. He takes it slow and steady, clearing a path for Sitka, encouraging her along. He holds his breath tight in his lungs with every slide forward. When he hears the hollow *whumpf* and feels the slope slide from beneath him and knows the very earth beneath his feet has given away, he goes somewhere beyond words. There's no story for this. He lets out his breath in a defeated sigh and then gasps once, for what he knows will be his final taste of air. Cold particles of snow numb his throat.

Michael experiences the slide in slow motion. The whole way down the slope, his mind plays one idea over and over. *But I was somewhere safe. We were being safe. We were in the trees.* When the torrent of snow stops and he finally comes to rest, he has a decent-sized pocket of air around his face. He settles in and waits for the others to come and get him. He'll use this in his marketing. "Coalton Realtor Battles the Mountain. And Wins." He'll have his secretary do up a press release. "Coalton Range Delivers its Worst But Can't Beat Michael LePlage."

He'll tell Baby Kodiak about it one day. He pictures his little tyke, on skis by age two, out ski touring by ten. Michael will put a different spin on the version he tells his little buckaroo. "Play safe," he'll say. "Never test the mountain. It'll win every time."

Picturing his son—a clean cut boy just as competent and comfortable on the mountain as Loco but without the piercings and the attitude, without the missing teeth—Michael begins to feel a little drowsy. Maybe he'll just close his eyes, sleep for a bit, conserve his energy. His transceiver is set to transmit. The others will find him soon. He never lets his thoughts tune into the faint buzzing at the back of his mind—the nagging suspicion, what if the others are all buried too? Now, he closes his eyes and thinks of Janet warming the soup, thinks of returning home to the hut and pulling up her shirt so he can rest his cheek against her massive warm belly and trace his finger along the new line, the one that divides her exactly in half.

Alison knows it, has known from the moment this crazy adventure began, that she's risking her life. Her brief moment of reprieve after yesterday afternoon's scare, her empowering belief that she'd faced her crisis and survived it, disappears as soon as she finds herself on this open slope, giant mountains loaded with snow towering above her. And this time, the sensation feels different than yesterday.

She hears the *toasssss* with such incredible ferocity and speed that there can be no end but the final thudding *t* of death. *ToasssssT*, that's what an avalanche sounds like. As the snow pulls her feet out from under her, shooting her body down the mountain, she feels clarity wash over her. She should scream. She feels the sound rising up from deep in her gut, but she swallows it, forcing it down. To scream would be both predictable and pointless. Her hangover suddenly gone, her mind narrows in on precisely this moment, the whoosh of sound and movement carrying her away. Her knees slam into her midriff, pushing her *Book of Great Ideas* hard against her ribs. She knows she should swim, but she doesn't have a chance. Everything happens too fast. Instead, she simply lets herself go, feels herself falling free and fast, out of control. She's more relaxed than she thought she would be. She and her *Book of Great Ideas* will both be buried—she knows that—but for some reason it's okay. It can't be anything else, can it?

Shanny sees it happen. She's revived at the thought of one more run before lunch, and stands slightly apart from the group, looking over her shoulder to the massive headwall above her. That's where she wishes she could be, not standing around in the trees with a bunch of newbie gapers. Her eyes scan the steep rocks, searching out the narrow strips of snow that she knows sit untouched, waiting for her.

That's when she sees it. The whole top of the mountain cracks open. A mile? Two miles? A gaping chasm from one side of the ridge straight across to the other. Adrenalin races through her body, turning her skin hot, her face flushed. She can outrun it. She knows she can. She pushes away from the group and points her snowboard straight down the open bowl before her. To hell with sticking in the trees. The group can have the trees. Powder flies up into her face, speckling her cheeks, wetting her lips, blinding her eyes. She boards faster than she's ever boarded before, imagining a whole mountain of fluff flying up in her wake. The entire slope has let go a landslide of confetti in homage to her. The celebration of Shanny.

She wishes SOR had his camera trained on her, so that he could capture her at her most invincible.

Even when the snow catches her, rips her off her feet, she hears a voice strong in her ears.

Power through it.

Swim.

Fight.

And she does. She fights for her life, hanging high on the snow, imagining herself swimming free of a thousand tons of snow at the mountain's bottom.

She feels the tree before she sees it. The force of the impact snaps her femur in two and then in two again. She feels the pain sear through her, hot and loud. But she knows the pain means nothing. She will die. Pain is simply the last indication that she's alive.

And then nothing.

SOR always thought things would move fast in an avalanche—and they kind of did yesterday—but today is different. He finds he has time to reflect, time to figure out what's going on. Real time has no meaning. Seconds retract and expand in ways that have nothing to do with a clock. The slide probably takes . . . what? Five seconds, ten? But he experiences it like a lifetime of reflection. He feels bad about Alison. It's not like he cares about her in any specific sort of way, but he doesn't wish her dead either. Not like this. And he knows that if she dies, he's to blame.

Instinctively, he grabs Sancho by the collar as soon as he hears the echo of falling snow above him.

What does an avalanche sound like: "Oh fuck!" he'd always said. "You're *toasssssst*," he'd said. But really it sounds like goodbye. It sounds like dirt shoveled onto his coffin.

He loses his grip on Sancho's collar as soon as the snow pushes him onto his back. His body moves more and more quickly, but he manages to stay on top of the snow longer than he'd have expected. Sancho's scrawny little ass is the last thing he sees before his world turns white. And then black.

"Findley! Rider!" Ella yells over her shoulder, expecting the animals to come rushing to her side. They don't come.

"They'll be back," Cosmos assures her, "They're just exploring."

Then she turns her positive energy to the skiers, who have started to cross the wide open bowl. She sees they will cross one by one. Lanny has gone first, the others lined up single file behind him. She directs all her good will towards Lanny and his yellow dog.

Neither Ella nor Cosmos believes herself to be in any danger, not inside the trees.

But nobody expects the slide of a century.

Cosmos' first thought is that she's been clumsy, that she will embarrass herself in front of the skiers by toppling over. Now she's standing, now she isn't. Everyone will laugh at the stupid, awkward woman on snowshoes.

So much for intuition. Before she knows what's happening, she's being carried full force in the path of the avalanche. By then it's too late. But, really, it was too late as soon as the mountain split open above her. Her fate had been decided. Hers and Ella's. And it's her fault. Ella would've left.

Cosmos whispers a small apology under her breath and hugs her arms around her own torso and holds on tight as her body careens down the slope.

F-Bomb knows right away that it's a big fucking avalanche. He feels it in his guts. A life-ender. "Native Intuition," the others would call it and laugh at him, bouncing their flat palms over their open mouths, like kids playing at Cowboys and Indians. They could laugh, but he felt what he felt. This time he knows the mountain has spoken. There's nothing left to say. He closes his eyes and prepares himself for one last ride.

Loco does everything right. With the first movement, he swims for all he's worth. He fights the snow, fights the pull of nature, fights the inevitability of death. He tries with every muscle in his body, every bit of will, to direct himself out of the moving snow.

When he feels the snow begin to slow—after what seems like an eternity of warp-speed downhill travel—he's still conscious. He says a prayer of thanks for that, and as he comes to a standstill he tries to punch one arm in the direction he hopes is up. He holds the other hand in front of his face. He knows this action will create an air pocket, something to keep him alive until the others arrive to dig him out.

Then he waits, slowing his breath, going over the list of things he's done right. He'd put his transceiver in his pocket rather than strapped to his chest, just like he'd told the others. He applauds himself for his own foresight because he knows his knees banged hard into his chest on the way down, probably broke at least his top two ribs. That could've easily bust his transceiver. And that would mean: *Arrivederci, Loco.* No hope of anyone finding him. Alive or dead.

He panics only a little when he realizes that he's come to a stop with his arms behind him, stuck frozen into a sort of futile superman pose. He should've tried harder to swing his arms towards the surface, punching hard, hoping to get a piece of mitt above the surface so rescuers could spot him easily.

With the remainder of his conscious minutes, Loco frets about this detail needlessly. Even if there was anyone to come looking, his hand is a full two metres underneath the snow's surface. His mitt would've been visible to no one.

Assuming there was anyone left to look.

Kevin and Claudette are saved such thoughts. They aren't even close to the others, but as the police will tell Janet the next morning, this slide takes out everyone in the area. Coalton has seen nothing like it this century.

Kevin and Claudette, though, don't have time to register the event at all. The rush of snow sends their machines flying above them. Their bodies race down the mountain in a tumble cycle with the heavy snowmobiles. Heads bash in, bones break, flesh tears off limbs. Even when the bodies are all recovered, well into the new season and after a late spring melt, theirs will be unrecognizable.

Fredrik is luckiest of all. When the snow begins to rumble, he sits just on the outskirts of the path. He feels the earth move him but ever so slowly. If he'd had his wits about him, if his hands had immediately clenched the throttle, he could almost have got away.

But instead, he stumbles with his gloves off and his hand on a water bottle. Somehow, he's thrown from the stream of snow—free of the avalanche path—and his machine rolls with him. It pins him. Stuck, he tries wiggling his legs, his arms. He can't feel his feet, can't move his neck. When he looks down, he sees that the snow has turned a sickening red.

His eyes take in the inevitable truth, his own life spilled on the mountain. He lifts his gaze from the blood-soaked ground and remembers the view from yesterday: the bluebird sky, the peaks pointed heavenward as sharp as arrowheads, the towering cedars. Rain beats his face, and he wonders . . . what is he doing so far away from home? He should be on a fishing boat, eating herring, the salty wind making his eyes water.

He imagines the phone call his mother will get.

Jag prater inte engelska. I don't speak English. She will say the practised phrase into the receiver and gesture helplessly at her husband forcing the receiver into his hands.

He will take it from her and shrug. *Jag prater inte engleska. I don't speak English*, he will repeat.

It isn't right that things should end like this. He's just so far away from his family. So terribly far.

29. The Retraction

Heinz sits staring at the mountain. His Heorot sign remains knocked down and after the work of his own foot late yesterday, it's pushed down so deep into the snow that it's barely visible. He decides that's where it'll stay. Let it get deeper and deeper in the snow for all he cares. Let all his stupid signs fall to the ground for what it matters to him.

Just then, he hears a booming explosion, as if the mountain has stomped its foot in approval. Then right before his eyes, a giant crack opens across the mountain's face, a grinning fracture from one side of the bowl to another. While he sits and contemplates that toothless gaping mouth—and it is, ever so faintly, pointing upwards—he swears he hears the mountain sigh, a swooshing breath of utter contentment.

All the world's a stage, he thinks, but not always in the way the Great Bard meant. More often than they think, humans are no more than a passive audience. The mountain, it appears, has called the final curtain on this performance. He lowers himself to the ground and leans back against his hut, setting his stick across his lap, fingering the dried scat at its point, and he waits to see what will happen next.

Mid-morning tomorrow a knock will rattle the door of Camelot. Janet will be nauseous with fatigue. She will have spent all night alone in the small cabin, cooped up like a rabid dog, pacing frantic circles from one side of its small cage to the other. With each circle of the hut, she will have stopped at the front window and pressed her hot forehead against the cool glass. *Please let them come. Please please please.*

She will have bartered with whatever higher power there was. *I'll take a broken leg. Even Michael. Michael could've broken his leg. I'll take that. And it's just taken the rest of the group all afternoon and all night to get him back. Safe and sound. Broken leg. But I'll take it.*

Or they could be lost. I'll take lost. They're simply waiting for daylight to find their way back. Lost.

As the sun falls, she'll hear a scratch to the door. She'll pull it open, hopeful, but it will just be the huskies. The two big animals will push past her, buckling her knees, and bringing the smell of wet wool socks with them. She'll poke her head out the door and scream. "MICHAEL!! MIIIIIIKE—ALLLLLLL. PLEASE, MICHAEL!!" She'll feel silly—powerless—talking to the empty night air. She will close the door.

As the night wears on, she'll offer more. *I'll take a death. If I have to, I'll take a death. Not Michael's death, but a death. Even a friend. Cosmos—you can even have Cosmos. Just please don't let it be Michael.*

She'll try to lie down on her bed, for the sake of Kodiak, will rub her hands across her belly in what she hopes to be a soothing fashion. She'll force calming pictures into her mind—Michael returning home with the morning sun, all smiles. *You won't believe what happened,* he'll say. *Get this. This'll be a story to tell our kids.*

But nobody will come with the sunrise.

By mid-morning, when the knock on the door does finally come, Janet will have cried herself dry. She will lift her head and look at the door, unsure how to respond to a knock, out here, as if someone had just arrived at her house in the suburbs, a neighbour coming over to borrow sugar cubes.

She will push the heavy door open, a burst of air and sunlight coming inside with the two men, two RCMP officers, their snowmobiles parked on a slant just above the hut's entrance. The older one will have a thick black moustache, one that looks like it must catch the food every time he eats. *I've seen him around,* Janet will think, and then silently reprimand herself for having such a mundane thought in a moment of obvious crisis. The other one will look young, too young to be wearing that uniform with such seriousness. *His face shines with youth*, she'll think. *Another mundane thought.* She will rein her mind in, ready herself for the only news that these RCMP officers could deliver.

The two men will cast their eyes downward, as if embarrassed by her blotchy and swollen face, her red-rimmed eyes.

"It was all over in thirty seconds," the older man with the black bushy moustache will tell her. "They wouldn't have suffered at all. They wouldn't even have known what was happening." He'll meet her eyes and stare, as if he would like to sear this information into her brain. "And it was a hundred-year event. There was no way they could've anticipated it. Not an event of that magnitude."

"Nobody could outrun something like that," the younger one will add, as if Janet may be angry that her husband hadn't tried hard enough. "The top of the mountain literally split open, a fracture a mile wide. Thousands of tons of snow fell on them. Enough to bury a town."

The older officer will shoot the younger one a look. Sometimes enough information was enough information. Nobody needs to know everything.

The full impact of the younger man's report will haunt Janet for years.

"Everybody?" she'll ask, knowing they'll understand her true question. *Is everybody gone?* The other questions—how do you know? where did you come from? who told you?—won't occur to her until much later. Just . . .

Is everybody dead?

The older man will nod, remove his hat, and hold it tight to his chest as if applying pressure to a bleeding wound.

But none of that will happen until tomorrow. For now, Janet knows nothing. She just sits, legs propped on a stump in front of the woodstove, hands busily creating a tiny baby's toque out of the softest of yellow wool (*knit one, purl one, knit one, purl one*). She sniffs the incense and thinks about the curried carrot soup she'll warm up for lunch, how perfectly it will go with the freshly baked sourdough rolls that Ella brought, how the spicy aroma will welcome the skiers back to the cozy hut.

In the quiet of the remote hut with a woodstove burning hot at her feet, she knits, she plans, and, much like Heinz, she waits.

Acknowledgments

A version of this novel was written as partial requirement for the completion of a PHD at the University of Calgary. Thanks to my brilliant dissertation supervisors Suzette Mayr and Murray McGillvray. Thanks also to other University of Calgary faculty members from whom I learned a great deal, especially Kirsten Pullen, Douglas A. Brown, and Pamela McCallum. Thanks to Barb Howe for taking care of all the details and keeping everybody on track.

I also wish to express my gratitude to the College of the Rockies' Professional Development Committee for granting the leave that enabled me to write the first draft.

Thanks also to the many ski-culture enthusiasts who put up with my never-ending questions and to my one-man writing group, Nic Milligan.

I'm grateful also to the friends and family who helped me with my "women's work," so that I could find time to do my writing work, especially Johnna Abdou, Carrie Will, Emma Padgett, Amanda Racher, Janet MacIntyre, Keya White, Sage McBride, Ruth Nina Pangan, and Sandralee Paul.

Thanks to the women at the Fernie Heritage Library where I did most of my writing and also to the wonderfully supportive and encouraging women of Polar Peek Books & Treasures.

Thanks to John Douglas for acting as an occasional research assistant, answering e-mails all the way from Rwanda (malaria and all). Other immensely helpful "research assistants" include: Marty Hafke, Jay Bourne, Paul Ragusa, Jim Thorner, and Ryan Merrill.

Thanks to Valhalla Mountain Touring for an awesome "research" trip, to Dr. Paul Michal for tips on trip assholes and prioresses, to Heather Kerr for "Jesus would've been a telemarker," to Kieran Summers of GIV'ER Shirtworks for the slogans, to Dr. Shelley Forrest for sewing the fingers back onto my writing hand, and to Ruth Linka at Brindle & Glass for believing in the project.